The Implausibility of a Dog Named Bo

To KATHI

WE CAN'T WAIT TO SEE YOU AGAIN.

Joe Hoffman
Bob Jacobs

For all the magnificent dogs
that shall live forever in our hearts
and minds as constant reminders
of how great we could be if only
we were more like them

Malmedy, Belgium
December 1944

A persistent crackle of gunfire pierces the cold night air as flares streak skyward, bathing everything in the stark, metallic light of an alien moon. Mortar shells explode all around and massive cannons rumble in the distance. A pitiful, ghostly-looking dog wobbles his way down a dimly lit street with his nose to the ground, shaking uncontrollably, delirious with starvation, searching every possible nook and cranny for food. And what a mangy mess he is: every rib visible through his filthy brown fur, dry tongue hanging out the side of his mouth, watery eyes incapable of focusing, ears caked with crud. He almost falls when a round explodes nearby and he has to lean against a wall to steady himself. Then he continues on, eventually sniffs his way to an open door, and stumbles inside.

Five battle-weary American soldiers, separated from their unit during the Battle of the Bulge and seeking refuge from the German onslaught, scamper furtively down the same street. They desperately need to find safe haven before the glow of dawn threatens to expose their position to the barbaric enemy that just slaughtered eighty-four prisoners of war. The town is all but deserted save for the odd assortment of allied stragglers and the dreaded Nazi snipers lurking atop the tallest buildings.

The Americans go from door to door, trying to find the best place to hide. Ira Spiegel motions to the others and anxiously points to a small shop across the street. They exchange nervous glances, bewildered by his sense of urgency. They have no idea what the word *Apotheke* means, but they trust him because he's the only one with a college education. He told them to call him Doc because that was his nickname back home; it wasn't. His wavy, jet black hair and those intensely focused, deep brown eyes that squint through thick, wire rim glasses all look out of place on a man wearing a khaki uniform. Someone like him should be wearing an attorney's double breasted suit or a white doctor's coat. In fact, he grew up fully expecting to become a brilliant physician, but it simply didn't turn out that way. His head was so far up in the clouds that his feet rarely touched the ground long enough for him to have even the slightest touch with reality. Always fancying himself as a gifted healer made even his wildest dreams seem perfectly reasonable and attainable. Though extremely intelligent, his prodigious cortical horsepower was no guarantee of success, not on the road to a career in medicine anyway. While he excelled in chemistry, biology, physics, and math, he didn't have enough money to pay for medical school. It nearly drove him crazy. He was meant to be a doctor. It was the only identity he had ever known.

He finally ended up becoming a pharmacist, a highly respected profession in the eyes of most people, but to him, merely a constant reminder of his pitiful station in life. He saw himself as nothing more than an errand boy for the doctors, filling their prescriptions and mixing their formulas while having to tolerate their condescension. Most of them were, in his contemptuous eyes, mere pill pushers and overpaid mechanics who only went to medical school because their families could afford the tuition. He swore to his wife that their only son would go to medical school. She, in turn, swore that the boy would have a happy childhood and that they would support him regardless of whatever he chose to do in life. Ira finally did come down to earth long enough to admit that she was right, though it took more than two years and several sleepless nights on the living room sofa to convince him.

One by one, the men follow Spiegel through the shadows and disappear into the shop. They silently scour the room, using only hand signals until they're sure no one is inside; no one but the trembling, half-dead dog, cowering in a corner, that slowly raises his head to look at them. He appears to be full-grown, what's left of him, and at least two years old. All he can make out are the men's fuzzy, grayish shapes moving around him, their muffled footsteps, and their garbled voices.

Billy O'Neal, known to everyone as Billy O, slowly kneels beside him, murmuring softly, trying to calm him down. The hulking, red-haired Irishman never had a dog of his own. The only dogs he ever knew were the poor starving mongrels that scrounged for garbage at the docks where he worked back in Boston. There was no room in his family's crowded apartment for a dog, let alone any spare food to feed one. If the depression was hard on people, it was much harder on homeless animals.

Billy liked to eat lunch alone, far away from the other stevedores. Most of the strays steered clear of him, but there was one ugly little cur that usually hovered nearby, stalking him, waiting for any delicious morsel to hit the ground, but he always shooed it away. One day, the dog crawled up behind him, snatched half a sandwich right out of his hand, and ran away with it. From then on, Billy sat with his back against the wall while he ate. But soon, he found himself saving part of his lunch for the dog because he admired his bravado. It became a daily ritual, a game of sorts, avidly played by both of them. Every time Billy threw him a morsel of food, the dog would grab it, act like he stole it, and run away. So Billy named him Grabber.

This dog can't run away; he can't even stand. All he can do is cringe, expecting the worst from the the large man, but also confused by the gentle tone of his voice. The dog flinches and closes his eyes when Billy starts to pet him, but the reassuring sound and the soothing touch gradually begin to allay his fear.

The other men ignore the dog. They're too busy complaining because the place reeks with the acrid stench of toxic chemicals.

Frank Kozlowski, the new platoon leader, elbows Spiegel and whispers hoarsely, "Hey Doc, why the hell'd you pick this place?

3

Spiegel raises a finger to his lips and whispers back defiantly, "Quiet! Look around you. It's a drugstore and, in case you haven't noticed, we're completely out of medical supplies."

Steve Rasco interrupts with a giggle, "A drug store, huh. So where's the soda fountain? Oh, what I wouldn't give for a chocolate milkshake."

Then Ben Harper chimes in, "Me, too. I love chocolate shakes."

Kozlowski scoffs at him, "Course you would. You remind me of a chocolate Easter bunny."

Rasco grabs Kozlowski's neck with one hand and cocks his fist, ready to deliver a punch, "You need to mind your manners."

Kozlowski wrestles with Rasco, "Let go of me. You can't sass a superior."

Billy jumps up and grabs Kozlowski by the shoulders, "Hey, you've only been in command for a few hours since the sarge got killed and there ain't nothin' superior about you."

Kozlowski saw his battlefield promotion as a way to finally be in charge of something. The youngest of four boys, he was little more than the family punching bag. If he complained to his parents when his brothers beat him up, they would slap him around even more and tell him to stop his bellyaching. No wonder he was so stupid. Every time he turned around, somebody was knocking him over the head. Naturally, he became a bully in his own right and also inherited his family's brand of nasty racism. There aren't many people that dirt-poor West Virginia coal miners can look down on.

Now the dog is even more scared because of all the ruckus and he whines plaintively. Everybody stops and looks down at him for a long moment. He looks back at them and whines even louder, pleading with them to stop. If men can't stand it when a woman or a baby cries, they hate it when a dog whines. It strikes a chord that's been there for thousands of years.

Kozlowski seizes what he thinks is a moment of weakness and tries to reassert his authority by drawing his knife and hissing at Billy, "I'll show you who's in charge. I'm gonna put that dog outta his misery before he barks and gives us away."

Before anyone else can make a move, Harper grabs Kozlowski's wrist and squeezes it so hard that he screams in pain and falls to the floor. Alabama sharecroppers have very strong hands from working long hours in the fields and Harper is no exception. In fact, his hands are so huge, they look like bear traps stuck on the end of his arms. Billy kicks the knife out of Kozlowski's hand and it sails across the room.

Harper releases his grip and shakes his head, "No way you're gonna hurt this dog." Then he kneels down next to the cringing mutt and gently pats his neck, "It's okay, little fella, don't be afraid. We'll protect ya."

The dog's eyes widen as if he recognizes Harper, or at least, that he somehow understands him. He even stops shaking and pants a sigh of relief which drives Kozlowski right over the edge. His eyes burn with rage and he tries to stand up, "Why, I'm gonna..."

Rasco steps over him and points a finger right between his eyes, "You better be quiet or we'll have to put you outta your misery."

When they hear this, Billy and Harper look at each other and burst out laughing.

Rasco bends down and puts his hands on his knees, "Either we pull together or we die together. Do you read me?"

Kozlowski glares up at him and grits his teeth.

Rasco continues, "Hey, answer me, asshole."

Kozlowski scoots away holding his wrist, "I get it. It's four against one and rank don't mean nothin'. You want it, Rasco? You got it. You be in charge. I don't care no more."

Spiegel knows enough psychology to understand what's really going on with Kozlowski and smiles at him, "Look, we've got a war to fight so we can't be fighting each other. We gotta pull together like Rasco said." Then he offers his hand to Kozlowski who's clearly surprised that someone is actually being nice to him. He looks at the other men who are solemnly nodding in agreement with Spiegel and clears his throat, "You're right." He takes Spiegel's hand, stands up, and looks at Harper, "Sorry, I never been around any Negroes."

Harper chuckles good-naturedly, "Oh, I understand. I never been around so many white people."

Everybody laughs until Kozlowski gets serious and looks at Rasco, "Alright, what's our next move?"

Rasco's expression changes from a smile to a determined frown, "Okay, here's what we need to do. You guys ready?"

The men look at each other and they all nod.

"Good. Spiegel, you and Kozlowski open the back door and see if you can find any supplies or food."

Kozlowski looks at Spiegel and says, "C'mon, let's go."

Rasco pats him on the back, "Thanks. Be careful."

"Harper, you keep a lookout by the front window; the Germans can't be too far away. Billy, you take care of the dog while I figure out how we can get back to our unit. I grabbed Sarge's maps after he got killed, but honestly, without a radio, it's gonna be a crapshoot at best."

Billy sits on the floor next to the dog, pets him, and reassures him with his kind voice. The dog looks at Billy and tries to focus on his smiling face, but it's still a blur. He isn't scared this time. He recognizes the warm sound and the familiar smell. He knows the man means him no harm.

Rasco sits at a small table next to Billy and the dog and pours over the maps. He reaches into his jacket and pulls out an apple. Then he cuts off a big piece and takes a bite. The dog smells the apple, looks toward Rasco and licks his chops. Rasco smiles down at him, "Now where's my manners? Would you like a piece of my apple?"

The dog licks his chops again and growls softly so Rasco bends over and offers it to him.

"Here you go, like my mother always says, 'an apple a day'..."

The dog snatches the apple and gulps it down before Rasco can say another word. He jerks his hand back and giggles.

"Hey, leave the fingers, will ya."

Billy looks up at Rasco, "Guess he don't care what it is. He'd eat anything at this point, but we gotta get him some real food and some water.

"I agree. It's about time we saved a life instead of destroying everything in our path. Besides, we could use a little luck and saving him might just bring us some."

He takes a deep breath and rubs his hands together, "Alright, let's see what's on the menu."

He rummages through his pockets and finds a can of K-rations fatty pork, the disgusting excuse for food the Army expects its soldiers to live on. He flips it to Billy who opens it, recoils from the putrid smell, and looks at the dog, "Sorry, this is what they give us to eat. No offense, but we call it dog food."

Meanwhile, Spiegel is trying to pry the padlock off the back door with his knife and Kozlowski stands behind him with his rifle at the ready. Spiegel tries and tries, but he can't open the lock.

Disgusted, Kozlowski pulls him away from the door, "Lemme at it. I'll use my rifle."

Spiegel gasps, "You're not going to shoot the lock off, are you? It'll make too much noise."

Kozlowski shakes his head and looks at Spiegel, "I ain't gonna shoot the lock off. I'm gonna bust it off." He easily shatters the lock with his rifle butt and smirks at Spiegel who's standing there with his mouth open, "You ready?"

Spiegel raises his rifle and nods nervously. Kozlowski kicks the door open and barges in. Spiegel hesitates for a moment and slowly creeps through the doorway. Kozlowski strikes a match and they look around the room, totally aghast at what the flickering light reveals. Nothing could

7

have prepared them for this. They look at each other, mouths agape, both afraid they've stumbled into Frankenstein's laboratory.

Kozlowski lowers his rifle and looks at Spiegel who's lighting a Bunsen burner, "What the hell is this?"

Spiegel gleefully holds up the flame so it fills the entire room with an eerie glow, "This is fantastic. It's the most amazing lab I've ever seen. Just look at all this weird equipment. I don't even recognize most of it. Somebody did some serious work in here."

"What kinda work?"

"I don't know, but I've got to find out."

"Ain't you a druggist?"

Spiegel laughs, "Please, I'm a pharmacist. I majored in chemistry, but this place is way out of my league."

The room is mostly intact save for one gaping hole in the roof that explains the small pile of rubble on the floor beneath it. There is a large, coal-fired oven, four crucibles, different types of distillation equipment, and various jars containing an odd assortment of animals and plants preserved in formaldehyde. Plus, there's a refrigerator, a fully stocked pantry, and a bed. Spiegel snaps his fingers and points to the back door. Kozlowski nods, walks over, and slowly opens it. He sticks his rifle out and waves it around before poking his head out. He quickly looks right and left, pulls his head back in, and shuts the door. He turns to Spiegel and shrugs his shoulders, "Ain't nothin' out back 'cept an alley."

Spiegel motions toward the pantry, "Why don't you grab some food and take it to the guys."

Kozlowski's face lights up, "Thats a great idea." He takes off his jacket and lays it on the floor. He grabs several cans of food, some sausages, and a big hunk of cheese, wraps it all up in his jacket, and throws it over his shoulder with a grunt. He starts for the door and looks at Spiegel, "Ain't you comin'?"

"No, I want to stay here and look around some more, but you go ahead."

Kozlowski shrugs his shoulders, "Okay, suit yourself," and walks into the other room.

Spiegel turns his attention to the large table in the center of the room that contains two antique microscopes and an old leather-bound notebook with the signs of the zodiac etched in gold on its cover. The mere sight of it makes his head spin. Entranced, he circles the table, never taking his eyes off the book, mustering the courage to touch it, not quite sure he should. He carefully sits on a stool at the edge of the table and cocks his head warily, almost as if he expects it to move. He takes two deep breaths, wipes his sweaty hands on his pants, and slowly reaches for it.

Once his pulse has stopped throbbing in his neck, Spiegel grabs the book and opens it before anything else can stop him. It appears to be some kind of diary filled with cryptic entries in French and Latin, surreal illustrations of people, animals, and monsters surrounded by astrological calculations and enigmatic medieval symbols. Then it dawns on him. This isn't a chemist's laboratory; it's the secret lair of an alchemist. He's not out of his league; he's standing on the threshold of another world.

He can't possibly explain this to the other guys and he probably shouldn't tell them anyway. They'll leave him alone, content to fill their bellies, while he quietly tries to unravel the glorious mysteries in front of him.

2

Rasco and Kozlowski sit at the table and noisily scarf down their food. Harper, still keeping a lookout, sits next to the window and eats by himself. Billy sits on the floor, feeding the rancid meat to the dog, and says, "Hey, Rasco, can I ask you a personal question?"

Rasco doesn't look up, "Sure, as long as I can keep eating. Kozlowski, go sit by the window so Harper can take a break and eat with us."

Kozlowski almost chokes as he tries to answer, "Wha...what the hell? I ain't finished eatin' yet."

Rasco looks up and gives him some serious stink eye.

He gets the message, grabs as much food as he can carry, and does as he's told without another word. Harper takes his place at the table and smiles at Rasco, "Kozlowski got another beef?"

Rasco grins back at him, "Nah, he started to blow a fuse 'cause I told him to switch places with you, but he caught himself. Billy wanted to ask me something personal and whatever we talk about is certainly none of Kozlowski's business. He's acting better since we chewed him out, but I still don't trust him." He turns to Billy, "So go ahead; there's no secrets between the three of us."

"Ah, thanks. It's just that, well, I can't understand why you'd want to be an actor? I mean, you sure look the part, but isn't it awful hard to get work?"

Rasco looks the part alright. He's what you'd call a real dreamboat: tall, muscular, winning smile, pearly white teeth, thick black hair, sky blue eyes. It was impossible for him to escape the comments and the stares, even in Los Angeles where he grew up. It was almost as if he didn't have any say in the matter. People who knew him thought he should be an actor. Strangers took one look at him and assumed he was an actor.

Billy is a working man. If he looked like Rasco, he'd still be a working man. He hated what he did, but he managed to work steadily during the Depression when millions of people couldn't find a job. His father died when he was a teenager which left him with no choice. He went down to the docks, took his father's place, and became the family breadwinner.

Rasco knows Billy's story and, as a result, has more respect for him than he does for himself especially since Billy was the first to befriend Harper when he joined the platoon. Negro soldiers were only used as truck drivers and stevedores until the very end of the war. They weren't even allowed to carry guns. General Dwight Eisenhower, the Supreme Allied Commander, changed all that during the Battle of the Bulge. There simply weren't enough white troops to replace all those killed and wounded during the bloodiest battle of the war. He made the monumental decision to give weapons to the Negro soldiers so they could join the white military units and fight in combat for the first time. Over 2,000 of them volunteered to go to the front and Benjamin was one of the first.

A lot of white soldiers thought that arming them was a terrible idea. The Jim Crow laws in the South prevented them from owning firearms. Now they were being ordered to fight for the country that had enslaved their ancestors for hundreds of years. Who could blame them for shooting white soldiers if given the chance, especially those with heavy southern accents? Billy didn't give it a second thought. He saw Harper for what he was: just another decent human being trying to survive this hellish mayhem and get back home in one piece to the wife he adored and the baby girl he hadn't seen for two long years. He constantly wondered what his daughter looked like or what kind of personality she had, but that didn't matter. He'd say things like, "I'll bet she's every bit as pretty as her mama," or, "I just know she'll be smarter'n me."

11

Billy also admired Harper for being so well-educated, having grown up in an area where most people couldn't read, let alone write. He said his mother taught him to read the Sears catalog before he started school. It also gave him a glimpse of a whole world of things he never would have seen in his small town. It contained over 100,000 items to include Mickey Mouse watches, live canaries, chocolates, electric trains, and every kind of toy imaginable. You could even buy an entire house right out of the catalog. Once he got started, he read everything he could get his hands on and finished all the books in the local library by the time he was ten.

Rasco shrugs his shoulders, "Honestly, it wasn't that hard to get work, well, at the start of my career anyway. You see, my mom was a terrific music teacher. I guess I took it for granted, but music was always a central part of our lives. She started me on the piano when I was 5 and voice lessons when I was 10. I never considered it performing when I was young; it's what we did as a family and it was a lot of fun. When my voice changed in high school, all of a sudden, I became a serious performer. I had to...my voice was that good. I mean, I'm just being honest, I'm not bragging, it was terrific. I went right from doing high school plays to auditioning in Hollywood. Remember, musicals were the big thing before the war. A lot of actors were extremely good looking, but if you could sing, you were in huge demand. That was the advantage I had over the rest of them. Hell, I was in my first film at the age of 18, and then another, and another, and then it happened.

Billy asks, "What happened?"

Rasco continues, "That was the problem; I worked too much and I blew my voice."

Billy looks befuddled, "How can you blow your voice?"

Rasco shrugs, "Oh, it's easier than you might think. Try singing at the top of your lungs for 8 hours straight without a break. They said I developed nodules on my vocal cords, kind of like callouses, that ruined my gorgeous singing voice. I'm lucky I can still talk. Oh, and then they fired me.

Billy grimaces, "Those bastards."

Rasco smiles and shakes his head, "Aw, they had to. I couldn't sing anymore, others could, end of story. It took me a while to find work until I finally got hired to be in a bunch of patriotic films that were produced in conjunction with the Defense Department. You guys probably saw 'em in theaters. They get you all worked up with a lot of sappy flag-waving and at the end, they tell you to go buy War Bonds. So, yeah, I was always able to get work, but it wasn't very important work. I'm not very good at anything else so I was lucky to get that."

Billy gets oddly serious and says, "Well, seems to me you're good at organizing stuff and you've got a lot of common sense. Look how you whipped this group of morons into shape."

Rasco is taken aback by Billy's observation. For once, somebody is actually speaking to him as a person, and not just a good looking commodity. Plus, Billy sees something in him that he never saw in himself, mainly because he never had any reason to be introspective. All he had to do was smile and doors seemed to open automatically. This is uncharted territory; it makes him feel uncomfortable and kind of guilty so he tries to dismiss it out of hand.

"Who me?   Billy, if I had any common sense, I wouldn't be an actor."

He pauses, looks down for a moment, then at Billy.

"Or maybe if I had more self-respect, I wouldn't be an actor."

"What do mean if you had more self-respect?"

Rasco smiles and shrugs his shoulders, "I was part of the Hollywood studio system. I was under contract and they owned me same as they owned the lights, cameras, and props. They told me what to wear, who to date, and what project to do. Basically, I worked in a factory that supported the war effort by making those propaganda films. I guess you could say I was helping and it was an important part of the nation's defense strategy, but the bullets weren't real, the battles were carefully staged, and the good guys always won."

Billy is amazed at Rasco's honesty and humility. The roughnecks he knew back in Boston would never dare show their cards like that.

"Well, sounds to me like you were doin' somethin' real important back home. How'd you end up here with the rest of us?"

Rasco answers shyly, "They kept telling us that we were doing our part and we were exempt from the draft. We didn't have to enlist, but it didn't feel right so I did anyway. I mean, these bullets are real, you guys are real and, for the first time in my life, I feel like I'm real."

Billy nods his head pensively, grabs his canteen, and pours water into his cupped hand so the dog can lap it up. When the canteen is empty, the dog licks his hand until every last drop is gone. He giggles and scratches the dog's head, "Hey, that tickles. Don't worry, I'll get you some more water." Then he looks at Rasco, "Know what I'd like to do when this mess is over?"

"What, you want to be an actor?"

"Right, fat chance. No, I'd like to be a vet."

Rasco teases him, "Hey, we'll all be vets when this is over."

Billy strokes the dog gently, "You know what I mean, a veterinarian. Have you heard about that G.I. Bill? They say it'll pay for us to go to college for free when the war's over. I can't think of anything else I'd rather do than take care of animals like this here mutt. He's not like any of the nasty dogs I saw at the docks. He's really special, but when you think about it, all animals are special. They all deserve the best care we can give 'em."

Rasco grins and shakes his head, "Whew, that sounds great. Here we are, killing people right and left, and all you can think about is taking care of poor, defenseless animals. Now I really feel like I had a worthless job back home."

Billy loses patience with him, "The hell you did. C'mon now, we all got different talents. You got a real way with people and you know how to get things done. Maybe you could work your way up to bein' a director."

Rasco makes a face and rolls his eyes.

"Like that'll ever happen. They'd never take me seriously enough to put me in charge."

Billy has had it with Rasco's virtually nonexistent self-regard. He's always had to use every bone in his body and every fiber of his soul to survive his miserable lot in life. "Aw, you're probably right. Why should they have faith in you if you don't have faith in yourself?"

Rasco turns toward Billy with his mouth agape; he's speechless.

3

Disgusted with Rasco, Billy gets up and walks into the back room.

"Spiegel, aren't you hungry? Whoa, what's goin' on in here?"

Spiegel totally ignores him so he tries again.

"Hey, Spiegel, you hear me? Spiegel."

Never taking his eyes off the book, Spiegel raises his hand to stop Billy, "Can't you see I'm busy? Whatever you're saying, I don't care. Please stop bugging me."

Billy shrugs, makes an obscene gesture toward Spiegel, and walks back into the other room.

Spiegel can't be bothered because he can't hear anything except the roaring sound of his own blood coursing through his body. A bead of sweat trickles off the end of his nose and he manages to intercept it before it splashes onto the precious book. He takes of his helmet and wipes his face on both arms of his jacket before he takes it off as well. Once again, he starts to mumble to himself, "This must be why I'm here."

He initially became interested in the mystical realm because of his grandfather, Saul Spiegel, who came from what he called the "Old Country" which happened to be Hungary. He used to delight Ira with fantastic stories about mysticism, magic, and, yes, alchemy. The old man often bore the brunt of cruel family jokes because everybody else thought he was off his rocker. His favorite grandson was the only one who defended him because he loved the stories and always begged for more. Thus, he knew from a very early age that he didn't want to be a typical doctor. No, he wanted to use any and all means at his disposal to go beyond the limits of conventional medical knowledge and rediscover the secrets of the ancient alchemists.

He majored in chemistry because his grandfather told him that it evolved from alchemy. Unfortunately, much had been lost in that long, convoluted transition. Modern chemistry, with its worship of the scientific method, never takes into account the elusive nature of the great truths; truths that can't always be reliably reproduced in the laboratory. Alchemy, like agriculture, is governed by the interplay of the seasons, the sun, the moon, the position of the planets, the delicate balance between heat and cold, moisture and dryness. Strictly speaking, it is an art, not a science. It seeks to explore the supreme, hidden reality that is the essence of ultimate truths and all religions. It is the perfect melding of the physical and spiritual planes. His grandfather told him that the old alchemists had a far better understanding of the true nature of matter than all the Nobel Prize winners in history.

Most people have never heard of alchemy. Of the small minority who have, most of them think it's the quest for a way to turn base metal into gold, that alchemists are merely trying to get rich. Nothing could be further from the truth. They didn't sell their knowledge nor did they try to profit from it. Instead, they only passed it along to those they deemed worthy, thus giving rise to the legend that modern alchemists were still doing the sacred work. The "Gold" they sought was actually a metaphor for the Elixir of Life, the Key to Immortality that would cure all ills and rejuvenate the body.

When medical school was no longer an option, it dawned on Spiegel that being a pharmacist might just be the clearest path to attaining his loftiest goals. He tirelessly combed libraries for any mention of alchemy. He grilled his chemistry teachers about their limited knowledge of the subject, usually earning a stern rebuke for having his head in the clouds or somewhere else more personal. He didn't want to be a common pill pusher like the rest of his class. Rather, he studied to be a compounding pharmacist so he could devise intricate chemical formulas with specific healing properties. He simply wanted to do whatever he could to further medical science, knowing full well that he would never be able to duplicate the work of the great alchemists, that is, until this very moment.

He devours the pages as rapidly as possible, looking for any clues about the true nature of the work. It appears to be a mystical cookbook of sorts, a narrative that chronicles the completion of the quest. Had the author actually accomplished the unthinkable? If so, where is it? Did he take it with him when he fled? If not, would he return for it? What if he's captured by the Germans and they're able to exploit the power of healing, of longevity, and God forbid, of immortality? Spiegel trembles at the thought, definitely his worst nightmare. All the more reason to search the entire place as quickly and as thoroughly as possible, but he can't tear himself away from the book that holds him so tightly under its spell. Ah, wait, how does it end? Feeling stupid for wasting so much time, he holds his breath and turns to the last page.

There it is, a drawing of the sun with flames radiating from a smiling face that looks strangely familiar. At first, he can't decide if it's wishful thinking or something he really did see during his research. No, he's positive, that's it, that's the sign of completion. It means that whoever worked in this lab successfully produced the Elixir and, if Spiegel can find it, he knows he will have the gateway to another level of existence. Then it dawns on him: the Elixir isn't the most important thing, the book is. Yes, this diary contains the magical procedure necessary to produce something that has eluded scientists for centuries. Without it, no one could possibly reverse engineer the process; modern chemistry simply isn't up to the task. He has every confidence that, given enough time, he can unravel the secrets that will allow him to concoct the magical potion himself. Therefore, he will guard it with his life and never let it out of his sight. A moment of panic seizes him until he decides to stuff it in his rucksack and stash it under the bed.

Now he has to find the Elixir. He tries to concentrate as he scours every inch of the lab, but his unbridled imagination races out of control. Has he found his alter ego? The person who worked here was obviously leading a dual life. He was the village pharmacist to the people who came into his store, but in his secret lab, he was a gifted alchemist, the embodiment of Spiegel's lifelong dream.

Where is it? Where would the wizard hide it? He closes his eyes and breathes silently, hoping for any answer, any clue. A loud ticking sound startles him out of his reverie. His eyes pop open and he sees an old clock on the wall, its pendulum swaying methodically behind a glass door. His heart pounds in his chest, almost drowning out the sound of the clock. Yes, clocks were symbolic of their work because they sought to reverse the effect of time on the human condition. He wants to go to the clock and see what's inside, but he can't move his legs. The fear of what he might find inside the clock seems to have paralyzed him. He looks down impatiently and slaps his legs with both hands as if he's trying to wake them up.

Finally, he summons the courage to approach the clock and take it down from the wall. It's heavy and, because of the moving pendulum, it feels strangely alive, like it has a pulse of its own. His hands tremble as he places it carefully on the table. He takes a deep breath, fumbles for the chair, and sits down facing the clock. He cocks his head from one side to the other and listens intently like he's waiting for the clock to tell him something. At last, he grasps it with both hands and turns it around so he can examine the back. There's a door with a small latch. Now he's drenched in cold sweat, his mouth as dry as sandpaper. Shaming himself into action, he wipes his hands on the front of his uniform and reaches for the clasp. It opens easily, revealing two test tubes with rubber stoppers, both filled with a milky liquid. His features slowly dissolve into a demonic grin that transforms his face into a macabre mask as his reality changes forever. All traces of fear have left his body only to be replaced with a monstrous feeling of intense gratification. This is it. This is his destiny. He holds the very secret of life in his hands.

He stares off into space and imagines what this will mean to his country, to his place in history and, ultimately, to the rest of mankind. Chuckling to himself, he remembers that he originally entered this room in search of medical supplies. Instead, he's stumbled onto something that could save his belligerent species from annihilation. Maybe it will turn the tide forever and make war a thing of the past. Maybe it's only the noxious chemical fumes playing tricks on his befuddled brain, propelling him into a state of ecstatic euphoria. At this point, he really doesn't care; he's determined to savor this delightful dream come true for as long as possible.

4

Billy walks into the front room, gives Rasco a dirty look, and sits on the floor next to the dog. Rasco shakes his head and winces. He knows everything Billy said about him is true, but he can't stand the cold shoulder especially since he'd like to thank Billy for opening his eyes.

He made Kozlowski and Harper switch places again since Kozlowski wasn't keeping an eye on the street. Now he's back at the table burping and continuing to stuff his face so Rasco walks over to Harper, puts a hand on his shoulder, and offers him a piece of cheese. Together, they eat in silence and look for any sign of the enemy.

Then they hear the dreaded wail of incoming mortars. Rasco pulls Harper away from the window and shoves him to the floor where he falls on top of the dog. Billy instinctively jumps on top of Harper to shield him from the blast. Kozlowski freezes and stares at the ceiling as a glob of food tumbles from his mouth.

The deafening concussion of an exploding shell turns the room inside out. The roof crumbles on top of the men, crushing Kozlowski and driving a jagged piece of smoking metal into Billy's back, his jacket instantly awash in a sea of foaming crimson. More screaming missiles sail overhead followed by thundering explosions all around them.

Harper comes to, his face contorted by the searing pain in his side as he struggles to get Billy off him. When he finally does, he grabs Billy's face and screams, "Billy O, look at me," but his eyes are already locked in the frozen gaze of death. Harper screams again, "Billy O, don't leave me. Aw shit. You gone." When he yells this time, he realizes he can barely hear his own voice due to the loud ringing in his ears and the constant fusillade of exploding shells.

Then he feels the dog under him, desperately gasping for air. When he pushes himself off the dog, he sees Rasco lying next to him with his eyes closed, his left leg pinned under a huge ceiling timber. He shakes Rasco's arm and yells, "Rasco, Rasco, c'mon Rasco, don't you leave me, too."

Rasco slowly wakes up and turns toward Harper, "Hey, what the...?" As he speaks, he notices he's almost deaf so he points to his ears and shakes his head. Harper nods and yells, "I know. I can't hear either," then he tries to move the massive hunk of wood off Rasco's leg. Together, they push as hard as they can until they're finally able to roll it away.

Rasco tries to stand, but his left leg gives way and he screams as he collapses.

"Harper, you gotta help me, my knee's shot."

Harper doesn't hear a word because he's turned away, holding his side, and struggling to get to his feet. Once he does, he sees Rasco grabbing his knee, rocking back and forth. Still holding his side, Harper extends his hand to Rasco and helps him up. They steady each other and hobble over to Koslowski. Rasco leans against the wall, grabs Kozlowski's hand that's sticking out of the rubble, and feels for a pulse. He shakes his head "No" to Harper who kneels next to Billy, gently closes his eyes, and removes his dog tags. He puts them in his pocket, looks up at Rasco, and they stare at each other with tears streaming down their cheeks until Rasco snaps out of it and yells, "C'mon, grab the dog. Let's see if Spiegel made it."

Harper bends down, cradles the dog tightly in his arms, and nearly faints from the pain when he stands up. Rasco grabs a piece of wood to use as a cane and puts his arm around Harper's shoulder. Together, they slowly climb through the rubble and head for the back room.

They can't believe their eyes when they enter the lab; it's still completely intact. Harper lays the dog on the table next to the clock, his mouth opening and closing convulsively, his legs pawing in midair, as he barely clings to life. Rasco looks around for Spiegel and finds him cringing under the bed. He kicks Spiegel's leg, which startles him, and makes him scream, "What happened? Who are you?"

Rasco kicks him again, "Spiegel, it's me, Rasco. Billy O and Kozlowski are dead. Get up. You gotta bandage my knee so we can get out of here."

Spiegel scrambles to his feet clutching the test tubes to his chest. When he sees the dog lying on the table, obviously in the throes of death, his face contorts into a maniacal grin, "Now's my chance to prove I've found the Elixir of Life. I'll give some to the dog and if it saves him, why, I can save mankind. I know my grandfather's smiling down on me." He looks up through the hole in the roof and screams, "Watch me, Gramps. Watch me make history. Soon, everyone on earth will know my name."

Rasco gasps in dismay, "What the...? Are you off your rocker? Didn't you hear me? C'mon, fix my knee. We gotta get outta here!"

Spiegel totally ignores Rasco, shoves Harper aside, and starts stroking the dog's head, "I can save you. You'll be fine as soon as you drink this. No, you'll be more than fine; you'll be immortal." He cradles the dog's head with one hand, pulls the stopper out of one of the tubes with his teeth, and pours the liquid into the dog's mouth. He chokes at first, but once he swallows, his eyes bulge wide open and glow with a golden intensity. Mesmerized by the liquid, he drinks the rest of it as fast as he can, despite the spasms convulsing his entire body.

Rasco and Harper are dumfounded by the dog's radical transformation and they look at each other in total disbelief. Rasco starts to yell at Spiegel again, but stops cold with his mouth agape, paralyzed by the sound of another mortar screaming toward them. He and Harper dive under the table and cover their heads with their hands. Spiegel staggers backward, watching the dog writhe uncontrollably as his body mutates. He gazes at the other tube in his hand and screams, "It's working. The magic is working and because I found it, I deserve it, too. Yes, not only will I be famous, I will live forever."

He laughs defiantly in the direction of the incoming round as he pulls out the stopper and raises the tube to his lips, but before he can drink, the projectile disintegrates the back wall, the tube spirals in midair, emptying its milky contents, and the blast launches him into the rack of specimen jars, shattering them and killing him instantly. Thus, as he exits life, the image of what could have been is eternally etched in his soul before it evaporates back into the alchemical ether.

The highly flammable formaldehyde splashes everywhere and catches fire. Rasco and Harper survive the blast, but they're both knocked out and the flames creep steadily toward them. The dog, blown off the table, licks his chops, and shivers uncontrollably as the liquid courses through his bloodstream, reaching every part of his body, transforming it, healing his wounds, and fueling his brain with a determination that boils up like a geyser, filling him with an exuberance that supersedes all trepidation and propels him into another level of existence. He springs to his feet, looks around the room with his bright golden eyes and, for the first time in his life, sees everything in crystal clear color, instead of the usual blurred, grayish tones.

He howls lustily at the ceiling and violently shakes his body from head to tail, and with each gyration, he grows larger and stronger as his muscles bulge and his fur gets thicker. When he stops shaking, he sniffs Spiegel's dead body and snorts in disgust. Next, he sniffs Rasco, grabs him by the collar of his jacket, and swiftly drags him out the back door as easily as if he were dragging an old army blanket. He trots back into the lab panting happily, grabs the semiconscious Harper who's mumbling nonsense, whisks him outside, and not a moment too soon. The building crumbles into a huge pile of flaming debris and everything inside is lost forever.

5

The distant voices from above lift Harper out of his stupor and propel him toward the surface. He always wondered what it would feel like to ride an elevator. He's been drifting for days through a series of wild, otherworldly dreams fueled by the painkiller that dripped steadily into his arm. The dreams terrified him at first, but in a deceptively lucid moment, he decided that he must be dead and that death is nothing more than an ever-changing picture show.

His vertical assent comes to an abrupt stop as he tries to open his eyes that have been glued shut ever since that horrific day. Faint images continue to drift in and out of his mind: the drug store, the good food, the first explosion that killed Billy O and Kozlowski, stumbling into the lab with Rasco, the blinding flash that killed Spiegel while he was messing with the dog, and finally, the disturbing memory of being whisked out of the building by some mysteriously powerful being.

Suddenly, a voice with a strong Cockney accent cackles loudly in his ear, "Oh, look, he's awake. Hello, Mr. Harper, how are you?"

Now his eyes have no choice; they pry themselves open just to see what kind of creature is making those horrendous sounds, Okay, this must be heaven because it's supposed to be white and everything he sees is unbearably, painfully white. Then a bolt of fear shoots through him when he sees a scary looking angel in a white cap with plump, pink cheeks and striking blue eyes hovering over him, grinning with a mouth full of crooked yellow teeth.

His mind races. If this is heaven, then it's the wrong one. What if he got here by mistake? What if all the other angels are this dreadful looking and he's doomed to be surrounded by them for all eternity? Oh no, could this be hell? It's supposed to be all hot and fiery, but who knows? Maybe it's just cold and full of ugly, noisy white angels.

Rasco, wearing a robe and standing with a cane on the other side of the bed, says, "Harper, Harper, it's me, Rasco. You okay?"

Harper jerks his head toward the familiar voice and tries to speak, but all he can do is smile weakly and make gurgling sounds deep in his throat.

Rasco pats him on the arm and says, "Hey, take it easy. We'll have plenty of time to talk."

Harper coughs again and again, finally clearing his throat enough to say, "Rasco, we're dead 'n this is hell, right?"

Rasco and the nurse roar with laughter. This scares Harper even more and confirms his worst suspicion: he's stuck here forever and now they're laughing at him.

Rasco gets very serious when he sees the sheer terror in Harper's eyes and says, "Hey, Ben, we're not dead. We survived and we're in an English hospital. You should thank Nurse Tinsley here. She's been taking very good care of you."

Harper's mouth drops open as he blinks away tears of relief. He looks back and forth from Rasco to the nurse, still suspicious, still not totally convinced he's alive. He finally gets up the courage to speak, but just in case he is dead, he tries to be real nice to the angel.

"Thank ya, Ma'am, I do appreciate your help."

He turns back to Rasco, and says, "Are we the only Americans in this hospital?"

The nurse senses his real concern, pats his head gently, and reassures him, "Oh no, me darlin', we got all kinds of brave heroes and we're eternally grateful to have you." Then she leans down and kisses him on the forehead.

Now he believes them. He also knows he's alive because the pain shooting through his side is a rude wake up call that makes him scream, "Eeyow, what's that? Was I shot?"

The nurse continues to pat his head and speaks to him very softly, "No, Mr. Harper, your spleen was crushed so we took it out along with two o' your ribs, but we had to get you off the painkillers so you're gonna have to tough it out for a bit."

Now he panics again and yells at her, "You took what? My spleen? What'd you do with it?"

Rasco grabs his arm and says, "Take it easy, you'll never miss it."

Harper comes right back at him, "Not gonna miss it? Then why was it there in the first place?"

The nurse clears her throat and speaks very slowly and deliberately, "Mr. Harper, your spleen protects against infections, but you'll do just fine without it, if you're careful."

"And just what do you mean by 'careful'?"

"Well now, you should try not to catch cold or it might be hard to shake."

Rasco giggles and says, "Ha, he lives in Alabama. All he has to worry about is heat stroke."

The nurse smiles at them and says, "You're two very lucky lads. You both survived this horrible war and soon you'll be back in the States where you belong. I'll let you catch up now."

She turns to leave, but pauses at Rasco's side and gazes up at him long enough to memorize every aspect of his perfect face, then walks away fanning herself with a hanky.

Harper waits until she's gone, then he turns to Rasco with a devilish grin and says, "Oo, she's in love with you."

Rasco actually blushes, bursts out laughing, and says, "Gimme a break, will you."

Harper starts to laugh with him, but the pain stops him and makes him wince.

Rasco keeps laughing and says, "See, that's what you get for being a wiseacre." Then he clears his throat and says, "Hey, seriously, can I tell you something."

Harper squints his eyes closed, puffs out his cheeks, exhales as much pain as he can, and says, "Okay, what is it?"

Rasco clears his throat again and says, "I just want to thank you for saving my life. The guys who found us said they figured you dragged me out of the burning building since I was out cold. Plus, my leg was busted up so I couldn't have saved myself, let alone anyone else."

Harper is stunned when he hears this. He doesn't know what to say, or in truth, he's afraid to say what he thinks really happened that day. He certainly can't tell Rasco that he vaguely remembers something dragging both of them to safety. On the other hand, he might as well take credit for saving him. He likes being thought of as a hero. It makes him feel a little guilty at first, but what the hell, why not shut up and enjoy it. It's about time the country had a Colored hero. Plus, no one could possibly dispute Rasco's story and the dog's probably dead anyway. After a long pause, he says, " Aw, it wasn't a big deal. You would've done the same for me. Hey, how's your leg? They say how long you'll have to use a cane?"

"Excuse me, Mr. Harper, but someone saving my life is a very big deal so get used to it. And as for my leg, I'll always have a limp and I'll probably have to use a cane for the rest of my life. Looks like I'm in for a big career change."

Harper is relieved to be talking about something else and says, "What're you gonna do when you get home?"

Rasco shakes his head and grins.

"You won't believe what I've been thinking. Look, as soon as I realized that my Hollywood career was over, I figured I'd just stay in the Army."

"You what? Are you nuts?"

"I know, huh. Sounds crazy, but Billy O put a bug in my ear and it got me to thinking. Hey, I really wasn't happy being an actor. I only did it because it was easy and I never gave anything else a second thought. Obviously, I can't fight because of my leg. Maybe they could find me a desk job in recruiting or something else. Who knows?"

Harper can't believe his ears. How could anyone give up the chance to get out of the Army with an honorable discharge and go home to his family? Whoa, that thought almost backfires in his mind. He knows his family will be deliriously happy to see him, but what if he can't do all the heavy work on the farm like he used to? He still feels guilty about leaving them to go fight a war they didn't understand or care about. Then he sobers up and realizes that, whatever it takes, he'll be able to get the job done.

"Hey, Rasco, that nurse say how bad I'm hurt? I mean, I gotta get back 'n work on the farm."

Rasco shakes his head and smiles at Harper.

"Ben, you're a hero. You're the one who saved the day back there and I'm sure you'll be fine when you get home."

"That's not what I asked. Ain't no heroes on a farm, just workin' folks. What'd she say?"

Rasco looks down at the floor and then slowly at Harper.

"Look, you were hurt real bad. You've been in this hospital for almost two weeks. It's hard to tell what you can do when you get home, but there are some great people here who will make damn sure you get back to normal."

Harper is taken aback; he's never heard such kind words from another man, let alone a white man. Now he's determined to honor Rasco's friendship and make him proud. The best way to do that is to get well, no matter what it takes, and get home to his family.

"Alright, I hear you. They better be real good 'cause they gotta find a way to get me ready for life back on the farm. By the way, did she say I could get outta bed?"

Rasco grins and says, "No, but she didn't say you couldn't. Wanna give it a try?"

Harper takes a deep breath and grimaces as he props himself up on one elbow. "Now's as good a time as ever. Gimme a hand."

Rasco grabs his hand and says, "Sure, real easy now."

29

They both groan as Harper tries to sit up, but can't and falls back onto the bed. He gives out a determined growl and tries again. This time he's able to sit up, catch his breath for a moment, and swing his legs over the edge of the bed. He looks up at Rasco and says, "What if I put my feet down and my legs won't hold me?"

Rasco grins at him and says, "Well then, I suppose we'll both end up on the floor."

Harper starts to laugh, grabs his side, and says, "Stop, you're killin' me."

Rasco shows him no mercy and says, "Aw, poor wittle soldier."

Harper can't help it now. He rolls around on the bed, screaming in pain and laughing uncontrollably until Nurse Tinsley bursts into the room and yells, "For the love o' Mike, have you crazy Yanks lost your minds?"

Rasco stumbles on his cane and almost falls as he and Harper laugh at each other like complete fools. All the pain, the horrors of war, the loss of their buddies, everything that's been stuck inside them, rolls out in waves of joyful hysteria.

The nurse stands there for a moment with her hands on her ample hips and bites her lip, trying not to join in the revelry, but once she lets out the first little giggle, it's no use, her dam bursts and she howls while dancing a little jig for them. Next, she grabs Rasco's arm and twirls herself around him while Harper claps his hands.

When she finally settles down and catches her breath, she pokes Rasco and says, "Did you tell 'im about the dog?"

Harper feels a jolt of anxiety when he hears this, gets very serious, and says, "What dog?"

Rasco steadies himself on his cane, pats himself on the chest as he tries to breathe normally, and says, "Oh, yeah, no, not yet." He takes a few more breaths and continues, "You're not gonna believe it, but they let Billy O's dog come with us and he's been waiting for you outside the hospital ever since. The medics who rescued us said, when they found us, we were both unconscious and he was standing guard. They tried to shoo him away, but he ignored them and jumped right into the field ambulance with us."

Deep down, Harper knows he wouldn't be alive if it weren't for the dog and he can't help himself; he looks up at the ceiling and chokes out the words, "Thank ya, Lord."

The nurse chimes in, "Amen! He sits there all day long, lookin' up at your window. He knows you're in here, he does. I've been feedin' 'im scraps from the kitchen when I go home at night. He's very sweet."

Yes, he's sweet, but that's only the beginning. The real reason he's waiting is because the bond they have is stronger than tempered steel, the bond that was forged when Harper saved his life and then, scant moments later, when he saved Harper's.

Harper's mouth hangs open as he looks back and forth from Rasco to the nurse, refusing to believe what she's saying. He swallows hard, looks warily at Rasco, and tries his best to deny the irrefutable truth, "Aw, you sure it's BIlly O's dog? There's no way he survived all that."

Rasco shakes his head and says, "Yup, he sure did, but you won't hardly recognize him 'cause he's so big and strong now. I don't know what happened back there, but come to think of it, Spiegel made him drink something right before that last explosion and he started to shake like crazy. There has to be a logical explanation, but I sure as hell can't figure it out. All I remember is waking up in the ambulance and there he was, staring down at me with those big golden eyes and not a mark on him. He was the most gorgeous dog I'd ever seen and he was huge. Anyway, c'mon, let's get you out of bed and you can see for yourself."

He and the nurse help Harper stand up and walk him slowly to the window. When he looks out, the dog sees him, sits at attention, pants happily, and wags his tail. Harper's heart skips a beat, but he's able to smile and wave feebly. The dog barks insistently and runs back and forth like he's begging him to come out and play. Harper chokes back his tears as he thinks of Billy O who saved his life the first time and also befriended the dog that saved his life the second time.

Rasco puts his hand on Harper's shoulder and says, "It looks like you've been adopted. I think you'll have to take him home with you. What do you say?"

Harper keeps staring out the window and says, "You're right. We belong together. He's my dog now."

As he says this, Harper finally understands and accepts the destiny they share that is both exhilarating and terrifying at the same time. It's the least he can do to honor Billy O's memory. If it weren't for him, Harper knows he and the dog would both be dead.

6

Harper sits in the back of a rickety old bus, looking out the window at the misty Alabama countryside glowing awake in the early morning. Yellow daffodils, the first welcome signs of spring, line the dusty dirt road that's taking him home. He's wearing his Army uniform, now adorned with a Purple Heart and a Bronze Star, that make him feel more embarrassed than proud. He always looked upon his service as just another job and, where he comes from, you don't get medals for doing your job, you get to eat supper. Most people in the country aren't aware that Negroes are now fighting in combat. Needless to say, the sight of Harper's medals come as quite a troubling surprise to many.

He turns to his traveling companion and says, "See those fields goin' by? You can grow anything you want in 'em, dirt's so good. Uh huh, it's a fact, you'll see."

His companion, sitting proudly next to him, drinking in the lush scenery with his golden eyes, pants his approval and whines expectantly.

"Hold on, we'll be there soon. I gotta go, too."

A dog riding on a bus in rural Alabama isn't all that unusual, but this big, burly creature with Army dog tags hanging around his neck is something else altogether. Harper managed to grab Billy O's tags after he died, promising himself to keep them forever in honor of his best friend who fearlessly protected him to the end. It only seems proper to let the dog wear them. After all, he was Billy O's dog.

If Harper's medals are a source of curiosity, often seasoned with a dash of hostile disbelief for most white people, the dog and his Army tags seem to soften even the nastiest bigot. This is due in no small part to the fact that this particular dog defies description. He doesn't look like any standard breed, yet he doesn't look like your basic garden-variety mutt, either. Plus, he's downright handsome. No one can resist him. The dog tags give complete strangers a great excuse to talk to him, scratch his ears, and even say a few kind words to his buddy who certainly wasn't prepared for all the attention. The most intriguing thing about the dog isn't the way he looks, it's the way he looks at you and looks into you as if he understands every word you say, as if there's no one else on the bus. Then, he looks from you to Harper, inviting you to talk to him as well.

When the bus finally rattles and wheezes to a stop at a deserted intersection in the middle of nowhere, it takes Harper and the dog a while get off because they have to say good-bye to all their new friends. The freckle-faced driver scampers up a ladder on the back of the bus and hands Harper his GI duffle bag. When he climbs down, he looks around to make sure no one on the bus is listening, and whispers, "I just wanna thank you for fightin' over there. Couldn't go myself, bad back 'n all. You take care, Son. You done us right proud 'n you got yourself one fine dog."

They stand there silently for a long moment until Harper smiles sheepishly and whispers, "Yessir, he is a fine dog. Thank you much."

Harper and the dog watch the driver climb back into the bus and close the door. Then he grinds into first gear and the bus lurches forward. Harper waves at the all hands waving out the windows until the bus coughs its way down the road and disappears in a swirling cloud of dust.

He grins at the dog and says, "Alright, let's find us a big tree."

He drags the duffle into the woods and the dog follows behind with his nose to the ground, inhaling all the great new smells. When Harper finds a large enough tree, he looks both ways, unzips his pants, and sighs his relief. The dog trots over to the other side of the same tree, peeks around at Harper, and lifts his leg.

Harper laughs and says, "Hey, this is my tree."

The dog laughs at him defiantly. When he's finished, he backs up to the tree and kicks dirt on it with both hind legs, the way a dog is supposed to. This makes Harper laugh even harder and, after he's finished, he kicks dirt onto his side of the tree.

The dog loves it and barks his approval.

"See, you ain't the only one who knows how to clean up. C'mon, we best get goin' 'cause we got a two mile walk ahead of us."

He turns toward the road, but stops dead in his tracks when he hears the unmistakable, heart-stopping sound coming from a big fat diamondback rattler coiled menacingly at his feet. Never taking his eyes off the angry monster, he backs up as carefully and as silently as possible. The snake has other ideas and strikes viciously at his leg, but before it can reach its target, it disappears in a gust of wind that knocks Harper to the ground. He crawls backward as fast as he can, stumbles to his feet, and sees the dog, twenty feet away, flailing the life out of the snake. When he's finished, the dog trots toward Harper with the dead snake's head visible out the side of his mouth and its limp body trailing between his legs.

"You got to be kiddin'. Drop that thing."

The dog, just doing his job, drops the varmint at Harper's feet, looks up at him, and pants happily. The snake's mouth opens and closes spasmodically as venom drips from its huge fangs. Harper stares at the snake and warily backs away as his mind wanders back to the image of Spiegel pouring something mysterious down the dog's throat just before that last mortar hit. He shakes his head, trying to erase the thought from his mind, and motions for the dog to follow him.

He drags the heavy duffel to the roadside and looks down at it with resignation. He managed to lug it this far, using all his strength and determination, mainly to save face and honor the uniform. He knows he can't drag it all the way home; he'll have to carry it and that sure won't be easy since he's weak and his side still hurts a lot, but he has no choice.

He takes a couple of deep breaths, hefts it up onto his shoulder with a grunt, and staggers under its weight. The dog watches him struggle to regain his balance, take a few difficult steps forward, and then stumble backward. Then the dog walks in front of him and stands sideways, effectively blocking his path.

"Hey, get outta the way. It's hard enough walkin' without you tryin' to trip me."

The dog doesn't budge. He looks up at him, looks down the road, and back up at him. Harper slides the duffel off his shoulder and lets it fall to the ground.

"What the? Oh, I get it. You think you can carry this better'n me, huh?"

The dog looks up at him, gives him a little snort, and starts panting. Harper realizes the dog has a point, as usual. He picks up the duffel and lays it across the dog's back, being careful to balance it properly, and adjusts the strap under the dog's belly like a cinch on a saddle. When he finishes, the dog snorts again and trots happily down the road like he isn't carrying anything at all.

Harper is shocked when he sees how easily the dog handles the load like he's a pack mule. Again, it dredges up the hazy recollection of being dragged to safety back in Belgium, something he either tries to forget or dismiss as nothing more than another crazy dream. However, it's no use denying what he sees now. He rolls his eyes and shakes his head.

He knows the dog is incredibly special, not just physically, but also in the uncanny way he relates to people. He wonders how the family will react to him. 'Sure, there were always dogs at the farm, mostly strays, puny little mongrels that weren't much good for anything except chasing cats and terrorizing chickens. But hey, this dog was Billy O's and now he's mine. I'm lucky to have him and I know the family will love him, too.'

Most soldiers returning home from the war are happily greeted by family, friends, and even the occasional brass band. Harper did write a letter telling his family when he would be home, but they never got it. Instead, they live in constant fear of the brown sedan that everyone dreads; the one that always carries two soldiers sent to notify a family of their loved one's death. Beyond that, they have absolutely no idea if he's loading ships, fighting, wounded, missing in action, or dead. Unfortunately, most imaginations tend to dwell on the worst possible outcome, leaving little space for optimism.

He beams and says, "Not so fast now. I gotta keep up, you know."

The dog looks back at Harper and slows down.

"Thats better. Now I can stay with you."

Harper has no idea what to expect when he gets home. He thinks about his wife, Bessie, and his daughter, Sally, who was only one when he left back in 1943. He realizes that Sally's three now, that he missed her first words and her first steps, and that he's missed his sweet Bessie every single day since he left. He hopes they're still living with his mama and daddy, but of course they are. His mama would never let that baby out of her sight.

His mother, Edna, was truly the stalwart leader of the family. His father, Jeremiah, as tough as he was on the outside, always deferred to his mother's good sense and was no match for her iron will.

When Benjamin's draft notice came, Jeremiah promptly tore it up and didn't tell him about it. Instead, he told Edna, "No son o' mine's gonna die for the country that made us slaves and still treats us like dirt."

Luckily, Edna was the only person who wasn't afraid of Jeremiah. She scolded him severely and demanded that he tell Benjamin what he had done. When Jeremiah finally admitted it to him, he was so moved by the depth of his father's love that it inspired him for the rest of his life.

The only time he ever saw his father cry was the day he boarded the bus that carried him off to the Army. There stood one of the toughest men in the state of Alabama, sobbing uncontrollably and screaming at his only son to come home safe. He certainly wasn't alone; the entire family stood there crying in the rain as the bus rumbled down the muddy road that led to the highway. Bessie held Sally high up in the air so her daddy could see her from the back window of the bus. It was an image that awakened him every morning and led him to his dreams every night.

He needs to rest and he's worried about the family's reaction to the dog so he tells him to stop walking. He slides the duffle off his back and sits on it with a groan. As he looks at the dog, trying to figure out how to communicate his concern, he realizes that, despite the dog's wacky unpredictability, he has absolutely no reason to be afraid of him because everything he does turns out great. He does things way too fast and he's way too smart, but anybody can have a slow, dumb dog. Harper knows he's darn lucky to have this one, especially since they've already been through so much together and then there's the undeniable truth that he probably wouldn't be alive if it weren't for him. Most of all, he has faith; the kind of faith that gives him the strength to weather tough times and makes him appreciate good fortune. And, without a doubt, this dog is one giant dose of good fortune.

Harper holds his hands out toward him. The dog wags his tail, slowly walks over, and stands motionless. He cradles the dog's head in his hands and looks straight into his eyes.

"Thanks for killin' that snake, it was real nice of you. Now we're gonna keep walkin', but I'm askin' you to go easy, especially when we get to the farm. See, my family's there and they got to get used to you so please take it slow, okay?"

The dog licks Harper's face, turns, and stands facing down the road. Harper smiles and says, "I guess you're ready for your load, huh?" The dog turns his head toward Harper, snorts once, and faces straight ahead. Harper stands up, grabs the duffel, ties it on the dog's back, and off they go. Harper looks up at the sky, shakes his head, beams down at the dog, and pats him on the head.

One thing's for sure, the dog aims to please though Harper can't figure out if he really understands or if he simply gets a kick out of carrying the load. Regardless, Harper talks to him all the way home, just in case.

7

Edna sits in her creaky rocking chair on the front porch, methodically shelling peas, never taking her eyes off her treasured granddaughter, Sally, who's sitting on the top step, singing to her rag doll. And, as she does during most of her waking hours, Edna silently prays for the safe return of Sally's father, her only son, Benjamin.

Like most Negroes living in this place and time, she managed to survive the Great Depression and she continues to struggle under the oppressive Jim Crow laws, but the past two years have been the most difficult of all. Both her daughters got married off and moved away leaving only her husband, Jeremiah, Benjamin's wife, Bessie, and her to do all the work. It isn't the back-breaking, dawn to dusk labor that bothers her so much; that's life on a farm. It's the constant, nagging worry about Benjamin's safety that weighs on her soul. It's like having an iron yoke around her neck, always there, seemingly heavier with each passing day. Not knowing is the most devastating part of it. Her mind can't help going to the worst possible places and thinking the worst possible thoughts.

"Gramma, look, a man's comin' and he's got a real big doggy."

Edna looks up and blinks her eyes twice, making sure the most wonderful sight imaginable is real. It is. It's Benjamin and there's a large dog with a huge duffel bag on his back ambling along beside him.

Peas fly everywhere as she jumps up and leaps off the porch screaming.

"Benjamin, you're home! My baby's home! Aw, thank you, Lord!"

She throws her arms around him, nearly knocking him down in the process, and making him scream in pain.

"Mama, Mama, easy now, I'm still hurtin' real bad."

She catches her breath and steps back to take a wide-eyed look at him.

"Why're you hurtin'? You been shot? What's wrong with you and where'd you get that fine dog? He ain't from around here."

He smiles at her through his tears and says, "Mama, you got to slow down. I'm hurt, but I'll be okay, just take some time."

Sally doesn't pay any attention to them. Instead, she walks straight to the dog, starts petting him, and talking to him as if she's known him her entire life. He sits down, lets the duffel fall of his back, and returns her affection by licking her gently. Her giggles catch Benjamin's attention and he nods toward her as he asks his mother, "Oh, Mama, that's Sally."

"Oh, Benjamin, it sure is. Go on, talk to her. She ain't shy and she ain't afraid of nothin."

He walks over, squats down next to the dog, and smiles at Sally. She smiles back at him and says, "He your dog, Mister?"

He can hardly speak because of the giant lump in his throat.

"Yes, Baby, and he's your dog, too."

Stunned into silence, Sally's mouth falls open and her eyes nearly pop out of her head as she glances back and forth from Edna to Benjamin. Then she jumps at Benjamin, wraps her arms tightly around his neck, and knocks him on his back. He gasps for breath and tries to speak, but Sally's little arms won't let go for fear he will disappear again.

"'You my daddy, you my daddy, you stay here with me and never leave."

Edna bends over, tickles Sally's ribs, and says, "C'mon, Baby, turn loose now. Your daddy can't breathe."

Sally loosens her grip, giggles gleefully, and showers Benjamin's face with kisses.

"You breathe, Daddy. You be fine."

Benjamin gasps, sits up, and giggles back at her.

"Thank you, Darlin'. You sure are a strong child."

She jumps to her feet and offers him her hand.

"I show ya how strong I am. C'mon get up."

Still giggling, he takes her hand and struggles to his feet.

"Thank you, Sally. I appreciate your help."

She looks up at him and smiles broadly.

"Ooo, you a big man, bigger'n Grampa."

He smiles back at her and says, "Yup, I'm bigger, but he don't like it."

Benjamin doesn't notice that Bessie has quietly tiptoed out of the house and is standing behind him. She whispers in his ear, "A big man's just fine with me."

Benjamin wheels around and says, "Aw, Bessie, you're the most beeyootiful woman in the whole wide world."

They hug for a very long moment until Benjamin pulls back and says, "I'm gonna look at you all the days o' my life 'cause I ain't dreamin' about you no more. Now you're a dream come true."

She stands back and looks him up and down with a straight face. This makes him nervous and he says, "What's the matter, Baby? What're you lookin' at?"

She clears her throat and says, "Somethin's not right. What happened to you?

Edna chimes in, "That's what I said. Somethin's definitely not right. Benjamin, please, tell us what happened to you."

He looks down at the dog, takes a deep breath before looking back at Edna, and says, "Mama, me 'n my buddies, we got hit real bad. The only reason two of us made it back was probly 'cause of this here dog. If it wasn't for him, why, I don't guess I'd be standin' here right now."

Bessie can't believe it and says, "You mean he came from over there?"

Benjamin nods his head and says, "Yes, Ma'am, they let me bring him home with me mainly 'cause he always stuck by me; he just wouldn't go away."

Sally tugs at her daddy's pant leg and says, "What doggy's name?"

Benjamin looks up at the sky and tries not to get choked up, "Uh, he doesn't have a name. We just called him Billy O's dog."

Sally tugs on his pant leg again and says, "Daddy, who Billy O?"

He wipes his eyes on his sleeve, takes a deep breath, and puffs out his cheeks as he slowly exhales. Next, he stoops down next to her, puts one hand on her arm, scratches the dog's head with his other hand, and says, "He was my best friend in the Army. He came from up north and we were real different, but he always treated me good 'n stuck up for me."

She also scratches the dog's head and says, "Where Billy O now?"

"Aw, Child, he's gone. He didn't make it. He gave his life to save mine. Thats why I kept his dog. See these name tags hangin' 'round his neck? They were Billy O's, but this is our dog now so we oughta give him a name. Hey, why don't you think up a name?"

She frowns and gets very serious for a moment, "Bill we o. Um, b ee o. B b o." She shakes her head, "Is kinda hard, Daddy. You help."

He rubs his chin and smiles, "I know, how 'bout we jus' call 'im Bo?"

She giggles, "Bo? Yeah, Bo's real good 'n real easy ta say."

She walks over to the dog and places her hands on either side of his face, "You Bo now. You my Bo."

He makes a happy little gurgling deep in his throat and licks her cheek.

"Ooo, Daddy, Bo give me a kiss."

Benjamin bites his lip and chokes out, "Dats 'cause he loves you, Baby."

Jeremiah walks into the house at dusk after plowing the fields all day and almost faints when he sees his son, still wearing his uniform, sitting at the kitchen table with Bessie and Edna, holding Sally on his lap. What's more, there's a big, strange dog sitting proudly next to Benjamin, as if he's always been a member of the family. It's the first time a dog has ever been in the house and for good reason. Farm dogs are outside dogs, dirty dogs, nasty dogs, scavengers, impossible to chase away. Not this dog. He's clean, handsome, and smiling happily at everyone.

If Edna was worried sick about Benjamin's safety, Jeremiah was embittered to the point of insanity, barely able to function on a daily basis. He called it the "White Man's War" and never saw any reason why his only son should have to fight it. Edna and Bessie did their level best to keep his spirits up, but nothing seemed to help. Every day was worse than the one before, that is, until today. This is the best day of his life, better than his wedding day, or the birth of his three children, or even the birth of his beloved little Sally, the only living soul capable of making him smile.

Hot tears of joy and gratitude stream down his face. He grits his teeth and shakes both fists under his chin until he can choke out his words, "Buh, Buh, Benjamin. Aw, praise God. Benjamin, you're home, you're home."

Benjamin stands up with Sally in his arms, walks around the table, and hugs his daddy who gives Edna a crooked smile through his tears. Bo stands up on his hind legs, puts a paw on Benjamin's arm, and licks Sally's face. Edna and Bessie both get up and embrace their family, together again, as never before.

8

A cool moonbeam pours through the open window forcing Bessie to squint herself awake and smile at the man in the moon grinning down at her. She rubs her eyes and rejoices that Benjamin finally came home. She ached for his touch last night, but when she came out of the bathroom he had already fallen into a deep sleep. She was mad at first, but that soon melted away as she snuggled into bed and fell asleep beside him.

She's wide awake now and she's waited long enough. He can sleep later. She reaches for him. He's not there? She sits bolt upright and looks around the room. Was she dreaming? Did he really come home yesterday? Then she hears the old rocker creaking on the porch. She puts on her robe, tiptoes into the front room, and peeks out the window. There's Benjamin, in his pajama pants, rocking slowly, and scratching Bo who's sitting by his side.

Bo's ears perk up, he turns around, sees Bessie in the window, and thumps his tail on the floor. Benjamin smiles at him.

"What're you lookin' at?"

Bessie walks out the screen door, stands behind Benjamin, puts her hands over his eyes, and winks at Bo.

"You guess what he's lookin' at."

Benjamin grins and chuckles.

"Okay, let me see now. You Mrs. Truman?"

"No, Sir."

"Uh, Mrs. Eisenhower?"

"Wrong again."

"Why, you must be Mrs. Harper."

Bessie moves her hands from Benjamin's eyes to his shoulders, bends down, kisses his cheek, and whispers in his ear.

"Right, you are, Mr Harper. You have just won the grand prize."

He cranes his neck and looks at her.

"And just what is that grand prize?"

She kneels at the side of the chair opposite Bo, smiles sweetly at Benjamin, and playfully bites him on the arm, making him catch his breath and stop rocking.

"I'm the grand prize, you fool."

He shakes his head and smiles at her.

"Aw, Baby, you sure are. I was so exhausted by the bus ride and the   long walk home that I just tried to catch a little nap before you came to bed. Guess it turned into more than that and when I woke up, you were sleepin' next to me."

She stands up, puts her hands on her hips, and says, "Well, why didn't you wake me up?"

He smirks at Bo and starts petting him.

"Help me out here, Boy. She's mad at me now."

She rolls her eyes and stamps her foot.

"Benjamin, do you see me standin' here?"

He ignores her and talks to Bo instead.

"You look at her and tell me what you think I should do."

Bo pants happily at Bessie and then at Benjamin who says,

"You're absolutely right. That's a great idea."

He stands up, takes Bessie by the hand, and leads her down the steps into the grass. She tries to wrinkle up her face into a frown, but she can't do it and bursts into laughter.

"Benjamin Harper, you're the craziest man in Alabama. Why're you teasin' me and why're you talkin' to him like that, like he's human?"

He grabs both of her hands and swings her in a circle as Bo runs around them in the opposite direction, barking happily. "He's the only one I could talk to since I left the hospital, but he's sayin' you're the one I need to talk to right now."

He brings her to a halt and grabs her by the shoulders. She stares at him with her mouth open, too astounded to speak. He gives her a sly little smile and pinches her on the cheek.

"Let's go inside and I'll tell you a story."

He puts his arm around her and leads her toward the porch. Bo runs up the steps and whines at them impatiently. Bessie laughs at him and says, "I guess he wants to hear the story, too."

Benjamin kisses her on the neck and whispers, "Aw, he already knows the story. He just wants me to tell it to you."

She smiles and says, "He did, huh? Ooo, he is a smart dog."

When Benjamin opens the screen door, Bo jumps ahead of them and runs into the house. They follow him to the bedroom, but he stops in the hall and sits at attention, happily thumping his tail on the floor, giving them his blessing. After Bessie enters the room, Benjamin gives Bo a little wink, and closes the door. Bo curls up on the floor with his head between his paws, lets out a contented sigh, and gazes at the man in the moon.

9

It's the kind of sweet sunny spring day that lifts your spirits, makes anything seem possible, and every dream attainable. A warm breeze carries the intoxicating aroma of jasmine into the bedroom and gently awakens Benjamin. Not sure where he is, he rubs his eyes and stares at the oddly familiar ceiling light. Then he sees Bessie sleeping beside him and jumps like he's been shot.

"Whaa, who, uh, what the…?"

She's jolted awake, nearly falls out of bed, and screams, "Benjamin, what in the world's wrong with you?"

Benjamin can't help himself; he gets the giggles and buries his head in his pillow which makes Bessie even madder. She picks up her pillow and beats Benjamin over the head until she dissolves into helpless laughter and collapses on top of him. The laughter doesn't last long.

There's a loud knock at the door followed by Edna's kiddingly stern voice, "Hey, when ya'll get done foolin' around, you need to get in the kitchen and eat breakfast, hear?"

Benjamin and Bessie stop for a moment, but don't answer, so Edna gives the door one last slap and yells, "It's gettin' cold now."

They listen until her footsteps dissolve down the hall, pull the covers over their heads, and start giggling all over again. Their raucous fun doesn't last long. Jeremiah's voice booms outside the door, "In case ya'll forgot, we live on a farm 'n there's lots of work to do."

Silence under the covers, then Benjamin responds with a sheepish, "Yes, Daddy, we're comin'."

This jolts Benjamin back to reality and forces him to focus on his greatest concern. How in the world can he get his family to understand that, while Bo is way beyond normal and way beyond anything imaginable, he's also the gentlest, most protective, and most loyal animal in all creation? He desperately wants them to love and trust Bo the way he does; he just doesn't know where to start.

He rolls the covers back, sits up with his head in his hands, rocks back and forth, and says, "Bessie, I gotta tell you somethin' and you can't tell anyone else just yet, okay?"

She rubs his back and says, "Sure, Baby, it's you 'n me here, just you 'n me. What is it?"

He looks at her for a long moment before whispering so no one else can hear.

"I guess you can tell that Bo's a real character, right?"

Surprised that the serious discussion he wants to have is about the dog, she gives him a puzzled look and says, "Uh, yeah, he's sure got a lot of personality, but that ain't no secret. Why're you makin' such a big deal out of it?"

He shakes his head and keeps whispering, "C'mon, lemme finish. His personality is just the beginning. It's the other things he does that, well, you'll have to see 'em to believe 'em."

Now she can't resist teasing him and she asks, "Oh, what, is he a circus dog? Does he do tricks like can he walk on his front legs and jump through hoops?"

He does his best to be patient with her, but she's in such a playful mood that, though this might not be the best time to have a serious conversation, he needs her to understand Bo before he does something really crazy and scares her. Plus, he needs her to help put the rest of the family at ease around Bo.

"No, he ain't no circus dog, but he probably could do tricks like that if he wanted to. You see, Bessie, he's way beyond that. He can move so fast that you can't hardly see him. And he's as strong as a bull, stronger than he has any right to be. Somethin' really strange happened to him over there and I can't explain it. All I know is that he has the kindest nature of any animal I have ever known and that you certainly don't need to be afraid of him. In fact, I promises you that he will always protect the family and be a great companion for Sally. You gotta trust what I'm sayin' and help me get the rest of the family to accept him."

Poor Bessie can only stare at him with her mouth open and shake her head. He hugs her and kisses her on the neck. She pulls back, looks at him for a long moment, smiles, hugs him tightly and whispers, "If you trust him, I'll make sure they trust him and love him like you do no matter what kind of wild stuff he does."

Relieved, Benjamin jumps out of bed, puts on his robe, and says, "Alright then, let's eat."

They walk into the kitchen and are amazed to find Sally sharing her flapjacks with Bo. She takes a bite and gives him a bite while petting him with her other hand and whispering in his ear. Amazingly enough, Jeremiah sits next to her beaming when you would expect him to scold her for feeding a dog at the table. It's clear that Bo has already become a devoted
member of the family.

Benjamin and Bessie quietly take their seats and look at each other blankly, not quite sure how to act. Edna, tending to another batch of flapjacks on the stove, wastes no time in welcoming them with a wry smile.

"Hope ya'll got some sleep what with dancin' in the moonlight 'n laughin' it up in the bedroom."

Bessie straightens her hair and tries unsuccessfully not to grin while Benjamin rolls his eyes, marveling at his mother's uncanny ability to see all and know all. He's never gotten away with anything because she catches him every time, but this time he's not embarrassed, nor is he shy about what's happened since he got home yesterday. He knows how lucky he is to be living right smack in the middle of the answer to all those fervent prayers he said while he was away.

Edna continues, "'Uh, Benjamin, if you're up to it, could you get your shotgun 'n get us some rabbits for dinner? Your daddy can't shoot as good as you 'n I've been wantin' some rabbit stew ever since you left."

Benjamin gives Bessie a sly wink and says, "Yes, Mama, but I won't need a gun. I'll take Bo outside after breakfast and I bet he'll catch all the rabbits you want."

She turns, frowns at him, and says, "For sure? How do you know he can catch rabbits? Most dogs can't."

Benjamin tries to look innocent and says, "Oh, I ain't worried. You'll see."

Jeremiah pipes in, "Any dog can catch rabbits is a good dog for sure."

After breakfast, Benjamin gets dressed and goes outside with Bo. He fishes his lucky rabbit's foot out of his pocket, looks around to see if anybody's watching, and lets Bo sniff it. Then he points to the woods and says, "Go get me one."

Without hesitation, Bo streaks into the woods, reappears in one fluid motion with a dead rabbit in his mouth, and drops it at Benjamin's feet.

He pats him on the head and says, "Good dog, now get me another one."

He instantly reappears with another rabbit and a small voice behind Benjamin says, "He a good dog 'n he a real fast dog."

Fear shoots through Benjamin's body when he hears Sally. She must have seen everything through the screen door. Now what? He knows he has to remain calm and act like everything's normal, like there's nothing unusual about Bo.

He grabs both rabbits, turns to face her, and says, "Yup, he's real fast, ain't he. Now we gotta take these to Mama so she can fix 'em for supper."

Sally grins bravely, opens the door, and says, "Okay, Daddy."

Thinking she's alright, he breathes a sigh of relief and walks inside with Bo, but after they pass, she stares blankly into space with her mouth open in sheer disbelief.

Benjamin looks back at her and says, "You comin', Sugar?"

She doesn't move a muscle; she doesn't even breathe until he whistles at her and says, "Sally Harper, you hear me talkin' to you?"

This jolts her back to her senses. She gasps for breath, closes the door, and walks inside never taking her eyes off him. This isn't good. He knows she's scared and confused by what she has just seen. He holds up his hand toward her and says, "I'll take 'em into the kitchen 'n I'll be right back, okay?"

She nods and stands there wringing her hands, her eyes glued to Bo until Benjamin returns and says, "Somethin' wrong, Sally?"

She bites her lip and looks at him with tears welling up in her eyes. Then she looks at Bo and shrugs her shoulders. Benjamin kneels down next to her, gives her a big hug, and whispers in her ear, "You don't have to be afraid o' Bo. He's just a real special dog, that's all."

She hugs him tightly and nods her head. He tries to pull back, but she won't let go. She just keeps staring at Bo over his shoulder. Suddenly, Bo sits up on his haunches, dangles his paws in front of him, and pants happily at her.

She can't resist him; she giggles and whispers in Benjamin's ear, "Wook, Daddy, Bo's doin' a trick for me."

She releases her hold on his neck and turns his head so he can watch Bo.

He grins and whispers back at her, "See, he's a funny dog 'n all he wants to do is make you happy."

10

Life for the Harpers is the best it's ever been. The crops are good and the livestock is healthy. The family only leaves the farm on Sundays for church and for the occasional trip into town for staples. Thus, for the most part, they're insulated from the virulent racial prejudice surrounding them.

Once Sally and Bessie get used to Bo and his special talents, they help Benjamin convince Edna and Jeremiah that, while he's truly an extraordinary dog capable of mind-boggling feats, he has a heart of gold and can always be trusted to do what's best.

Before long he proves to be indispensable. Benjamin, painfully aware that he can't do heavy lifting like he used to, asks Edna to sew two burlap bags together so Bo can wear them like saddle bags and carry everything from fresh vegetables to firewood. As a result, they're able to get more work done than three strong men.

Jeremiah, still in his early forties and strong as the proverbial ox, never says a word about Benjamin's injuries. Instead, he happily rides his tractor from dawn till dusk, keenly aware of how lucky he is to have his son back home again. He also takes every opportunity to make sure that Sally knows how far her people have come. He plowed the fields with a mule when he was a boy. Now, every once in a while, he'll hitch up that rusty old plow to Tillie, his beloved mule, and dig up a few rows just to show her how it was done. And he'll perch her up on his shoulders so he can listen to the sweet music of her giggling above him.

Bo, ever mindful of Sally's safety and well-being, walks alongside Jeremiah, never taking his eyes off her. If Jeremiah starts to stumble, Bo leans into him and steadies him so she stays put. He greatly admires Jeremiah for the loving way he puts everyone else in the family first, before himself. Likewise, Jeremiah instinctively understands Bo as few people could. They're almost like two sides of the same coin: man and beast, but kindred spirits on some unimaginable level, both eager and willing to help others.

When Sally tells Jeremiah that she wants a garden of her own, he makes a harness and a small plow for Bo to pull. Together, they grunt and sweat their way around that field until Sally has the most beautiful little garden imaginable because Bo makes the rows perfectly straight and clean. He even lets her ride on his back so they can get places faster and have more fun. Of course, he never runs too fast and he has an amazing ability to balance her perfectly so she won't fall off.

They're inseparable, always in their own little world, laughing, sharing secrets, and playing jokes on the rest of the family. They love to hide things like Jeremiah's pipe and Bessie's slippers and then giggle while their victims stumble around scratching their heads, trying to find the lost items. Sally will think of something, merely point to it, and Bo will steal it. He crawls silently under tables, around chairs, right under your nose and you'll never notice until it's too late. Sally tells him to be "imbizzable" and that's exactly what he does. But when you least expect it, the pipe or slippers will magically reappear. Everyone in the family knows who the culprits are, but no one has ever seen them do it.

Bessie finally catches them in the act one Sunday afternoon. She looks out the window and sees Benjamin taking a well deserved nap on the front porch. His straw hat has slipped off and is lying on the hammock next to him. Then she sees Sally point to the hat and watches Bo tiptoe over, deftly grab it without disturbing Benjamin, walk silently across the porch, and give it to Sally. She takes it from him, kisses him on the head, and they scurry into the back yard. Bessie runs through the house to see where they're going and sees them sneak into the laundry shed. She can't help it; she laughs so hard she has to steady herself as her eyes fill with tears of joy.

Bo isn't just the alpha dog in the barnyard, he's the alpha dog everywhere and nothing gets by him. He won't let any harm come to the family and especially not to Sally. One day, they go for a long walk in the woods to pick wild strawberries for one of Edna's scrumptious pies. Sally skips merrily down the path when, all of a sudden, Bo stops in front of her, perks up his ears, and then streaks off into the woods. She calls to him, but all she hears are horrendous noises coming from deep in the forest: snarling, barking, and squealing...then silence. Just as she's about to call out again, Bo appears in front of her, licking his bloody chops and a deep wound on his hind leg. She starts crying and throws her arms around his neck, but he starts walking slowly toward home, pulling her with him in the process.

When she sees the house, she lets go of him, runs up the front steps, and screams for help. Edna and Bessie open the door and try to calm her down as she struggles to tell them what happened between sobs. When they turn to look at Bo, they're startled to see him sitting calmly in front of them, panting happily as usual. Sally said he was all bloody and had a wounded leg, but he looks perfectly normal now; there's no blood and his leg is fine. The women look at each other in wide-eyed amazement and try to calm Sally down as best they can.

Benjamin and Jeremiah come running around the side of the house to see what all the commotion is about. Sally tells them exactly what she told the women. They look back and forth from her to Bo, to the women, and shake their heads, attempting to make sense of yet another surreal situation. After Sally regains her composure, Jeremiah asks her to show him where it happened, but she tells him she's too scared to go back without Bo. He tells her that's fine; he and her daddy will accompany her and Bo into the woods.

They set off after warning the women to stay inside, just in case. As they walk along, both men sneak a look at Bo whenever possible, but neither of them can see anything wrong with him. He isn't limping, there's no blood, and no sign of a fight. When they get into the woods, Jeremiah has the good sense to tell Sally to wait with her daddy while he and Bo go ahead. He looks down and says, "Bo, show me where the fight was."

Bo looks up at him, snorts, and leads him deep into the woods. Jeremiah has always lived on a farm and he's seen most everything that could happen out in the country, but nothing could have prepared him for this. Bo stops for a moment, turns and looks up at him, as if to say, "Get ready, this isn't going to be pretty."

Jeremiah steps into a clearing and almost faints when he sees the carnage in front of him. There lies a dead wild boar the size of a horse. His neck has been torn in half, his fearsome 5-inch tusks are dripping with blood, and he has deep, gushing wounds all over his body. Jeremiah looks down at Bo, pats his head, and says, "You are somethin' and I sure am glad we're on the same team, you and me. Thanks for protectin' Sally. Looks like we'll be eatin' pork meat for a good while." Bo likes the sound of that and licks his chops.

Before long, Bessie can't seem to keep her breakfast down and a little bump appears in her belly which propels Edna over the moon with excitement. Nothing makes a grandmother happier than the prospect of another child in the family. Jeremiah is so thrilled that he starts building a new crib in giddy anticipation of the blessed event. Likewise, Sally is overjoyed to learn that she will soon have a little brother or sister to play with.

Bo senses something growing inside Bessie and tends to her day and night, watching her closely, nuzzling her through the nausea, steadying her when she gets really big and has trouble walking. He knows how fragile she is and how precious is the gift she bears. After a few months together, she starts telling him things she's never told another human being. Things like her darkest secrets, her daring hopes, her most fervent prayers. And she's absolutely positive he understands every word. Perhaps it's the way he gazes into her eyes when she speaks, or the way he draws near when she whispers something very personal.

A screaming baby boy finally arrives in the midst of a heavy thunder storm, causing Benjamin to pinch himself to make sure he isn't dreaming, that this really is his fortunate life. The war has continued to fade away in his mind, but not the memory of his buddy, Billy O'Neal, who made the ultimate sacrifice to save him and who befriended the greatest dog in all creation; the same dog that now makes anything and everything seem possible.

And thus, on this rainy night in the spring of 1946, William Jeremiah Harper takes his first breath in a country with a shameful past, but a bright future as the proud leader of the free world.

11

After five years of relative peace on our planet, North and South Korea go to war in June of 1950 with Russia and China backing the North, and the US and the United Nations backing the South. A few days later, a dreaded, brown Army sedan mysteriously pulls up in front of the Harper farmhouse. Edna looks out her kitchen window, gasps in horror, and covers her mouth with both hands. She knows about this car and the terrible news it always brings, but her fear is mixed with confusion and her mind races. 'That new war just started and we got no kin in the Army, but what if they want Benjamin to go fight again? Lord, help us.'

She lowers her hands and screams, "Bessie, c'mere right quick."

Bessie comes running from the back of the house with Billy, now a four-year-old toddler, slung on her hip. There's a loud knock at the front door and Edna nearly jumps out of her skin.

"What's wrong, Mama? Who's there?"

Edna shakes her head and her mouth quivers.

"It's the bad news men from the Army. They must be comin' to get Benjamin."

Bessie stamps her foot and shakes her finger at Edna.

"Uh uh, no way they're comin' for Benjamin; he's done his service and he's done with them. Let's go see what they want. Fools probably got the wrong house anyhow."

She grabs Edna's arm and marches her to the door. Expecting the worst, Edna reluctantly straightens herself and nods when she's ready. Bessie hurls the door open, ready for a fight, but she and Edna gasp when they see a pretty young raven-haired woman standing there with a big grin on her face.

"Why hello, I'm Sonja Daye, please call me Sonny, and..." she pauses long enough to pull the ramrod-straight soldier next to her into view, "this is Sargent Bellows. We're looking for Mr. Benjamin Harper. You see, I'm with the *Stars and Stripes*, the official Armed Forces newspaper, and I'm going to write a story about the Distinguished Service Cross that the US Government would like to give Mr. Harper for his valiant service to our country because he risked his own life in order to rescue a wounded member of his platoon from a burning building during an enemy attack. This is his house, isn't it? We had a real hard time finding it and we had to ask a bunch of people in town. Finally, one of your neighbors, Mr. Johnson, was kind enough to draw us this little map here. See?"

Edna and Bessie, stunned into complete silence by this incredible barrage of words, look down at the map, then at each other with their mouths open and their eyes darting back and forth, as they try to comprehend what's happening.

Sonny is talking a blue streak because this is only one of several stops she and Bellows are making in Alabama and they're on a very tight schedule. They flew to Birmingham in a small transport plane along with several young soldiers who wouldn't stop leering at her, but she didn't care. She's used to that kind of attention since she's what you call a "real looker" and sharp as a tack on top of it.

After working at the paper for almost a year, this is her first assignment outside of Washington, DC, and one that doesn't feature an Army wife's recipe for tuna casserole or an interview with a grumpy old General. Now she's finally writing about some of the brave men who fought so heroically during the war. Unfortunately, except for the change of scenery, it's still pretty much the same dull, tedious work that she was doing in DC and it certainly has nothing to do with great news reporting.

She grew up in Chicago and her dad, Charlie, is a sportswriter who cut his teeth on the Black Sox scandal that almost brought down major league baseball back in 1919. Like most men, he really wanted a son, but his wife, Lizzy, gave birth to a beautiful baby girl who was named after Sonja Henie, the Olympic champion figure skater. Charlie never did get a son since Sonya ended up being an only child, but it didn't matter because he was absolutely nuts about his spunky little tomboy. As soon as she was old enough, he took her to all kinds of games and she was thrilled to sit in the press box with him. She knew more about sports than most of the boys in school and she was a good baseball player, too. Charlie gave her the nickname Sonny, not as a play on the phrase "sunny day," but for the son he never had. She loved it when he introduced her to people because he would say, "I'd like you to meet my children; her name is Sonny."

She majored in journalism at Northwestern and often wrote editorials about the poor and disadvantaged for the school paper, a byproduct of her dad's habit of favoring the underdog. She dearly wanted to be a reporter when she graduated, but no newspaper would hire her because all the reporters were men and the only women in press rooms were secretaries. Sonny was definitely not cut out to be a secretary. There were a few women who wrote human interest stories that were called "puff pieces" to basically fill up space. The thought of doing that made Sonny nauseous, but it was exactly the kind of story she had to write when she finally got the job at the *Stars and Stripes* after being unemployed for several months.

She left Chicago without a second thought, moved to Washington, and was initially excited to work at the Pentagon. Her editor was well aware that she was a very talented writer, but as time wore on, he realized that she was rather bored and obviously restless. He hoped this trip would stimulate her and keep her interested in the job. So far, that definitely hasn't happened.

Out of nowhere, Bo gallops onto the porch with Sally on his back and skids to a stop at Sonny's feet. Sally hops down and says, "Hi, I'm Sally 'n this here's Bo. Ya'll lost?"

Sonny kneels down next to Sally and says, "Why, hello Sally, I'm Sonny and I'm so glad to meet you and Bo. I don't think we're lost. Sargent Bellows and I came here to give Mr. Harper a medal. Is he your daddy?"

Sally gives Sonny a puzzled look and turns to Bessie. "What's she sayin', Mama?"

Bo interrupts by putting his paw on Sonny's arm, gazing at her with his dreamy, liquid gold eyes, and then licking her face. She doesn't quite know how to react and, to everyone's amazement, she seems to be at a loss for words.

Sally giggles, looks up at her mother, and says, "Mama, Bo likes her…she's nice."

Bessie and Edna smile at each other and Bessie says, "Alright, Sally, if Bo likes her, then she's okay."

Edna offers her hand to Sonny and says, "Here, please stand up and, please slow down a bit, will you?"

Sonny, a bit embarrassed, takes Edna's hand and stands. She draws a deep breath and speaks in a very measured tone.

"Oh, I am so sorry, Ma'am. I know I talk too fast when I get excited.

Sally tugs on Sonny's skirt and asks, "Why're you 'cited?"

Sonny wrinkles her brow and smiles sweetly.

"Sally, the Army wants the whole country to know that your daddy is a real war hero and I'm so excited because it's my job to tell his story."

Sargent Bellows, ever mindful of the clock, clears his throat and says, "Excuse me, Ladies. Is Benjamin Harper here and, if so, is he available?"

Jeremiah's gruff voice assaults the two visitors from behind.

"You ain't got no business with him. He's done with the Army so get back in your car and get outta here."

This startles Sonny and she jumps in fear, but Edna puts her hands on her hips and gives Jeremiah "the face:" a look of utter disdain, usually delivered with one or two raised eyebrows by a very strong woman, that tells you to shut your trap and straighten up. Jeremiah's scowl fades into a look of resignation as he looks at the sky and starts whistling. The Sargent senses an opening and turns to Jeremiah.

"Sir, I am here to honor Mr. Harper and give him a special medal."

Unable to resist, Sonny chimes in, "Yes, Sir, and I'm here to write a newspaper story so a lot of people will learn about Mr. Harper's bravery."

Jeremiah stops whistling and mutters angrily under his breath, knowing he's been warned to behave himself, as Benjamin walks up behind him, snaps to attention, and salutes the Sargent.

"Sir, Private Benjamin Harper. Welcome to my home, Sir."

The Sargent returns his salute with a warm smile and strides down the steps to shake his hand.

"At ease, Mr. Harper. I appreciate the salute, but you're a civilian now and we're here to honor you, Sir."

Jeremiah gets even more suspicious when he hears this big white soldier speaking to his son with such reverence and respect. However, the soldier has the opposite effect on Edna and Bessie who are overcome with pride, but Sally has heard enough so she grabs Sonny's hand and says, "C'mon, Miss Sonny, me 'n Bo'll show you the garden we planted."

Sonny smiles at Sally and looks at Bessie.

"Why, I'd love to see your garden. Ma'am, is it okay if we run out there for a couple of minutes?"

Bessie cocks her head to one side and holds up her hand, reminding Sally to keep Bo in check so he doesn't do anything too astounding in front of these strangers. Then she turns to Sonny and says, "That's fine with me. She doesn't need to hear any more of the stuff they're talkin' about."

"Thanks, Mama", says Sally with a knowing wink as she jumps on Bo's back. "Follow us, Miss Sonny."

They bound down the steps and gallop toward the garden. Sonny can't help laughing as she pulls up her skirt and trots after them.

"I'm coming, Sally."

When Sonny finally catches up, she finds Sally standing in the middle of a row of corn, pointing to weeds that Bo quickly pulls up and spits on the ground. Sonny can't believe her eyes. She's been around a lot of dogs, but this one's doing things way beyond the usual fetch and roll over tricks. Then Sally points to the little plow and harness lying next to the garden shed.

"Shame you missed us plowin' earlier this spring. Bo 'n me got real good at it."

Not wanting to sound like a dumb city gal, Sonny tries to act nonchalant when she says, "Yes, I'm sure you and Bo make a great team."

She walks over to the plow and examines it carefully. Then she looks down at Sally and says, "Where did you get this little plow? It's so cute."

"Grampa Jeremiah made it from an old shovel. He makes all kinda stuff."

At that very moment, Jeremiah's booming voice can be heard in the distance and it sounds like he's raising a real ruckus this time. Sally runs to Bo, jumps on his back, and says, "Let's go see what's wrong." They tear off toward the house with Sonny in pursuit once again. When they get there, Jeremiah is standing in front of Sargent Bellows, shaking a finger in his face, and giving him what for.

"He don't need your lousy medal. He's already got enough of 'em. Like I said, he's done with the Army and as of right now, you are trespassin' on my property."

Benjamin jumps in front of Jeremiah and holds up the medal in his hand.

"Daddy, the Distinguished Service Cross ain't just any medal. Plus, it's mine and it don't concern you. These people came a long way to give it to me and I really appreciate it. Someday, maybe you will, too."

Edna yells, "Jeremiah Harper, get in the house."

There's nothing like the voice of authority to freeze a man in his tracks. Without hesitation, Jeremiah silently obeys and doesn't even grumble under his breath. Edna calmly turns to her guests and says, "Excuse me, Miss Sonny, Sargent, would you like some ice tea?"

Sonny's mouth hangs open, but nothing comes out prompting Benjamin to say, "Thanks, Mama, 'bout time we acted polite." He motions toward a couple of chairs and says, "Let's sit here on the porch and have some tea. That okay with you folks?"

Still mute, Sonny smiles weakly, nods her head, and sits down. Sargent Bellows grabs a chair and says, "Thanks, that'd be swell." Benjamin sits next to Sonny in his rocker and says, "Hope you like sweet tea, that's how we make it." She fumbles for words and says, "Oh, uh, I'm sure I'll like it just fine." Bo lies down facing them with his head between his paws, perks up his ears, and moves his eyes back and forth when they speak. Edna, Bessie, and Sally go into the house and Bessie soon reappears with three glasses of tea. She hands one to Sonny who nods and smiles, she hands another to the Sargent, gives the last one to Benjamin, and kisses him on the cheek before going back into the house.

Sonny takes a nervous sip of her tea and coughs as her eyes bug out. Benjamin laughs and says, "Yup, now you know what real sweet tea tastes like." She looks at him and cracks up, "Wow, I guess. Why, it's the sweetest thing I've ever tasted and it's really good."

He slaps his leg, "Oh, yeah, drink two glasses of this tea and you'll get lots of work done. That's for sure."

She knows she has to regain her composure, but it's no easy task as she tries to recover from the awful taste of the dreadful, liquid sugar now churning in her stomach. After all, she has to interview him for her story and the way things happen around here, this may be her only opportunity. She makes herself take a deep breath and slowly nods her head.

"Ah, so that's your secret. No wonder you have such a great farm. I bet you missed it a lot when you were in the Army. What was that like?"

Instantly transported to another place and time by a simple question, Benjamin's jovial attitude dissolves into a scowl as he looks off into space and starts rocking faster.

"Like hell on earth, like bein' another kind of slave. Never been more 'n ten miles from home before I went to war. That ocean trip made me so sick, whew, just wanted to die. Only reason they gave me a gun was 'cause too many white soldiers got killed. Before that, all I did was load 'n unload boats. I nearly froze to death that first winter. Yup, they lost so many white boys, they had to give us guns. We laughed because we knew they were afraid we'd shoot them instead of the Germans. Bet my daddy would've shot some white boys if he'd had the chance."

Bellows clears his throat and looks out over the farm, trying his best not to react to Benjamin's hostile words. Sonny's blood runs cold as she witnesses the rapid transformation of this sweet, caring man into an embittered survivor of horrors she can't begin to imagine. Until now, she was only allowed to write syrupy stories of happy families reunited after the war that basically ignored what any of the soldiers had been through. She usually interviewed the wives and children with the soldier in the background either smiling adoringly at his family or staring blankly into space. She was thrilled when she was told to fly down to Alabama with Sargent Bellows so she could write important stories about actual war heroes who were going to receive special medals for valor. It was about time she got a proper assignment befitting a real reporter. What she wasn't told, however, was that all the recipients were Negroes who would become part of a larger government agenda.

Bo knows Benjamin is upset so he sits up, puts his paw on Benjamin's knee, and gives him a little snort to snap him out of it. Benjamin abruptly stops rocking and realizes he's spilled way too many beans. Before now, he was mainly concerned about not letting Sonny or the Sargent witness any of Bo's unusual talents. The family had already discussed what they would do when any strangers were around Bo to keep him in tow and make sure he acted like a normal farm dog. They knew that pulling a little plow and letting Sally ride on his back might be pushing it, but he was so good natured that he made those things appear rather ordinary.

Now Benjamin has to back up and find a way to convince Sonny to keep most of what he just said out of the newspaper article she's supposed to write. He believes she means well, but she's obviously intimidated and somewhat confused by what she's already seen and heard. Maybe if he can calm her down, she'll listen to reason and write a sterile account of her visit without too many details: the exact opposite of what she has in mind, but he doesn't know that.

He pats Bo on the head and says, "Okay, you're right, I'll behave." He turns to them and says, "Uh, Bo just told me to mind my manners. I shoulda never said that part 'bout my daddy shootin' white people."

He pats Sargent Bellows on the shoulder and says, "And you got nothin' to worry about, okay?"

Bellows chuckles and says, "Aw, I'm not worried. I'm sure your father's a good man."

Benjamin smiles and says, "Yeah…good 'n ornery. I'm sorry he put ya through the wringer. Now, Miss Sonny, please don't put that in the paper."

She clears her throat and says, "No, uh, I won't. We're here to honor you, not to make trouble for you."

"Good, 'cause if people in town got wind o' that, it would bring us a heap o' trouble. Instead, I should be tellin' you 'bout all the great things that happened to me. Yes Ma'am, my two best friends in the Army were white and guess what?"

"What, what's that," she stammers, relieved to see him return from his rant to the wonderful man she met in the first place.

He chuckles to himself and says, "One of 'em was Billy O'Neal. We called 'im Billy O. Now ain't that somthin'?"

She wrinkles her brow and cocks her head to one side.

"Billy O? Lemme guess."

"Yup, we, I mean, Sally named the dog Bo, she had a hard time sayin' Billy O, 'cause he's the one who rescued the dog in the first place and to top it all, he gave his life to save mine."

"And your son?"

"That's right. He's l'il Billy."

"What was so special about Billy O'Neal?"

"He was the first white man ever gave me a second thought or treated me like a real friend."

Sonny stares at him with her heart pounding at the realization that he's telling her the indisputable and despicable truth. She was duly forewarned about the plight of Negroes in the deep South: Jim Crow sanctioned segregation, horrible schools, the inability to vote, frequent lynchings that went unpunished. Now she can taste it, feel it, see it in his eyes, and hear it in the reverent tone of his voice when he speaks of Billy.

"Why do you think he was different?"

"See, he worked at the docks in Boston with all different kinds of folks and he said they were all treated the same by the bosses…terrible." He chuckles and looks at her. "But one time, I got real mad at him."

"Why, what did he do?"

"Aw, I just took him wrong. I told him how bad it was for us folks down here and he said it couldn't be any worse than bein' what he called "Shanty Irish" up in Boston. Course, I never thought anythin' could be as bad as here, but the more he told me, the more I got it."

"Benjamin, I hope you don't mind, but what happened to him?"

"When the attack started, I fell on top of the dog 'n Billy jumped on top o' me. He gave his own life ta save mine. Get it? He's the only reason I'm sittin' here. Cause o' what he did, me 'n Rasco, we the only ones lived ta tell about it."

Sonny lights up and says, "Steve Rasco, the man you saved. That's why we're here, the reason you're getting the medal."

"Yeah, right, he's my other white friend, but…." He stops himself from going any further, his eyes glaze over, and he stares down at Bo, mesmerized by the haunting memory of being dragged out of the building.

"I'm sorry? But what?"

He's totally alone in his head, lost somewhere back in Belgium, deaf to her questions until she touches him on the arm.

"Benjamin, are you okay?"

This jolts him back to reality and he jerks like he's been shot.

"What was that? Who are…?"

"Benjamin, it's me, Sonny. It's okay."

Her heart pounds up into her ears as she tries to comprehend what just happened. She's heard stories about soldiers unwillingly reliving battles and acting irrationally, but she's never witnessed someone in the midst of such a trauma. This is a whole lot more than she bargained for.

"Oh, Miss Sonny, sorry, uh, I guess I had a bad recollection. It was awful rough over there." Back to his senses, he's relieved he didn't say any more than he did. He almost told her the truth that still terrifies him, the truth about Bo. That was a close one.

"Yes, yes, I'm sure it was and you certainly deserve this medal. We're so proud of you. The whole country is proud of you."

Benjamin nods pensively and it hits him: he should definitely take credit for saving Rasco. Maybe people will respect him if they think he's some kind of hero. Maybe they'll even change a little. Even more important, maybe it'll help him forget the terrifying images ingrained so deeply in his soul. Maybe the nightmares will go away…what a relief that would be.

Sonny sees him drift away again and knows she has to wrap this up. "Benjamin, please don't worry about the story I'm going to write. You're a wonderful man and you deserve the peaceful life you have here with your family. I would never do anything to change that or to harm you in any way."

He heaves a sigh of relief, grabs Bo, gives him a bear hug, and whispers in his ear, "You're right, she is a good woman."

"Look, I hope I deserve Bo's opinion of me, but I promise you I will write the best story I can, one that you and I can both be proud of. Deal?"

He stands up and smiles.

"Yes Ma'am, that's a good deal alright. Thank you."

"No, thank you, Benjamin. Thank you for being so honest with me and, well, thanks I guess for just being you. Hey, I hope you don't mind, but I'm supposed to get a picture of you and Sargent Bellows, you know, with the medal? Do you think we could do that?"

He smiles sheepishly and says, "I suppose. Could you send me a copy? Mama would like that."

She gives him a big grin, pats him on the arm, and says, "Of course, I will. I'll even have it framed for you. How's that?"

"That'd be fine. Do I have to get dressed up for the picture?"

"Oh, no, no, you're great just the way you are. Give me a second and I'll go get the camera."

She skips off the porch and grabs the camera from inside the car. She returns quickly and starts fussing with the men, telling them how she wants them to pose: shaking hands, both holding the medal, smiling at each other, then at the camera, until she's afraid she's worn out their patience.

She clears her throat loudly and says, "Ahem, thank you, gentlemen. I got all the shots I need. Sargent, we should be going, shouldn't we?"

They both look at her with a start, pull their hands apart rather awkwardly, and Benjamin almost drops the medal, but he catches it just before it hits the ground. He smiles at Sonny and says, "Wait till I get Sally. I know she'll wanna tell you goodbye." He runs into the house and comes right back holding Sally by the hand. She and Bo run to Sonny and she says, "Now don't forget me 'n Bo, okay?"

Sonny kneels down, puts her arms around them, and says, "I could never forget you and Bo. Both of you are adorable."

Bo licks Sonny on the cheek and makes her giggle. Sally looks at him and says, "Yup, he's the best dog in the whole world; he's my hero."

When Sonny and the Sargent get in the car and drive away, Sonny hangs out the window and waves to Sally who runs after the car with Bo at her side and yells, "Don't forget us. You promised."

Sonny pulls her head back into the car and says, "Whew, nice family, but that dog is something else."

12

Bo never sleeps, not because his acutely heightened senses keep him awake; he simply doesn't need to sleep since his body constantly rejuvenates itself anyway. One of the first things he noticed about all the other dogs at the farm was the astounding amount of time they spent snoozing, twitching their eyes and legs, woofing softly, blissfully dreaming their lives away. He soon learned to emulate them to a degree by lying out of the way so as not to irritate the family. Nobody wants a dog that's always in their face, demanding attention.

Tonight, as he always does, he lies at the foot of Sally's bed listening to her rhythmic breathing while she dozes peacefully above him. All of a sudden, his ears perk up and his head snaps to attention when strange, frantic whispers waft through the open window, alerting him that something very wrong is happening outside. He springs to the window and puts his paws on the ledge. When he peers into the night, he can make out several people standing in front of the barn and they're all carrying large sticks. One of them strikes a match, they set their sticks on fire, and begin torching the barn.

Bo leaps out the window and snarls viciously at them. They scatter everywhere, but one of them, a gangly teenage boy, sprints toward the house. Bo intercepts him and sinks his teeth into the arm holding the flaming torch. His bite all but severs the limb and the boy lets out a bloodcurdling scream. Next, Bo darts from one boy to another, ripping the sticks from each of them in turn before they know what hit them. Then he lets out a series of ferocious, earsplitting growls and vicious barks prompting them to cover their ears in pain before grabbing their wounded companion and scurrying into the night.

One of them screams, "Harper, you ain't no hero. Next time we'll burn your house down."

Jeremiah bounds through the front door in his nightshirt, brandishing his old shotgun. No one has ever dared breach his beloved bastion and he's fully prepared to defend his home by whatever means necessary.

He yells, "Oh, yeah? Come back here again and I'll fill ya full o' buckshot."

Benjamin, Bessie, and Edna run out of the house in their night clothes and head straight for the burning barn. Benjamin grabs a bucket, fills it in the watering trough, and frantically runs back and forth, drenching as much of the fire as possible. Bessie and Edna soak gunny sacks in the trough and swat at the flames. Bo hears Tillie braying hysterically inside the barn so he runs in, unlatches her pen, and chases her outside to safety. Then he jumps into the trough to wet his fur, runs back inside the barn, and rolls around in the burning straw to snuff out the flames. Jeremiah grabs another bucket and runs back and forth from the trough to the barn with Benjamin. Bo runs out of the barn with his coat on fire, jumps into the trough again, but the water's almost gone so he rolls around in what's left and heads back into the barn.

Sally runs outside in her nighty and screams when she sees Bo on fire, "Daddy, Bo gonna burn ta death. Ya gotta save 'im."

Benjamin doesn't hear her because he's so busy grunting and pumping with all his might to refill the trough as fast as he can. She runs up to him, latches onto the pump handle, and tries to help him pump faster.

"Daddy, ya can't let Bo burn. Please, Daddy."

"Let go, Sally. I know ya tryin' ta help, but I can pump faster by myself."

She lets go and punches his leg, "What about Bo? Ya can make another barn, but ya can't make another Bo."

She's right. He pumps his bucket full of water and yells, "Bo, get out here."

He staggers out of the barn, covered in flames, and collapses in front of Benjamin who empties the bucket on him. Everybody gasps in horror and surrounds Bo's charred, smoking body.

Jeremiah pumps another bucketful and slings it all over Bo, "Ya stay with us, Bo. Hear me? Ya stay right here."

Bo's mouth opens and closes in the throes of death as Edna clasps her hands over her mouth and does her best not to cry out loud. Of all the horrible injustice and pain she's felt in her life, seeing Bo suffer like this hurts more than anything ever has.

Sally screams and Bessie picks her up and holds her tightly, "Hush, child. He gonna be fine. You'll see."

Benjamin kneels down next to Bo and fights back his tears, "Ya hear that, Bo? Ya gonna be fine. Ya gonna be jus' fine."

Bo looks up at Benjamin, his golden eyes barely visible through small slits in his crusty, blackened face. He raises his head, licks Benjamin's hand, and tries to stand, but collapses in a heap. His body begins to tremble and he makes little groaning sounds deep in his throat that grow louder and louder as violent spasms twist him every which way until it looks like he might break in half. Benjamin jumps to his feet, runs to Bessie and Sally, and envelopes them in his arms so neither of them can see Bo's agony. Likewise, Jeremiah hugs Edna and turns her away so she can't watch either. Now, father and son, duty-bound to protect their women and shield them from witnessing Bo's last horrific moments on earth, stare at each other for the strength to get through it themselves rather than watch him die.

They all remain motionless as if cast in stone, listening to every groan and gasp coming from Bo until there's nothing left to hear but their own pounding hearts and Sally's soft little whimpers. Benjamin finally looks at the barn and breathes a sigh of relief. The fire has been reduced to a pile of glowing embers and most of the building still stands. Yes, they've saved the barn, but at what cost? A wave of nausea surges through him, fueled by an incomprehensible sense of guilt. Why did Sally have to tell him the obvious fact that Bo was so much more important than a rickety old barn? Why didn't he stop Bo from running into the fire? But then again, who could stop Bo from being Bo, from always caring and helping?

Jeremiah jolts him back to his senses when he whispers hoarsely, "Benjamin, look at me."

When he does, he sees Jeremiah grinning like a fool and nodding toward Bo. Benjamin frowns at him, musters all his courage, and looks at Bo. If he weren't holding on to Bessie and Sally, he probably would have collapsed. There's Bo, sitting proudly, panting happily, and looking perfectly normal. He's clean, he's dry, and his lush fur glistens like it always has. Benjamin clears his throat and yells, "Look, everybody, look at Bo."

Afraid at first, they all turn slowly and nearly faint when they see him. Sally jumps down and throws her arms around his neck, "Bo, you, you fine. No fire can kill my Bo."

Bo whines softly and hugs Sally with one of his paws and it's too much for Edna. She throws her head back, raises her arms, and yells, "Praise God Almighty, ya done sent us a miracle. He ain't no dog, he's an angel from heaven."

In the end, they were able to save about half of the barn, but it was a soggy, stinking mess that would take a lot of hard work to rebuild. It wasn't the first time white people had used fire against the Colored folk in that area and it certainly wouldn't be the last.

The saddest and most tragic part of the whole ordeal was Sally's loss of innocence. The family had done everything possible to shield her from the vicious hatred surrounding them. As a result, she treated everyone the same. When Sonny made that surprise visit, Sally instantly took to her and gladly befriended her because Sally didn't see color, she only saw people…that is, until those white boys set fire to the barn. Now she spends most of her time talking to Bo and nobody else. It seems like he's the only one that can provide her with any measure of comfort.

Jeremiah was upset, too, and not just about Sally or the barn. He couldn't understand why they attacked the family now and why one of them said Benjamin wasn't a hero. Were they angry because he was one of the first Negroes to fight in their White Army? And so what if he did? His blood runs every bit as red as theirs.

Truth be told, Sonny was an unwitting accomplice to a rather cruel ruse devised by the Defense Department that effectively painted a target on the Harper farm. The Korean War had quickly turned into a national emergency and every eligible man was required to register for the draft, but unlike World War II, the war-weary American people had little or no interest in supporting the newest dustup. This was especially true in rural Negro communities where there was certainly no rush to get involved. The government was also at a distinct disadvantage because there were obviously no voting records for people who weren't allowed to vote. In other words, thousands of Negro men were virtually invisible unless they chose to register on their own.

Someone at the Pentagon got the bright idea to give out special medals to some of the Negro soldiers who had been in combat toward the end of the war and widely publicize them in order to get other men in their communities to enlist. Sonny was told that Benjamin's story would only be published in the Stars & Stripes, but much to her dismay, it was sent to all the major wire services and hundreds of local newspapers. To make matters worse, the Harper's home town paper plastered the story right on the front page along with a picture of Benjamin holding his medal and shaking hands with Sargent Bellows.

There had already been several accounts of Colored soldiers being harassed or even assaulted for simply wearing a uniform. It didn't matter that they fought and died like everyone else. Many people, especially in the South, didn't even consider them to be human, let alone full citizens. Benjamin's story really infuriated those racists because white boys weren't given any special medals and they fought during the whole war, not just the last few months.

Lynchings, burnings, and other unthinkable atrocities were still all too common in the South. For the most part, the Harpers were insulated from the virulent hate surrounding them since they were almost completely self-sufficient. They grew their own food, sent their children to segregated schools, and, of course, attended a Negro church. Plus, everyone knew Jeremiah Harper was a proud, defiant man who would defend his family at any cost and was best left alone. And whenever he and Benjamin went to town, they always took Bo with them just to be on the safe side. People were amazed at how big, strong, and downright handsome he was, but if he saw someone who looked like trouble, he would stare them down and freeze them in their tracks until they backed off. Those blazing, golden eyes could give anyone the chills.

Sonny's article changed everything. At first, there were whispers about "teachin' them Harpers a good lesson." Soon, several plans were hatched, one more devious and cruel than the next. Finally, it was Danny Carter who convinced his friends that they should be the ones to take care of those uppity Harpers once and for all. Danny was a nasty thug who got away with everything because his father, Trig, was not only the sheriff, he was also a member of the Klan. Danny was tired of living in his father's shadow and this was the perfect opportunity to earn his stripes, to become a certified badass in his own right. Maybe then he could go to Klan meetings as a full member and not just a spectator like he'd been doing since he was a little kid.

His only redeeming quality was his ability to throw things: first rocks, then baseballs, and unfortunately for the Harpers, flaming torches. He wasn't much good at anything else, couldn't stand to be in school, just wanted to grow strong enough to get out from under his father's abusive hand that reigned terror down on him at the slightest provocation. Danny was tall, gangly, buck-toothed and plagued by an embarrassing stammer. Trig always said he looked like a character right out of the Li'l Abner comic strip and called him "Dogpatch" after the fictitious town where Li'l Abner lived.

Trig got his nickname due to his itchy trigger finger. He was notorious for shooting anything that moved, many things that didn't, and rumor had it, more than one unlucky soul. Unlike his pathetic son, he was a large, powerful man who could mow you down with his brute strength. Oddly enough, he was also extremely glib and surprisingly adept at using words to bully people.

Like most of the people in town, he quit high school to work in the local mill, but he hated the daily, monotonous grind right from the get go. Everybody clocked in at 6 AM, got a half hour for lunch, and clocked out at 6 PM. You had to ask permission to use the restroom and, if you were sick for a day, the company docked you for two days pay. Finally, after gutting it out for almost five years, he started holding secret meetings after hours, whipping everyone into a frenzy, convincing them to use work stoppages that brought the mill to a grinding halt. This made him something of a local legend, a kind of hero among his fellow workers for standing up to management and demanding better working conditions. When the owners found out that Trig was behind all the unrest, he was not only fired, he was beaten within an inch of his life by the thugs who were brought in to restore order at the mill. Everybody else gave up the fight and grimly spent the rest of their lives chained to their noisy machines, hating their jobs even more, but deathly afraid to lose them.

Not Trig…losing that lousy job didn't faze him one bit and neither did the beating. Instead, he became determined to find a way to be in charge and not answer to anyone. Then it dawned on him, while getting wasted on moonshine one night, that nobody messes with cops. When he came to the next morning, he downed a pot of strong coffee, drove over to the sheriff's office, and demanded to be hired as a deputy. Not only was he hired on the spot, he quickly got the reputation for being the best deputy in the squad.

His head got so big he even dared to run against the current sheriff in the next election. Most of the townspeople were too scared not to vote for him since there was no such thing as a secret ballot. Everybody was expected to vote and every vote was recorded by the mayor. You wrote the name of your candidate on a piece of paper, signed it, and stuffed it into the ballot box. At the end of the day, the mayor emptied the ballots onto his desk and read them aloud to his secretary who kept a running tally. Of course, Trig paid the mayor a visit the day before the election just to make sure the count went his way. After announcing the winner, the mayor burned all the ballots and that was that.

Before long, the sight of the Trig's car in your rearview mirror with its red light flashing was enough to give anyone a heart attack. He would stop people for no good reason at all. He'd simply get bored and go looking for trouble and, if he couldn't find any, he'd manufacture some of his own.

Luckily, Danny's friends knew enough to tie a belt around his arm to stop the bleeding before taking him to the hospital. This saved his life, but not his arm nor what was left of his spirit after Trig stormed into his room, pointed his signature sawed-off shotgun at him, and raged like a madman.

"Ya dumb sumbitch, now you'll be even more useless than ya was before. You'll never be able to earn a livin' and I'll have to support ya forever. Shame that crazy dog didn't finish ya off instead of just tearin' your arm to shreds. Now I gotta go threaten them folks and act like I give a damn about ya."

He punctuated his tirade by spitting a big dollop of hot tobacco juice into Danny's face before clomping out of the room in his mud-caked boots. The boy couldn't do anything but lie there, crying silently, also wishing the dog had ended his miserable life. Trig stopped at the nurse's station half way down the hall and bellowed to no one in particular, "Ya'll can keep that pathetic whelp. I ain't got no use for 'im."

13

Bessie and Edna aren't a bit surprised when they look out the window and see Trig's car creeping up the road toward the house. As he gets closer, they can see him looking back and forth, searching everywhere for something. They expected he'd show up sooner or later because a friend who works at the hospital warned them that Trig's boy, of all people, was the one Bo mauled.

Never taking her eyes off the sheriff's car, Bessie turns her head to the side and screams, "Benjamin, get in here. Trig's comin' and you know he's lookin' for Bo."

Benjamin and Jeremiah both run into the front room and Benjamin says, "Where's Bo and the children?"

Edna says, "They're supposed to be in the barn feedin' the horses and milkin' the cows. I just hope they stay in there until we can get rid o' that nasty cracker."

Benjamin holds up both hands and says, "Mama, you gotta calm down. Let me handle it."

Jeremiah shakes his fist at Benjamin and says, "Calm down hell. Lemme get my shotgun and I'll handle it."

Benjamin grabs his fist and whispers, "Daddy, no! All three o' you stay in the house and I'll go deal with Trig. Bessie, you keep an eye on the barn. All hell will break loose if he sees Bo."

He raises his eyebrows and stares them down. One by one, they nod reluctantly and he whispers, "Thank you." He walks out the screen door, puts his hands in his pockets, and stands on the porch as Trig pulls to a stop in front of the house. Benjamin knows this is the most important battle of his life and, if he loses it, his entire family could be lost, wiped out, gone forever. He only risked his own neck in the war. Now, one wrong word, one wrong move and…

Trig sticks his head out the window and says, "Benjamin, take yo hands out yo pockets 'fore I git out this car, hear?"

Benjamin nods once and carefully does as he's told. Trig kicks his door open and grunts himself out of the car with shotgun in hand. He looks around and says, "Ya'll here alone?"

"No Sir. Family's in the house."

"Where's yo dog?"

"Probably off in the woods huntin' rabbits."

"Ya know what he did to my son last night?"

"No Sir. I know he chased off some boys. Your son one of 'em?"

Trig chuckles to himself and walks up onto the porch. Benjamin steps to the side and faces the barn so Trig won't. It works; Trig stands across from him, patting his gun barrels in the palm of his hand.

"Yup, yo dog 'bout chewed his arm off. Now, Benjamin, we got us a real problem here and I need yo help."

Benjamin doesn't waver, looks him right in the eyes, and says, "Oh no. Sir, I am truly sorry 'bout your son. What can I do to help?"

It's a good thing Trig is blocking Benjamin's view of the barn door or he'd see Bo poking his head out, watching them intently, waiting for a signal.

Trig's eyes narrow and he takes great pleasure in saying, "Lookee here. Yo dog got ta pay for what he done 'n ya'll know it. I ain't gonna look for 'im in them woods so I'll give ya two days ta bring 'im ta me, dead or alive."

He turns his head to the side and spits a wad of tobacco juice on the porch for good measure. When he does, Benjamin notices Bo and his heart skips a beat. It's a good thing Bessie's been keeping an eye on the barn; she leans out the side window and waves at Bo to get back inside. He instantly obeys her and disappears.

Benjamin takes a deep breath, nods his head, and says, "Yessir, I'll go get 'im and bring 'im to ya. Yessir, I will."

Trig clears his throat, hocks another wad on the porch, and says, "Benjamin, I know my boy was up ta no good, but we gotta keep da peace, you 'n me…unnerstand?"

Benjamin nods and starts to speak, but before he can, the screen door flies open and Edna storms out carrying a pan of dishwater, flings it at the tobacco juice and splashes Trig's boots in the process. She looks surprised and says, "Oh, hey, Sheriff, didn't see ya there," and goes back into the house.

Benjamin and Trig are both mortified, albeit for very different reasons, as they look at the door in sheer disbelief. Benjamin is not only afraid to look at Trig, he's afraid to move a muscle. After an extremely long, uncomfortable moment, Trig clears his throat and says, "Well, I best be goin' now. Glad we had dis here talk."

Benjamin clears his own throat and says, "Yessir, I'll see ya real soon."

Trig walks down the steps to his car, turns to Benjamin, and says, "Two days." He gets in with another grunt and slowly drives away, looking everywhere until he disappears in the dust.

Benjamin looks at the barn, but doesn't see Bo. He opens the screen and goes inside to find Edna, Jeremiah, and Bessie staring at him with tears of rage burning in their eyes. He collapses on the couch, puts his head in his hands, and begins to growl to himself, "Man can't have my dog. Gotta figure a way ta save Bo 'n protect the family at the same time. If I don't kill Bo, Trig'll kill us."

Bessie sits next to him, puts her arm around his neck, and says, "Benjamin, I know you're right. I saw Bo pokin' his head out the barn so I waved at 'im and he went back inside. 'Bout scared me silly."

Benjamin looks at her and says, "Thanks, Baby. I saw him for just a wink and then he was gone. Don't know what would've happened if Trig'd seen 'im. Lord knows it would've been ugly." He looks up at Edna and grins, "And Mama, was ya tryin' ta give me a heart attack or what?"

She giggles and says, "No, Honey, I was tryin' ta give Trig a heart attack. Think I almost did."

They all laugh nervously, grateful for any break in the tension. Then Jeremiah claps his hands and says, "Benjamin, you're right. If we only do one good thing for the rest of our lives, it'll be savin' Bo 'n the family, too."

Benjamin stands up, gives Jeremiah a bear hug, and says, "I know, Daddy. Jus' leave it to me. I'll take care o' Trig. Now gimme all the buckshot ya got and I'll get goin'."

Jeremiah gets excited and laughs, "What? Ya gonna shoot 'im?"

Benjamin smirks and says, "No, Daddy. That ain't what I'm thinkin'. I got a much better idea. You'll see."

Bessie wraps her arms around him and says, "Benjamin Harper, I almost lost ya in the war and I don't intend ta lose ya now. Please don't get in trouble with Trig. Ya know what he'll do."

He pats her on the back and says, "Don't worry, Darlin'. I'm gonna play a little trick on 'im, that's all. A trick that'll save Bo's life and ours." He looks over her shoulder at Jeremiah and says, "Now gimme that buckshot."
Jeremiah nods silently and leaves the room, but Bessie won't let go of Benjamin. He rubs her back and nibbles on her neck until she giggles, "You better have a real good trick up yo sleeve or else you'll have ta answer ta me, hear?"

He tries to keep a straight face, but it's no use. He giggles right back at her, "Oh, no, I don't want that ta happen. I'll trick 'im good. I promise."

Jeremiah returns carrying a burlap bag and a shotgun and silently hands them to Benjamin. He knows how serious this is and there's nothing left to say so he punches Benjamin on the shoulder and nods. Benjamin gets it and nods back.

He turns to Bessie and says, "Keep the children in the house till I get back and lock Bo in the barn. Make sure he's got plenty of food and water, don't know how long he'll be in there, okay?"

She clenches her teeth and bravely whispers, "I will, soon as ya leave. Come back ta me safe."

He gives her a peck on the cheek, winks at his parents, and heads out the door toward the woods. Jeremiah gives Edna a reassuring pat on the shoulder, goes outside, and parks himself in a rocker on the front porch. A couple of hours later he hears one shot, two more, and another two, then nothing. He stops rocking at the first shot and starts again after the last two, silently praying that Benjamin's alright.

A lot of wild dogs live in the woods. Some of them used to hang around the farm long enough to steal food or kill a few chickens, but they quickly learned to stay away when Bo got there, wisely preferring to go after rabbits and squirrels instead. Benjamin hears them when it's dark and the wind's right, barking and howling at the moon while they hunt. It's definitely a team effort because he can make out several different dogs from the way they sound. Maybe they learned to hunt in packs from being around wolves or simply from necessity. So far they've never attacked any people, but the children certainly aren't allowed to go in the woods alone.

As soon as it gets dark, Benjamin walks into view holding a rope over his shoulder, dragging a large carcass behind him. Jeremiah jumps up when he sees Benjamin and runs toward him, but skids to a stop when he gets a good look at what's on the other end of the rope.

"Benjamin, what in the world? What is that anyway?"

"Daddy, it's the way I'm gonna save Bo's life. See, I went lookin' for the pack o' wild dogs that lives out in the woods. I figured I'd find one looked like Bo, shoot 'im up good, and get Trig ta believe it really was him. Trouble was, they found me first. Guess they thought I was gonna be their dinner tonight. This here is what's left of the biggest one. He was somethin' fierce, jumped right at me. Lucky I got off a shot before he got ta me. When the other dogs ran off, I shot him up real bad so Trig couldn't tell if he was Bo or not. I think I got lucky and I believe it'll work."

Jeremiah can't believe his ears or his eyes. He grabs Benjamin's shoulders and says, "War changed ya, didn't it. Made ya smarter and made ya stronger. Ya left a good boy and ya came back a damn good man. It'll work alright. He's the same color as Bo 'n almost as big, but know what else ya gotta do?"

"What?"

"Put them dog tags on 'im; that'll ice the cake 'n Trig'll go for it. Let's hide 'im in the shed; don't want nobody else ta see this mess. Come mornin', we'll throw 'im in the truck and ya can take 'im ta Trig. Uh, just one question 'fore we go inside: what da hell are ya gonna do with Bo?"

Benjamin grabs Jeremiah's shoulders and grins at him.

"That reporter. Ya know, Sonny? Gonna call her and tell her ta come back here and finish what she started. She's gotta drive down here right quick and take Bo home with her. Otherwise, I only bought us some time by killin' this here mutt."

Jeremiah hugs his son and says, "I know you're right. Aw, it's gonna hurt us all so bad, 'specially Sally, but she needs ta know life is tough. Survivin' this'll be a good lesson."

14

The phone rings and rings until Sonny wakes up enough to grope for it in the dark. She clears her throat and mumbles, "Uh, um, hello?"

"Miss Sonny?"

"Who's this?"

"It's Benjamin."

"Benja...who?"

"Benjamin Harper from Alabama. You know, you were at my house?"

"Oh, Benjamin, uh, yes. What time is it? Is everything alright?"

"Hell no! Everything's gone wrong since your article hit the local newspaper."

"The what? No, it wasn't supposed to. How'd it get there?"

"I don't know, but it did and it's caused us a heap o' trouble."

"Trouble? What kind of trouble?"

Through gritted teeth, he carefully recounts everything, starting with the boys' attempt to burn down his house that was thwarted by Bo's heroic efforts, the sheriff's visit, the upshot of their conversation, and the dead stray hidden in the shed.

"I had to do somethin' to protect my family. Bo can take care of himself. That's for sure, but that's what worries me the most. If the sheriff finds out Bo's still alive, he'll come after him and I'm afraid of what Bo might do."

"Why? What do yo mean? Bo's such a wonderful dog. I can understand why you'd be worried about him, but it sounds like you're more worried about that nasty sheriff."

"Oh, that ain't the half of it, Miss Sonny. To be honest, I never told ya the whole truth about Bo. He can do things you'd never believe unless you saw 'em for yourself."

"Like what?"

Now she's fully awake and her reporter's curiosity is going full steam. Sure, she's sorry about all the anguish the article has caused, and yes, she feels guilty about telling him the article was only going to run in the Stars and Stripes, but that's what she was told. No, she had no idea it also went out to local newspapers, but what's this big secret about Bo? There could be a real story here, not just another piece of fluff, and the timing couldn't be better. When she returned to DC from Alabama, she landed her dream job at the Associated Press. Now her mind runs wild, hoping this will be the gigantic scoop that will get everybody's attention.

Meanwhile, Benjamin is doing his best not to get any angrier, but he can't help wondering if she's lying and knew all along that the story would be sent everywhere.

"Benjamin, please tell me what Bo can do."

The redemptive power of the trust he once felt for Sonny that soothed his troubled soul is only a distant memory, replaced now with a feeling of betrayal that festers deep down in the very core of his being. He doesn't say a word, for what seems like an interminable amount of time, and the silence is about to drive her crazy.

"Benjamin, how can I help? Please, say something."

Her sincerity gives him a glimmer of hope. He dearly wants to believe her, to trust her again. At this point, he's out of options. He has no choice and he knows it. He looks up at the ceiling, prays he's doing the right thing, and says, "Miss Sonny, you gotta drive down here and take Bo back with ya. That's the only way my family will be safe 'n he can go on livin'. I'll tell ya everything I know 'bout him and all the amazing things he done when ya get here. Now, gotta be honest, might be dangerous even for a white woman like you, but I got no one else ta call. Ain't gonna let 'em hurt my dog. It'll be awful hard on me and my family ta see 'im go, but I can't think o' nothin' else. You know he likes ya a lot, don't ya?"

Surprising tears of guilt mixed with frustration well up in her eyes and stream down her face. She grabs a handful of sheet, tries to stem the flow, and collect herself. It's useless, they just keep coming, blurring her vision and making it impossible to speak.

"Miss Sonny? You still there?"

She blurts out a guttural "Yes, yes, hard to talk, hold on."

She blows her nose in the sheet, starts laughing, and says, "What would my mother say? I just blew my nose in my sheet."

"You what?"

She clears her throat and slaps herself on the cheek in an attempt to get it together, "Oh, please don't make me say it again. I'm sorry, I'm just a mess, Benjamin."

"You a mess? You done got us into one helluva mess. Now get down here now 'n make it right."

Her mind is spinning because it's obvious that he's not going to tell her any more over the phone. If she wants the story, she'll have to go down there again, but she can't imagine keeping that big crazy dog in her apartment. He'll probably tear up the place. Wait a minute, there's no need to take him back to DC once she has enough information for the story. If he's such a terrific dog, she could drop him off in the middle of nowhere and he'd be fine. Plus, nobody would ever know the difference. She takes a deep breath and says, " This a lot to process, I mean you have to understand that I…"

"Just tell me straight. You comin' or not?"

Shocked by his blunt words, she holds the phone away from her ear, stares at it for a moment, puts it back, and says, "Alright, alright, I'll leave first thing in the the morning and drive as fast as I can, but only if you promise to tell me everything about Bo before I take him back with me. Okay?"

He exhales a sigh of relief and says, "I promise. Drive fast," and he bangs the phone down before she has a chance to say anything else.

When Benjamin tells everyone that Bo will soon be gone forever, the entire family basically goes into mourning, as if someone had died. His fur stays wet from them hugging him and sobbing on his broad shoulders. He does his best to make everyone feel better by licking them and nuzzling them, all to no avail. They're inconsolable and even he can't turn the tide. Sally nearly breaks Benjamin's heart when she tells him she can't cry any more because she's run out of tears. She clearly understands it's best for Bo and for the family, but it doesn't make the pill less bitter, or the pain less severe.

Jeremiah, ever the strong patriarch, hides his grief as best he can and does everything in his power to comfort the rest of his family. It turns out to be a good way to rid himself of his bitterness by substituting it with love. The more he consoles them, the better he feels and he's astounded by the pure happiness pouring into him during this time of gut-wrenching sorrow. Edna clearly sees the welcome change in him that she hopes will finally bring him some peace and help heal the entire family.

She, in turn, reminds everyone that Bo instantly approved of Sonny when they met and, for that very reason, they shouldn't hold a grudge against her. On the contrary, they should welcome her and thank her because she's doing a wonderful thing. Easy for Edna to say, but terribly difficult to accept, especially for Sally whose anger often boils over into a demonic rage. As far as she's concerned, there is no rationale and no logic for any of this; it's just wrong.

Poor Benjamin isn't faring well either, but his mental anguish is the least of his worries. It was already dark by the time he pulled up in front of Trig's house. There were two children playing on the front porch under a bare light bulb that dangled from the ceiling. When Benjamin got out of his truck, they screamed, "Daddy, Daddy, is a Niggah here," and ran inside. Seconds later, Trig barged out of the house with his sawed-off shotgun at the ready and laughed when he saw Benjamin. He turned his head toward the house and yelled, "Is okay. I know dis here Niggah. Ya'll play inside now."

He was wearing filthy, grease-covered bib overalls, no shirt, and no shoes. He stepped down off the porch, stood in front of Benjamin, patted the gun barrels in the palm of his hand, and said, "Got sumpin fer me, Benjamin?"

Trig's eyes were glassy and his breath reeked of moonshine, prompting Benjamin to take a step back. Before he answered, he noticed the two kids watching wide-eyed through the screen door with their mouths dangling open. Trig looked at them and laughed again, "They ain't never seen one a yo kind 'round here. Now, whatcha got?"

Before leaving the farm, Benjamin took Mike's dog tags off Bo and put them around the dead dog's neck. It had already started to decompose and the stench was so bad that Trig gagged when Benjamin pulled the carcass out of the truck and threw it at his feet. Half its face was blown off, but it did have an undeniable resemblance to Bo.

Benjamin reached down, ripped the tags off the dog's neck, and said, "It's a dishonor to leave these on such a rotten dog 'cause the soldier they belonged to was a hero." He shoved them into his pocket, paused, looked Trig right in the eye, and continued, "We're square now, right?"

Trig nodded, still trying not to retch, and said, "Yup, we're square. Ya'll done what I said 'n that's the end of it. Well, 'cept fer one mo thing."

"What's that?"

"Is time fer yo lesson, Niggah."

Trig gripped his gun with both hands like a bat and smacked Benjamin upside the head knocking him back against his truck. Blood gushed from the wound, trickled into his ear, and deafened him on that side. Stunned by the blow and disoriented by the gurgling sound in his ear, Benjamin couldn't defend himself as Trig grabbed the barrels of his gun with one hand, held the grip in his other hand, and rammed the muzzle into Benjamin's stomach, forcing him to bend over and fall to his knees gasping in pain.

"At's where ya'll belong…on yo knees, Niggah. He swung the gun with both hands, smashed Benjamin in the face, and knocked him to the ground. Then he kicked him again and again. Benjamin had never felt such unbearable pain. It was even worse than getting his spleen crushed in the explosion.

As if in a dream, Benjamin heard children's voices chanting in the distance, "Kill 'em, Daddy. Kill dat Niggah. Kill 'em. Kill 'em."

Trig leaned down close to Benjamin's bloody face and whispered hoarsely, "Case ya'll fergot, dis town's mah plantation 'n ya'll mah Niggahs. Now git back in yo truck 'n git rid o' dat awful thing."

Benjamin somehow managed to navigate his way home after throwing the mangled dog in the river. His mind, filled with hatred and disgust, raced with mixed thoughts of revenge and resignation. He knew he didn't dare lift a finger to defend himself; doing so would only add more fuel to Trig's fiendish fire so he had to endure the beating and pray that Trig wouldn't kill him. Still, he couldn't help fantasizing about getting his massive hands around Trig's neck and choking his sorry life away, even though he knew it would earn him a one-way ticket to his own lynching.

His thoughts also drifted back to the first German soldier he killed in Belgium. While standing guard one night, he heard something rustling in the bushes behind him. Suddenly, a soldier lunged at him with a dagger. All Benjamin did was raise his rifle and let the attacker skewer himself on the fixed bayonet. It was just light enough for Benjamin to see the realization in the man's eyes that he had, in effect, killed himself. His last words were, "Schwartzer Teufel."

Benjamin didn't know whether to laugh or cry when someone translated it for him. It meant "Black Devil," a name he'd been called numerous times back home. At that moment, he sensed that killing the German was, in part, a kind of retribution for everything White men had done to his people and he fully understood the cruel irony that he was now part of the US Army, the White Man's Army.

One of his eyes has swollen completely shut and the blood in his ear has hardened into a crusty glob by the time he parks next to the barn. He doesn't want anyone to see him in this condition, especially not Sally. He figures he'll stay in the barn until he gets well enough to rejoin the family. With his last ounce of energy, he opens the truck door, loses consciousness, and falls to the ground.

He awakens and realizes that he's lying inside the barn on a bed of fresh hay and he sees Edna tending to his wounds while humming *Rock of Ages*. Bo is sitting next to her and makes a happy little gurgling sound in his throat and thumps his tail when Benjamin opens his good eye, gasps, and says, "Mama, where am I?"

"You safe now, Baby. Bo came in the house and pulled me out here. You was passed out just inside the barn door."

Benjamin's not thinking too well, but the last thing he remembers is falling out of the truck. How did he get in here if he was out cold? Then it hits him: Bo must have dragged him to safety just like he did back in Belgium.

"You need to rest. Bo and me'll take good care o' you. Don't you worry 'bout nothin' at all. We right here. We always be right here."

"Mama, Trig beat me bad 'n there wasn't nuthin' I could do about it."

"I know, I know, same as always, but we got to be thankful he didn't…" She chokes up and looks away, trying to regain her composure. She's the unbreakable, immovable center of the family, everybody else's source of strength. She can't allow herself the luxury of desperation or weakness; she always has to exhibit an air of unwavering fortitude, not for herself, for her family.

Bo nuzzles his way under her hand and brings her back. She clears her throat, smiles at him, and says, "Oh, Bo, you right. We got to get this man on his feet so he can get back to work 'stead o' lying around here in the barn, wastin' time."

Benjamin smiles as he drifts off to sleep, knowing that he's safe with his mama tending to his wounds and Bo standing guard.

Bolts of searing pain wake him up the next morning and he sees Bo sitting motionless next to him.

"Bo, where's Mama?"

He looks toward the house and looks back at Benjamin.

"Ah, she went back inside, huh."

He nods his head and snorts.

Benjamin pats his own chest and says, "C'mere, Boy."

Bo moves closer, places his head on Benjamin's chest, and closes his eyes. Benjamin gently scratches his ears and tries to envision life without him. He used to think losing Billy was the worst thing that ever happened to him. This is far worse. Bo isn't just a pet or a friend, he's an integral part of Benjamin's very being. Maybe it's the burden of the real truth about Bo that churns deep within him; the truth he hasn't dared to share with anyone else for fear that, either they'd think he was crazy, or worse yet, they'd believe him and become as tormented as he is.

Of course, he talks to Bo about their secret and everything else for that matter. No wonder life without him seems inconceivable. Maybe he should tell the family the whole truth, maybe they would understand enough to help him cope with this horrendous loss. They've all seen Bo do some amazing things. No, killing a huge wild boar is one thing; changing from a sickly, half-dead mutt into this gorgeous, robust animal in a matter of seconds is something else altogether, something Benjamin has often wished he hadn't witnessed. No, he can't possibly expect them to shoulder that burden, too.

Lucky for him, Bessie, though poorly educated and semi-literate, has an uncanny ability to understand the human condition, especially in terms of survival. Above all, she understands Benjamin and feels his inexplicable pain as deeply as if it were her own, though she'll never know it's true nature. What she does know is that their life must go on and, likewise, so must Bo's. She senses that he has a greater purpose and should be out in the world, free to help other people. To her, this dire situation is an obvious blessing that isn't disguised at all; it's as plain as day. She knows her challenge is to convince Benjamin that this is not the tragedy he feels, but an opportunity to appreciate the wonderful times they've had with Bo, build on them for the future, and send him on his way with all their love.

Benjamin told her that he was going to tell Sonny the whole truth about Bo; anything less would be terribly unfair to both of them. She must be fully and honestly prepared for life with this unique animal or there could be disastrous consequences. She seems to be a smart, confident woman who should be able to comprehend whatever Benjamin tells her, regardless of how scary or implausible it may sound. Bessie also has a sneaking suspicion that the process of coming clean will allow Benjamin to move forward and free himself from the nagging secrets he's borne for so long.

It takes Sonny two full days to get there and she's completely exhausted when she arrives in the midst of a glorious pink sunset. Edna runs down the porch steps, gives her a hug when she gets out of her car holding a small suitcase, and whispers, "You're a very special young woman, Sonny. No, you're more'n that, you're an angel."

Sonny hugs her tightly and whispers, "Oh, thank you, Edna. I'm no angel, but I was afraid you'd hate me because of all the trouble I've caused."

Edna pulls back and says, "All you did was tell the truth about my Benjamin. Shame those people couldn't stand to hear it. They're the problem, not you." She turns toward the house and screams, "Hey ya'll, Miss Sonny's here."

Bessie, Sally, and Billy emerge from the house hand in hand and wait on the porch. Jeremiah follows and stands next to them. They try their best to smile at Sonny through quivering lips, but it's no use. Jeremiah wipes his eyes on his sleeve, bravely walks down the steps, and holds out his hand.

"Here, Miss Sonny, lemme take your bag inside."

Instead of handing him the bag, she drops it to the ground and gives him a hug. "Oh, Jeremiah, you were all so happy the last time I was here. I'm so sorry it has to be this way now."

"Don't be sorry, Miss Sonny. Ain't your fault. We're happy to see you anyway. Come inside now. You must be awful tired."

"Oh, you are so right. I can hardly see straight."

He picks up her bag and takes it inside while Edna leads her up the steps where Sally confronts her and says, "Miss Sonny, you done a horrible thing. They tried to burn our house down 'cause o' you 'n now you takin' Bo away from us."

Edna stamps her foot and says, "Child, hush up now. Miss Sonny's not to blame. It's those other people who's filled with hate. She's different. She's on our side."

Sally stamps her foot defiantly and runs in the house. Sonny starts to speak, but nothing comes out. Instead, her mouth hangs open and she shakes her head at Edna who tries to reassure her.

"Don't pay her no mind, Miss Sonny. She'll understand all this when she gets older, but right now...she's in a world o' hurt."

"Edna, I feel terrible for Sally and for your whole family. I can't imagine what you're going through. It's always horrible when someone's dog dies, but I know losing Bo like this is even worse and now you're all in danger. By the way, where are Bo and Benjamin?"

"They stay in the barn day 'n night. They don't ever come in the house. We take 'em food 'n stuff to drink when it's dark so nobody knows they're in there."

"I'm so sorry. That must be really hard for everybody."

Edna ignores what Sonny says and pulls her in the house. "C'mon, I got something for you."

As soon as they walk into the kitchen, Edna picks up a tray containing two sandwiches and two glasses of milk and says, "Here's some dinner for you and Benjamin. Please take it out to the barn; he's spectin' you. By the way, you need to prepare yourself before you see him. He's hurt real bad."

"Why? What happened to him? Can you tell me?"

Edna is suddenly torn between two very strong emotions and her eyes narrow into a deep scowl. On one hand, she feels like she should prepare Sonny for the shock of seeing Benjamin in his mangled condition. Yet, she can't resist the temptation to make her feel guilty for putting the family in such a bind.

"I can tell you a lot. You best prepare yourself for a shock when you see Benjamin 'cause Trig, that sick bastard of a sheriff, beat him up somethin' fierce and he's hurtin' real bad. I mean, he's a mess 'n I doubt he'll ever be the same. He didn't dare defend hisself. No, Ma'am. Folks like us jus' gotta take it. If he'd fought back, Trig woulda killed him and then come over here and killed us all. Benjamin's lucky to be alive. A lesser man woulda died right there on the spot."

Sonny is so stunned she stubs her toe on the table leg when she reaches for the tray. "Oh, uh, I'm so clumsy, uh, but I won't drop it. I promise." She takes it from Edna and holds it firmly with both hands. Jeremiah gets up, opens the door for her, and says, "Thank you, Miss Sonny. You need to get on with it so you can leave first thing in the mornin'."

She smiles faintly, wondering what he means by "get on with it" as she struggles to balance her load and navigate through the door. The porch steps are also a challenge in the gathering dusk. The barn looms ahead, framed by a chorus of fireflies as she feels her way through the dewy grass. She wonders how she'll be able to knock on the door without dropping everything. She doesn't want to set the tray on the ground, but as she nears the barn, the door mysteriously opens. She looks inside and sees Bo sitting proudly, his golden eyes glistening from the light of a kerosene lantern, his tail thumping happily.

"Come in, Miss Sonny," whispers Benjamin.

She carefully walks through the door and there stands Benjamin, or rather, a man who resembles Benjamin. His head is bandaged, one of his eyes is gruesomely swollen shut, and he's bent over. Sonny is horrified and can't think of anything to say. Benjamin places his hand under the tray and, without a word, takes it from her in one easy motion. Bo can't wait any longer. He gives a little snort and, after Benjamin nods his permission, he runs to Sonny, leans into her leg, and groans affectionately until she reaches down and scratches his ears. She kneels next to him, gives him a proper hug, and says, "Oh, hello, Bo, I'm glad to see you, too."

Benjamin sets the tray on the table next to the lantern, sits on a rickety old chair, and eats quietly while Sonny and Bo get reacquainted. When he's finished, he clears his throat abruptly, stands up, and says, "Now, you sit here and eat your dinner while I tell you the real truth about Bo. That way, you won't have so far to fall if you pass out when you hear it. Oh, sorry 'bout the way I look; I'll explain that first."

Stunned, she stares at him for a moment before snapping out if it and saying, "The real truth? Why would I pass…?"

He holds up his hand to cut her off, then points toward the chair. She gets it. This is serious. She takes his advice and takes a seat. Bo moves in step with her, sits at her side, and noses her hand until she pets him some more. She takes a deep breath and raises her eyebrows at Benjamin to let him know she's ready to listen.

First, he tells her exactly how he got beat up by Trig without sparing any of the gory details and how Edna and Bo have been taking care of him because he was injured so badly he couldn't take care of himself. Plus, he's had to stay in the barn so Sally wouldn't see him like this. He wants Sonny to understand the gut-wrenching fear that envelopes his family on a daily basis. It's the way it's always been and there isn't anything they can do about it.

He is hopeful that Trig will leave him alone, but there's no guarantee. He also admits that, after what Trig did to him, he's more terrified for the safety of his family than ever before. All the more reason for Sonny to take Bo with her because Trig would probably shoot every one of them if he ever saw Bo again.

Tears trickle down her cheeks and she starts to say something, but Benjamin holds up his hand again and she remains silent. He warns her once more that what he is about to tell her is the truth only he and nobody else knows, and not to be scared by it, but to accept it as part of the sacred trust they share. She nods, swallows hard, and tries to steady herself.   Bo stands up, goes to the door, and looks at Benjamin who says, "Gotta go?" Bo nods and gives him a little snort. "Okay, go on, but hurry back." He noses his way out the door and Benjamin looks at Sonny and says, "He'll be back soon. You go ahead and eat. Don't want you to hear this on an empty stomach."

She pulls herself together, takes a bite of her sandwich, and eats in silence. For some reason, she feels safe and comfortable sitting here with Benjamin. Neither of them speak, but every so often, they look at each other and nod, acknowledging their strange, yet amazingly strong relationship.

Benjamin clears his throat and does his best to prepare her, "Hey, I hope you're ready 'cause I'm about to take your mind somewhere it's never been before."

She nods her head rapidly, partly out of anxiety, and partly out of an insatiable desire to know every fantastic detail, whatever it may be. "Okay, ready as I'll ever be."

He describes that fateful day back in Malmedy when Bo was miraculously transformed from a starving, mangy mongrel into the spectacular specimen he is now, and immediately after the transformation, how he saved Steve Rasco's life, then Benjamin's life, thus changing his entire world forever.

He recounts all his futile efforts to forget what happened over there and to conjure up every possible reason for his survival other than the one he always knew in his heart was true. He isn't a war hero; Bo is. Yet despite all his formidable powers, he's the kindest, gentlest, most loyal friend anyone could ever have. Benjamin finishes by saying that he's at peace with her taking Bo because he finally understands that Bo belongs to no one; he belongs to everyone.

Sonny jumps when she feels something brush her arm. She looks down and it's Bo, sitting next to her, dripping wet, innocently watching her with his big golden eyes.

Benjamin smiles, "Yeah, he does that. He appears outta nowhere without makin' a sound. Looks like he went for a swim in the pond…dog loves the water. But like I jus' told ya, the most important thing ya need ta know 'bout him, Miss Sonny, is that he ain't mine 'n he ain't yours. We just have to be satisfied with the time we get ta have with 'im. Now, if you don't mind, I'd like to spend the last bit o' my time alone with 'im. Anyway, you need ta go get some rest so you can leave at dawn. Oh, just one more thing: he likes ta eat apples. G'night."

She doesn't say a word as she rises, pats Bo's head, and shakes Benjamin's hand before leaving. Once she's gone, he motions for Bo to come to him. Bo sits in front of him and waits for a command, but instead, Benjamin lowers his face next to his, hugs his neck, and sobs uncontrollably. Bo whines softly in return until Benjamin sits up and wipes his eyes.

"We had a great run, didn't we, Bo. You're gonna go home with Miss Sonny in the mornin' 'n take care o' her from now on. We'll miss you somethin' fierce, but we're happy you were here for as long as you were. The best years of my life are the years we've been together. You ain't a dog, you know. You're some kinda angel. Lord knows, you're better at bein' human than we are 'n you taught us all how to be better people. Please do the same for Miss Sonny. She's a fine woman 'n she'll be a great friend, too."

He curls up with his arm around Bo and soon falls asleep until Bo hears footsteps outside. He jumps up and shoves Benjamin with his paw to wake him. Instantly alert, he grabs a hatchet and slowly opens the door only to find Sally standing there in her nightshirt, gazing up at him with a look of stark terror on her face.

"Daddy, wus wrong? How you get hurt?"

"Baby, what're you doin' out here? Ahh, I got hurt 'cause I fell off the tractor. I'll be fine."

"Please, Daddy, lemme spend the last night with you 'n Bo, please?"

"Aw, sure you can. C'mon in."

She puts her arms around Bo and leads him to a big pile of hay where she lies down and pats a spot for him. He snuggles up next to her and she exhales one deep sigh and falls asleep. It's fine if Sally wants to sleep next to Bo on his last night there, but Benjamin can't sleep now. He'd rather gaze into Bo's golden eyes for as long as possible, memorize every aspect of his handsome face, and the wonderful sight of Sally sleeping so peacefully next to him.

Sonny can't sleep either, but for a very different reason. She stares daggers at the ceiling, trying to digest what just happened in the barn. Her head spins so fast she feels like she's had too many drinks. Obviously, she can't write Bo's story; it would be radioactive. And there's no way she could ever ditch him. She knows she's in for a wild ride and realizes her life with him will have to be very guarded. No wonder Benjamin never told anyone else.

Leaving at dawn now seems like an impossible task, yet one that must be done for safety's sake, for everyone's sake. She finally wills herself to sleep only to be gently awakened by Bessie in what seems like an instant.

"Miss Sonny, Miss Sonny, time to wake up."

"Oh, no, oh, really? Oh, Bessie, hi, what time is it?"

"It's time to wake up."

"Yes, yes, you already said that, didn't you. Okay, here I go. I'm getting up now."

Bessie can't help giggling at Sonny as she staggers to her feet.

"C'mon in the kitchen now. Edna's made you a good breakfast and some o' her strong, and I do mean strong, coffee."

"I feel like I just ate dinner. You people sure eat a lot, don't you."

"Yes Ma'am, we farm people eat a lot 'cause we work a lot."

Sonny manages to follow Bessie into the kitchen and everybody, including Bo, is already at the table; everybody but Benjamin.

Sonny catches her breath for a moment and says, "Oh, good morning everyone. What time is it?"

Edna replies dryly, "Why, Miss Sonny, it's time to eat breakfast. Can't you see?"

Sonny smiles, shakes her head in defeat, and plops down in the chair between Jeremiah and Sally who ignores her and looks away.

Edna places an enormous plate of food in front of her that's brimming with pork chops, biscuits, fried potatoes, all smothered in gravy, and there's a piece of warm apple pie sitting next to it. She hesitates for a moment, not sure where to start. Jeremiah grins and says, "Somethin' wrong, Miss Sonny?"

"Oh, uh, no. I've just never seen such a big breakfast."

Jeremiah continues, "You better get started or Bo might grab it from you."

"He wouldn't, would he?"

"Nah, jus' kiddin'. He's got real good manners."

Sonny musters her courage and, after tasting that first delicious bite, attacks her food like a ravenous farm hand prompting Edna to utter an all-knowing, "Uh huh...there you go, Child."

Sonny chuckles and mumbles through a mouthful of food, "Ummm, so good."

As she continues to gobble everything down, it strikes her that the Harpers possess a kind of strength that's foreign to her, a strength forged out of the necessity for survival, a necessity she can't even begin to comprehend. She almost feels unworthy compared to them. They have indomitable courage and a regal sense of honor. What's more, except for Sally, they're happy this morning despite losing the greatest dog in all creation, a dog that's been a cherished member of their family for years. How do they do it? Is it faith? No, it's much more than that; it's destiny. Some are destined to have an ethereal sense of truth, forged amidst the cauldron of hate that surrounds them, the truth that life is family and family is life.

After breakfast, Edna, Jeremiah, Bessie, and Sonny assemble on the front porch to say their good-byes. Suddenly, Bessie's eyes get very big and she clasps both hands over her mouth as she looks over Sonny's shoulder toward the barn. When Sonny turns around, she sees Benjamin hobbling toward them, using a hoe for a walking stick. She's shocked when she sees him in the early morning light. He looks so much worse than he did last night in the barn. He looks like walking death and every step he takes is more painful than the one before. Bessie and Jeremiah start to sob, but Edna strides down the steps toward Benjamin and courageously helps him the rest of the way. When they get to the bottom of the porch, Jeremiah grabs the hoe from Benjamin, and muscles him up the steps.

Overcome, Sonny gently puts her arms around Benjamin's neck and sobs quietly on his shoulder, "Benjamin, you sweet, dear man. You will always be my hero."

He pulls back and tries to smile at her, "Aw, now Miss Sonny, ain't no heroes on a farm, jus' workin' folks like us." He looks at Bessie, "Now where's Bo 'n Sally? Hope they not hidin' somewhere."

Bessie only has to whistle once. Bo gallops around the side of the house and up onto the porch with Sally on his back. He skids to a stop and she hops off and hides behind her mother's skirt. Bessie tries to be stern, but Sally's so adorable it's virtually impossible to get mad at her.

"Sally Harper, why you hidin' back there and were you tryin' to scare us or what?" It's no use, she smiles proudly at Sally and says, "Or were you jus' puttin' on a show?"

No, Mama, I was takin' one last ride, that's all."

Benjamin winks at Sonny and says, "Miss Sonny, I warned you, gonna have your hands full with that dog."

She shakes her head until she convulses with contagious giggles that infect Benjamin and Bessie. Soon, everyone's laughing, though they really don't know why. It seems like the right thing to do and it comes as a welcome relief from all the tension.

In an attempt to regain her composure so she can have some last words with Benjamin, Sonny grabs him by the arm and pulls him to the side. After they both calm down, she clears her throat and reaches for his hand. She holds it with both of hers and looks up at him.

"Benjamin, I am honored that you have entrusted Bo to me and
I give you my solemn promise that I will love and protect him unless and until I'm not able to do it anymore. Then I will send him on his way, just as you have, with the complete faith that he will always be safe."

He reaches down with his other hand and rests it on top of hers.

"We are honored to know you, Sonny. You will always have a special place in our hearts and we can't thank you enough for takin' Bo. Now we have to hope 'n pray the rest of our family will be safe. "

"Benjamin, just know that my prayers will always be with you." She sees Sally peeking out from behind her mother so she blows her a kiss, but Sally makes a face and sticks her tongue out. Sonny shakes her head sadly, walks to the car, opens the door, and nods to Bo. He gives Sally one last lick, bounds toward the car, and jumps into the front seat. Sonny sadly waves to the Harpers and gets in.

She takes off down the dirt road as Bo sticks his head out the window and howls plaintively at the family.

Benjamin yells, "C'mon, everybody. Wave to Bo."

Sally jumps off the porch and runs after the car screaming.

"Bo, Bo, I love you forever."

He hears her and howls once more as the car disappears in a cloud of dust.

Sonny looks in her mirror and watches the Harpers fade from sight. Then she glances at Bo and doesn't believe what she sees. He's staring straight ahead and it looks like there's a tear rolling down his face.

"Bo, are you, I mean, are you really…?"

He ignores her, sticks his head out the window, and gleefully gobbles the wind like any dog would.

15

Sonny's '48 Hudson rumbles through the Alabama countryside like a tank heading off to battle. Bo can't decide whether he likes the front seat better, because of the great view of the road ahead, or the cavernous back seat with plenty of room for him to leisurely stretch out. He loved riding in the back of Benjamin's truck, but it was kind of lonely. This is much better because Sonny chatters constantly about everything on her mind. It isn't so much what she says, since he doesn't understand most of it, it's the fact that she's comfortable enough with him to speak so freely. And it's different than people talking in front of him, thinking he doesn't get what they're saying. She talks to him like she expects, or at least hopes, that he understands.

After driving for two days, she stops for gas in a small North Carolina town. A swarthy attendant wearing blue jeans and a torn t-shirt stumbles out of the station, wipes his mouth on the back of his hand, and stammers, "Uh, hi there. Wow, you sure are…"

"Fill 'er up, please."

"Ah, city girl, eh?"

"Just want some gas." She opens the door and almost hits him with it, "There a restroom inside?"

He giggles, "Ain't exactly a ladies room, but yer welcome to it."

She gets out and slams the door for effect, "Ain't exactly a lady."

That wipes the smile off his face and she heads toward the station. When she walks in her heart nearly stops. There's a newspaper on the counter with the headline: "Wild Animal Kills Alabama Sheriff." She grabs the paper and reads the story four or five times, hoping subconsciously that it will change if she keeps reading it over and over again. It doesn't. It plainly states that Sheriff Hiram "Trig" Carter died after being viciously mauled by an unidentified wild animal, probably a bear.

A bead of cold sweat trickles down her back and makes her shiver as she looks out the window at Bo who's sitting in the driver's seat with his head out the window, staring back at her. Her brain nearly explodes as she struggles to process everything. Then she forces a smile and waves at him. He pants happily in return.

'Good, you're not suspicious.' She turns and heads for the restroom. 'Omigod, it must have happened when he left the barn for a while after Benjamin told me what Trig did to him. Bo knew he wasn't going to be there to protect the Harpers so he did what he had to do. Can't blame him. He made sure that sadistic bastard would never harm Benjamin or his family again. Wow, glad he's on my side. Gotta be cool when I go back. Don't want him to think something's wrong. Come to think of it, nothing's wrong. Matter of fact, everything's pretty damned good. Well, as good as crazy shit can possibly be.'

She quickly relieves herself, walks outside with a big smile on her face, and opens the car door, "Go on, your turn." Bo bounds out of the car, tears around behind the station, and returns in an instant. Then he sits in front of her and licks his chops.

"What? Oh, you thirsty?"

He nods and gives her a friendly little growl.

"Okay, wait a second."

She grabs his pan out of the trunk and waves at him, "Follow me."

They walk over to the side of the station where she places the pan under a spigot and fills it. He gulps the water, stops abruptly and looks at the attendant for a moment, then continues until he licks the pan dry.

"Want some more?"

He simply burps and trots back to the car.

"Well, 'scuse you."

She follows him and hands the attendant a five dollar bill, "Thanks for cleaning my windshield. Keep the change."

He grabs the money from her, "Thank ya, Ma'am."

After she opens the door and Bo jumps in, she pauses for a moment and looks up at the sky as if she's looking for help, 'Keep calm. Act normal. This sort of thing happens all the time. Yeah, with this dog, it actually does. Guess I should get used to it.'

As she reflects back, struggling to process everything Benjamin told her and everything else that happened since she arrived yesterday, she can't help but wonder, 'What on earth will he do next? Ha, I'm sure it'll be way beyond my feeble imagination.'

"Need somethin' else, Ma'am?"

His voice jolts her back to her senses, "No, uh, thanks, just wondering if it's gonna rain."

She gets in and starts the car, aware that Bo's looking at her. She turns to him and smiles, "Now we can drive until it gets dark. Let me know if you have to go, okay?"

He doesn't move a muscle; he keeps looking at her. Another bead of sweat pops out on her forehead and trickles down her nose. Her heart pounds up in her throat and she wipes away the sweat, "Sure is hot. The sooner we get moving, the cooler it'll be."

She puts the car in gear and slowly pulls out of the station onto the road. Using every ounce courage she can muster, she reaches over and scratches his head, "You're such a good boy. I'm glad you're my dog now. I know you're sad and I know you're gonna miss them, but now we're family and we have to stick together. We're in for a hell of a ride and I'm really looking forward to it. We're gonna have a lot of fun. I promise."

He scoots close to her and licks her cheek which makes her heart pound even faster. She turns to him with tears welling up in her eyes, "Thanks, I needed that."

He scoots over to his side, sticks his head out the window, and howls so loud her ears ring.

'Jeez, I can't believe him. The sheer volume could knock someone down. What if he cuts loose in the city? Nah, I'm not worried; he minds better than any dog I've ever known. Just have to teach him how to behave.'

And they continue to chug along like they've been traveling together for years.

When they finally arrive in DC, Bo eagerly sticks his head out the window and sniffs the concrete forest looming overhead. The huge hunks of stone don't look like trees and they certainly don't smell like them either. In fact, the air stinks and makes him sneeze because the buildings belch out smoke, as do the cars, busses, and trucks. What a horrible place for a dog who can smell a rabbit a mile away.

Sonny can't help laughing at Bo's obvious distaste for the air in the nation's capital; she thinks it's kind of cute. He doesn't think it's a bit funny and snorts his disapproval. Next, he notices all the people hurrying everywhere, talking excitedly, bumping into each other, and never missing a beat. Sure, he's seen clumsy people when he went into town with Benjamin, but these folks are different, faster, most of them are white, and they're all wearing church clothes. He knew the word "church" meant that, every once in a while, the whole family would get dressed up and leave the house for a few hours. He also knew the word "bath" meant they would take turns splashing around in the indoor pond the night before he heard the word "church." Most dogs have to be taught words; Bo simply listens to what people say and learns on his own.

Sonny pulls to a stop in front of her apartment building.

"Well, here we are. This is where we live."

Bo looks at the bland brick edifice and back at Sonny.

"What? Don't you like it?"

He looks straight ahead and sighs.

"Look, I know it isn't a big, wonderful farm, but you'll get used to it."

She gets out of the car and nods at him, "Come on, let's go."

He reluctantly jumps out and looks around while she opens the trunk, grabs her overnight case, and a bag containing several cans of dog food and a special treat. When she slams the trunk, he bolts for the nearest tree, lifts his leg, and issues a stern warning to all who care to sniff: there's a new dog in town.

After he's finished, they walk to the front door and she opens it, "Well, go on in." He looks around almost as if he's considering making a run for it, finally puts his head down, walks slowly into the building, and stands motionless.

"Hey, don't be so glum. You'll love this place. The people are really nice and a lot of dogs live here, too. Plus, there's a big back yard. C'mon, let's go. My apartment is on the second floor."

Nothing. Either he doesn't understand or he couldn't care less, that is, until he walks in and sees the long flight of stairs in front of him and starts wagging his tail. Steps are familiar to him, not that he ever used them properly. He would always jump onto the Harper's front porch and skip the four steps entirely, even if he had Sally on his back. If that was something he and everyone else took for granted, this looks like it will be a real hoot. He walks to the foot of the stairs, crouches, gathering himself for the one-story leap, and gives Sonny a devilish look. She knows what he's about to do because she also remembers his flying leaps onto the porch. "Wait, Bo, don't you dare! You could scare somebody to death if they saw you do that."

He sits down and groans his disgust. Just when he was about to have some fun in this dreary place, she has to be the voice of reason, not that he clearly understands what she said. However, her cautionary tone does resonate enough to give him pause. Why exactly did she stop him? Then it occurs to him that none of the other dogs at the farm could do what he did. So, he shouldn't let people see him doing those things. Instead, he should make himself "imbizzable," as Sally used to say, and that will be even more fun.

However, now that he knows Sonny's afraid he'll do something scary, he can't resist the urge to tease her. He crouches again, as if he's about to jump, and gives her that same devilish look. Her mouth drops open and she claps her hands. "Bo, don't you dare!" He pants happily, thrilled she fell for it, and slowly walks up the stairs, pretending for a moment that he's a normal dog. "Oh, you're such a brat," she whispers with a sigh of relief.

She opens the door and he ambles in, takes a quick sniffing tour of the entire apartment, returns to the front door, and promptly lifts his leg on it.

Her mouth drops open, "Are you shitting me?" He looks at her quizzically. "Oh, no no no no, uhhh, figure of speech."

He lowers his leg, walks into the living room, and hops up on the sofa with a contented sigh.

"Well, make yourself at home, why don't you."

She runs into the kitchen and returns with a roll of paper towels and some liquid soap. Before she starts cleaning up the mess, she snaps her fingers, "Hey, Bo," he raises his head and she points at the puddle, "Don't ever do that again, only go outside. Understand?" He snorts and rolls his eyes up at the ceiling. Of course he won't do it again. A dog only has to mark his territory once. Guess she doesn't know that.

When she's finished, she scurries from room to room, tidying up the rest of the place for some odd reason, like she's expecting important company. Then she goes into the kitchen, fills a large bowl with water, and yells, "Here, Bo." He instantly appears, slurps the bowl empty, and stares at her with water dripping from his jowls.

"Uh, guess you want some food, too, huh?"

He sits at attention and licks his chops, doing his best to train her as quickly as possible. It works. She opens two cans and empties them onto a plastic dish. He rewards her for obeying his command by inhaling the food in a couple of gulps and pushes the empty dish toward her with his nose.

"More?" He nods his head and grunts.

"Wow, not shy, are you."

After he polishes off the next two cans of food, he signals his appreciation with a lusty belch.

She can't help laughing out loud, "I'm so glad you like my cooking, but you really should learn some manners. Oh, I almost forgot your dessert." She kneels down next to him and hands him an apple that he gobbles up, seeds, stem, and all. Then he rewards her again with a big lick on the cheek that makes her laugh even more.

She takes him out for a walk before turning in, but when she opens the front door he disappears in a blur around the side of the building. A few seconds later, he prances back in and right up the stairs. Speechless, she giggles and shakes her head before following behind him.

The next morning she awakens with a start when she realizes that she'll have to leave him alone in the apartment all day. Her life has been a dizzying whirlwind since Benjamin called her and she hasn't given much thought to the practical details of having a dog, let alone, Bo. Hopefully he won't lift his leg again or worse, but she's usually gone for ten hours or more and that's a lot to ask of any dog. Well, he'll just have to hold it or, on the downside, she'll have some serious housecleaning to do when she returns, a risk she'll have to take until she can figure out another strategy.

She sits up and screams when she sees him sitting next to the bed, staring at her. "Whoa…Bo, why are you…? Oh, why do you do anything?" He pants innocently until she pats the bed. "C'mere, handsome." He rests his chin on the bed and rolls his eyes at her while she scratches his ears. "Look, I have to go to work today and you'll have to stay by yourself. I'll leave you more food and plenty of water, plus, I'll open the windows 'cause it can get stuffy in here. I'll be back as soon as I can so please try to be good. No more accidents, okay?" He doesn't flinch or change the dreamy expression he gets when someone gives him a good scratching.

After getting ready for work, she gives him one more pat on the head, locks the door, and heads downstairs, hoping that all will be well when she returns that evening. She fires up the Hudson, waits for it to settle down to a dull roar, and pulls away from the curb. She's running late so she drives as fast as she dares without risking a ticket.

Suddenly, she notices something out of the corner of her eye that's moving alongside her. She looks over and nearly runs into a parked car when she sees Bo streaking down the sidewalk. Here's a dog, larger than a St. Bernard, running faster than a greyhound. She carefully swerves into an open spot on the side of the road, screeches to a halt, and jumps out of the car. He also skids to a stop and sits at attention.

"Bo! I told you to stay and here you are, running on the sidewalk at fifty miles an hour. You just can't do that."

He shows absolutely no contrition, no cowering, or acting like he's been a bad dog. Instead, he sits there motionless, a furry sphinx, not out of breath, not even panting. Then he trots to the car and jumps into the front seat like nothing's wrong. There's obviously no sense in continuing her rant so she calmly gets back in the car. Perhaps ignoring him will work. She drives on, eyes straight ahead, without saying a word.

Still, she can't erase the nagging thought of him jumping from the second story window. Any other dog would have broken a leg, or worse. Not this one, he just barrels through life unscathed with total abandon. An upcoming right turn gives her an excuse to sneak a peek at him, but when she does, he looks at her and smiles innocently. Who could stay mad at that face? It isn't fair and he knows it.

Trying to keep her composure, she says, "Well then, it looks like you're going to work with me. Yes, that's where I go almost every day, to work. It's how I pay for things like rent and dog food. My new boss is a tyrant and everybody's scared of him. You'll have to be on your best behavior, if there is such a thing." She glances at him to get his reaction, but he's hanging out the window, trying to get used to the noxious city air. "Bo, are you listening to me?" He pulls his head back inside and sneezes at her, covering her face with a fine spray of slobber.

16

Sonny strides confidently into the newsroom with Bo prancing beside her like he owns the place. Mouths drop open, typewriters stop tapping, and eyes bug out as an eerie hush envelopes the entire office. This can't be. The new girl has dared to walk in with, of all things, a dog? She's either drunk or completely daft. Old man Miller will hit the ceiling, where he spends most of his time anyway.

She can't help a nervous little giggle. "Well, morning everybody. Now that we appear to have your undivided attention, I'd like you to meet Bo, my new dog. He didn't want to stay home by himself so here we are, uh, for the time being anyway."

A pall of stunned silence still hovers over the room. Some people exchange nervous glances, petrified of being included in this wanton act of disobedience. Despite the obvious tension in the room, Bo doesn't waste any time and tries to make a friend. He sidles up to a man with a half-eaten sandwich on his desk, stares at the food, and licks his chops. Somewhat terrified, the poor soul can't decide which would be worse, sharing the sandwich with this pushy dog, or not giving him any and risking a nasty growl or a bite on the hand.

"Bo, mind your manners. That's his food, not yours. I'm sorry, Frank, I assure you he's not hungry and don't worry, he would never hurt you. Pet him a little, you'll see. Go on."

True, he doesn't look like a mean dog. In fact, he's so friendly, who wouldn't want to pet him? Frank cautiously extends the back of his hand and gets a reassuring sniff in return. Bo deftly slides his head under Frank's hand leaving him no recourse but to scratch away. Bo's groans of approval quickly draw a smiling crowd that soon disintegrates into a rowdy shoving match as everyone tries to get their hands on him. He starts doing some adorable little tricks that whip the crowd into more of a frenzy: shaking hands with one paw and then the other, lying on his back so more people can scratch his belly, rolling over and over, sitting up and begging. Sonny also gets caught up in the circus, laughing uncontrollably until she's holding her sides.

Jake Miller, firmly ensconced in his office as usual, with the blinds drawn and his door closed, can't believe the raucous commotion coming from the newsroom. Maybe there's been a big accident or, better still, an attack of some kind. Could it be the Russians? Editors live for that kind of exciting news and his pulse quickens as he flings his door open screaming, "What is it? Is there a fire? Did we get a call from the police or the Pentagon or..." He can't believe his eyes when he sees his entire staff fawning over a huge, gorgeous dog. "What the hell is that dog doing in here? How'd he get in?"

Much to his dismay, the party doesn't stop; everybody's having such a good time, they're oblivious to his screaming. This makes him even more furious. He elbows his way into the crowd until he's standing next to Bo who looks up at him and pants happily. For a split second, Jake is disarmed and almost succumbs to Bo's charm, but he quickly recovers and thunders, "Somebody better tell me what's going on here."

Total, abrupt, deafening silence chokes the life out of the party. Everybody freezes in place, afraid to breathe, afraid it might be their last breath as an employee of the Associated Press. Sonny bravely works her way toward Jack and flashes a guilty smile.

"You? You did this? Miss Daye, have you lost your...?"

"Mind? On the contrary, Mr. Miller, I've never felt more sane in my entire life. For the first time since I started working here, everyone's happy."

The veins in his neck bulge to the brink of rupturing. You could almost envision steam spewing from his ears as the expletives spew from his mouth. "Goddam it, I'm not happy and look at them now. Are they happy? No! They're not happy either, they're scared stiff because you and your dog have put their jobs at risk." He points to his office. "There's a huge stack of resumes on my desk, all from very qualified people who are dying to work here." He wags his finger in her face. "Now get rid of this mutt or you'll be the first to go!"

That's it. Bo has had it with this blowhard so he snarls at him with canines bared. Nobody threatens Sonny, nobody. Everyone, including Miller, gasps for breath. Everyone but Sonny, who can't help smiling proudly at her furry guardian. But before anyone can utter a word, all the phones in the office start ringing. Still frozen in place, people look at each other, afraid to move a muscle, until Sonny grabs one of the phones and says, "Newsroom, Sonny." She nods her head, picks up a pencil, and starts taking notes. "It crashed where? 12th Street, three blocks from the Capitol and it crushed two parked cars? Is the pilot still alive? He is, but he's trapped and the helicopter's smoking badly? Is the fire department there yet? Okay, thanks for the tip." She flings the phone on the desk, "C,mon, Bo" and they run out the door. Inspired by Sonny's bravado, other people start answering phones and taking notes. Miller tries to say something, but realizes it's hopeless, storms into his office, and slams the door.

Sonny drives like a maniac toward the plume of black smoke curling into the sky. Sirens wail in every direction compelling Bo to stick his head out the window and add his own lusty howls to the chorus of neighborhood dogs.

Suddenly, Sonny sees a firetruck a couple of blocks ahead of her. She careens around other cars, swerves in right behind the truck, and tails it to the scene while laughing wickedly at her own bravado, "Thanks for carving a path through the traffic. I know it's illegal to follow so closely, but hey, if this is the last story I'll ever file for the AP, I'm not about to let a little thing like the law slow me down."

Her daring maneuver pays off and she's the first reporter on the scene. The police aren't there either, only horrified onlookers. The smoldering Sikorsky, completely entangled in a web of sparking power lines, teeters precariously atop two parked cars. The terrified pilot is screaming for help and desperately trying to free himself from his safety harness. Several firemen, understandably scared of being electrocuted, carefully edge toward the pilot, but they're repulsed when a spark ignites some gas leaking from the engine and it bursts into flames. The crowd gasps in horror as the fire creeps closer and closer to the gas tank behind the pilot.

Despite shouted warnings from the firemen, Sonny and Bo run around the wreck to get closer to the pilot, but the heat is so intense she stumbles backward, falls to the sidewalk, and watches in shocked disbelief as Bo jumps through the flames into the cockpit, rips the pilot's harness to shreds, pulls him out of the chopper, and drags him to the firemen.

Then he rushes back to Sonny who scrambles to her feet and they dash to safety as the gas tank explodes, engulfs the entire chopper in flames, and sets both cars ablaze. The stunned firemen can't believe what they just witnessed and they gaze at each other in awe as they tend to the terrified pilot who's convinced he was just saved by a wild animal.

"I thought I was a goner. What the hell was that?"

One of the firemen grins and shakes his head, "The biggest, strongest dog I've ever seen; that's what it was. Why, he dragged you out of there like you were a stuffed toy. I'd buy him a huge T-bone if I was you."

When Sonny looks back and marvels at the flaming mass of twisted metal, she's forced to grapple with the undeniable magnitude of Bo's heroics. She kneels next to him and scratches his head, "Benjamin warned me about you, but I never really believed him, well, until now. You've got to be the most amazing creature on earth."

He gives her a big lick of gratitude and puts his head on her shoulder. She puts her arms around his neck and hugs him tightly, "Aw, Bo, I love you."

He moans softly in response. Startled, she pulls back and smiles at him, "Does that mean you love me, too?"

He nods and gives her another lick.

She rolls her eyes, "What did I ever do to deserve you? C'mon, let's go talk to the pilot." They walk to the firetruck where one of the men is tending to him while the rest of them frantically try to put out the fire.

She pulls out a pad and pencil, "Excuse me, Lieutenant Banks, what's your first name?"

The fireman starts to shove Sonny aside, but the handsome young pilot takes one look at her and says, "No, she's fine, uh, you can call me Jimmy." He sees Bo and almost jumps out of his skin, "Omigod, you are a dog. He yours? Who are you? What's your name?"

Bo pants happily and holds up his paw. When Jimmy grabs it , Bo envelopes him in a big hug, bowls him over, and licks his face. When Jimmy finally catches his breath, he looks up at Sonny and says, "He is your dog, right?"

"Yes, he's my dog."

"What kind is he?"

"Uh, I don't know. He's one of a kind."

"No shit! Oh, sorry. Now what's your name."

"I'm Miss Daye with the Associated Press."

"How'd you know my name and rank?"

"Your name tag and the silver bar on your collar. Based at Andrews, right?"

"There you go again. How'd you know I flew out of Andrews?"

"It's the closest base. Where are you from, Lieutenant?"

"Why, I hail from Tucson, but I live here now and I still didn't get your first name."

"What went wrong? Why'd you crash?"

His mouth drops open and he looks at the fireman for help, but he's still in shock himself, "Hey, answer the lady. I also need to know what happened so I can file my report and it's gonna be a lulu."

Jimmy swallows hard and clears his throat before responding, "Aw, well, it's like this, you see, uh..."

The fireman chimes in again, "Get to the point, Son. We don't have all day."

Sonny leans down and puts her hand on Jimmy's shoulder. "C'mon, you can tell us. You'll feel better when you get it off your chest."

He looks into those big brown eyes, believing every word she says, and nods his head decisively, "You're right, you're both right. Let's see, I checked all the systems before I took off, the weather report was good, but I hit a vicious updraft and it threw me sideways. The controls were pretty useless and it was all I could do to avoid crashing into those houses over there. I aimed for the street; I really did and I almost made it, well, except for the cars I hit."

The fireman chuckles, "Hey, you did a great job and that's what I'm gonna put in my report. How 'bout you, Miss?"

Sonny smiles approvingly, "You bet. Jimmy, I think you should be proud of the job you did here today. I'll bet you served in the war, didn't you."

"Yes, Ma'am, I flew EVAC missions on D-Day in the exact same kind of machine. Shame this one didn't make it."

"Well, you made it; that's all that counts." She looks at the fireman, "Looks like he'll be alright; you gonna take him to the hospital anyway?"

He shakes his head and says, "Nah, I think he can walk there by himself."

Jimmy takes the bait and struggles to his feet, "Sure, I could do that. Takes more 'n a little crash to keep me down." With that, he staggers to one side and the fireman winks at Sonny as he catches him before he falls.

"Yeah, guess we'd better give him a ride. Hey, never seen a dog do anything like that. You train him?"

"Not really, he sorta came that way. He just likes to help so I always take him with me. Uh, truth is, he refuses to stay at home so I guess I should say we go everywhere together."

Jimmy pipes in, "Hey, he sure is a great lookin' dog… just like you."

"Wow, thanks for saying I'm a great looking dog."

The fireman tilts his head back and roars with laughter, "Lieutenant, I think we'd better get you to the hospital before you cram both feet in your mouth." He muscles Jimmy away despite his attempts to apologize, "Aw, that ain't fair. You know what I meant. Gimme your phone number. I wanna buy your dog a steak and I'll buy you anything you want."

Sonny can't resist; she blows him a kiss and yells, "Hope you feel better, Jimmy. Bye now."

17

Sonny managed to sneak back into the newsroom with Bo slithering behind her, "imbizzable" once again. Her magnificently drawn account of the crash leapt out of her mind and onto the paper without any need for revision, allowing her to send it out less than an hour after it happened thus scooping every other news service and earning her the undying gratitude of one Jake Miller. Flabbergasted by her audacious bravery and her brilliant story, he had no choice in the matter. She praised the astounding talent exhibited by Lt. Banks who somehow guiding his crippled chopper into the street, thus sparing nearby dwellings and their inhabitants from certain catastrophe. She likened flying a disabled helicopter to being trapped inside a giant, drunken bumblebee. She also highlighted his brave service during the D-Day invasion when he flew the same model Sikorsky. No wonder he was able to perform such an incredible feat. He was just another brave pilot back then, but Sonny's story turned him into a real, modern-day hero.

One by one, the phones started ringing. As soon as one call was finished, another one came through. It was a madhouse. Newspapers called, as did radio and TV stations, the mayor's office, the Pentagon, senators, congressmen... all wanting to know more about the fearless writer who risked her own life in order to write the story and the amazing dog who dragged the pilot to safety. She was so swamped, other reporters had to answer calls and make interview appointments for her.

Sonny had always been a very serious, though not necessarily gifted writer. Witnessing Bo's intrepid abilities firsthand changed her and inspired her to emulate him, though she didn't realize it at first. Typically, news stories read with the same rat-a-tat, staccato rhythm of the typewriters that spit them out. Her story flowed with the lyric beauty of a violin solo, conveying warmth and nuance, as if it were written solely for each individual reader. And how surprising it was that she went far beyond the usual "who-what-when-where" basics of normal news stories. She incorporated very real, very human elements that made you admire Jimmy's courage and, shamelessly, Bo's as well.

In truth, the vivid portrait she painted of Lt. Banks' valiant efforts to spare the lives and property of innocent civilians was a subconscious tribute to Bo. The image of him fearlessly saving the pilot's life was etched in her memory and persistently roared up in front of her eyes. He didn't have to be told, he did it all on his own and he did it so swiftly, she couldn't help wondering if he might be capable of moving at the speed of sound. And if he actually moved that fast, would he cause a sonic boom? After finishing the story, she realized that she was powerless to ignore the ever expanding truth about Bo. It was clearly better to embrace her new reality, to use that truth as a constant source of inspiration, and to accept the fact that she was now part of an extraordinary team.

Her story about Lt. Banks was no aberration, no fluke; Sonny was the real thing and now everybody knew it. She went from rookie to star reporter in the space of one action-packed day, but in reality is was all due to Bo's heroics. Without him, it would have been just another story in all the papers. Miller started giving her the plum assignments and nobody seemed to care. Who could argue with her talent, her fearless determination, and the unrivaled beauty of her prose. Plus, his job got a whole lot easier due to the newfound morale in the office.

Everybody's attitude improved mainly because they started having fun at work, a direct result of Bo's unpredictable antics. He not only became the office mascot, he also became the class clown, up to his old tricks like hiding purses, glasses, coats, hats, you name it. Someone's typewriter even ended up in the hall with a half-written article still in it. Usually, he did all this without being seen, but sometimes he enlisted one person as an accomplice to help trick another, creating a constantly changing conspiracy of mischief-makers. He had learned to communicate so well with Sonny that, eventually, he was able to do the same with other people. Yet no one ever missed a deadline, everyone's work improved, and the accolades kept rolling in.

To be sure, things were going great at the Associated Press and Sonny's life was turning out to be so much better than she ever dreamed possible. Her career was on fire, Bo was above and beyond anyone else's idea of what a dog should or could be, and that was without their knowing the real Bo, the Bo revealed only to Benjamin and Sonny. He either performed his wildest exploits so fast the eye couldn't follow or while no one was looking, but what everyone did witness was an utterly charming and lovable dog that simply made their lives better.

And it was a great time to be in the news business. The Korean War was in full swing and Senator Joe McCarthy was conducting his reign of terror up on Capitol Hill. He accused countless people in the State Department of being Communists and had everyone running scared. True, there were Russian spies in DC and American spies in Moscow, but McCarthy's allegations were poorly substantiated. He was basically an obnoxious, egotistical blowhard who robbed several innocent people of their jobs and drove others to suicide. Sonny found a way to thwart his reign of terror when she uncovered the fact that he tried to have death sentences commuted for several German SS officers who were responsible for the 1944 Malmedy massacre of American prisoners of war. Boy, did that ring a bell. She nearly threw up when she remembered what Benjamin had told her about the massacre and that Bo came from there. Now it was personal. She wrote a blistering story about McCarthy that resulted in the Senate press corps voting him "the worst US senator" currently in office.

Unfortunately, the atmosphere of paranoia toward the Russians, often called the "Red Scare" and justified on many levels, continued to victimize many of the wrong people. While McCarthy held sway in the Senate, the House Committee on Un-American Activities (HUAC) targeted several prominent screenwriters in Hollywood who were eventually blacklisted because of previous or suspected Communist affiliations. Many of these individuals were denied work for many years. Some of them actually wrote screenplays for some very famous movies, either under assumed names, or as poorly paid ghostwriters.

One of Sonny's English professors from Northwestern, William Shapiro, took a sabbatical from teaching to work on a huge project at a major Hollywood studio. As luck would have it, he ended up on a team led by a very famous writer who also happened to be an avowed Communist. Running scared and unable to stand up to Congress, most major studios caved in under the unrelenting pressure and fired anyone who was remotely connected to a known Communist. Shapiro was caught up in the purge and wrote a scathing letter to the Washington Post in his own defense and in defense of everyone else who was fired.

Unlike the other writers, his letter became the stuff of history and was seen as a badge of honor in the academic community. He was welcomed back at Northwestern and became something of a cult hero, particularly among journalists and especially to Sonny who sent him a copy of her article on McCarthy and thanked him for being such an inspiration to her. Of course he remembered her. Who could forget the striking young woman whose ability and enthusiasm were even more profound than her looks. She included a snapshot of her and Bo with the caption "my partner in crime" that he proudly displayed on his desk as an example to his students.

18

Sonny has emerged as the darling of the AP in the two years since she wrote the article about the helicopter crash not just because of her wicked talent, but also due to her selfless attitude and willingness to help her fellow reporters. In fact, she's developed into something of a ghostwriter herself, constantly revising and polishing other people's work at the request of her newfound champion, Jake Miller. The once grouchy editor has now become her most ardent admirer, as well he should, since she's happy to let him reap all the praise for the stellar work coming out of the office.

She doesn't seek nor does she need the limelight, preferring to operate quietly within the private world she shares only with Bo. It's not that she isn't ambitious; nothing could be farther from the truth. Her career comes first, perhaps to a fault. She doesn't have time for a serious relationship, only an occasional dalliance. Her life is focused on finding unique opportunities to write groundbreaking stories and there's no room for any emotional baggage that might hold her back. She likes men alright and she has no trouble finding one to scratch a certain itch she gets from time to time, but nothing beyond that.

Bo barely tolerates her dating. He's so jealous and possessive that he does everything possible to intimidate her suitors. He growls at them, bumps into them, trips them, and stands in front of Sonny with canines flashing so they can't get close to her. He's seen enough people come and go in his life and he's haunted by the specter of her falling in love with some guy and disappearing. She tries to reassure him, but he doesn't listen, he keeps interfering whenever possible. Locking him out of her bedroom is the only way she can have a man to herself, and even then, Bo whines plaintively and paws at the door. So much for romance.

There have been numerous rumblings in the intelligence community about extremely well-trained Soviet agents living quietly in DC and staying under the radar due to their convincing ability to blend in. One of the tricks American soldiers used during the Second World War to ferret out German spies was to play baseball with them because they couldn't throw like our guys. The Russians learned that lesson and made their spies play baseball until they were really good at it. They also schooled them in every aspect of our culture from movies, to books, to folk legends like Paul Bunyan. They look like us, they talk like us; they even have kids who were born here. Some of them work in the US government; others may have regular jobs, but they specialize in getting close to government employees through any means possible. They bump into them in bars, talk to them in church, try to befriend them, date them, and try to find ways to blackmail them.

Max Kushner, another AP reporter and close friend of Sonny's who happened to be John Garfield's nephew, was inspired by two of his uncle's films: *Pride of the Marines* and *Body and Soul*. Garfield, a tremendously talented actor, was famous for playing the guy who wouldn't give up no matter what. Knock him down and he always got back up. Likewise, Kushner had the tenacity of a bulldog when he went after a story or a chess opponent since he longed to win a Pulitzer Prize for journalism and to be a chess Grand Master.

His fanatical chess playing took his mind off his job and gave him a brief respite from the DC rat race. However, he always had chess on his mind, even when he was at work. He rehashed games he'd already played and planned strategy for games he was currently playing. Sometimes, when he was at his desk, he'd stop typing, glower at his hands, and scold them under his breath for making stupid moves and losing a particular game as if it were their fault, not his.   No wonder everybody thought he was nuts. And they were right; his brand of genius was indeed a form of insanity.

He played chess three times a week with a friend of his at the State Department and late one night, in the middle of a boring game, the man mentioned something in passing about a rooming house where several undercover Russians agents were supposedly living. Realizing that he just let the wrong cat out of the bag, he told Max to steer clear because of an ongoing federal investigation which made Max even more inquisitive. He begged for the address until his buddy finally capitulated after making Max promise that he would never divulge his source or go anywhere near the house. Max would have agreed to anything, knowing full well that he'd never keep his promise. How could he? This wasn't an ordinary story, this was a matter of national security, and quite possibly, his best shot at the Pulitzer that would secure his place in history.

He didn't dare tell anyone else at the AP lest they steal his thunder. This was his baby, his treasure to dig up and share with the world. He formulated his strategy the same way he planned an attack on the chess board: always several moves ahead, taking into consideration every possible contingency.

Not that he was expecting anything in particular, but he was very surprised when he saw the house for the first time. It was in a decent neighborhood and there was a faded "Rooms" sign hanging in the window, but the shades were drawn and the place looked deserted. His first move was to position his car a half a block away and watch through a small pair of binoculars, carefully noting the various times everyone came and went, what they wore, what they carried in and out, and what kind of car they drove. Strangely enough, they all used a side door and never the front door. After two weeks of vigilant surveillance, he was sure there were three women and three men living there, and he never saw anyone enquire about a room. Why would they? The place wasn't exactly inviting from the outside.

His next move involved posing as a newspaper reporter and talking to various local businesses like the grocer, dry cleaner, and liquor store, in order to write a human interest story about them and how they benefitted the neighborhood. He told each of them that he had grown fond of the area and even thought he might like to live there, but before he signed a lease, he thought he should rent a room for a few days just to be sure and could they suggest a reasonable rooming house.

The owner of the grocery store immediately suggested that very house because the two nice ladies, sisters, who owned it were regular customers. They told him they came here from Milwaukee about five years ago which made sense to him because they both had that hard, northern accent. He smiled broadly and told Max he'd better like soup if he stayed there because the women always bought potatoes, beets, cabbage, and cheap cuts of beef for the soup they served every day. This stunned Max for a moment as he recalled his grandmother's beef borscht, the staple of many Eastern European kitchens and, by all accounts, the national soup of Russia. When he snapped out of it, he asked the owner if he knew any of the boarders and he said only the one man who came in every day for a cup of coffee and the paper. He was polite, but very curt and standoffish.

Max only half listened to what the guy said because the idea that these women served borscht every day drove him right over the edge and he stupidly abandoned his intricate game plan. His ego took over and the voice in his head told him if he wanted to become famous for uncovering a huge Russian spy ring, then he had to take some huge risks; that's what great journalists do.

He decided to interview them just like he did the other merchants and tell them he's doing a story on small businesses and their impact on the economy. He would ask them if he could take some pictures inside the house, find out what amenities they offer, and talk to some of their boarders.

This time he parked right in front of the house and confidently strode up the steps to the front porch. He knocked on the door for some time until he heard the sound of several locks and chains being undone. A woman in a house dress opened the door and eyed him suspiciously while she listened to his request and nodded in agreement, but she poked her head out to make sure he was alone before letting him in. His body was found a week later on the side of a country road in Virginia, an apparent hit and run victim.

Sonny almost lost it when she heard about Max. They were the best of friends and had cooperated very closely on several major stories. While she admired his tremendous zeal, she was usually frustrated by his cavalier disregard for organization. He was a great reporter in his own right; if anyone ever had the proverbial nose for news, he did. He would go out and meticulously gather all the important facts about a story, bring them back to the office, flash that sheepish grin of his, and dump his messy notes on her desk. As far as he was concerned, that part of his game was over and it was up to Sonny to organize the mess so he could write his final story.

It worked every time except one. Sonny was used to deciphering his barely legible scribblings on everything from notepaper to napkins. She drew the line, however, at the napkin with notes on one side and the remains of a messy hotdog on the other. She loved the challenge of assembling a cohesive narrative from all the disparate bits and pieces he gave her, a jigsaw puzzle of news if you will, but that time it was more than her stomach could handle.

His suspicious death did more than turn her stomach; it filled her with a volcanic rage because she didn't believe for a moment that it was an accident. The FBI didn't think so either. Max was found wearing jogging clothes and sneakers which made no sense to anyone who knew him. He couldn't run. He had painful bone spurs in both heels. It was all he could do to walk without limping and there was another sad irony surrounding his death. The only exercise he ever got was bending his elbow, and every time he did, his mouth flew open and something flew in. He loved to eat and drink to excess; everybody knew that about him. It was part of his mystique, his legend. Writers and newspaper reporters were notorious lushes and Max was rightfully proud of his membership in that fraternity.

Three weeks after his body was found, a horde of indistinguishable FBI agents descended upon the AP office and stayed round the clock. They had faces you couldn't describe, plain as day with no unique features unlike their controversial boss, J. Edgar Hoover, whose ugly mug resembled that of a petulant bulldog. They all wore the same dark suits and ties, white shirts, and the requisite shiny black shoes. Plain they were; dumb they weren't. They took Max's desk apart, right in the middle of the newsroom, examined every single piece with a magnifying glass, and dusted it for fingerprints.

Next, they interviewed everyone extensively, constantly probing for exact details. Different agents would ask the same question several different ways, always looking for inconsistencies. Sonny was their favorite target, ostensibly because she had worked so closely with Max. Or, perhaps they just used that as an excuse to spend as much time with her as possible. Most men do tend to act a little goofy around her. She cooperated at first, but she got angry after putting up with them for several days. 'Did they really consider her to be a suspect or were they mostly flirting? Either way, how dare they. Yes, she had often threatened to wring Max's neck. Nobody could blame her for that, but murder him? No way.'

One day, when all the agents file into Jake's office and close the door, it's the last straw. She jumps out of her chair and barges right in, "Alright, what the hell's going on here? I'm tired of being harassed."

Jake quickly closes the door behind her. All the FBI agents are standing at attention and a burly, distinguished-looking man is sitting at Jake's desk, rifling through a pile of paperwork. He's wearing a black turtleneck and a Basque beret, the cherished memento of his clandestine work with the French Resistance during the Second World War. Round tortoise shell glasses that you would expect to see perched below the bushy, unkempt eyebrows of a philosophy professor, loom above the vicious scar that starts at the corner of his mouth and stretches beyond his missing left ear lobe. And it's impossible to ignore the Colt 45 automatic poking out of his well-worn leather shoulder holster. The man's very presence is one of overwhelming intimidation; he literally exudes danger.

Without looking up, he says, "Hi Sonny, heard a lot about you."

She frowns at Jake who looks at the man with trepidation. She clears her throat and says, "I'll bet you have. And who the hell are you?"

"The US government; that good enough for you?"

She plops down in a chair across from him and says, "Oh, so you're the government. I always wondered what you looked like. Do you have a first name or should I call you Mr. Government?"

"You can call me John."

Really? John what? Doe?"

"Let's just say, for the sake of this operation, my name is John. It's much better that way. Please believe me. And actually, I work for a very small part of the government: the CIA. We're working closely with the FBI to find out why Max Kushner was murdered. Got any ideas?"

She realizes something's not right. The CIA doesn't work on domestic murder cases. They're concerned with foreign espionage and catching spies. She swallows hard and says, "Why are you involved? Do you think Max was a spy?"

He chuckles, looks around the room at the squirming agents, and says, "Why, no. On the contrary, we think he was murdered by spies."

"Spies? What makes you so sure?"

Jake steps in and says, "Sonny, please, we're in the middle of something. You really shouldn't be..."

"No, she's fine," says John. "Let her stay. She knew Max better than anyone else. Now, Sonny, I'm going to tell you what we know and you tell me if anything springs to mind, okay?"

She nods her head and says, "Sure, fine, but you gotta answer my questions, too. Deal?"

He chuckles again, nods his head, and continues, "First of all, we did an autopsy and found that Max died of suffocation a few hours before his body was run over by an automobile. Plus, he still had a ring around his neck, undeniable evidence of the Russians' favorite interrogation technique. You see, they tie a plastic bag over the head of the subject until they turn blue. Most people will tell you everything after going through that a couple of times."

"Fine, but why Max ? I'm sure you guys don't do autopsies on every supposed hit and run victim."

"No, of course not. We already knew what Max was up to because one of our men at the State Department mistakenly told him about a suspicious rooming house we've been watching. Luckily, our guy told us what he had done." John stops for a moment and glares at the agents. "And yes, we make mistakes just like everybody else in the government, but this one has set us back a good bit. We have no idea what Max told the Russians when they interrogated him, not that he knew that much, but like I said, we have to assume that he divulged everything he could recall."

"Why were you watching them in particular?"

"Well, we've known for a long time that Russian spies were living here and posing as Americans. Sometimes they live together as families, or they live in the same apartment building, or in this case, they live in the same rooming house. We checked into multi-unit properties in DC that were purchased after the end of the war and this one really stood out. It's owned by two sisters, Becky Marks and Sarah Fells, both widows, who told everyone they came here from Milwaukee when they bought the house five years ago. Trouble is, there's no record of them in Milwaukee or anywhere else before that. It's like they suddenly appeared out of thin air. Oh, and they paid cash for the house. Who does that? Not two middle-aged women."

"So let me get this straight. You were already watching the house so you ended up watching Max watch the house. Why didn't you stop him? And when he didn't come out, why didn't you go in and save him?"

Silence. The agents squirm, Jake looks nauseous, but John doesn't blink and calmly replies, "Because we were thrilled someone finally got inside; we were looking for the best way to get in there for several months. We're convinced that this house is the main hub of a very large, interconnected web of Soviet spy cells scattered throughout North America. And they're clever to the point of being brilliant. They exhibit stupendous spy craft, like the mysterious way they communicate with each other, the way they've blended in, right under our noses, and definitely under our radar for who knows how long.

Aside from the two sisters, the other four people living there all have legitimate jobs. One of them, a Swiss-born aeronautical engineer named Walter Schenkel, even works at the Pentagon...if you can believe it. There we were, in awe of them, probably being too careful, waiting for the perfect opportunity, and along comes Max who does his homework and simply waltzes in the front door. Talk about brass balls. No, he obviously wasn't a trained operative, but as far as I'm concerned, a great reporter is the next best thing."

That's all Sonny needed to hear. She smiles wickedly, leans forward in her chair, places both hands on the desk, and says, "John, you are one ruthless bastard." Everyone in the room gasps, everyone but John who doesn't flinch. Sonny continues, "And I like that about you. Now, since you still don't have a plan...I do."

Feet shift, throats are cleared, giggles are stifled, and all eyes are on John. Sonny doesn't wait for a response. She rises, opens the door, and Bo bolts into the room, stands by her side and growls softly at the strange man. She pats his head and says, "It's okay. I think."

John frowns and says, "Your dog looks quite formidable. Can I assume he won't bite me?"

Sonny smirks, "That depends."

John raises his eyebrows and says, "On what?"

"…on how you behave."

He narrows his eyes, "Then rest assured, I will be on my very best behavior. My men told me he was the smartest dog they'd ever seen, but they never told me how formidable he was. Where'd you get him?"

She sits down and Bo sits next to her, his stoic gaze locked on John. "A friend gave him to me."

"Really? A friend just gave him to you? That's some friend. Did you train him?"

"Yes and no."

"What do you mean?"

"I can't really say. He definitely has a mind of his own. He's trained me more than I've trained him."

"So what's your plan? You going to sic your dog on those bad ole Russians?"

"No, not unless I have to. Hey, you just said a great reporter is the next best thing to a trained operative and here we are. Think of Bo and me as a package deal you can't afford to refuse. You ready for my idea?"

"Pins and needles."

"The only way to get in that house is to paint them in a corner so they can't refuse. My idea is to pose as a blind woman who's in town for some kind of radical treatment or whatever. They'd never suspect that a blind woman could be a spy nor could they turn her down. And I'm sure you have people who could teach Bo how to be a seeing eye dog in nothing flat."

"Wait a minute. You don't know what you're talking about. It takes months to train seeing eye dogs and we don't have that much time. Plus, we already have access to well-trained dogs that could do this. Our main challenge, if we ever agree to your hair brained scheme, will be to get you ready for this in a few days."

"I hate to say it, but you don't know what you're talking about and, to be fair, how could you? You don't know Bo like I do. If you did, you'd agree with me. Here's the deal: get your best guy to train Bo for a day and you'll see. Otherwise, we're out."

John rolls his eyes and says, "Okay, aside from your apparent death wish, how in the world do you think you could pass for a blind woman and, if you somehow survive this crazy scenario, what's in it for you?"

"The same thing Max was after...the story of a lifetime."

"I think you need to spend some quality time in a rubber room at the funny farm."

"Hey, John, or whoever you are, my thinking has obviously eclipsed your best laid plans; this is the one great idea you geniuses never thought of. If you weren't so insecure, you'd agree with me."

Jake steps forward, defiantly puts his hands on his hips, and says, "John, you've met your match. Sonny is absolutely right. I assure you, she and Bo can pull this off. Now, not to fault you or any of your people, but I'll wager you don't have an asset like Sonny and you damn sure don't have a secret weapon like Bo."

John pushes back from the desk, crosses his arms, and sighs. "Sonny, I will take your outrageous idea under advisement. Everybody but Jake and Agent Hollis please leave the room.

19

It only takes John three days to formulate a plan to get Sonny into the rooming house and, hopefully, out safely with the critical intelligence. The operation will require a massive amount of coordination and a large dose of raw luck, but it's the best option they've ever had. Sonny was right about that.

She's thrilled when John calls her into the office and tells her the plan is a go. The first thing she says is, "Glad you finally saw the light, but once I get in there, you're not expecting me to crack any of their codes, are you?"

"No, don't be silly. You'll use an incredibly small Minox spy camera to photograph their documents. We'll do the decoding, thank you. We also want you to find out how they're sending messages from the house. They must have some kind of a secret transmitter that allows them to communicate with their comrades around the country. They're simply too coordinated, too connected, and that's the only possible explanation."

"You'll need to protect me at every turn, but how can you? You know I'm not an actress and you've already said these people are really good at what they do. I'm beginning to have second thoughts. What if they catch me and shoot me on the spot? How can you stop that from happening?"

"Look, if they do catch you, they won't shoot you because they'll want to find out how much you know about them. We'll be posted nearby, listening to everything, and I guarantee we'll rescue you."

"I have one very important question."

"Yes?"

"How will you be listening?"

"Bo will be wearing a small, inconspicuous microphone on his collar that will allow us to hear everything that happens. We'll be inside a Water Department van parked close to the house and we'll storm the building at the slightest hint of trouble."

"What's the Water Department got to do with this?"

"Oh, the night before you stay at the house, a water main down the block will spring a huge leak and it will take a couple of days to fix."

She laughs impishly. "Well, fancy that. You have a crystal ball."

"Look, we obviously have an entire scenario in place that should work very well and it won't take a lot of acting on your part. One of our agents, posing as a nurse from Georgetown Hospital, already called the house and inquired about the 'Rooms' sign in the window. There was a lot of commotion in the background until a woman got on the phone. She said the sign was an old one and they didn't have any rooms, but the agent pressed hard, saying she has a patient, a girl, who's blind and desperately needs a room for a very short time while undergoing experimental treatments at the hospital.

The woman said to hold for a minute. There were muffled conversations and when she came back on the phone, she asked how long the girl would need to stay. The agent guaranteed it would be less than a week and begged her to reconsider because this girl can't afford a hotel. After a long pause, punctuated with more unintelligible whispers, the woman finally said one of her tenants was away for a couple of weeks so she could sublet the room for a few days.

We will take you to the house in a hospital ambulance. You'll be wearing dark glasses, using a white cane, and Bo will have a typical guide dog harness. You'll tell them you were recently blinded in an accident back home in Illinois and how lucky you are to be here because Georgetown is the only hospital in the country that offers this program. It'll seem authentic if you're clumsy since this is all new to you. You simply can't react to visual stimuli and that's the end of it."

"Sounds like it'll be the end of me, Stanislavsky."

"Is that a Russian joke?"

"Ha, yes and no. Don't you know who he was?"

"Oh, you mean the Russian actor and teacher. Yes, as a matter of fact, we often use his method to train our spies. However, due to time constraints, we don't have that luxury in this instance. Back to what I said a moment ago, we have to rely on your ability to ignore visual stimuli. If you can do that, you will hopefully be able to find out how they transmit information and we can bring them down. If you make a serious mistake and they catch you, well, once again, we will always be there to protect you.

Sonny, here's the gist of the current situation: we have the bomb, the Russians have the bomb, and whoever strikes first wins. Fact is, they are determined to conquer us, and whether you believe it or not, it is the undeniable truth that demands immediate action if our nation is to survive."

She stares off into space, already rehearsing the part in her mind, delving into memories of every blind person she's ever observed, imagining how she and Bo will interact with each other as well as the Russians. Her outfits shouldn't be well coordinated, just slapped together in haphazard fashion, no makeup, hair parted wrong…

John clears his throat. "Sonny? Hello?"

Her gaze slowly turns toward the sound of his voice as her mind winds back to the present and her face darkens into a wicked smile.

"When do we start?"

Sonny and Bo are riding in the front seat of a Georgetown Hospital ambulance that's being driven by Agent Hollis who's dressed all in white like a real ambulance driver. Six additional agents are crammed into the back where the gurney would normally be.

She's bedeviled by a spate of second thoughts. 'Shit. Shit. Shit. And why didn't I take any drama classes in college? Because I thought they were a waste of time since I wanted to be a journalist who deals in fact not fantasy. Shakespeare was right: all the world is a stage, and if I'm a flop, I'm in big trouble. On the good side, these glasses are so dark, I might as well be blind. Maybe they'll force me to act like it. On the bad side, if they don't, I may end up dead like Max.'

It's only been three days since she agreed to do this, but so much has happened, it feels more like three months. John brought in his best team to give her a crash course in what it's like to be blind. They showed her how to use the white cane, how to work with a guide dog, when to stumble, and how to best ignore her surroundings. But she rebelled when they told her how to interact with Bo. Guide dogs aren't pets, they're employees and should be treated as such. If a dog makes a mistake, he must be sternly reprimanded with a sharp rebuke and a swift jerk on his harness. She would never dream of treating Bo like that. How could she? Then they reminded her that Bo was the key ingredient in the operation, the extraordinary dog who would quickly understand his new role. They also reminded her that she was the weak link, not Bo. She was the one who needed the most rigorous training.

However, to everyone's surprise, Bo presented his own set of challenges for the team like refusing to wear the leather harness. They would put it on him and he would promptly rip it off with his razor sharp canines. After this happened the third time, Sonny asked to talk to him and see if she could get him to tolerate it. First, she scratched his ears until he started making that familiar groaning sound and his eyes slowly closed. Next she whispered in his ear what a good dog he was and how important the harness was to her. She pleaded with him to do it for her. Talk about acting; the poor dog was putty in her hands. She motioned to one of the agents to attach the harness while Bo was in that semi-conscious state and it worked. When she stopped scratching him, he opened his eyes and stood proudly like he was born to be a guide dog.

Unfortunately, he wasn't used to being restrained by any kind of a leash, let alone that unwieldy contraption, and he rebelled by refusing to move when Sonny grabbed the handle. He would follow her to the ends of the earth as long as she didn't hold on to the handle, but he planted his feet and turned into a stubborn mule if she so much as touched it. This time, her scratching and whispering did nothing to persuade him.

She was almost ready to throw in the towel when one of the team members pulled her aside, handed her a small paper bag, and told her to look inside. She opened it and recoiled from the odor. It was boiled beef liver. The agent said they call it "dognip" because it's utterly irresistible. Trying not to lose her breakfast, she grabbed a piece of the stinking meat and held it in front of Bo's nose. Not only did it work, when they went home that night, Bo repeatedly grabbed the harness and took it to Sonny, angling for yet another smelly morsel.

Now to the hard part: training Sonny. First, they showed her how to use the little Minox. She loved it and her devious reporter's mind was instantly awash with all the surreptitious ways she could take snapshots with it. Next, they blindfolded her, gave her the white cane, and locked her in a darkened room filled with furniture, thus forcing her to navigate her way around all the obstacles. When she asked to be let out, she was told to sit at the table and the door would open.

What a cruel trick; there was no table, so she kept trying everything she could think of to find it. She used the cane, her hands, and her feet. She even crawled around on the floor until she finally cried out, "There's no goddam table in here." The door opened and she ran out of the room blinking at the bright lights and cursing the agents who were laughing hysterically and applauding her salty language.

On the following day, they drove her and Bo to a residential neighborhood, blindfolded her again, gave her the cane, told her to walk down the sidewalk with him, and stop when they came to the curb. She did a great job finding the curb, but against orders, she ventured into the street only to be scared out of her wits by an agent honking the horn on a car parked right in front of her. She screamed at him, "What are you trying to do? Give me a heart attack?"

"You were told to stop at the curb. Now go back and see if you can do it right this time."

"Yeah? How'd you like this dog to take a big chunk out of your rear end?"

She turned around in a huff and walked up and down that sidewalk for most of the afternoon until she finally got the hang of it. She and Bo eventually mastered the teamwork necessary to pull it off, proving once again that they could tackle just about anything.

She peeks at the driver out of the corner of her eye and says, "Agent Hollis, shouldn't you be wearing your cute little white cap?"

This is no time to be flippant. He isn't some low level lackey who's only driving the ambulance. He's the agent in charge of the team that trained her for the operation and he's uniquely qualified for the job by virtue of his degrees in psychology, theatre, and law.

"Miss Daye, you're supposed to be blind. Shouldn't you behave accordingly?"

"Hey, just trying to ease some of the tension before you throw me to the lions. And after all we've been through, you can call me Sonny."

"That's not going to happen. It has to be Miss Daye. First of all, I'm a professional, not to mention an employee of the US government. Secondly, I'm from Texas and I was raised to treat women with respect. And third, there are several agents listening to every word we say. Now, as far as I know, you volunteered to throw yourself into the arena, didn't you?"

There it is: the truth, or a good part of it anyway. Though strictly speaking, she didn't volunteer. It was more a case of her jumping headlong into the fray.

"Yes, I volunteered, it was all my idea, but that doesn't mean I'm not going to be nervous."

"Look, being nervous can actually help you do the job, if you use it correctly, or it could get you into some serious trouble if you don't. Tell them you're nervous about undergoing the experimental procedure for your eyes. You'll be using that emotion to your advantage and they may even have some sympathy for you. But if they take your show of nerves as a sign that something suspicious is going on, you could get hurt."

"Thanks for the pep talk. Now my heart is thumping even harder than it was before."

The ambulance rocks to a stop in front of the rooming house and Hollis pats Bo on the head. "Bo, we're depending on you to keep her safe. Oh, and Miss Daye?"

Sarcastically, "Yes, Agent Hollis."

"Break a leg."

Before she can respond, he puts on his white cap, grabs her overnight bag from behind the seat, and gets out. She takes one last deep breath, opens her door and struggles to get out with her purse slung over her shoulder, while holding onto her cane and Bo's harness. Hollis walks around the ambulance and carefully escorts them up to the front door. Still holding the bag, he rings the bell and then stands behind Sonny and Bo. They wait for what seems like an interminable amount of time and nothing happens. Hollis steps forward, rings the bell again, and knocks loudly on the door. He and Bo look up when they hear a window opening above them. Amazingly enough, Sonny resists the urge to look up and gives herself a little pat on the back, 'Ha, didn't look. Good blind girl.'

An older woman sticks her head out the window and yells, "Hello, can I help you?"

Hollis clears his throat and says, "Yes Ma'am, this is the young woman who needs to rent a room while she's undergoing therapy at the hospital."

The woman says, "Okay, hold on a minute" and she slams the window shut.

Several people can be heard walking around inside, talking in hushed tones, opening and closing doors.

Hollis plays his part to the hilt and pats Sonny on the shoulder. "Don't worry, Miss. You'll be fine."

She sincerely wants to believe him and responds with a real sniffle, "I hope you're right."

The noise coming from inside the house ceases and they hear someone fumbling with several locks on the front door. When it finally opens, a nice looking man wearing a shirt and tie steps into view, smiles, and says, "Hello, sorry to keep you waiting. Please come in."

Hollis helps Sonny and Bo through the door, shakes hands with the man, and says, "Thank you, Sir. You're very kind."

"Well, thanks, I'm Arthur Mullins, but I just live here. Sarah's one of the landladies and she'll be down in a moment."

Hollis says, "How do you like it here? Is the food any good?"

While the men chat away, Sonny gladly takes this opportunity to calm herself by reaching for Bo and scratching his head, trying to get her heart to stop pounding in her ears so she can concentrate on the challenge in front of her.

Arthur smiles and says, "This place is real quiet and the food is great, if you like down-home cooking, that is. Sarah also runs the kitchen and believe you me, nobody goes hungry around here. Where are you from Ma'am?"

Just when she thought she could relax for a minute, she's jolted back to reality by his question. She knows she has a typical Chicago accent; there's no getting around that.

"Me? I'm from Chicago. Can't you tell?"

"Oh? I never would have guessed, but then I'm no expert on midwestern accents. I'm from northern California and people say we don't have an accent. We just speak plain old American, I guess."

He turns toward the sound of someone coming down the stairs and says, "Why, here comes Sarah now. I'll let you folks get acquainted. Hope to see you later." The woman is wearing a white bibbed apron with a ruffled collar over a dowdy house dress that makes her look like a run-down version of Betty Crocker. As Arthur passes her on the stairs, she gives him a playful slap on the arm and says, "You weren't bad-mouthing my cooking, were you?"

He chuckles and says, "Uh uh, you know I always clean my plate."

She winks at Hollis and says, "That's the truth. Hi, I'm Sarah Fells. What's your name, Honey?"

Sonny awkwardly extends her hand in the general direction of Sarah's voice and says, "Hi, Sarah. I'm Sonya Knight. It's nice to meet you."

Sarah grasps Sonny's hand gently with both of her rough, gnarled hands and replies, "Why it's real nice to meet you and that's a fine looking dog you have there. What's his name?"

"Oh, his name is Bo. Yeah, people always tell me he's handsome."

"Now what kind of treatment are you here for."

Hollis steps up and says, "Excuse me, Ma'am. I'll try to explain it as best I can. It's an experimental therapy using ultrasound waves to stimulate the retina so more light gets in. It's already worked pretty well on some people and helped them regain at least some of their sight. Anything's better than nothing, right?"

Sonny grins, rocks back and forth, and says, "You can say that again. What I wouldn't give for just a glimmer of light."

Sarah looks at Hollis and says, "Well, that sounds great, but how long will it take? You know I can only squeeze her in for a few days."

Hollis replies, "Oh, we'll know right away if it'll work, say two or three days at most?"

Sarah nods decisively, "Okay, then. Let's get you situated, Miss Sonya. It'll be two dollars a day, three meals included."

Sonny gushes, "Oh, that's wonderful. Thank you. Thank you so much. This means the world to me."

Hollis turns to Sarah and says, "You're very kind and we appreciate it. By the way, I'd like to pick her up at nine tomorrow morning. Is that okay with you?"

"Sure, breakfast's at seven. Here, give me her case. The room's right here on the first floor."

Hollis hands her the case and says, "Thanks again, Ma'am. Hope you sleep well, Sonya."

Acting stunned by her good fortune, Sonny smiles, waves in his direction, and says, "I'm so relieved, I'm sure I will. Bye now."

After Hollis lets himself out, Sarah takes Sonny by the hand and leads her down the hall to her room, watching her like a hawk for any telltale sign that she's a plant. Once inside, Sarah walks her around, letting her feel each piece of furniture, making sure she knows where everything is. Next, Sarah takes her out into the hall and walks her to the bathroom. Bo dutifully walks beside Sonny, doing his best to act like a regular guide dog. When they get back to her room, Sarah asks if she has any questions.

"Why, yes. What time is dinner? I'm starved."

"Six o'clock on the button. I'll have someone knock on your door at ten till. How's that?"

"Oh, thank you. That would be great. Now, if you don't mind, I'd like to rest until then."

"Sure, you take it easy. I'll see you at dinner then."

"Oh, and Sarah?"

"Yes, Hon."

"Thanks for taking us in."

"Don't mention it. Glad to help."

She walks out, closes the door behind her, and Sonny collapses on the bed. She takes off her dark glasses and smiles incredulously at Bo who pants happily and slaps one of his paws on the bed as if to say, 'Way to go, Sonny.' She gives him a big hug around the neck and whispers, "So far so good."

The knocking sound creeps into her brain from far, far away. She tries to ignore it, but then she's jolted awake when she hears a woman say, "Time for dinner."

"Yes, uh, ahem. Coming. Thank you."

She scrambles out of bed and steps on Bo's tail in the process. He gives her a warning yelp and gets out of the way while she desperately searches for her dark glasses. She's disgusted with herself for falling asleep and realizes that she's totally unprepared for act two: a cozy little dinner with six scary Russian spies. She reminds herself to pay close attention to everything she does and keep her eyes closed so she doesn't react to any movement around her. As she looks around the room for her glasses, she notices there's no mirror.

'Great, no way to tell how I look. The hell with it. I have more important problems like ah, there's the glasses.' She puts them on, grabs the cane and Bo's harness, takes two very deep breaths, and theatrically fumbles her way out the door.

She stands frozen in the hall, realizing that she has no idea where the dining room is. It's probably not to the right where the bathroom is, so to the left they go. There's a trade-off between bumping into things because she supposedly can't see them and knowing how to use her dog and her cane to navigate around most obstacles. Experienced blind people rarely bump into things because they know what they're doing. Agent Hollis told her to say she just got Bo and she's still learning how to work with him. Hopefully that will explain why she stumbles around with such difficulty.

All of a sudden, a door opens and someone speaks right next to her. "Hi, you're the new girl and…"

Sonny flinches like she's been shot. "Wha, uh, oh, you scared me."

"Oh, no, I'm sorry. I'm Becky Marks. Sarah and I run the house together. She told me to take you to the dining room, but she certainly didn't tell me to frighten you."

Sonny stops to catch her breath and says, "Thank you, uh, Becky. That's alright. I can definitely use your help. Sarah gave me a little tour of the place, but she didn't tell me where to go for dinner."

"Here, I'll take your cane and you can hold onto my arm. Okay?"

"Wonderful. Now I can relax a little, but I'm sure I'll bump into things. I just got this dog last week and we're still learning how to work together."

"What's his name?"

"It's Bo and people tell me he's really handsome. What do you think?"

Becky laughs, "Wow, he certainly is and he's so big. I'll bet he's smart, too."

"Well, he's a lot smarter than I am. Hey, I'll bet we're in the dining room. It sure smells good."

"You're right. C'mon, I'll help you with your chair."

She carefully leads Sonny to the table, pulls out a chair, and helps her sit down.

"Oh, thanks. Is it alright if Bo sits next to me? Is there enough room?"

"Sure, he's fine right where he is."

Sonny looks straight ahead, doing her best to emulate a blind person, and says, "Bo, sit."

He minds instantly and remains motionless, waiting for his next command. Five other people are already seated and talking softly with each other. There are several platters in the middle of the table containing fried chicken, mashed potatoes, green beans, salad, and there's also a large gravy boat.

Becky clinks her water glass with her knife and says, "Excuse me, everyone. I want you to meet Sonya who will be staying with us for a few days. Please tell her your names."

Sarah giggles and says, "Aw, hi Sonya, this is Sarah."

Sonny smiles and nods her head. "Hi Sarah. Everything sure smells good."

An older man with a gravelly voice says, "Sonya, I'm Walter Schenkel. I am from Switzerland and I am the best looking man at the table."

Sonny giggles and says, "Oh, I love your accent. Hopefully my therapy will be successful and I'll be able to see if you're telling the truth."

A woman speaks up. "Ha, I'm Phyllis Swanson and Walter's lying through his teeth. Now the man sitting on my other side is Arthur, and he's almost as handsome as your dog there."

Everybody laughs and Arthur says, "Hi Sonya, I'm the guy who let you in and I must disagree with Phyllis. I'm nowhere near as good looking as Bo."

Sonny says, "Hi Arthur. Now you sound like an honest man. No offense Walter."

Everyone laughs again and a man says, "Sonya, Hi, I'm Paul Grenier. Now, I will not brag about my looks, but as you can tell, I am French and I definitely have the most beautiful accent, no?"

Sonny says, "Oh, no. I mean, yes. I mean, you just got me in a lot of trouble, Paul. "

The Russians are putting on quite a show, though in reality, it's a horror show, and Sonny is perfectly terrified by their pseudo-friendly patter. One thing's for sure: you put a random group of Americans at a table and there's no way they'd get along this well. The Russians should have taught that in their little spy school. Trouble is, this means they definitely are the real thing. It also means she'll have to up her game and be even more vigilant.

The FBI only gave her minimal background info on everybody, just enough to make it difficult for her to act surprised when they tell her what kind of work they do. First of all, they told her that Arthur is the boss and definitely the most important person in the house. He has worked at a big accounting firm in Maryland for several years, and like Sarah and Becky, he simply appeared out of thin air. He was trained by the KGB as a cryptologist and he's in charge of all the coded messages that are sent and received at the house.

Mousey little Phyllis is the true sleeper in the group. She works as a secretary in a law office, but she's actually an eminent physicist who discovered a brilliant method of transmitting top secret data back to Moscow. In the early 1950's, the US implemented a series of microwave relay networks that operated through a chain of repeater stations across the country to transmit telephone and television traffic. Phyllis discovered that she could transmit Arthur's coded messages by piggybacking on the microwave networks and nobody ever caught on. Once the message gets to a station on either coast, it's relayed to a Soviet ship waiting offshore that radios it to KGB headquarters.

Walter managed to worm his way into the Pentagon by playing the "Swiss" card and trading on his government's neutrality. True, he is an aeronautical engineer, but he's also a rocket propulsion expert having debriefed several Nazi missile scientists who were captured by the Soviets after the war. Due to his security clearance at the Pentagon, he's been able to stay abreast of the latest American missile technology and transmit top-level secrets back to Russia.

Paul works at a local gym as a trainer and weightlifting coach. He was a Communist sympathizer back home in France and one day, he walked right into the Russian embassy in Paris, and volunteered his services. The KGB took one look at him and decided to train him to be a ruthless interrogator. He usually starts by injecting his victim with a chemical the Soviets refer to as SP-117, a compound we would call "truth serum." A small dosage makes it impossible for the subject to lie, but unfortunately, it doesn't take effect immediately. If time is short, he goes from interrogator to torturer. His massive strength enables him to break bones with ease and quickly elicit whatever information his poor subject might have. Another quick method is the old "plastic bag over the head" suffocation trick. It also gets fast results and isn't as messy as compound fractures. Max must have died an excruciating death.

Becky and Sarah, brilliant half-sisters and multilingual translators, systematically organize intelligence from other agents in the field and turn it over to Arthur. Their father was a rabid Bolshevik and close ally of Lenin who made sure his children always had every advantage, particularly when it came to their education. As a result, Becky and Sarah went to the very best schools in Moscow and both girls developed their language skills by listening to their father's conversations with foreign diplomats. However, as good little Communists, they also had to work on a typical Russian collective farm, tilling the fields, feeding the animals, and cooking for everyone. They probably work the longest hours of anyone in the house since they also buy the groceries and cook all the food. As part of their preparation for deployment in DC, they were rigorously trained to cook American food in case they ever had to feed one of us. Obviously, there's no borscht on the menu this evening.

Becky dutifully fills a plate for Sonny and places it in front of her just as Sonny realizes that the FBI team forgot one very important thing: they never taught her how to eat like a blind person. Oh well, she remembers her dad saying the best defense is a strong offense so she gropes for the fork that she intends to wield with perfect dexterity. It should be on the left side of the plate, but it's not there. She tries the right side, still no fork. 'Can't peek, no matter what,' she keeps telling herself. To make matters worse, a pregnant silence engulfs the room. 'They must be watching my every move. They're hanging me out to dry, that's what they're doing.'

In sheer desperation, she whispers to Becky, "Hey, where's my fork? Are you playing a trick on me?"

Becky laughs, "Oh, Sonya, I'm so sorry. I gave you a plate of food and forgot to give you a fork. Here, hold out your hand."

Sonny offers her shaking right hand to Becky and says, "That's okay, sorry to be such a burden."

"You're not a burden. I'm just forgetful."

She hands the fork to Sonny, but she isn't expecting it at that moment and the fork falls out of her hand. Before she can think, she leans down, opens her eyes, and grabs it right after it clatters to the floor. A bolt of sheer terror engulfs her. Forget the fried chicken; she may have cooked her own goose. She slams her eyes shut and tries valiantly to weasel her way out of it by saying, "Hey, what a lucky grab," and holds up the fork like it's a trophy.

Silence. Everyone is stunned for a moment and for good reason. She must have seen the fork in order for her to pick it up so quickly though her eyes were below the top of the table when she opened them which made it impossible for anyone to see her do it.

They don't quite know how to act so they start a silent conversation: of raised eyebrows, pursed lips, shrugged shoulders, nods, winks, and grimaces, trying to decide on the right response. They want to know what she's up to every bit as much as she wants to know the same about them. Should they ignore what happened and act like they buy her feeble excuse? That's probably their best play and Sarah breaks the ice.

"I know how you did it. You heard where it hit the floor and that gave it away."

Becky chimes in, "That's right. Your hearing is much better than ours, isn't it?"

Sonny heaves a sigh of relief and says, "Oh, I just got lucky. I've only been blind for a short time so I doubt my hearing's improved yet. I guess it'll have to get a lot better if these treatments don't work. You know what they say, 'The Lord giveth and the Lord taketh away'."

Becky says, "Here give me that fork and I'll give you a clean one, okay?"

"Yes, thank you. I'll try not to drop this one."

Meanwhile, the agents listening in the van go berserk trying to figure out what just happened.

"A fork? Did she use her sight to pick up a fork she dropped? I think she blew her cover. This sounds really bad. Should we go in now? I don't know, it sounds to me like she handled it, although, they may be suspicious and, at the same time, smart enough to let her think she got away with it. Let's see how this plays out. Going in now might ruin our only chance of stopping them. They'll simply move their operation somewhere else and be much more difficult to infiltrate. As long as the dog is with her, we can hear everything that happens, and if something goes wrong, we can hopefully get in there before it's too late."

The conversations resume around the table and Sonny's heart rate eventually falls below a hundred. She's glad when she finds two drumsticks on her plate; they're much easier to handle. At this point, the last thing she's worried about is table manners and she inhales whatever she manages to scoop up with her fork. It's all really good just like Arthur said. Plus, the more she eats, the less she has to talk and the more she can listen. Soon, the combination of tension, rich food, and yawn-inducing conversation begins to have an almost narcotic effect on her and she can hardly keep from nodding off.

She clears her throat and says, "Well, Sarah, it's a good thing I'm only going to be here for a few days."

"Why's that, Hon?"

"This food is amazing. If I lived here, I'd get fat in no time at all. Oh, no, I hope I didn't insult anyone."

They all laugh and Walter says, "Don't worry, Sonya, we're all in pretty good shape despite Sarah's great cooking."

"Oh, thank goodness. Now, if it's okay, I'd like to get some rest. This has been a really long day."

Finally back to the relative safety of her room, Sonny collapses in a chair and pensively scratches Bo's ears as she tries to digest not only her absurdly fattening dinner, but also the cataclysm of the day's events. She's astounded by the enormity of everything that's happened in the past few hours and it makes her feel as though she's been living a shallow, dull existence up until now. So much for what most people would call a normal life. This is life lived to the nth degree, firing on cylinders she never knew were there and, with any luck, it will actually continue beyond tonight, though that might not be a safe bet considering her stupid mistake.

'This was not a good idea. No, it was a great idea that went terribly wrong, or did it? Maybe they didn't notice that I saw the fork, and if they did, they all covered it up perfectly with their inane chitchat that was boring at best, utterly banal at worst. Maybe they are that damn good. Have they mastered "us" to the point of being indistinguishable from the rest of the American population? The FBI and the CIA seem to think so. I knew they were desperate. Why else would they agree to this ruse? Yeah, right, their pat answer is Bo, the dog that makes the inconceivable seem possible. Oh, and John said a tenacious reporter is almost as good as a trained operative so putting my life on the line is a risk he's willing to take. Easy for him to say; he's sitting out there in a van, drinking coffee and eating doughnuts. The only thing he's risking is a heart attack.'

She puts her hands on either side of Bo's head and stares deeply into his eyes, "That little mishap with the fork almost gave me away. Maybe it did, but nobody acted liked they noticed. Oh, no, what if they really are that damn good? Gotta be smarter from now on…right?" Bo nods his head and gives her a little lick to cheer he up.

The guys in the van are stunned when they hear this. It confirms their worst suspicions and prompts more heated discussions about whether or not they should barge in now or wait and see how it plays out tomorrow. In the end, John decides to let her continue as planned.

Sonny's little talk with Bo had the opposite effect on the Russians who were eagerly listening to every word she said thanks to the bug Phyllis hid in her room. After dinner, they went straight to the basement, walked through a concealed hole in the wall, and down the steps to their secret communications bunker below. This fortress is more impenetrable than a bank vault because its reinforced concrete walls, floor, and ceiling are three feet thick. The heavy steel door actually came from a bank in Poland and was cleverly delivered to the house in a piano crate. Plus, there's an escape tunnel that surfaces in the woods a hundred feet away that also delivers fresh air to the room. And if they do have to escape, once they're in the clear, they'll detonate a large incendiary device inside the bunker that will obliterate everything.

Now they know they'll have to do whatever it takes to get what they want from Sonny. Initially, they fought tooth and nail during the phone call from the nurse at the hospital. Most of them thought it was sheer lunacy to let a stranger in the house, but Arthur decided it would be better to have the "patient" stay here and, if she is a plant, they'll be able to find out everything she knows. After they're satisfied that they've wrung every last detail out of her, the poor blind girl will have a terrible accident and fall down the basement steps to her death. Yes, it will be messy, but messy is one of their specialties.

It was a sleepless night for all concerned. Sonny was so afraid she'd miss breakfast that she wound her alarm clock too tight, something snapped inside, and it stopped ticking. She finally calmed down once she realized that she probably wouldn't have slept anyway and she used the time to rehearse her act for the next day. Bo watched her intently as she went through various motions and silently practiced her responses to every possible scenario she could imagine. Humans can be so entertaining.

John and his crew stayed on high alert throughout the night in case they had to spring into action if anything hit the proverbial fan. By the time the sun came up, the inside of their van smelled like a cross between a locker room and an outhouse because their "facilities" consisted of a five gallon paint can…that had no lid.

The Russians usually work straight through the night since Moscow is seven hours ahead of DC so this night wasn't any great departure from their normal routine except for the heated discussions they had about various ways of getting the most information from Sonny.

To be on the safe side, Arthur instructed Phyllis to collect any new intelligence that hadn't been relayed yet and transmit it tomorrow night along with everything they intend to wring out of Sonny. Otherwise, if they have to hastily abandon their fortress, that critical information might be lost forever.

Walter nearly jumped out of his skin when Phyllis told him to hand over everything he had. He had secured some incredible intelligence at the Pentagon that very morning, but he never got the chance to tell anyone due to Sonny's disruptive visit. It described the Top Secret Atlas Project being developed by the US: our first serious attempt at making an ICBM (Intercontinental Ballistic Missile) capable of delivering nuclear warheads to the Russian mainland. Though still early in the design phase, these details would give Soviet scientists invaluable access to our progress and our ultimate goals.

Right on schedule, Becky knocks loudly at ten till seven, "Sonya, breakfast."

"Uh, okay, I'm ready."

Is she ever. For the last five minutes, she's been standing at the door holding onto Bo's harness while he sits patiently at her side. She takes two deep breaths, fumbles around with the door long enough to signal her clumsiness, and swings it open.

"Is that you, Becky?"

"Yes it is." She grabs Sonny's arm and abruptly pulls her and Bo into the hall. "Wait here. I'll shut the door." She slams it so hard it startles Sonny. Then Becky clutches her hand and says, "Here, I'll lead the way."

Sonny is so preoccupied with her acting that she's oblivious to Becky's harsh manner. She even congratulates herself for really being on her game, convinced she can keep her eyes closed, regardless of anything that might happen. That will free up her mind so she can concentrate on her conversations with the other people and eating without any more mishaps. All she has to do now is get through breakfast and soon she'll be safely back in the ambulance with her buddies.

Then she nearly faints as a pang of fear grips her. 'What if they poison my food? What if I do something stupid again and they shoot me on the spot? Bo couldn't save me if either of those things happened.' She suddenly stops in her tracks, forcing Bo and Becky to stumble.

"Sonya, are you alright?"

Luckily, Sonny remembers what Hollis told her about using nervousness to her advantage. "Uh, well, I'm not sure. Honestly, Becky, I'm really dreading this visit to the hospital. If they can't cure me, I'll be blind for the rest of my life and I can't bear the thought of it."

Becky knows she should probably say something sympathetic at this point, but sympathy isn't in her nature so it takes her a moment to come up with a suitable response. Finally, she says, "Sonya, you must be positive. Don't lose hope."

In for a penny, as they say. Sonny seizes the moment, throws her arms around Becky, and cries real tears. So real, in fact, that Bo leans against her leg and whines his support.

Again, Becky isn't sure what she should say. She pulls away from Sonny and sternly repeats something she heard constantly during her KGB training, "Don't cry. You must be brave."

That hits Sonny right between the eyes. 'Yeah, get it together, Daye. You're in the World Series; this ain't the Minors.'

"You're right, Becky. You're so right. Thanks, I needed that."

'Oh, if she only knew.'

There's nothing like a good cry and Sonny's has a cathartic effect on her by the time she and Becky walk into the dining room where the other five Russians are already seated at the table, droning along with their usual dull conversations, only stopping long enough to greet Sonny before resuming. Though she feels much better, their cool indifference catches her a bit off guard and her pulse begins throbbing again. 'Why aren't they talking to me? Maybe my food is poisoned and they don't want to waste any time with small talk since they know they'll be extremely busy as soon as I croak.'

Just when she's about to pop a blood vessel, Paul speaks up to her right, "Sonya, excuse us. Sarah's coffee is so strong, we can't stop talking."

Saved by the Frenchman. "Oh, Paul, that explains it. Please fill my cup so I can catch up with you."

Paul continues, "It's right here." His large hand grasps hers and guides it to the cup sitting in front of her, but his hand lingers a bit too long and he still doesn't let go when he says, "Careful, it's hot. Do you take cream and sugar?"

Startled at the size and warmth of his hand, she mumbles, "Uh, yeah, uh, sounds good. I mean, yes, I take both. Thanks."

Little does Sonny know that this is actually a kind of sick foreplay for Paul, a prelude to the disgustingly perverse things he plans to do to her. After all, in order to rise to a position of prominence within the Soviet power structure during the regime of Joseph Stalin, a man credited with killing tens of millions of his own people, you're either the baddest bastard on the block or you're banished to Siberia… if you're lucky. Otherwise, bye-bye, Comrade. What's worse, Arthur and everyone else in the house relish Paul's performances and love to watch him work his sadistic magic on some poor wretch. Phyllis was so aroused by the sheer artistry Paul displayed while tormenting Max Kushner that she seduced him after Max finally succumbed and gladly died.

Sonny can't believe the effect his touch is having on her. It actually feels good and she almost giggles at the absurdity of the situation. How can she possibly be responding to a Russian spy she's trying to catch? She never expected anyone to make a pass at her in the midst of all this intrigue. Sure, it happens all the time in real life. But here? No way. Maybe he's toying with her; trying to get her to open her eyes. 'Fat chance, Casanova.'

She pulls her hand away and says, "Oh, just one sugar and not too much cream, thanks."

Becky speaks up to her left, "Here, I'll do it. You'll have to excuse Paul. He suffers from being French, you know. They all think they're God's gift to women. In reality, he's as ugly as a toad."

The table erupts with laughter and Paul mutters, "Merde," under his breath. He does resemble a toad because he has large bumps all over his body. In his case, however, they're mounds of knotted muscle. Sonny's glad Becky put him down. It gives her a moment to collect herself and hopefully get through breakfast without any more unwelcome distractions.

She's almost exuberant when she and Bo get into the ambulance. As they pass the Water Department van parked next to a barricade around a manhole, she leans close to Bo's collar and says, "Hey, John, we just passed the van. You in there?"

Agent Hollis grits his teeth and says, "Miss Daye, can you ever stop the wisecracks?"

She ignores him and says, "Whew, am I glad to be here. I think I've run out of adrenaline. Is that possible?"

He keeps his gaze fixed on the road and responds dryly, "We can only hope your adrenalin rushes didn't give you away. By the way, I liked it when you cried with Becky; that was some great acting."

"Acting? I wasn't acting. I simply used the opportunity to let loose some of my pent up tension. Isn't that what you told me to do?"

"I wasn't fishing for a compliment."

"No, you would never do that, Mr. Perfection."

"Miss Daye, please."

"No offense intended; just lettin' off some steam. Hey, are we going to the hospital now?"

"No, we're going to a secret location where the team can debrief you. There's no way we could do that effectively at the hospital."

"Okay, makes sense."

"I'm glad you think so."

Sonny is amused when the ambulance pulls into the garage of a swanky Georgetown house. After the garage door lowers automatically and all six agents crawl out of the back, she swoons, "Wow. Nice joint, Hollis. You live here?"

"Of course not, but if you'd like to keep living, you'd better stop being so flip and get serious for once."

Once inside, Sonny and Bo are ushered into a large room where all the curtains are drawn and several people are sitting around a large round table. John, obviously in charge, is flanked by strange men on either side of him. Everyone has a legal pad in front of them, except for the two women who are there to record everything with stenotype machines.

When Sonny sees them, she can't help herself. She looks right at John and says, "Are you going to put me under oath before I testify?"

Both women respond with quick keystrokes and John smiles patiently, "Sonny, please have a seat. I seriously doubt you'll lie to us; that's not why we're recording this and you know it. Oh, there's a bowl of water next to your chair for Bo. Now, may we begin?"

"Fine, think I could have a glass of water?"

One of the women gets up, goes to a side table, fills a glass with water from a large pitcher, and places it in front of Sonny who says, "Oh, you're a waitress, too, huh."

The other woman types away and Sonny gives her a dirty look. The woman stares back impassively and doesn't flinch.

Sonny stares back at her and says, "Aren't you going to record the fact that I made a face at you or do you only record what I say?"

Once again, the woman types while staring blankly at Sonny.

John slams his palm on the table and growls, "Sonny, enough already. We have work to do. Now tell us what happened with the fork last night."

"Wow, you cut right to the chase, don't you? Yes, well, when Becky handed it to me, I wasn't expecting it, and I dropped it. Then I bent over, picked it up, and realized that I had opened my eyes. Honestly, I seriously doubt that anyone saw me since I was leaning down when it happened, but I did pick it up right away which is why I said it was a lucky grab. Then, as you probably heard, Becky and Sarah chimed in and sort of validated my alibi."

John glowers back and forth at his people and then at Sonny before saying, "C'mon, do you really think you got away with it? These people are pros. They can smell a rat a mile away."

"Yes, I think they bought it. I'm still alive aren't I?"

John abruptly stands and says, "This operation is over. You're too stupid for your own good and we're running the risk of losing a lot of ground in our investigation if we continue with your little charade."

Sonny jumps to her feet and so does Bo. "If I'm so stupid, why did I come up with the best idea yet for getting inside the house. You're embarrassed because I made all of you look stupid."

The silence is more than deafening once the women finish their last keystrokes. John and Sonny stare defiantly at each other while everyone else looks straight ahead, frozen in wide-eyed disbelief. After what seems like an eternity, Bo snorts in disgust, walks over to the water dish, loudly laps up half of it, and licks his jowls. Without taking her eyes off

John, Sonny grabs her glass of water, downs it, and wipes her mouth on her sleeve. John allows himself a slight grin, picks up his glass, and offers a toast, "Here's to you, Sonny. You've got some big ones. Alright everybody, you heard the lady. Let's get ready for tonight."

After lying on her bed for several hours fully dressed, Sonny sits up, swings her legs over the edge, and whispers to Bo, "Okay, I'm gonna go see what I can find. Wish me luck." Then she orders him to be quiet by holding one finger up to her mouth before carefully opening the door. She steps out, looks up and down the hall, and gives him the "stay" sign. He makes a soft gurgling sound deep in his throat to show his displeasure at being left behind, but he stops when she holds up her finger again. "Now you stay right here and be quiet. I won't be long." She winks at him, walks out, and silently closes the door.

John goes ballistic when Sonny leaves without Bo, "Hear that? She didn't take the dog with her. Talk about shit for brains. Better saddle up, Boys. We'll probably have to barge in there any minute now and save her sorry ass."

Sonny sneaks into the dining room and through the kitchen to see what's behind it, but all she finds is a large pantry and the back door. As she retraces her steps, she notices another door off the kitchen. She opens it slowly and sees a flight of stairs going down to the basement. The stairwell is completely dark except for a flicker of light at the end.

She's torn between her morbid curiosity and her last shred of common sense, 'Oh, crap. Why didn't I bring Bo with me? Because I was stupid...that's why. I should turn right around and get him. No, I'm already here. I'll just see what's down there and if I find anything, then I'll go get him.'

When she gets to the basement, she notices a large bookcase that's pulled away from the wall and there's a jagged hole behind it. She tiptoes over to the bookcase, looks through the hole, and sees yet another flight of stairs going down even farther. It's lit by a string of bare light bulbs and it looks like a mineshaft. The steps are made of raw lumber and the stairwell was obviously hacked right out of the bare earth, the walls and ceiling are nothing but packed dirt and rocks.

Having thrown all caution to the wind, the first creaky step only makes her more determined to forge ahead and she steadies herself by patting the clammy walls as she goes down. When she finally exits the stairwell, she stands before a huge steel door that's slightly ajar with light streaming from inside. She creeps toward it, listens for any telltale sounds, but it's completely quiet. She waits for several more minutes and still hears nothing. When she finally gets up the courage and slowly swings the door open, a hand reaches out, grabs her by the wrist, and pulls her inside. The door swings shut behind her with a loud thud and several heavy bolts slide into place.

The lights are so bright, she has to squint as she looks around and counts all six Russians who were patiently lying in wait for her.

She does her best to keep her composure and blurts out, "Hey, what's going on? What is this place?"

Paul leers at her and says, "How stupid do you think we are, Sonya, or whatever your name is? Here…have a seat." He forces her to sit in a large metal chair that's bolted to the floor, deftly ties her hands behind her, and yells, "Play the tape."

Phyllis walks to the large table, presses a button on the tape recorder, and Sonny's heart nearly stops when she hears her own voice, "That little mishap with the fork almost gave me away. Maybe it did, but nobody acted liked they noticed. Oh, no, what if they really are that damn good? Gotta be smarter from now on…right? Okay, I'm gonna go see what I can find. Wish me luck. Now you stay right here and be quiet. I won't be long."

Paul walks around in front of Sonny, smirks, and slaps her face so hard her lip splits open and blood trickles down her chin. "Thanks for giving us that warning. We suspected you would find your way down here, but it was so kind of you to let us know exactly when you were coming."

She's so stunned by the blow that she shakes her head convulsively back and forth, spraying blood everywhere, as she tries to clear her mind, but it's no use. She's paralyzed with fear and the realization that she'll probably never see the light of day again. Thinking straight is impossible.

Meanwhile, Bo senses something is amiss. He paces back and forth, whines softly, stops to sniff the air for clues, then paces some more. He wants to go find Sonny, but he was told to stay in the room so stay he must.

Paul grins sardonically, pulls up another chair, and sits facing her. "Sonya, my dear, I have many delicious ways to deal with you. Now, this can go quickly and easily for you, or I assure you, it can go very slowly and extremely painfully."

He reaches into his pants pocket, pulls out a switchblade, and springs the 4 inch stiletto blade into action.

"Either way, you will end up dead just like your reporter friend Max. The choice is yours. Now cut the bullshit. How are you and Max connected?"

She spits a mouthful of blood on the floor and screams, "I'm a reporter just like Max…that's our only connection. I swear."

He leaps to his feet, grabs her by the throat, and holds the knife within an inch of her left eye. "By the time I get done, you will tell me every last thing you know about us."

Phyllis edges closer to Paul, puts her head on his shoulder, and says, "He's such an artist and I love to watch him work. It makes me feel so alive knowing that soon you will be so dead."

Sonny almost retches as a shocking wave of terror envelopes her entire body. She knows her only hope is sitting way on the other side of the house and she screams, "Bo! Bo! Bo! Bo!"

Bo's ears perk up, then he growls thunderously and grabs the doorknob in his mouth, but the door won't open. He tries again and when the knob breaks off, he flings it across the room in disgust and scratches the door so furiously that sawdust fills the air. Once he begins to break through, he backs up, hurls himself at the weakened spot, and explodes into the hall.

He sniffs the floor and follows his nose through the house right to the cellar door. Down he goes in one fell swoop...his paws hardly touching a step. He sees the hole in the wall and senses Sonny is somewhere beyond. This time he carefully glides down the steps until he's in front of the steel door and he hears Paul yell, "Give me the bag."

Phyllis grabs a clear plastic bag and a roll of adhesive tape from the table and hands them to Paul. He thrusts the bag over Sonny's head and viciously wraps the tape around her neck as she gasps in horror.

Bo growls so thunderously that everyone inside the vault can feel the floor vibrate. Then he gets up on his hind legs and fiercely scratches the door until sparks fly.

Paul laughs, "Oh, listen. It sounds like your precious dog is trying to save you, but he won't. Only death will save you. We got a lot out of Max and now you'll give us the rest. Nod your head if you're ready to talk."

Instead, she defiantly tries to suck the bag into her mouth so she can bite a hole in it, but once she does, she realizes that it's no ordinary bag and, try as she may, she can't bite through it. Next she holds her breath for as long as possible and when she finally exhales, she showers the inside of the bag with blood. She also tries in vain to free her hands, desperately kicks her legs, and shudders uncontrollably until she passes out.

Paul rips the tape from around her neck, pulls the bag off her head, and slaps her face. Her body jerks in series of violent spasms until she becomes motionless again.

164

Paul screams, "Give me the water?"

Walter grabs a large bucket of water and hands it to Paul who rears back and savagely empties it right into Sonny's face. She comes to gasping for breath and coughing uncontrollably. He grabs her by both shoulders and shakes her so hard he almost snaps her neck, "Now tell me everything you know or you get the bag again."

Sonny inhales as deeply as she can and spits blood in his face, "Go to hell, asshole." She takes another deep breath and screams, "Bo, save me! Bo, save me now! Bo, Bo...please, Bo."

Paul wipes his face on his sleeve and growls, "Ha, you'll go to hell long before I do." He shoves the bag over her head and wraps the tape around her neck, all in one fluid motion. She tries to break the chair loose by rocking back and forth, determined not to lose consciousness. She tries so hard to free her hands that her wrists start bleeding. She viciously kicks at Paul, but he laughs and moves away. The last thing she sees before she passes out is his sick, twisted face followed by blurred images of her parents and their home in Chicago.

Bo runs back up the steps, turns and hurls himself toward the door, hitting it with all his might. The door groans under his assault, but it holds.

Walter yells, "I'm sick of that goddamn dog making so much noise. I'll put an end to him right now. Maybe then she'll realize how alone and helpless she really is."

He pulls his Makarov pistol and opens the door. Bo immediately pounces on him and knocks him down, but Walter is able to fire one hollow-point slug into Bo's neck that mushrooms to three times it's original diameter and leaves an exit wound the size of a quarter as bloody bits of flesh and fur explode into the air.

Arthur screams at Phyllis, "Transmit the Atlas file... now! We're out of time."

She runs to the table and frantically pecks away on a strange cipher machine that's attached to the microwave transmitter. Despite the blood spurting from his wound, Bo grabs Walter's wrist and tears off his gun hand. It falls to the floor, still clutching the pistol, leaving him with nothing but a gory stub. Next, he jumps on Paul and tears off the hand holding the knife in exactly the same way. Becky and Sarah leap into the fray and frantically try to stop the bleeding from their mangled limbs. Arthur heads for the tunnel, but Bo takes a big chunk out of his lower leg, rips his Achilles tendon to shreds, and he falls to the floor screaming.

Next, Bo runs to Sonny, tears a gaping hole the bag, and licks her face. Nothing…she isn't breathing. Her head falls forward, her chin rests on her chest. He licks her so hard her head flies back and then falls forward again. He sits in front of her and growls loudly. Nothing. He growls louder and louder until she finally comes to gasping and screaming, "Bo, what the…? How did you…?" Then she notices the blood pouring out of his wound. "Omigod, you're bleeding. What…?"

He runs behind her chair, rips the ropes from her hands, and helps her stand. She grabs a handful of fur on his back and he leads her past the screaming Russians writhing on the floor in massive pools of their own blood. Sonny looks up and there's John and several FBI agents scrambling down the steps toward them with guns drawn. The agents have their standard issue .38 caliber revolvers, but John sports the famous .45 caliber Thompson submachine gun.

He yells, "You alright? Dog get shot?"

She leans against the wall to steady herself while she rips the rest of the tape off her throat and mumbles, "Yeah, uh, gotta go." She grabs Bo's fur with both hands and he drags her up the stairs as more agents hurl past them and barge into the room. One of them slips on the blood and falls next to Paul who's holding what's left of his right arm and cursing in French. John shoves the agent out of the way and stands over Paul, "Wow, guess the dog didn't get your tongue, but he did get your hand."

Paul snarls at him and continues his French tirade. Another young agent, who's obviously never seen such carnage, puts his hand over his mouth, gags, and tries not to throw up.

John turns to him and says, "Agent Burns, why don't you go get some fresh air and, while you're out there, you might want to call for a couple of ambulances, but take your time. There's no hurry."

This infuriates Walter who screams and tries to lunge for John, but also slips on the blood and falls to the floor clutching his own bloody stub. John calmly stomps on his neck and says, "You'd better stay right there. We wouldn't want you to lose too much blood, now would we."

In the midst of all the commotion, Arthur screams at Phyllis who's still typing, "Atlas. Atlas."

With that, John calmly raises his gun and, with a quick burst from his Tommy gun, blows her brains all over the wall. Then he pulls the plug on the cipher machine.

Arthur whimpers, "Atlas."

The table contains an incredible array of spy paraphernalia: a large radar scanner with a flickering screen, the tape recorder, a microwave transmitter, and the cipher machine. Plus, there's a treasure trove of code books in Russian, English and French, the file containing top secret information on the Atlas project that Phyllis was trying to transmit, and a list of other covert Russian operatives and their American aliases.

John turns to the agents milling around the room and says, "Nobody touch anything on this table until I examine every last bit of it. Now get those sumbitches out of my sight."

One of the agents bends down and grins at Walter, "How the hell am I supposed to cuff a guy with only one hand? Guess I'll just have to put 'em on your feet."

Walter curses a blue streak in Russian and kicks his legs wildly. Another agent steps over him and points a pistol at his face, "You better hold real still so my buddy can cuff your feet or I'll gladly shoot off your other hand. Up to you, Boris."

Sonny and Bo make their way up the second flight of stairs, past another wave of agents, through the kitchen, and out the back door. She collapses on the steps and watches Bo run into the yard and shake himself like he just came in out of the rain, but he shakes so fast that his entire body is enveloped in a fine crimson mist. After he stops, she starts to cry and says, "Come here, Boy."

He happily gallops to her and sits at her feet. She kneels down and when she reaches out to pet him, he licks her bloody wrists.

She sobs, "Oh, Bo, first you save my life and now you're healing my wounds. What would I do without you?" She chuckles, "I wouldn't do anything because I'd be dead. Here let me see how bad you're hurt." She feels his neck with both hands, but try as she may, she can't find any blood or any trace of a wound. She stands up, blinking through her tears, and runs her hands over his entire neck refusing to believe what she sees...or rather, what she doesn't see. She wipes her eyes on her sleeve, looks at him again, and her mouth drops open. There he sits, as happy and gorgeous as ever. His fur is completely dry; there's no wound, no blood, nothing.

"Omigod," she gasps as she stumbles backward, trying not to faint, "Benjamin told me about...uh, what you did to that wild boar and that Sally said you were seriously wounded, but when you got back to the house, you were perfectly fine. I never really believed him. I thought he was spinning some kind of yarn."

She wipes her eyes again and frantically looks around, realizing that she has to get him out of there before anyone else sees him. She scratches his ears, kisses him on the head, and they run out to the street. And they run and they run until she can't run anymore. She finally staggers over to a telephone pole and holds on so she won't collapse. He sits next to her and looks around nonchalantly like this has been a perfectly normal evening. When she notices that he isn't panting, that he's not the least bit out of breath, she collapses to the sidewalk, rolls over on her back, and giggles hysterically.

After she catches her breath, a warm feeling of safety and serenity washes over her. She muses about having to run away from the rooming house when she saw Bo's instant rejuvenation so no one else could witness his surreal transformation from being a severely wounded, bloody mess back to his normal, robust self in a matter of seconds. That she was subjected to unspeakably horrific torture at the hands of an inhuman, sadistic murderer doesn't bother her in the least. Most people would carry the burden of such a harrowing experience for the rest of their lives, yet it doesn't faze her at all. How could that be?

The obvious answer is Bo. His limitless courage, his ironclad loyalty, his willingness to protect her from any and all threats coupled with his otherworldly talents and abilities have given her the courage to face any imaginable obstacle with a confidence that is as strong as his dedication to her well-being. Now that she's truly experienced the liberation of Bo's love and devotion, Sonny is free to fearlessly pursue anything she wants.

Suddenly gripped by the enormity of the situation, a wave of nausea wells up in her throat, but she grits her teeth and looks toward the sky, "Max, we just got revenge for what those goddam Russians did to you." She looks down long enough to take a few deep breaths and collect herself before raising her eyes again, "You were one great reporter and I miss you, you big slob." She blows a kiss, then smiles at Bo, and gives him a big hug.

20

The cab pulls up in front of the White House and when Sonny gets out, she's bombarded by a barrage of flash bulbs. Suddenly, a hush falls over the crowd and everyone does a double take, wondering if she's Audrey Hepburn. And why shouldn't they? She's dressed in a stunning, floor-length red gown, her sleek raven hair is done up in an elegant French twist, and that breathtakingly beautiful face is gorgeous enough to stop traffic.

"Hey, Sonny, you look great. Where's Bo?"

She stops, scours the crowd, and tries to place the familiar voice. One of the photographers raises his camera in the air and yells, "Sonny, over here, it's me, Alan."

She spots him and laughs, "Oh, hi Alan. Why thank you. I couldn't find a tuxedo for Bo so he had to stay home."

The sea parts and all eyes are riveted on her as she walks up the steps and disappears through the front door.

Someone yells, "Al, who is she and who's Bo?"

"She's a reporter at the Associated Press and Bo's her dog."

The man shakes his head and mumbles, "Wow, that's some honey. Think I'll apply for a job at the AP."

To be sure, Sonny's recent appointment as chief White House correspondent was due to merit. It was also a bit of a consolation prize for the Pulitzer she fully expected to win for her groundbreaking exposé about the Russian spy ring that she was forbidden to write. Citing national security, the US government issued an airtight gag order on any and all details surrounding the infiltration and raid on the rooming house, the subsequent rounding up of scores of other Russian agents, both here and abroad, and the effective destruction of their intricate web of deceit.

The joint CIA/FBI task force that ran the operation had fully intended for her to write the story; it had all the trappings of a propaganda coup that would have been an extremely valuable victory in the Cold War. As it turned out, it was painfully obvious that the US had seriously underestimated the scope of the Russian spy campaign until Max Kushner's suspicious, untimely death shined a spotlight on the rooming house. And who knows what could have happened if their operation had failed. At the very least, it would have forever besmirched the integrity and competence of our entire intelligence community. Instead, the success of this operation made them look like a bunch of dunderheads who simply got lucky because of a young reporter and her dog.

Agent Hollis, who supervised the team that trained Bo and Sonny for the operation, had trained K-9 dogs during the war and when he was grilling Sonny about Max Kushner, he noticed Bo's extraordinarily unique behavior patterns that were so far beyond instinctive, they were magical. First of all, he and Sonny communicated on a level that was almost telepathic. Then there was the way he could appear and disappear, literally in plain sight. One minute he would be lying at Sonny's feet, and a moment later, he was gone. How did he do that? Where did he go? It gave Hollis the creeps, but he had to stay focused on his job and get to the bottom of Kushner's murder. Still, it was too much to ignore and when Sonny came up with her idea to pose as a blind woman with Bo as her seeing eye dog, it dawned on him that it just might be the break they were looking for, the tactic to get inside the rooming house that had eluded them.

Once the operation was over and everybody in the joint task force fully comprehended the surreal way it went down, the verdict was unanimous: Sonny and Bo were a tremendously powerful, military grade weapon that had to be classified Top Secret and, likewise, every detail surrounding the incident had to be accorded the same designation. Forget the embarrassment of underestimating Soviet espionage capabilities, when John and his crew saw what

Bo did to the Russians, he became the main reason they could never let Sonny write the story.

Talk about baptism under fire, here she is, attending the first official function at the recently renovated White House, and boy is it a doozy: a state dinner honoring Sir Winston Churchill no less, the newly re-elected Prime Minister of Great Britain. Yes, she yearned to be in the middle of the action, but you know what they say about being careful what you wish for. Sometimes, when you actually get it, you start to feel that you're in way over your head. In Sonny's case, that thought lasts about two seconds and she's back to full steam ahead, business as usual, especially when she tries to imagine what it would be like if Bo were here with her, snatching hors d'oeuvres, ending up in the kitchen, begging for more, and getting them. She envisions him, not in a tuxedo, but sporting a gold bow tie, the same color as his fiery, golden eyes. That would do the trick.

It doesn't matter if they're together or apart; there's an ever-present, conscious bond that isn't separated by space or time. And he was so adorable earlier this evening when he saw her all dressed up for the party. He sat at attention, thumped his tail on the floor, and happily panted his approval. In response, she curtsied and said, "Why, thank you, kind Sir."

She taps the shoulder of a young waiter carrying a tray of Champagne glasses and he nearly stumbles when their eyes meet. She grabs his arm to steady him and says, "Oh, sorry. Did I startle you?"

He laughs nervously. "Um, uh, yes, to be perfectly honest, you did, but it was my pleasure. If you don't mind my asking, who are you anyway?"

She smiles impishly. "Why, I'm Sonny Daye. And who are you...anyway?"

Before he can answer, she grabs a glass of Champagne and walks into the dining room where an aide guides her to a seat at the head table no less. And there they are, Truman and Churchill, less than ten feet away, joking in hushed tones as if they've been friends their entire lives.

Churchill, born into landed aristocracy, the magnetically inspirational public speaker who gave the British people immense hope and courage during the darkest hours of the German bombings that turned London into a devilish cauldron of raging fire storms, but who now presides over the rapidly shrinking British Empire upon which the sun was never supposed to set, sits next to President Harry Truman, the plain talking, poker playing farm boy from Missouri, who was instrumental in forming the United Nations, NATO, and funding the Marshall Plan that rebuilt Europe after the war; the man who dropped the big one, not once, but twice, thus ending the Second World War, and ushering in mankind's apocalyptic era.

The human species now has the ability to totally erase itself from the face of the earth and that horrifying reality is clarified by the fact that the US and Russia, archenemies in the Cold War, both have the bomb. It isn't a question of if it could happen, but more a question of how it could happen.

Her pulse quickens, her eyes dart from one man to the other, trying desperately to overhear their secret conversation. Oh, if she could only read lips like Bo. They seem very relaxed, almost nonchalant, but these highly skilled old foxes are brazenly discussing the gravest of issues right in front of everyone and she's sure of it.

Once again, her instincts are correct. It's a good thing Truman has a masterful poker face because Churchill just casually mentioned that he will soon announce Britain's intention to test its own nuclear device before the end of the year. Truman's unflinching response, every bit as casual, is delivered with a knowing smile: something about needing to pull another chair up to the table between him and Stalin. He isn't the least bit surprised because he already knew everything Churchill told him before the old sot whispered the first word. Great Britain might be our closest ally, but intelligence gathering doesn't differentiate between friends and enemies.

Dinner parties, even glittery state dinners, tend to be stuffy, boring, and wholly uneventful. This one proves to be quite the opposite in every respect and, by virtue of the tense global situation, it has to be. Truman and Churchill know they have Stalin, the vicious tiger, by his despicable tail and that cooperation between the US and Great Britain is more important now than it was during the war because the stakes are even higher. Difficult to fathom, true nonetheless.

Sonny devours the heady atmosphere with unimaginable delight as she witnesses history unfold, but all too soon, dinner ends abruptly when President Truman rises and proposes a toast to Prime Minister Churchill causing everyone else in the room to stand up quickly and try to grab any glass in front of them to join in the toast. This results in several glasses of wine and water being spilled unceremoniously and rather noisily. Truman, always ready with a quip, says, "Maybe we shouldn't toast. It sounds like some of you have already had too much to drink."

Expecting to get a laugh, Truman is surprised when he notices that most of the people are watching in horror as the corpulent Churchill struggles to get out of his chair. If anybody's had too much, it's the notoriously drunk Prime Minister. But, once again, he saves the day, "Mr. President, I assure you I have had far too much to drink, but let's toast anyway and give the rest of these bloody amateurs a chance to catch up."

The room erupts with the kind of laughter that happens when a great tension is relieved and people are free to giggle away their pent up emotions, but the boring, perfunctory toasts quickly subdue the levity until the orchestra begins to play in the grand ballroom. Sonny, one of the few people actually listening to the tipsy buffoons, didn't come here to dance; she came hoping to ferret out the truth, but she might as well enjoy herself a little so she joins the eager crowd filing out of the dining room.

As soon as she enters, she becomes the undisputed belle of the ball with suitors galore lining up to spend a few brief moments twirling her around the floor. She hardly ever wears high heels and it's all she can do to maintain her balance as she wrestles with the clumsy oafs trying to make time with her. Most of them are shorter than she is and they stumble to keep up with her in their alcoholic stupor. The dance marathon goes on for so long she can hardly catch her breath, when out of nowhere, a voice from above brings everything to a standstill.

"Excuse me, but I have to cut in."

She wearily turns to face the next potential masher, but when she looks up and gazes into those crystal blue eyes, she knows her life will never be the same. He felt the much same way, but even more so, when he first saw her at dinner…simply because he recognized her. Yet how could that be possible? She's both a complete stranger and eerily familiar all at the same time. He's sure they've never met. He would remember that exquisitely gorgeous face, but this goes far beyond the superficial; he feels as though he's known her forever. Yes, it's not the face that he knows; he knows her, as profoundly as he's ever known anything in his entire life. It's amazing how fast the human mind can work when it senses the past, present, and future all at once, momentarily blotting out the rest of reality in the process.

He subtly elbows her current dance partner out of the way, leans down, and whispers in her ear, "You look like you could use a break. Let's find a table and have a drink."

He could have said, "Let's go jump in the reflecting pool by the Lincoln Memorial," and she would have uttered the very same response, "Sure, lead the way."

As she takes his arm, something unexpected happens, something otherworldly. She, too, feels as if she belongs with him, that they are and have always been a couple. She's been around a lot of men…beautiful women usually are, but she's never felt completely captivated before. Luckily, she notices the cane in his other hand and his slight limp which kicks her reporter's instinct into high gear, flooding her brain with even more questions and diverting her attention, for the moment anyway. 'Where should I begin? No, I'll let him start the conversation since he made the first move and clearly has an agenda. On the other hand, maybe he's just another wolf, albeit a gorgeous one. Ah, so what if he is? I'm obviously ready for that and a whole lot more.'

He threads a path through the crowded dance floor and then to a small table with two chairs facing each other. She's somewhat amused to see a silver ice bucket with a bottle of Champagne on the table along with two glasses and she can't help thinking, 'Oh, this guy's good, real good.' He guides her to a chair and seats her in one fluid motion. Next, he pulls the other chair around the table and sits next to her, reaches for the bottle, pops the cork, and fills both glasses without spilling a drop.

He hands her a glass, but before taking it, she removes her gloves, and brushes his hand with her fingers before she accepts the glass. He's transfixed by her careful, methodical demeanor and his eyes drift from her hand holding the glass up to her smiling face. He returns her smile, raises his glass, and says, "I believe a toast is in order."

"Do you, now."

"Oh, yes, I do. I..."

"Sir, you might have the courtesy to introduce yourself first."

He sits there with his mouth open, paralyzed by her incredible nerve and her steely confidence. In truth, he might not be so intimidated if he knew that she's actually torn between feelings of dizzy exhilaration and sheer panic, to the point that she's about to burst into tears or laughter and she can't decide which would be more catastrophic.

"I'm Steve Rasco. Who are you?"

The laughter wins and she lets it out with abandon.

He's shocked. "What's so funny? Are you amused by my name?"

She does her best to calm down, clears her throat, and says, "I'm Sonny Daye. Nice to meet you." and starts laughing again.

He puts his glass down and says, "Right, laugh all you want, but my real name is Steve Rasco. Now, what's your real name?"

Then it hits her and her heart jumps into her throat. She can't respond because there's no way to express what's going through her mind. At this point, all she can do is wonder, 'Is life nothing more than a crap shoot or is it a preordained path? He's that Steve Rasco. Ben Harper's Rasco, the other guy Bo saved back in Belgium. Oh, I gotta take him home, uh, sure, I would have anyway, but wait'll Bo sees him. He'll recognize him. I know he will. This is way too delicious. I can't wait, yet, I think I'd better make doubly sure it really is him.'

She has to put her glass down and wipe her eyes with one of her gloves, realizing that now she's laughing so hard she's crying. She finally looks up at him, grits her teeth, and nods her head emphatically.

"What? What are you trying to say? You really are Sunny Day?"

"Yes, yes I am, but Sonny's spelled with an 'o' and Daye has an 'e' on the end. It really is my name, Steve Rasco." She puts her hand on his. "It really is, I swear. Now, I hope you don't mind. Can I ask what happened to your leg?"

"Do I get extra points if I tell you?"

"No, I mean, yes, but that's not why I'm asking. I'm a reporter and I'm naturally curious."

"In that case, it happened back in Belgium in December of 1944. I'm lucky to be here so I really can't complain about walking with a cane. You see, I was one of only two survivors from my original platoon. The other guy, Ben Harper, saved my life when he dragged me out of a burning building after we took a direct hit. I kept in touch with him for a while; I'd call him on the phone, but then he became distant and finally told me to stop calling. I think he was uncomfortable about what happened back there and talking to me reminded him how awful it was. I'm really sorry he pulled away. After all, like I said, the guy saved my life."

Suddenly sobered by the reality of the situation, she leaves her hand on his, picks up her glass with her other hand, and says, "Amazing, thanks. Then how about a toast to Ben Harper?"

He picks up his glass and says, "Yes, let's toast to Ben and to the future. May it always be this wonderful."

She clinks his glass and says, "Steve, I'll drink to that."

She accepts his offer to drive her home without the slightest hesitation and they mostly talk about their careers as a way of easing the tension. He tells her about his injury-induced transition from active duty to a desk job at the Pentagon and eventually to the Voice of America where he's been instrumental in formulating much of the propaganda we broadcast into the Soviet Union and other countries. He tells her he never thought his acting career would amount to anything, but it gave him a tremendous background that serves him extremely well in his new job. In short, he learned how to put on a show and that's precisely what he does now, only this show isn't light entertainment, it's entertainment that plays for keeps. It's a vital and powerful instrument of our foreign policy.

When she tells him she works for the Associated Press, he makes a crack about her also being in the propaganda business since the government probably what tells her to write. On the contrary, she responds, the government has never told her what to write, but recently, they did tell her what not to write. Before he can ask what that means, she laughs and takes great joy in saying she can't tell him any more because it's classified, though not nearly as classified as the delicious thought running through her mind, 'You're gonna shit when you see Bo.'

They pull to a stop in front of her building and she puts her hand on his arm and says, "Wait, I have something very important to tell you before we go upstairs."

"Oh, no, you live with your mother."

"No, silly boy."

"Then you must have a roommate. Is that it?"

"No…"

"Oh, don't worry. I'm a gentleman and …"

"Stop, just stop."

"What?"

"I have a dog."

"You have a dog. That's it?"

"No, that's just the beginning."

Sonny is so overwhelmed by the giddy anticipation of Steve's reunion with Bo that she has trouble walking. High heels are always a challenge, but doubly so when your pulse rate is off the charts. They climb the steps to the second floor and she pauses before she puts her key in the lock, "Bo, I have a new friend with me. Be sweet now."

Now he's really confused and understandably apprehensive about this mystery dog. 'Why did she tell him to be sweet? Would he attack if she didn't say anything? Is that what he normally does? Attack?'

He clears his throat and says, "Ahem, before we go in…?"

"Yes?"

"Has he bitten people before?"

"Yes."

"A lot?"

"A few."

"Has he ever…?"

"Yes."

Unable to wait any longer, she unlocks the door and swings it open. Bo immediately leaps at Steve, knocks him flat on his back, and licks him right into a state of panic. He knew it was Steve from the very sound of his voice out in the hall.

"Sonny, call him off. I can't breathe."

"Bo, let him up. Why, you act as if you know Steve."

Bo gives him one more lick for good measure, backs away, reluctantly sits at attention, and pants happily at both of them.

Sonny helps Steve struggle to his feet, as tries to reclaim his sense of dignity, and says, "Wow, I see why you to warned me. At least he didn't bite me."

Sonny smiles coyly, "Not yet, anyway."

"What is that supposed to mean?"

"Steve, now don't be mad, but I've been toying with you."

"What? How?"

"Steve."

"Yes."

"Take a good look at Bo. His name is short for Billy O. Ring a bell?"

Steve bends down to get a better look at him and reads the dog tags around his neck. Shocked, he stands bolt upright, turns to Sonny, and says, "No way. It couldn't possibly be…"

She beams at him and says, "Yes, it is."

With some difficulty, Steve goes down to one knee and holds out his arms to Bo. "C'mere, Fella."

This time, Bo walks cautiously to him, sits up on his haunches, puts his paws around Steve's neck, and hugs him. Steve hugs him back and chokes up. Bo rolls his eyes up at Sonny before nuzzling his head against Steve's to console him.

Sonny bends down and puts her hand on Steve's shoulder. "Steve, there's a lot more you should know before we go any further."

Those last three words definitely get his attention. He pulls away from Bo, tries to compose himself, and stands up. "There's more?"

"Oh, there's a lot more and I think you should sit down," as she takes his hand and leads him to the sofa.

He sits next to her and says, "Fine, go ahead, this oughta be good."

"Ha! Good doesn't begin to describe what I'm about to tell you."

Bo celebrates the reunion by lying on his back, jackknifing his body back and forth on the carpet, and moaning his approval. When he's done scratching, he flops over on his stomach, puts his head between his paws, and listens as Sonny, without hesitation or reservation, gets up, paces back and forth, and starts with her first trip to Alabama when she worked for the Stars and Stripes, and continues until she brings Steve right up to this moment. She only skips Bo's last incredible exploit with the Russians. Telling Steve everything else relieves the onerous burden of secrecy she's borne for so long, a burden she willingly accepted as a small price to pay for having Bo in her life.

She bends over and snaps her fingers in front of Steve's glassy eyes. "Yes, Ben didn't save your life; Bo did. He dragged both of you out of that burning building in Malmedy."

"What? What are you saying? No, sorry, you're wrong. Ben saved me. He's a decorated war hero. Didn't he tell you?"

"Steve, he told me the real story and now you're the only other soul on earth who knows the truth." She takes a deep breath and says, as nonchalantly as possible, "Any more questions?"

He raises his arm and places it on the back of the couch. "Yes, will you sit here with me?"

She smiles seductively, "That's an easy one. Of course I will."

When she snuggles up to him, he gently puts his arm around her and says, "You'll never know how much I appreciate everything you've told me. I've been struggling for years with the memory of what happened back in Malmedy. Did Ben tell also you about the change in the dog's, uh, Bo's appearance?"

"He told me a lot, but I'd love to hear your recollection of what happened."

"Well, it's the real reason that day's haunted me ever since. And now, after what you've told me, I can begin to make sense out of it, but then again, not really."

"What do you mean?"

"Though what I'm about to tell you may help you come to terms with everything you and Ben have witnessed, it still won't explain what happened in the first place. When we entered that pharmacy, the only thing we found was a half-dead, flea-bitten excuse for a dog cowering in a corner. He was so far gone, most people would have put him out of his misery, but Billy O'Neal was instantly drawn to him and started taking care of him. Here was this big, burly Irish dock worker from the absolute worst part of Boston, a guy who could scare the hell out of you with a look, and he was talking to this wretched mongrel like it was his own baby."

"C'mon, the change? Tell me what happened. I can't wait."

"Okay, okay, we took two direct hits. The first one killed everyone but me, Ben, Ira Spiegel, and the dog who was as good as gone anyway. Now, here's the scary part: just before the second blast, Spiegel forced the dog to drink a vial of strange, milky-looking liquid. The blast knocked me out and when I came to in the field ambulance, my leg was killing me and there was this dog, and I do mean this dog," He points at Bo. "completely alive and healthy, staring at me with those big golden eyes, and panting happily like I was his long lost buddy. Then I heard a grunting sound from the other stretcher and there was Ben, smiling at me like a damned fool and he said, 'We made it, Rasco. We made it.'

Sonny, I'm convinced that the mysterious liquid turned him into this magnificent creature and that Ira Spiegel knew it would, but tragically, he didn't survive. By the way, we figured the dog was at least two years old when we found him back in 1944. Here it is 1952, Bo's got to be at least ten years old, and he looks the same as he did in that ambulance; no grey whiskers, not a one. In short, he hasn't aged a day. Go figure."

"Wow, yeah, Ben told me how old he was and I think about it all the time. But Steve, what do you think was in that vial?"

"Who the hell knows. While the rest of us were trying to survive and find a way to get back to our company, Spiegel stayed in the back of the pharmacy by himself and messed with test tubes. That's all I can say and it still keeps me up at night when I think about it."

Sonny shivers. They stop and stare at each other for a very long moment as the reality of their connection sinks in. Steve finally reaches up and caresses her cheek with the back of his hand, then grasps her neck, and gently pulls her to him. They kiss for an even longer moment and when she opens her eyes, she smiles and says, "Wow, the past is almost too much to comprehend. I think we should go delve into the future." She stands, takes him by the hand, leads him into the bedroom, and winks at Bo before closing the door.

Soon, he hears playful giggles that quickly morph into primal animal sounds: the kind of guttural outbursts that surely echoed off distant cave walls at the dawn of mankind, the same feral chorus that has guaranteed our survival for countless millennia.

It's a good thing Bo never sleeps because no dog could snooze through all the racket they're making. He walks into the kitchen to get a drink and stops in front of the bedroom door on his way back because their screams have dissolved into muffled moans accompanied by intense, heavy breathing. He listens for a moment, decides they're fine, and returns to his favorite spot in the living room.

21

"Go wake him up." Sonny and Bo have just returned from their morning walk and, for the first time in a long time, she's prepared breakfast for two, not that she's trying to play house or make Steve feel comfortable. It's merely the best way to move him out the door quickly so she can get on with her day. And the first order of business is a tall one... attempting to coherently analyze everything that's happened since yesterday. She's keenly aware that it doesn't matter whether this is exquisite serendipity or their preordained path. The only undeniable fact is that applying third dimensional logic to a fourth dimensional situation is an exercise in futility.

'How or why we got here isn't important. This is where we are and there's no turning back. My dull, well-ordered life has careened out of control and it scares the hell out of me. Last night was terrific alright, but my job, for what it's worth, is the most important aspect of my life. Yeah, gotta focus on that, if for no other reason than to maintain some structure and a shred of sanity amidst this torrid turn of events.'

Plus, she has work to do, polishing her latest story and, even though it's Saturday, she's itching to get to the office, type it up, and hand it in. The sooner she does, the sooner she can forget about the trash they expect her to regurgitate from the press briefings at the White House. Her appointment there was supposed to be a prestigious promotion, but now she's languishing in the position and feeling like she's only a highly paid parrot barfing back inane boilerplate. She isn't a real news reporter anymore; she's merely a cog in the machine that delivers the government's bullshit. It's basically the same thing Steve does at the VOA, except she's peddling domestic propaganda to her fellow

Americans. While his work is heroic, hers is an embarrassment.

There are 15-20 different reporters from various news agencies posted at the White House and they all get the same information. Their main challenge is to fashion those bullet points into a coherent narrative that will hopefully be somewhat interesting to read. Her Russian escapade spoiled the daylights out of her, not that she yearns to risk her life again for the sake of a story, a story that never was written. Now it almost doesn't matter. She relished the thrill of the hunt, the intrigue, the danger. Not being able to write the story was horribly painful until she realized it was the process that thrilled her. Most reporters can write a pretty good story, that goes without saying, but living in the middle of great stories, having a front row seat as history's being made...that's what Sonny hungers for.

Jake thought her assignment at the White House would be a step up. As far as she's concerned, it's taken her off her game. She was so close to Churchill and Truman last night, truly spitting distance, but she wasn't allowed to speak to them, let alone interview them. You would think they'd want to say something on the record as a quick way to lay out some nifty platitudes, if nothing else. No way. Not in the cards for her or any other member of the press corps. Instead, they'll get an official outline for their story on the state dinner.

Government bigwigs would go nuts if she wrote a factual account of what really happened: all the drunks she saw, how they misbehaved, who said what, and to whom. Then there was the fat Senator who offered to set her up in a luxury apartment in return for certain sexual favors. If she ever wrote a story like that, it would literally set the newspapers on fire. It would also incinerate her career in the process.

Bo sits inches away from Steve's comatose face and gives a little snort. Nothing. Another, louder snort. Still nothing. He slams a paw on the mattress inches from Steve's nose and finally gets him to open one eye.

"Wha... who the...? Steve recoils from the furry face in front of him and looks around the room, still not quite sure what planet he's on, let alone what day it is. He's been sleeping, or rather hibernating, for a scant two hours, not nearly enough to recover from last night's gymnastics. Sonny kept him up all night, depleting him to the point of exhaustion. He hasn't expended that much energy since basic training and now this crazy dog is determined to get him out of bed.

"Where is she? Where's Sonny?" Bo gives him a friendly little woof and pants happily. "Okay, okay, I'll get up." He swings his legs over the side of the bed and puts his head in his hands. When he opens his eyes, Bo's gone and the smell of fresh brewed coffee wafts in through the doorway.

He stumbles around the room and manages to find his boxers and t-shirt. He tries to smooth his hair back, but it refuses to obey and he looks like he just survived a tornado, which isn't far from the truth. Bo reappears, barks once, and runs away. "Yeah, yeah, gimme a minute." He clears his throat, throws his shoulders back, and strides out of the room as confidently as he can without using his cane.

He walks into the kitchen and there's Sonny, sitting at the table, dressed in a crisp blouse and a skirt, writing feverishly in a notebook with Bo sitting at her side. Her hair is pulled into a sleek, high ponytail tied with a black velvet ribbon. She knows Steve is standing there, but she continues writing until she finishes by putting an emphatic period at the end of a sentence. She puts her pen down, looks up at him with a deadpan expression, and says, "Coffee?" not "Good morning, Darling." or "Hi, Honey." just "Coffee?"

He blinks and shakes his head. "Sure, uh, and good morning to you."

She picks up her pen, nods toward the percolator on the counter, and says with a sarcastic smile, "Morning. Help yourself and there's some scrambled eggs 'n bacon if you want. I've already eaten" and she returns to her work.

He looks at Bo as if to say, 'Help me out here, Buddy.' Bo cocks his head to one side and gives him a look that says, 'What's your problem?'

Steve tries to save face by busying himself in the grub department making as much noise as possible, whistling, humming, dropping his silverware on a plate until she gets the hint and slaps her pen down on the pad.

"Steve…"

"No, I get it…"

"Really? How could you? Look at everything that happened last night: the State Dinner, Churchill, Truman, us. Is it always like this when you sleep with a woman? Don't answer that."

Steve chuckles and turns away.

"What? You think it's funny?"

He tries to stifle it, but another giggle finds its way to the surface. "May I speak now?"

"It better be good."

"It wasn't good, it was great and, for some odd reason, you can't handle it."

"Get out."

"I rest my case." He throws his dish on the counter and leaves the kitchen.

Bo has been watching this unfold as if he's at a tennis match…back and forth, back and forth, from Sonny to Steve, Steve to Sonny. He watches Steve leave and looks back at Sonny. She throws her hands up and blurts out, "Men! You're all alike…you're animals. I already have a dog; I don't need another one."

Steve appears in the doorway, "Now don't tell me I'm the same as all the other guys you've been with."

"Hey, watch it. You make it sound like there've been a lot and why are you still here?"

"I'm still here because you're still talking to me and I don't care how many there've been. I refuse to believe you brought all of them home after knowing them for only a few hours."

"Hell no, you're the only one."

"Okay, so men aren't all the same and women certainly aren't. After last night, it's obvious to me that every once in a blue moon, an extraordinary woman emerges from the pack."

"Oh, so now I'm a dog."

"No, you're more like a wild cat."

"Is that a bad thing?"

"Ha, I obviously like it when you get wild. Look, I don't want to ruin what might be the best thing that's ever happened to me and, if I may say so, perhaps to you as well."

She gives him a defiant grin. "Think so, huh?"

He nonchalantly reaches down and scratches Bo's ear until his eyes fall to half mast as he moans and nuzzles Steve's leg.

Sonny rolls her eyes. "Well, so much for my ferocious dog."

She looks up at Steve. "Does every living creature adore you?"

He laughs, "No, hopefully just the ones I adore. By the way, I have adored this dog ever since I watched him change Billy O'Neal into a better person. And on top of that, now I find out he saved my life. Then there's you."

She bats her eyelashes at him. "Does that mean you adore me, too?"

"No."

"No?" She thunders.

"Take it easy. Adore is the future tense of smitten and you'll just have to settle for that until further notice. Why? Do you adore me?"

She sticks her nose in the air, trying not to laugh. "No, slightly smitten at best." She looks at Steve. "Now what the hell do we do?"

"Uh, after breakfast?"

"No, I mean in general. You know."

He raises his eyebrows and shrugs, "Uh, uh, I don't know. Do you?"

"You're not being much help."

He grabs a strip of bacon off his plate, feeds it to Bo, and grins, "Kinda help do you want?"

"Hey, I usually don't feed him at the table."

"Why not?"

"Oh, for heaven's sake…probably because somebody told me not to."

"Maybe you should've asked him.

"Steve!"

"What?"

"I'm scared."

"Boo!"

"Steve, stop teasing me."

"I'm not teasing; I'm trying to get you to relax. You're all worked up and you have absolutely no reason to be scared, certainly not of me."

"Oh, I'm not scared of you. I think I'm scared of us. I mean…aw, crap, I don't know what I mean."

Bo slaps a paw onto her leg and laughs at her. She gives him a dirty look and clenches her jaw, trying not to crack up. It doesn't work. She throws her head back and lets loose. When she finally composes herself long enough to look at Steve, he sticks his tongue out and looks cross-eyed at her which sends her into another fit of convulsive laughter.

He quits while he's ahead and deadpans, "Think I'll take a quick shower." Then he calmly walks out of the kitchen leaving Sonny in a state of utter confusion. All she can do is stare at him with her mouth open until he's gone. When she finally snaps out of it, she looks down at Bo, and says, "What just happened?" No response. She rolls her eyes, "Oh, you're no help either." He snorts at her, walks over to his water bowl, loudly washes down the bacon, burps, and leaves.

Steve walked back into the kitchen fully dressed, stood behind Sonny, and rubbed her tense shoulders. She instantly yielded to his touch and moaned softly, still amazed at the effect he has on her. One thing would definitely have led to another if Bo hadn't demanded their attention with several loud barks. As they ran out the door, laughing like silly teenagers, Sonny realized she hadn't forewarned Steve about Bo's idea of a walk, but then again, she wasn't thinking too clearly at that point. He noticed that she didn't put a leash on Bo, but he was preoccupied with his own thoughts and forgot about it when they left the apartment.

Sure enough, when she opened the front door of her building, Bo disappeared as usual. Steve was clearly taken aback and gave Sonny a look of sheer terror. You can tell someone about Bo's capabilities, but when they see them firsthand, it's a dog of a different color. She felt a little guilty about not preparing him better for Bo's rocket speed so she tried to play it down.

"Yeah, he likes to take a quick run around the neighborhood, but he always comes back." Her attempt failed miserably. Steve's look didn't change, he didn't flinch, and he appeared to have stopped breathing. An absurd thought crossed her mind and it was all she could do not to laugh out loud. 'Great. I almost killed him last night and now my dog has given him a stroke.'

She grabbed his arm and said, "Steve, snap out of it. I tried to warn you. Okay, maybe I should have stressed the part about his speed, but hey, he's fast, real fast, scary fast. And anyway, if he didn't trust you, he'd never let you see him do that. He has an amazing awareness of his surroundings and if any strangers are watching, he won't do anything spectacular; he acts like a normal dog. The point is, he likes you. Get used to it, Soldier." Then she lost it and laughed right in his face.

Boom! His heart started thumping and he gasped for breath, but it wasn't her laughter that brought him back, it was the "get used to it." She tipped her hand with that simple phrase. She wanted him to stick around and now they were both way beyond smitten. Good thing he didn't leave when she told him to. She was still holding onto his arm as he motioned toward the street and said, "Shall we?" as he led her down the steps to the sidewalk.

They had a lovely stroll in the crisp evening air, smiling at each other from time to time, not saying a word, for nothing needed to be said. When suddenly, they felt a gust of wind rush over their heads from behind and watched as Bo soared to a landing thirty feet in front of them. He spun around, placed his front legs flat on the sidewalk, lowered his head between them, put his rump in the air, and wagged his tail furiously: the universal canine signal for "Let's play!" Sonny let go of Steve's arm, leaned forward, raised her hands in claw fashion, and growled, "I'm gonna get you."

Bo jumped to his feet, galloped toward them, and sprang five feet over their heads. Steve ducked, but Sonny didn't flinch and confidently watched Bo sail over them. Steve looked around to see where he landed but he had disappeared again. After clearing his throat to collect himself, he looked at Sonny and said, "You know, I don't think 'fast' does him justice. I think 'vanishes into thin air' is much better."

"There you go. You're beginning to understand." She took his hand and they continued down the sidewalk at a leisurely pace, their heads spinning, trying desperately to make sense of everything. Their respite was short-lived because they both felt something weighing on their clasped hands. Sonny innately knew what it was; Steve had a sneaking suspicion and couldn't resist glancing down. Yes, it was Bo, walking between them, resting his chin on their hands. It was his way of giving them his blessing, as if it were a perfectly normal thing to do. If he likes you, he has the uncanny ability to make the extraordinary seem normal due to his consummate knowledge of the human condition. He doesn't try to shock you with his feats; he shares them with you in a very gentle way. But if he doesn't like you or you try to harm someone he loves, you could find yourself in the midst of a living hell, subjected to horrific waves of metaphysical mayhem.

When they got back to her apartment, Sonny told Steve she needed to go to her office and turn in her article. He did the honorable thing, said he admired her commitment, and offered to drive her, though he would've preferred to head right back into the bedroom. When she hesitated, he suggested they take Bo, get some Chinese food, and eat dinner at his place. It was a bit late to be coy so she accepted his invitation and quickly stuffed a change of clothes into a small bag.

There were always a few people in the AP office regardless of the time of day. That night there were only a couple of young copyboys toiling away. Bo instantly made his rounds, looking for any choice morsels on the floor, and checking the wastebaskets for leftovers. The boys blushed when Sonny said "Hello" as did most men in the office regardless of their age. Steve chuckled to himself and patiently sat in the corner reading a newspaper while she typed her article. Having finished his search, Bo walked over to Steve and plopped down next to him with a contented sigh. This caught Sonny by surprise, albeit a very pleasant one; she was accustomed to her dog lying at her feet when she worked.

A few minutes later, she ripped the paper out of the typewriter and declared, "Finished. Now the whole world can read my incredibly interesting story about all the renovations at the White House right down to the 18th Century Chippendale table that was donated by some old lady in Vermont. Steve, this is precisely the kind of earth-shattering news I report on a daily basis."

He didn't know if he should laugh or frown sympathetically so he took her lead and added his own sarcasm, "And that's exactly the kind of earth-shattering news our country needs to know on a daily basis. You should be proud."

After they left the office, Steve drove to his favorite Chinese restaurant and took Sonny inside to order. The lady behind the counter smiled and said, "Ah, Mr. Steve, who's your new friend?"

That didn't sound very good to Sonny. It made her feel like she was nothing more than his date du jour, that this restaurant was part of his normal routine before taking a woman back to his place for fun and games. The worst part of it was the undeniably jealous feeling she had toward women she didn't even know, those nasty trollops who preceded her in Steve's life. How was that possible? She had been with him for less than 24 hours and she was already being possessive? Well, the shoe had never been on that foot before. Boys, and later men, had always been a convenience, not a necessity for her. Many tried and, until now, all failed to keep her interest for more than a short time, let alone corral her. She didn't have a clue why Steve was different or why her feelings for him weren't merely different, they were alarmingly uncontrollable. Her primal "fight or flight" instincts failed her. She was paralyzed and couldn't decide which one was right.

Steve knew exactly how it must have sounded and racked his brain for the right comeback. "No, Mrs. Ling, this is my old friend, Sonny."

Totally surprised, Mrs. Ling's mouth dropped open and she knew she had to come up with the correct response lest she make a big mistake. "Yes, yes, Sonny, I'm so glad to meet you. What can I get you?"

Something snapped and Sonny decided to fight for her luscious Lothario so she responded with a wry smile, "Oh, Steve knows what I like. He'll order for me."

Steve grabbed a menu and quickly scanned it. 'What a pisser she is. Okay, everybody likes shrimp. Yeah, that's a safe bet and eggs rolls, too.' He looked at Sonny with his own wry smile and said, "Ah, here it is. They have your Sweet and Sour Shrimp. Will one egg roll be enough or would you like two?"

She couldn't resist, "Oh, better make it two. I've worked up quite an appetite since yesterday."

He struggled to keep a straight face and turned to Mrs. Ling, "Yes, uh, you heard the lady. She'll have two egg rolls along with the shrimp and I'll have my usual Beef Subgum."

Luckily for them, their food was ready in no time and they could stop making small talk, trying not to burst into fits of raucous laughter. That happened when they got back in the car and Bo thought they'd both lost their minds. He sat motionless in the back seat until they were able to sober up long enough for Steve to drive. At that point, he lay down with a groan, hoping they'd keep it together so he could relax.

Sonny wasn't expecting anything in particular when Steve parked in front of a modern building in a nice neighborhood, but she and Bo hesitated when he opened the door to his apartment. It was a one room studio and the focal point was a gorgeous, unmade king size bed. To the left, a brown leather sofa and a mahogany coffee table with newspapers and magazines. Next to it, the latest Motorola TV-record player combo in a large cabinet. To the right, several shelves containing books and records behind a matching leather chair. There was a small table and only one chair in the kitchen. If it weren't for the framed photograph on the wall of an attractive older woman playing the piano, the place would have screamed, "bachelor pad."

Bo took one look, snorted his disgust, and backed away from the door. Then he looked up at Sonny and frowned. After living on the farm, it was bad enough being cooped up in her apartment, but this place was way too small. Steve realized they were shocked and tried to smooth things over as he ran inside and frantically attempted to tidy up.

"Look, Sonny, I obviously wasn't expecting company and I really didn't think about it when I asked you to come over here."

Still standing in the doorway with Bo, she smiled, "Steve, don't worry about it." She looked over his shoulder, "Wow, is that your mother?"

He grinned proudly, "Yup, sure is. She's my hero; gave me the gift of music. Sonny, please come in."

She couldn't help thinking, 'Omigod, no abstract prints, no Lautrec posters, just a prominently displayed picture of his mother. Is he the ultimate dreamboat, or what?'

"Sonny?"

"Huh? Oh, that's great. You'll have to tell me all about her, but let's go back to my place. We'll be more comfortable there. This isn't big enough for the three of us."

He shrugged and laughed, "Yeah, you got that right. Hey, I'm really…"

"Steve, stop. No apologies. No explanations. Food's getting cold so lock your door and let's go."

"Guess I should pack a bag."

"Better pack a big one. No offense, but we're never coming back here again."

After they got back to Sonny's and finished dinner, she asked Steve if he'd like to see the rest of her apartment. He said he would since he wasn't exactly paying attention earlier. First, she showed him her home office with built-in bookshelves, file cabinets, and a beautiful desk with a Smith-Corona typewriter. There are several framed photographs hanging on the walls along with her diploma from the University of Chicago.

He pointed to one of the pictures and said, "Your parents?"

"Yes, I'd like you to meet Elizabeth and Archie Daye."

He played right along, "Why hello, Elizabeth. Nice to meet you, Archie. You sure have a gorgeous daughter."

She punched him on the shoulder. "Hey, watch it. You'll have to clean it up if you ever meet them."

"Ow! That hurt. You pack a pretty good punch."

"Then behave or I'll bop you again."

He grabbed her in his arms and pulled her close. "Now, you can't get a good swing at me."

"Yeah, what about my knee?"

"You wouldn't."

"You're right. I would never hurt that part of you. It's one of my favorites."

"Good to know. Now tell me about your parents."

"Why do you want to know about my parents?"

"I want to know everything about you, that's why."

"Ahhh, there'll be plenty of time for that."

"Oh, so you're planning to spend a lot of time with me."

She got very serious and said, "Steve, it's not a matter of spending time with you; I'm with you...period. Therein, lies the difference."

His face went blank and he froze for a moment as he realized his life would never be the same, then he smiled and said, "Back atcha', Baby."

"You know, when a man pulls a woman this close, he usually kisses her."

It's difficult to kiss when both people are smiling so broadly, but they managed somehow.

Steve is the first to wake up the next morning and he's very glad he did when he sees Sonny lying next to him. It's his first opportunity to watch her sleep, to drink in every minute detail of her flawless face and to watch her chest rhythmically rising and falling with each breath.

She's beyond irresistible and it's impossible not to be intoxicated by her ample charms. He pulls a feather out of his pillow and tickles her nose with it. She brushes it away with her hand, but doesn't make a sound. He tickles her nose again. She giggles, opens her eyes, and says, "Hey, what day is it?"

"Um, pretty sure it's Sunday."

"I gotta pee and I'm starved."

She jumps out of bed, runs into the bathroom, and slams the door. He gets up, struggles into his boxers, and stumbles out of the room. He goes into the kitchen hoping to figure out breakfast and it's not easy since he doesn't know where anything is. He opens the fridge and has to chuckle. It looks like the breakfast she made yesterday was the last of her morning food. There's three different kinds of cheese, four bottles of wine, and some fruit. Next, he opens almost every cabinet and finds absolutely nothing that he would consider eating before noon.

She walks in wearing a black kimono and says, "Don't waste your time. I haven't been to the store in over a week. Let's hit the diner."

He turns around intending to make some wisecrack, but when he sees her in that kimono with her tousled hair and smudged makeup, he realizes he's all done. He's totally, helplessly in love with her and there's no two ways about it. A smile slowly lights up his face until he's grinning like a complete fool.

"Steve, hello, how 'bout it?"

He blinks himself back to reality and says, "How 'bout what?"

"The diner, remember?"

"Yeah, uh, definitely the diner."

After breakfast, Steve offers to take her grocery shopping and it backfires when he grabs a cart and says, "Okay, I'll buy everything. Tell me what you like to cook?"

"Who me? Nothing. Oh, wait, I get it." She gets the giggles. "You always buy the groceries and your date does the cooking."

"What? No, not uh…"

She completely loses it and laughs so hard, she has to grab his arm to steady herself, "Well, just so you know, you've already had everything I can cook...bacon and eggs. You're lucky I didn't burn the goddam toast like I usually do."

"Seriously, didn't your mom teach you how to cook?"

"No way. In fact, she was thrilled when TV dinners came out. Honestly, so were we. Dad always said she only cooked properly in the lab; she's a biochemist."

"You're kidding."

"No, I'm serious. She can ruin anything and I'm the same way. Like mother like daughter. Luckily, there are a lot of great restaurants in Chicago. Hell, my dad and I even stuffed ourselves with junk food at ballgames so we wouldn't have to eat Mom's cooking when we got home. Needless to say, our family ate out whenever possible and our fridge was always filled with doggie bags.

Now, my dad can cook, sort of. He grills steaks, chops, and hot dogs. And, he roasts baked potatoes right in the charcoal. They're terrific. Of course, he can only grill when the weather's nice. Nobody cooks outside in the middle of a Chicago winter."

Okay, your mom's a scientist. What's your dad...a doctor?"

She laughs, "Not even close...he's a sportswriter."

"Wow, tell me about him."

"Well, he was a great baseball player in college, a scrappy little second sacker as they say, but just before he was supposed to get a shot at the majors, he developed a serious heart murmur and had to quit. That kind of gut-wrenching disappointment probably would have ruined most people, but not Archie Daye. No siree. He had majored in journalism because he planned to be a writer after his baseball career was over so he started writing freelance articles and submitting them to various newspapers around the country. He had a distinct advantage over other writers since he knew sports from the inside out, as a real participant, not just an observer. Before long, he got an offer from the Chicago Sun Times and he's been there ever since."

"Wow, sounds like your parents are a great example of opposites attracting."

"You got that right. My mother has a focused, logical career path shaped by her fierce determination to rise to the top of her field. Daddy, on the other hand, is, now don't take this the wrong way, a free spirit, almost an artist, in the way he approaches his work. He's every bit as serious about his craft as my mom is, but he loves what he does so much and his enthusiasm is so infectious that he makes it look easy. Nothing ever seems to be easy for her. She fusses, she fumes, she agonizes over every last detail, always looking around that last corner, making sure she hasn't missed anything."

"I hate to pry, but do you think she's happy, do you think they're happy?"

"Whoa, that is rather personal, but, um, now that you mention it, no, I don't think she's happy with her work, or with her marriage. Now don't get me wrong, my parents definitely love each other. However, I've always felt that she harbored a kind of resentment against him because having to constantly worry about his health was such a burden or that being married in general might have held her back. Hell, she might even resent me; nothing holds a woman back like having a child. I think she always considered herself to be the primary breadwinner in the family even though Daddy made more money. Therefore, she didn't dare take any professional risks because she felt that, at any moment, Daddy could get real sick or even die and that she'd be saddled with the onerous responsibility of raising little old me by herself. But knock wood, he's as strong as an ox, one of the healthiest people I've ever met."

She looks around, realizes they're standing in the middle of a grocery store, and says, "Why am I standing here, spilling my guts to you? This is crazy."

"No, it's not crazy, it's wonderful, you're wonderful. I'll stand here and listen to you until they kick us out when the store closes."

"Oh, you're not playing fair; men aren't supposed to be interested in anything beyond this." She frames her face with her hands and bats her lashes. "And this." She gestures toward her figure.

"Hey, I'm not playing. You'd better get used to this man being interested in everything about you."

"Okay, you're on, but now it's my turn. I assume you have parents. Tell me about them."

"Uh, I had parents. They're both gone."

She caresses his cheek with her hand, "Oh, Steve, I'm sorry. I feel terrible about the way I said that."

He takes her hand in his and says, "Nah, don't worry about it, really. My dad died of cancer when I was ten and my mom died of a heart attack four years ago. She was a real trooper, she was. After he died, she had to support us by giving music lessons in our home. We got along just fine and, hey, look at the wonderful opportunity I had to learn so much from someone who was such a gifted teacher. Whenever I could, I listened to her giving lessons to other kids and adults, too. Yeah, some parents were so impressed with the way she inspired their kids that they asked her to teach them as well. I've often told people that I grew up in a conservatory. I never said it to impress anyone; it's the truth."

He points at the fresh turkeys in the butcher's case and says,

"Out of curiosity, what did your family do for the holidays? Did your mom ever cook a turkey?"

"Ha, only once. She threw it in the oven, told us it would take three hours, and suggested we go to the movies. When we got home, there was a firetruck in the driveway and the house was filled with smoke. She had set the oven on "Broil" because she heard that you should broil a turkey. It looked more like a crusty bowling ball than a bird. After that, we always seemed to end up at other people's houses for holiday dinners. I think everybody took pity on us when they heard about the firetruck."

They're inseparable from that point forward and Steve does everything in his power to spoil Sonny by taking her to all his favorite restaurants and on weekend adventures. They usually go to the Catoctin Mountain Park next to Camp David. Being out in the woods is a great antidote for the frenetic hustle and bustle in DC. That's why President Eisenhower named his personal retreat after his grandson and stays there as often as possible. Hiking is a challenge for Steve, but he adjusts by using a cane with a large, flat base that doesn't get stuck in the wet soil. He always carries a military rucksack filled with food, water, and treats for Bo. Sonny brings a backpack with everything necessary for a proper picnic, even flatware and napkins.

Bo loves their frequent forays into the wild, especially if there's a large pond or a lake. He'd rather be in the water than almost anywhere else and he swims so fast he leaves a wake behind him like a speedboat. He also does something else in the water that's rather extraordinary. He starts off doing a normal dog paddle and, before you know it, he's hopping across the top of the water like a big, furry bullfrog and howling with delight. Before long, Steve's car always seems to have that musty "wet dog smell" that permeates everything. He and Sonny couldn't care less. Wet or dry, Bo's their dog, even if he is part frog.

And he's beginning to feel almost as happy as he was when he lived with the Harpers. Now that was some family, the kind you don't run into very often. The love, the deep abiding love, that's what Sonny and Steve have in common with them. No wonder he's beginning to feel comfortable. Leaving the Harpers left a devastating wound that turned into a nagging vacuum, yet they'll always be an integral part of his very soul. Perhaps he'll feel that close to Sonny and Steve some day. It's a lot to hope for, but if it happened once, maybe it'll happen again.

22

Most honeymoons start immediately after the wedding and last about a week. Though there was no wedding, Sonny and Steve spend the next several months in a blissful, honeymoon-like bubble together with Bo who gets happier and more devoted to them with each passing day.

He was nobody's dog when he stumbled into that Belgian apothecary during the bitter winter of 1944. Born on a farm two years earlier, life was perfectly normal at first. His mother took great care of her puppies, feeding them, licking them, helping them learn to walk, letting them explore the barnyard, protecting them from the mean old rooster. His memories of nursing himself to sleep, waking to the toasty smell of the other warm bodies piled around him, and cutting his teeth on the apples that fell off the tree next to the house were his fondest memories because when he was only three months old, the lush, golden wheat fields surrounding the farm became wretched, pockmarked battlefields. He was lucky to escape with his life, never to see his mother or any of his brothers and sisters again.

Since that time, he was always on the run, always scavenging for food and water, never hearing a kind word, never getting a friendly pat on the head. He knew the only place to find drinking water was indoors because everything outside was frozen solid, but he didn't find a single drop when he went inside and he was paralyzed by a sense of impending doom he had never felt before. A dog can go for days without food, but not water. Then, as he was preparing to take his last breath, a group of men crept in the front door and silently slithered about.

One of them, Billy O'Neal, was instantly drawn to him, gently nurtured him, and protected him from another man's threats. He had only heard French spoken and had never heard Billy's strange language, nor had anyone ever spoken to him in such kind, reassuring tones. Ultimately, Billy sacrificed his own life to save him and Benjamin Harper who first shielded him from the incoming mortar rounds.

After the blast that killed Billy and the nasty man, Benjamin carried him into the back room with Steve's help. There was another man hiding under a bed who had a wild, maniacal look in his eyes. The man jumped up, started talking to him, and forced him to drink something strange, but after he downed the first gulp, he had an uncontrollable urge to drink every last drop and, when he did, he was swathed in a glowing warmth that drastically changed his entire body and his mind until he became the magnificent animal he is today.

While all that was happening to him, he saw the look of boundless joy on the man's face in vivid color as he also started to drink something, but a blast killed him before he could. Now, the gobs of blood erupting from the man's body were bright red instead of dark charcoal. Steve's eyes were crystal blue. The men's uniforms were tan instead of gray. In addition to his radical physical transformation, Bo's very nature was forever ingrained with the desire to help others and he instantly, effortlessly dragged Benjamin and Steve to safety after the blast killed the crazy man and started the fire that engulfed the building in massive orange flames that destroyed it.

He accompanied Benjamin back home and soon became an integral part of the Harper family. He loved living on their farm, not only because they were so wonderful to him, but also because it felt familiar, like the farm where he was born. He never would have left the Harpers, but he had to because it was the right thing to do for them and for himself. He felt an instant kinship with Sonny when he met her and, though it was terribly painful to leave the Harpers, he trusted her and knew they would be great together. He still doesn't like the city, but Sonny lets him roam about to his heart's content and never tries to rein him in. Now that Steve has returned to him and joined the life he and Sonny have made, he feels complete again. He's a member of another great family.

Sonny and Steve never actually argue. Instead, they playfully joust with words while keeping a straight face, trying their best to make the other one crack up. The first to laugh loses.

However, they come close to an impasse when Steve makes an actual proposal thinly disguised as a very sensible suggestion.

"Are you crazy? My mother will kill me." roars Sonny.

Steve stands his ground, "Why? Why wouldn't she want us to get married instead of 'living in sin' like she always says?"

"Hold your horses there, Cowboy. Did you just propose to me by saying, 'Maybe we should get married?' Aren't you supposed to get down on one knee and ask me?"

"Yeah, and if I got down on one knee, you'd have to help me up. How romantic would that be?"

Sonny grits her teeth, determined not to giggle, "Are we having our first fight?"

"Absolutely not. You're simply having trouble grasping the obvious because unfortunately, you're kinda slow."

Her mouth drops open, she laughs, she loses, and Bo happily barks his approval. Steve chuckles and points at him, "See, Bo completely agrees with me."

She wraps her arms around him and holds him tightly, "Oh, Steve, I love you and, since you did ask me in a roundabout way, my answer is 'Yes', but you don't know my mother." She pulls back and looks up at him, "You'd think any woman in her right mind would be thrilled to have her daughter marry you...not Elizabeth Daye. As far as she's concerned, marrying you would pose a huge threat to my career."

"I don't get it. Why am I a threat?"

"Remember...I told you she has always resented being married and having a child. Now, before you think she's some kind of evil witch, let me explain. I know she loves me and she's crazy about my dad, but I also know she lives with the nagging suspicion that she could have gone farther and had an even more illustrious career if she were single. So yes, she's trying to relive her life vicariously through me and she doesn't want anything to stand in the way of my professional success, even if I have to sacrifice my personal happiness in the process."

"I'm sorry. That's way beyond selfish; it's downright tragic. She has so much more than most women and she's still not satisfied."

"Yes, it is tragic. I'm just warning you that we'll have to tread carefully and be very patient with her because, goddam it, we're gonna get married!"
And she gives him one of those long, deep kisses that always leads to something else.

Nowadays, men and women with good breeding from fine upstanding families simply don't live together because Puritan morality abounds. Women wear white gloves when they leave their neat, suburban enclaves to go shopping downtown. Their loyal, gray-suited husbands go to work five days a week and they expect to find a clean house and a hot dinner on the table when they return. Their boys play Little League baseball, join the Scouts, and except for a few oddball greasers who try to look like James Dean, most of them are good, clean-cut kids. The girls wear poodle skirts, bobby socks, saddle shoes, and they take sewing and cooking classes in Home Economics so they can follow in their mothers' footsteps.

Sonny and her mother are definitely the exception. They both have stellar careers any man would envy. It isn't easy, but the rewards far outweigh the sacrifices and, in particular, help them weather the resentful, whispered condemnations coming from other women who feel threatened by them.

Her mother knew from the beginning that she and Steve were living together and begrudgingly tolerated it in light of Sonny's continued success while always hoping they'd break up at some point. And it wasn't like they were living together in Chicago where all her friends and colleagues would find out about it and think it was scandalous.

If that was barely tolerable, then getting married will most definitely be over the line. Sonny knows her mother will do anything and everything to discourage her when she announces it, so she diligently rehearses her speech in front of Bo for a couple of days. He's a great audience and never tires of hearing the same thing over and over again. By the time she makes the phone call, she has a solid plan in mind and knows exactly what she's going to say. As a result, she's perfectly calm and relaxed, but just to be on the safe side, she has Steve and Bo sitting with her for moral support.

Her mother snaps at her, "Sonny, if you actually go through with this, it's only a matter of time until your career goes right down the toilet."

Undaunted and thoroughly prepared, Sonny continues, "It's too bad you have to say things like that instead of congratulating me and giving me your blessing. Here's the deal, Mom. You have a wonderful husband, a loving daughter, and an enviable career. Sorry that's not enough to make you happy. Now, you can either help me plan a small wedding in Chicago and enlarge your family with the addition of one terrific guy and one amazing dog, or continue down this pathetic path until you're all alone. The choice is yours. Let me know when you've made it."

After what seems like an eternity, Elizabeth sniffs and clears her throat, "Yes, it is my choice. I'll let you know when I make it," and she hangs up.

Sonny jerks the phone away from her ear and glares at it, "Thanks, Mom. Thanks for your support. Same to you," and she slams it down.

Bo whines sympathetically, doing his best to comfort her.

"Oh, thanks Bo. You're so sweet."

Steve is in shock. "Aw, c'mon, she hung up on you? She can't possibly be that mean."

"Ha, listen to this. One time she asked my high school boyfriend if he knew what the Periodic Table was. He said he thought it might have something to do with a woman's certain time of the month. She lit into him like a screaming banshee and he never spoke to me again."

Steve shrugs it off, "Aw, I'm not worried because I know we can withstand an assault from her or anyone else, for that matter."

It dawns on her that he's absolutely right. Perhaps her mother blindly assumes that she knows what's best for her only child simply because she's a renowned scientist. Oddly enough, her mother's narrow-mindedness makes it real, this thing with Steve, whatever it is. Up until now, Sonny has been gliding along, enjoying the ride, existing blissfully within the confines of her private, romantic cocoon. But when her mother barges into her life and shines a spotlight on her fantasy, it instantly morphs into reality. It not only clarifies how she feels, it also dispels her panic and fills her with an unusually warm, confident feeling. Her mother will simply have to accept the situation and that's that.

Archie had always been painfully aware that Elizabeth wasn't entirely happy with him or with her life in general and he's sorry for that, but luckily, his happiness has never been contingent upon hers. On the other hand, his happiness has always been inextricably linked to Sonny's. If she's sad, he's sad. If someone hurts her, the pain hits him right in the gut, especially if Elizabeth is the culprit. So when he found out about her reaction to Sonny's wedding news, he got so mad he was stiff-legged.

After three days of wrangling and sleeping alone, Elizabeth finally capitulated after multiple unsuccessful attempts to convince Archie she was right. In the end, she not only agreed to behave, she started getting excited about the wedding. Obviously there's a very strong wedding-planning gene in every mother's DNA, even if she's a cold-hearted scientist. Of course, one person's idea of a small wedding can be quite different from another's. Sonny was thinking 15-20 people; Elizabeth sat down at a typewriter and banged out 85 names without stopping. Archie knew better than to trust her with any of the details, especially after seeing the list, and quickly put his foot down.

"Here's how this is going to go. You tell Sonny to send you the names of the people she wants to invite, what kind of food and drink she wants at the reception, and who should officiate. Got it?"

It's interesting that dogs have been a part of the human equation for almost as long as men and women. They didn't start out being pets, let alone members of the family. First, they were trusted sentries that signaled approaching danger. Next, they became hunting companions, and eventually, loyal guardians, oftentimes the last line of defense. It seems wholly inadequate to call them "man's best friend" because they've always been so much more to us. Though, in truth, dogs are better friends than most humans. They're more loyal, more dependable, and more loving. They've evolved to the point that they naturally embody the best of humanity. You could honestly say they're better at being human than we are and, since they've evolved more than we have, there's a lot we could learn from them if only we'd pay attention.

Then there's Bo. Simply being around him makes people better. He leads by example, often to the point of throughly embarrassing people around him. It's kind of hard to be petty and selfish when you see him cheerfully doing so much for others.

Even a tough cookie like Elizabeth couldn't resist his charms. She was left alone with him while Archie took Steve and the other men in the wedding out for a bachelor party the night before. Likewise, Sonny went out with her friends for a bachelorette party. She wanted to have the wedding at home and there was nothing for Elizabeth to do but relax with a glass of Sherry and prepare herself for the next day's festivities. The judge will arrive around noon and perform the ceremony at 12:30. Food will be provided by a caterer, drink: a bartender, flowers: a florist, music: a harpist.

Elizabeth thought it would be a good idea to get engrossed in a book as a way to stop her mind from racing. Yes, she had agreed, even given her word, that she would actively participate in tomorrow's merriment and not be a spoilsport. Still, she couldn't stop worrying about her legacy, a legacy that had little to do with her own career and everything to do with Sonny's.

When she reached for the decanter to refill her glass, she was shocked to see Bo lying in front of her, his head between his paws, his eyes locked on hers. He was keenly aware of the tension between Sonny and her mother and he couldn't abide it. Anything that disrupted or threatened Sonny's happiness was intolerable to him and Elizabeth's behavior was absolutely intolerable. That did it for him. It was time to show her the error of her ways in no uncertain terms. Drastic times call for drastic measures. He knew it would be risky to let her see what he could do, but if that's what it takes, then so be it.

"Where did you come from? How can such a large animal appear out of nowhere? I think it's rude to sneak up on people like that."

He raised his head, frowned, and gave her a throaty little growl.

"Oh, you think I'm the rude one, eh?"

He nodded his head and panted happily, stunning her into a state of disbelief coupled with a small dose of panic.

'Must be the Sherry. Damned dog couldn't possibly understand what I said, but just to be sure…'

"Bo, do you think I'm a nice person?"

He rolled his eyes up at the ceiling, obviously avoiding the issue.

"Bo, answer me."

He lowered his eyes, stared at her for a moment, and shook his head. She gasped and dropped her glass. He didn't move a muscle, he just kept staring right into her soul.

She went completely blank and time stood still until he licked her hand and jolted her back to reality. When she jerked her hand away, he gently rested his head in her lap and rolled his big, golden eyes up at her. Summoning all her courage, she slowly placed her trembling hand on his head and began scratching his ears. As usual, he closed his eyes and moaned softly.

"Do you think there's any hope for me?"

He instantly raised his head and nodded. That's all it took. The dam broke, the tears streamed down her face, and she hugged him tightly. She cried away her fears, her anxiety, and most of all, her need to live though Sonny. Now they were both free.

When she stopped sobbing and pulled away from him, he licked her face until she laughed and cried some more.

"Oh, you've made a mess of me. Now, this has to be our secret...okay?"

Right on cue, he gave her one last lick and nodded his head with a little grunt. He figured she wouldn't tell anyone what just happened. Who'd believe it anyway? Humans are so easy to train.

"Good. Now, if you'll excuse me, I have to wash my face and fix my makeup before the rest of them get home."

He trotted to the front door and looked back over his shoulder at her.

"Oh, you have to freshen up, too, huh?"

He turned toward the door and gave it a swat with his paw.

She giggled, "Alright, alright," opened the door and, of course, he disappeared in an instant. Hopelessly disarmed, she stared blankly into space and nodded, "Definitely the Sherry."

The wedding went off without a hitch. When the judge asked for the rings, Bo appeared with a small box in his mouth, gave it to Steve, and everyone swooned. Elizabeth was behaving so nicely, she made Archie nervous, but soon he and everyone else stopped waiting for her to explode and got on with the party. She knew something no one else knew: Bo had forever changed her and she realized she had been the prisoner of her own conceit, but no more. She and Bo were conspicuously inseparable during the reception, sharing food, whispered secrets, and knowing glances. It didn't take Sonny long to figure it out; she knew Bo must have worked some of his magic on her mother.

That was the turning point. After the wedding, she and Steve had a real honeymoon. They drove up to Lake Geneva with Bo, rented a cabin, and shut out the rest of the world for an entire week. Afterwards, they stopped at her parent's house on their way back to DC and Sonny and her mother finally made peace, once and for all. It had a lot to do with Elizabeth's newfound sympathy for Sonny's career struggles that enabled her to offer Sonny some great advice.

Your father tells me you're frustrated with your job."

"He did? Uh, well. Yeah, I am. It's been kinda tough lately."

"Sonny why do you think your father is such an outstanding sportswriter?"

"Is this a trick question?"

"No, I'm not trying to trick you. I'm trying to be helpful. Listen to me. Archie's different because most hacks merely list the box scores and the winning pitcher. Archie tells you why the pitcher won, who taught him to throw that devastating curve ball, and how he broke into the majors. You always made straight A's and that allowed you to write your own ticket. Keep doing your level best at work, keep writing about the people behind the stories the way your father does, and something else better will come along. It may not happen on your schedule, but I guarantee you, it will."

Sonny was shocked and flattered at the same time. Her mother had never offered her the first bit of encouragement, that was her dad's job. Elizabeth led by example and fully expected Sonny to follow in her overachieving footsteps which, in fact, she always had. This was different; this was an actual pep talk that was both highly unusual and greatly appreciated.

Sonny and Steve now take regular trips back to Chicago with Bo to visit her parents and the five of them have grown into a tightly knit family. That closeness has afforded them the courage and support to soldier through their respective career difficulties. Box seats at Wrigley Field can make anyone forget their troubles, at least for nine innings anyway.

After toughing it out at the White house for almost two years, Sonny is suddenly gone a lot because the President is able to travel more than ever before. He is the first to install an air-to-ground telephone and an air-to-ground teletype machine in his plane so he's never out of touch and free to go wherever he wants at a moment's notice. The trips range from an overnight jaunt to a sixteen day sojourn around the world. Now she feels even more trapped than she did before, but it's part of her job and she has to remember what her mother said about hanging in there until something else pops up.

At least when Sonny leaves home on one of her trips, Steve can take care of Bo and vice versa. He was happy to do so when they first started dating, but that was before her trips got longer and more frequent. Now it really bothers him that she's out there being the star and he's left behind playing second fiddle, a glorified babysitter for Bo. Not that they don't have fun together. If you have to take care of a dog, you could certainly do a lot worse than this one.

However, there's no such thing as taking Bo for a simple walk in the park. The unusually handsome pair tends to attract a lot of attention from the women they encounter. Most of them are too shy or too intimidated to approach Steve directly, but some try to use Bo as a wonderful, metaphorical icebreaker.

"Oh, you'll have to excuse me, but you have the best looking dog I have ever seen. What's his name?" Or they speak directly to Bo. "Hey, Boy? Are you wearing his dog tags? I bet he's a war hero."

When Steve tries to laugh off the advances, it makes him even more attractive and the women even more determined. That's why he started carrying a tennis ball with him. If a woman persists, he tells her he can't talk, that his dog needs a lot of exercise, and he hurls the ball while totally ignoring everything she says. Bo retrieves it and brings it back to Steve again and again. This goes on until the woman gives up which doesn't take very long; being ignored is strong medicine.

Most of the time, however, Bo is content to sit quietly with Steve and watch the rest of the dogs run around and play fetch with their owners. After all, he can outrun all of them and there isn't much fun in that. One day, he notices an adorable three-legged dog with a red bandanna around his neck, sitting on the sidelines and whining because he wants to play, too. The old man sitting on the bench next to him pets him and tries to sooth him by talking softly, but he still whines plaintively.

Steve watches in awe as Bo streaks into the group of dogs and grabs a loose ball. Then he playfully walks over to the three-legged dog and drops the ball at his feet. The dog pants happily, picks up the ball, and starts chewing on it. Mission accomplished, Bo trots back to Steve and plops down beside him.

Steve looks over at the old man who waves at him and mouths, "Thank you."

Steve waves back and nods his head as a lump wells up in his throat. 'That guy probably thinks I told him to do it. Ha, I should be that smart.' He reaches down and scratches Bo's ears, "You're the best dog ever."

Steve's work at the Voice of America has become even more crucial to the nation's security because the Cold War is being waged so ferociously by the United States and the Soviet Union, but it simply doesn't have the sizzle or the notoriety that Sonny's does. It can't. Everything he does is top secret. He's like a mysterious puppeteer, pulling the strings behind the scenes as opposed to being in front of the camera like he was in Hollywood.

Thus, he despises the job that he now regards as a boring, dead-end situation. He can't help it. He feels like he's going nowhere, and worse, he's beginning to feel like the housewife waiting impatiently at the dinner table for her husband to come home: food getting cold, candles lit, open bottle of wine, nervously checking the clock, complaining to the dog. He's never felt so vulnerable.

'Something's gotta give. When Sonny gets home tonight, I'll tell her I'm miserable and I'm gonna find another job. She'll understand. She knows I miss the limelight and there's nothing wrong with that. Hell, I miss the daylight. Everything I do makes me feel like I'm hiding in the dark.'

After returning from a summit conference in Switzerland with the President, Sonny's jolted awake when the plane touches down and she's so groggy from jet lag that she feels like she's drunk. All she wants to do is get home as quickly as possible, jump into a hot shower, and sleep for 24 hours, but when she gets there, Steve opens the door and blurts out his unhappiness before she can say anything. She's so startled and so punchy that she laughs in his face.

"What? You think this is funny?"

She giggles uncontrollably and throws her arms around his neck, "Hi, Sonny, how was your trip? Are you tired? Bo and I have missed you so much"

Shamed back to his senses, he swings her around in a circle and giggles right back, "Aw, you must be worn out. Bo and I are so glad you're home. I'm gonna change jobs as soon as possible."

He thankfully sets her down and she recovers long enough to mumble, "That's wonderful, Steve, just wonderful...now can I please take a shower and hibernate for the rest of the winter?"

23

Steve stays at the Voice of America for as long as he can, goaded by his superiors and encouraged by Sonny, he manages to tough it out for another two years until some of the propaganda seeds he has sown begin to have a transformative effect on some unintended targets as 1956 proves to be a watershed year full of tumultuous cultural, ideological, and geographic changes. The Hungarian Revolution that starts as a student demonstration is viciously crushed by Soviet troops. The images of Soviet tanks mowing down innocent civilians in the streets of Budapest make one thing perfectly clear: you can't stop a tank with propaganda.

That fact, along with feeling personally responsible for kindling the unrest, push Steve right over the edge. He stands up in the middle of a VOA board meeting and rails, "Don't the rest of you realize what happened over there? Our broadcasts helped convince the poor, defenseless people of Hungary to rebel against the Soviets and we hung them out to dry when the shit hit the fan. Where were our soldiers? Where were our tanks? These people were fighting with pitchforks and we didn't lift a finger."

It doesn't take long for word of Steve's diatribe to get out and everyone is astounded. Here's a guy who's universally admired, a pillar of the intelligence community, openly questioning and even condemning a sacrosanct program. Sonny's boss, Jake, hears about it from his contacts at the CIA and asks her what's wrong with Steve. She shrugs it off by saying he was understandably devastated when Hungary fell and he feels somewhat responsible for giving them false hope. Even Ernie Shiller, his old boss from the VOA who now runs the biggest radio station in DC, calls him one night...ostensibly to see if he's alright.

"Hello."

"Hi, Steve, Ernie Shiller."

"Oh, Hi Ernie, what a surprise."

"Hey, you doin' okay? I'm hearing rumblings that you've become a disgruntled employee."

"No, I'm not okay. What? Somebody tell you I flew off the handle in the middle of a board meeting?"

"Matter of fact, a couple of people told me. Steve, they're getting very concerned about you."

"Wow, news sure travels fast in this town."

"Tell me about it. You used to be so happy there. Why the change?"

"I'll tell you why. I feel like I've been naive, and even worse, like I've been used. You know, I believed we were doing a helluva lot of good in the world. Now I've stopped believing because I'm convinced we're merely doling out a lot of false hope that we aren't prepared to back up. I honestly don't think I can do it anymore. Isn't that why you left?"

"Hell no, it was all about the money."

"The money? Really? How much do you...oh, sorry, it's none of my..."

"125 grand plus expenses."

"What? Nobody makes that much in government, not even the President."

"Steve, listen to me. I've got a great idea. Let's have dinner at Duke Zeibert's and I'll tell you all about it. What do you say?"

"Now that you have my attention, sure, when?"

"How 'bout Thursday at seven?"

"Works for me. I could use some cheering up. Thanks, Ernie."

Old affable Ernie, the big, heavyset guy who's the perennial life of any party, rarely does or says anything just for the hell of it; he always has a very specific agenda in mind. And what a salesman he is. In a town known for its professional arm-twisters, he's widely regarded as one of the best. His amazing ability to stay several steps ahead of everyone else made him a highly respected and revered leader at the VOA. Everybody knew they were being manipulated, yet nobody seemed to care. In fact, he did such a great job, the agency foundered for a time when he left. He had a hunch the radio business was about to grow exponentially and he wanted to be right in the middle of it.

If there's one thing Ernie can smell a mile away, it's his next great opportunity. He was an Army Intelligence officer during World War II and when the State Department took over the Voice of America in 1945, he knew it would have an extremely important role in maintaining our postwar influence throughout the world. After he was discharged later that year, he went straight to Washington and easily landed a job at the VOA due to his innate ability to sell himself and his experience handling top secret information.

Steve isn't used to eating dinner surrounded by the DC power elite including members of Congress, lobbyists, foreign ambassadors, and business titans. No wonder Sonny was jealous when he told her they were going to Duke's. She'd give anything to be here, doing her best to overhear all the dealmaking and horse-trading. This is one of the places where the real business of government gets done. As Steve looks around the room through the wafting cloud of blue cigar smoke, it irritates the hell out of him that these fat cats are his real bosses. They decide how much money the VOA will get and they specify exactly how every last dime will be spent. He does their dirty work and they never lose a wink of sleep over it, like he does almost every night. Now he's even more interested in what Ernie has up his sleeve, but Ernie catches him completely off guard.

"Do you watch the Tonight Show with Steve Allen?"

"Uh, yeah, it's amazing, he's amazing. Why do you ask?"

"I want to know if you can tell me why the show is so successful."

"Uh, no, never gave it much thought, but I bet you're gonna tell me."

"It's simple. For the first time on television, someone's actually talking to the audience and there's a real dialogue going on, a two-way conversation. You could have the same kind of show on radio. We have the technology that will allow people to call the station and you can talk to them right on the air. Your show would logically start at midnight and run into the wee hours. That's when all the real characters are awake. It'll be wild."

"Whoa, I dunno Ernie. Sounds awfully risky."

"Yes, that's the point. Remember how popular radio theater was? The whole family used to huddle around the radio and hang on every word? Now people will go crazy trying to get on the phone with you. For the first time ever, the audience will be an integral part of the drama. They'll be the stars and you'll be the director. Nobody's ever done it and you're just the guy to do it. What do you say?"

" Aw, I don't think people would listen to that kind of show. What about music? Everybody's going nuts about the music being played on the radio. Won't we miss the boat if we don't play Rock and Roll?"

"Steve, we play Rock and Roll all day long and we're making a mint. Sure, you'll play some music, too, but it will be the regular stuff we play during that time slot. You know, easy listening music that'll fill the space between phone calls. Don't forget, your show won't be about people merely listening; they'll be clamoring to be part of it. You and your listeners can talk about anything you want. It'll give a voice to all the people who don't have one. Your show will be one big American soapbox where everyone's welcome to blow off steam. Of course, you'll have to cut off the people who talk dirty or make threats. We can't have that, but it'll also add to the excitement. We already have live TV and now we'll have live radio. Oh, by the way, I know what you're making and I'll double it."

Steve turns a few heads when he yells, "You'll double my salary. Are you drunk?"

"Keep your voice down. You're not among friends here."

He leans toward Ernie and whispers, "No shit. These are the assholes who pull my strings. But you're serious? You're really serious?"

"Yes, of course I am. Here's what we'll do. You and Sonny come down to the station and I'll give you the Cook's tour."

"Oh, that might backfire. She'll probably think it's crazy."

"Aah, no she won't. Steve, you're a married man now. The two of you should make this decision together and she'll appreciate being included. Don't you agree?

Ernie could sell ice skates to a man stranded in the desert. However, when Steve and Sonny go to the station that weekend, they're both aghast when he walks them right past a nice, modern studio where a DJ is on the air, and takes them into a large storage room filled with dusty old equipment. There's a broken turntable, two beat-up microphones, some kind of control board with a lot of switches and several round dials, one of which has a cracked face. The huge clock on the wall looks like it came from a railroad station. There's only one piece of new equipment in the room and it definitely looks out of place. It's a reel-to reel tape recorder… Ernie's secret weapon.

Sonny gives Steve a look that clearly says, 'You've got to be shitting me.'

He nods and clears his throat, "Ernie, I don't…"

"Hey, Steve, this is going to be your new studio, your office, your own private space to do with as you please. I'm not gonna stick you in that little studio the other DJ's use. We'll clear out all this junk, replace it with the best equipment there is, plus a big telephone system, and you can order any kind of furniture you want. The only thing that'll stay is this tape recorder. Know why?"

Steve chuckles, "No, Ernie, but I bet you're gonna tell me."

"Yep, and you're gonna love it. We'll record all your shows. Can you imagine how valuable those tapes will be? We can play back the best ones any time we want. Hell, maybe we'll even put some of them on a record and call it *Steve's Greatest Bits.*"

Sonny winks at Steve, "Ernie, don't you mean *Greatest Hits?*"

"No, it'll only contain the funny ones, the comedy bits, and the controversial ones that'll really get people stirred up. Get it? Look, every station's making money playing Rock and Roll, but only during the day. Companies don't buy ads at night because there aren't enough listeners. I know you'll draw a huge audience and we'll be able to sell ads 24 hours a day. Steve, this is the perfect job for you. With your talent, great looks, and personality, the public will love you. What's more, your knowledge of local and international news will allow you to comment intelligently on almost any topic that might come up. Steve, you're the only man on earth who could do this job."

And with that, the masterful salesman shuts up and grins like a fool.

It's an unusually quiet drive home from the station. Whenever Sonny tries to get a conversation going, Steve either cuts her off and says he has a lot of thinking to do or he ignores her completely. She's really excited and doesn't understand why he's being such a grump. Sure, Ernie's a big bag of wind, but everything he said made perfect sense and she can't imagine what's bugging Steve.

In fact, his head is spinning out of control. He's scared, excited, worried, enthused, and skeptical, all at the same time. No wonder he can't talk to Sonny. He wouldn't know where to start. This whole thing reminds him of a high stakes poker game and he's never been much of a gambler.

She finally yells at him, "Steve!"

Shaken from his reverie, he jerks the steering wheel and almost hits a parked car. "Dammit, Sonny, you scared the hell out of me. What's wrong?"

"That's my question…what the hell's wrong with you?"

"Nothing's wrong with me. I'm just, uh…"

"Just, uh what? You hate your current job, you get a fabulous offer for a terrific new job from someone you know and respect, and you have to think about it? Like I said, what the hell's wrong with you?"

"Jeez, take it easy, will you. It is a lot to think about. And, yeah, I do hate my job, but this one sounds like a gigantic pie in the sky. What if I can't handle it? What if nobody listens to the show?"

"It's a good thing you're so handsome because you can be so stupid. You had the balls to volunteer for the Army when you could've gotten out of it. Now you're scared of working at a radio station?"

"Wow, you're tough."

"Well, one of us has to be."

He cracks up. He loses.

They continue to talk about it for the rest of the weekend until Sunday night when Steve can't take it anymore and uses Bo as an excuse to get away from Sonny's relentless pressure. The woman just won't give an inch.

"I know, I know. Nothing ventured, nothing gained. Tell you what, I'm gonna take Bo for a walk and clear my head. That okay with you?"

"Absolutely, because once you clear your head, you'll agree with me."

He takes a deep breath, knowing any response would be futile, and heads out the door with Bo.

She smiles wickedly as she watches them through the window until they disappear around the corner, "Fine, Bo'll knock some sense into him."

Steve's idea of clearing his head is venting to Bo, using him as a sounding board, hoping against hope that some clarity will emerge.

"I think Ernie's crazy. Yeah, he's so aggressive, so driven to bring in more revenue that he's gone crazy. Uh, crazy like a fox. If the station makes more, he'll make more and all he's risking is a little money for a new studio. But me? Hell, I'm risking everything. I can just imagine trying to get another job after making a very public fool of myself. Know what I mean?"

He looks down and Bo acts like he hasn't heard a word.

"Hey, I'm talking about some really important stuff here. Could you at least pay attention?"

Bo just keeps walking, looking around, doing his thing, sniffing here and there, lifting his leg again and again.

Steve's so determined to get a rise out of Bo that he ignores being ignored, "So, Ernie got his idea from Steve Allen who happens to be a brilliant guy and a very talented comedian. Then there's me: a washed-up actor who now specializes in propaganda. But Ernie did say the callers will be the stars of the show. They'll carry the load and I'm sure they'll relish the chance to have their voices heard…uh, if they actually call in. That's a mighty big 'if' and why is Sonny so excited about all this? That make any sense to you? Maybe she totally fell for Ernie's bullshit. No, she's not that gullible. Wait, I get it. She's obviously sick and tired of me being so unhappy and she's probably thinking that anything's better than the status quo. Right?"

Bo still won't look at him or give any hint that he's paying attention.

"Sure, go ahead, ignore everything I'm saying. Thanks for all your help."

That does it. Listening to Steve's whining and complaining is bad enough, but Bo can't stand sarcasm; the tone grates on him. He wheels around, abruptly sits in front of Steve, and makes him stumble to a stop.

"Hey, look out. You trying to trip me?"

Bo looks up at him and growls.

"What? You mad at me, too?"

Bo throws his head back, paws at the dog tags around his neck, and then stares daggers at Steve.

"What are you…? Omigod, Billy O's tags."

Bo barks softly and pants happily.

"Ah, I get it. He never complained. Okay, okay, I'll take the job."

Bo holds up his paw to shake on it. Utterly defenseless, Steve smiles and shakes his paw, "Thanks, Buddy, you're right as usual."

Bo nods and heads for home.

Steve follows him with a shrug, "Oh, guess we're done here."

When Steve walks in the door with Bo and sees Sonny sitting on the couch, he holds up both hands and says, "Now, before you start in on me, I want you to know that Bo and I had a little talk and we decided that I should take the job."

She's so thrilled, it's all she can do to restrain herself from doing cartwheels around the living room, but he's obviously being as nonchalant as possible so she doesn't want to seem too excited. Of all the things she'd love to say like: 'It's about time you came to your senses.' or 'You wouldn't listen to me, but you listened to Bo?' she tries to be as cool as he is and smiles sweetly, "Oh, that's good news. Wanna watch some TV?"

Steve calls Ernie later that night.

"Hello."

"When do I start?"

"Oh, hi, Steve, how are you?"

"Ernie."

"Ah, now you're gung-ho, eh?"

"Isn't that what everybody wants me to be?"

"No, it's what you'd better be, in your own heart. Forget about the rest of us."

"Yes, goddam it, I had a lot of help, but it's my decision so let's get on with it, okay?"

"That's what I wanted to hear, but remember, you'll need to give proper notice; you can't just walk out the door. In the meantime, why don't you drop by the station after work later in the week and we'll get the ball rolling. How's that sound?"

"You got a deal. Call you in a couple of days."

"Steve…"

"What?"

"I'll do everything in my power to make you a success."

He turns and smiles at Sonny and Bo, "Ernie, success is the only option."

The following evening, Steve and Sonny take Bo for his usual walk. However, this time, the ever-curious Sonny is on a mission and she steers them into a local record store where she buys a copy of Elvis Presley's *Hound Dog*. When they get home, she puts it on the turntable and cranks up the volume. Bo instantly loves it, though he doesn't really understand most of the lyrics. If he did, he might not like it so much, but he knows the word *dog*, and now every time he hears the song, he dances around on his hind legs and howls along with the music. Sonny thinks it's the cutest thing she's ever seen. They have a blast dancing together and, without realizing it, they've just become part of a much bigger phenomenon.

A seismic shift in American culture, brought about by the confluence of three disparate events, also occurs in 1956. The first momentous event happens when the recording industry unveils the 45 RPM record. Until now, only large, expensive records containing several songs or complete symphonies are available to the public. The 45, as it is known, changes everything because it contains one song on one side and another on the flip or "B" side. Plus, it sells for pennies, making it affordable to almost everyone…

especially teenagers. Cheap record players soon follow, allowing the kids to play a stack of several 45's, one right after the other. This leads to group dances called sock hops where kids kick off their shoes and dance like crazy in their bobby socks.

Rock and Roll provides them with a welcome diversion, a great way to take their minds off the nuclear arms race and gives them a momentary respite from all the fear mongering heaped on the country by the government and the media. The Second World War, with its massive utilization of all our resources, catapulted us out of the Great Depression and into a period of unparalleled prosperity. After the Korean War ended in 1953, the nuclear buildup and the new "Space Race", as it is called, keep the American cash register ringing louder than ever.

The second, and perhaps the most important event, happens when Elvis Presley, a singing truck driver from Memphis, Tennessee, blasts onto the scene and makes "Rock and Roll" the music of a new generation with the release of one song: *Hound Dog.*

Three years earlier, Elvis walked into Sun Records in Memphis carrying a beat-up guitar and spent $4 to make a record for his mother. The owner, Sam Phillips, who already had a lot of experience producing records for prominent artists like B.B. King, Howlin' Wolf, and Ike Turner, instantly recognized something unique about the shy, introverted young man.

It was during a late night recording session in 1954 that the real Elvis emerged, the Elvis who would change the world. After trying out several songs without much luck for most of the day and well into the night, he finally had the idea to let loose on an old blues number by Arthur "Big Boy" Crudup called *That's All Right, Mama.* Maybe he was so tired he was punchy, but instead of being reserved and shy, he started jumping around the studio like a mad man as his two side men grabbed their instruments and struggled to keep up with his manic gyrations.

The Elvis Presley who walked out of the studio that night was completely different than the one who had walked in that morning. Nobody knew it at the time, but that was the moment "The King" was born. Two weeks later, the 45 with *That's All Right* and *Blue Moon Over Kentucky* on the flip side debuted on Memphis radio and sold over 4,000 copies the first week alone.

The third, and perhaps inevitable, event happens when record companies and radio stations figure out how to work together and make mountains of money off the new rage that's sweeping the country. The guys who play the records on the radio are called disc jockeys or DJ's and they can create instant recording stars simply by playing a song over and over again. Particular 45's literally fly off the shelves after the kids hear it continually on their local radio station and some of the DJ's are becoming almost as famous as the people making the records.

In order to get in the groove, Steve spends every spare moment learning as much as he can about the radio business. He finally understands why all this is happening, both to him, and to the rest of the country. Rock and Roll liberates people from their cares and worries and gives them a real sense of belonging, of being part of a community. Plus, it's daring, controversial, and a little naughty. That's exactly what his show will be. Yes, he's venturing into uncharted territory, but isn't that what art and entertainment are supposed to do: open doors we never knew existed and take us places we've never been?

Most DJ's have a simple, predictable schedule for their shows. They play a set number of records, do a set number of commercials, perhaps read a few news spots, and every single minute is planned ahead of time. The difficult part of their job is to find their niche, the distinct personality that sets them apart from all the rest. Morning DJ's can range from cheery and upbeat to raucous and outrageous. During the day, they tend to be more low-key because most people are listening at work. All bets are off at night; that's when the real characters come out to play. Their audiences pay more attention to the music and to them.

Steve knows his most serious challenge will be to separate himself from the rest of the people in radio. First of all, he isn't going to be a regular DJ like all the other guys. He'll be a unique radio personality with a new, extraordinary format. Sure, having brutally frank, on-air conversations with callers will set him apart, but it's not enough. Then it hits him: each show should have a particular topic or theme. It could be a newspaper story, a famous person, a movie, a best selling book, anything under the sun...the more timely and controversial, the better. After he names the topic, the show will become an untethered stream of radio consciousness. Yes, he'll have to do some commercials, but otherwise, he'll be free to talk to someone for as long as he wants, or play any record he wishes. And, unlike the DJ's, he'll be more of a facilitator. The real focus will be on his callers.

True to his word, Ernie spares no expense in providing Steve with everything he needs and wants in his new studio including a gleaming chrome Shure Super 55 microphone, custom headphones, two turntables, a phone console with ten lines, a high back leather chair and a seven foot leather couch, even a small fridge, and Ernie's masterstroke, the reel-to-reel tape machine that'll record all of Steve's shows.

For his part, Steve mentally prepares for his new job with the same level of seriousness he had before he went into battle. Back then he risked his life on a daily basis yet this somehow feels much the same. True, it's his professional life on the line here, but he's still scared despite the deal he struck with Bo. He was single during the war and only had to worry about himself. Nobody's ever attempted this on radio and if his show's a flop, thousands of people will know about it, he"ll look like a fool for leaving the VOA, and what's worse, he could embarrass Sonny. However, in reality, she was obviously more disturbed by his unhappiness when he worked there.

The clock strikes midnight, the red "On Air" light goes on, and with a forced smile in his voice, he booms, "Good morning, Washington, this is Steve Rasco and I'll be with you Monday through Friday from 12 to 6 AM. This is our chance and it really is our chance, yours and mine, to talk straight about anything and everything under the moon... your likes, dislikes, frustrations, complaints, whatever's on your mind. Yes, it's the middle of the night and most people are asleep, but you and I are here together, free to shoot the breeze until the sun comes up. How's that possible? Well, I have ten phone lines here in the studio so you can call in and talk to me right on the air. Yes, you heard me, so get a pencil and take down this number: it's five five five, five one, zero zero. That's five five five fifty-one hundred. Got it?

We do have a few simple ground rules. You'll need to be civil and respectful of each other and, please, no profanity. If you swear, I'll have to cut you off and that's the last thing I want to do. Oh, by the way, every show will start off with a certain topic and tonight I'd like to talk about your favorite thing in the whole world. Doesn't matter what it is. I'm not here to judge. I just want to get to know you. Now, if you don't want to talk about your favorite thing, then tell me what's on your mind and we'll talk about that. Fair enough? Alright, here we go. The lines are open and the number is five five five, five one, zero zero. That's five five five fifty-one hundred. Talk to me, DC."

Ah, the best-laid plans...after introducing himself and explaining his show's dramatic new concept, the phone refuses to ring and the radio audience, if there is one, hears nothing but a big dose of debilitating dead air. Utterly panic-stricken, Steve stares at the phone, trying his telepathic best to get a single line to light up, but they're all as dark as the cloud creeping into his soul. A bead of sweat sprouts from his forehead, dribbles down his nose, splats on his script, and spurs him into action.

"Hey, tell you what. I'm gonna play a record and give you some time to think about it. Here's Pat Boone crooning his new hit, *Ain't That a Shame*."

He drops the needle onto the record and, if it weren't for his bum leg, he'd probably drop to his knees and pray for help. He's never felt so alone in his entire life. It's like being the pitcher on the mound with the bases loaded, no outs, and Mickey Mantle's standing in the batter's box with a 3 and 0 count which means he has three chances, yes, three big swings to blast that lopsided hunk of horsehide out of the park and put four big ones on the board for the Yanks.

Steve stands up and paces around the studio as several random thoughts bounce around his brain. 'What record should I play next if nobody calls by the time this one's over? But it's such a perfect song. Maybe I should keep playing it 'cause it's probably what people will say about my short-lived radio career. Clearly, I should plead insanity and walk out of the studio. It wouldn't be far from the truth. No, no, I'm not insane, but how stupid of me to think the phones would be ringing off the hook right away. Better get my shit together, think of another topic or pick another record, and keep going since there is no Plan B.'

He sits back down and starts rummaging through the pile of 45's on his desk, but something catches his eye and he giggles, "Omigod! There's a call on Line 1!"

He's so thrilled, he jerks the needle off the record and it makes that horrible screeching sound. Then he clumsily grabs the phone and almost drops it, "Hi, this is Steve. You're on the air."

A sultry female voice whispers, "Hi, Steve, this is Vicki."

Precious seconds tick away as Steve tries to regain his composure which is extremely difficult because there's something disturbingly familiar about Vicki's voice…it sounds like Sonny. 'Holy shit, it really is Sonny.'

"Why, hello, Vicki. Thanks for calling. Tell me, what's your favorite thing?"

"Well, Steve, to put it politely, I'm a streetwalker, a prostitute, a courtesan, if you will. My regular customers call me Wicked Vicki. You can call me an-y-thing you want."

He grins, 'Yeah, it's her alright. What a babe.'

"Wow, you're a prostitute. Thanks for starting off my first show with a bang. Oh, no, I can't believe I just said that."

"Steve…"

"Yes, Vicki."

"My feet hurt all the time so I'm not too happy when I'm on the stroll, as we say, but Steve…"

"Yes, Vicki."

"Since you asked, my favorite thing is being off my feet…if you know what I mean."

He has to pinch himself to stop from laughing, "Yes, I think I know what you mean. Sorta takes your mind off your aching feet, right?"

"Oh, yeah, does it ever. And Steve…"

"Yes, Vicki."

"Ever heard the phrase, 'My body is a temple?'"

"Uh huh, I believe I have."

"Guess what, Steve."

"What, Vicki?"

'You can rent my temple by the hour."

Try as he may, the longer he tries to stifle his laughter, the worse it gets. He grits his teeth so hard his eyes fill with tears and he almost chokes.

"Steve…"

He bites his hand in a feeble attempt to get it together and whispers, "What?"

"Is there anything else you'd like to ask me, Steve?"

He clears his throat, "Why, yes there is. What bothers you the most about your job?"

"Oh, that's easy. The cops who hassle me unless I bribe them…one way or another, if you know what I mean."

"Yeah, I get your drift. Tell me, isn't there something else you'd rather do?"

"Oh, of course…I'd like to get a rich, good looking man like you to take care of me."

"Whoa there, Vicki. I'm already taken. Well, will you look at that, there are two other callers waiting. Sorry, gotta go."

"But Steve…"

"Sorry, Vicki. Everybody deserves a chance to speak. Bye now."

Feeling a combination of relief and giddy anticipation, he hits the first blinking line, "Hi, this is Steve. You're on the air."

The scolding voice of an older woman slams him right back down to earth, "Prostitution is illegal and you think this tawdry woman is hilarious? Shame on you."

Luckily, he's well-prepared for this because he knew, at some point, it was bound to happen: people disagreeing so vehemently it could get ugly. But in the opening minutes of his very first show? Welcome to live radio.

"Hey, there's no shame in giving anyone an opportunity to speak. It's a First Amendment right we all have regardless of who we are or what we do for a living. I don't make the laws and I don't enforce the laws. Now, if you'd like to have a civil conversation about the issue of prostitution, I'm all ears. If not, I'll go to our next caller."

There's an audible click as that person hangs up.

"Aw, she's gone. That's too bad. Let's see what our next caller has to say."

Now three lines are lit up and we're off to the races. Steve goes to the next caller and the next and, in what seems like no time at all, he glances up at the clock and is amazed that he's been on the air for almost three hours, but he really needs to take a break so he plays another record. He can't help laughing at himself. With all his careful planning, he never considered what it would be like to sit still for six straight hours.

After doing a few laps around the station to stretch his legs and clear his head, he walks back into the studio, sees four lines winking at him, and he replays Sonny's call in his mind, 'She not only saved my bacon, she also calmed me down, and really did start the show with a bang. I didn't think it was possible, but I just fell in love with her all over again.'

When Steve quietly opens the front door, Bo bounds out of the bedroom, rears up on his hind legs, and hugs Steve who barely manages to stay on his feet as he whispers, "Hey, take it easy. Did you listen to my show?"

Bo pulls back and licks Steve's face until he gasps for breath, "Whoa, guess you liked it, huh?"

Bo jumps down, sits up on his haunches, and barks twice.

"Shhh, you'll wake…"

Sonny runs out of the bedroom, fully awake, fully dressed, and jumps into Steve's outstretched arms, "Steve Rasco, we need to celebrate."

He gives her a bear hug and laughs, "Oh, yes we do, Vicki Rasco." They keep hugging and giggling until she pulls back, smiles wickedly, and whispers in her 'Vicki' voice, "Hey, wanna play in my temple?"

Before long, people with normal 9 to 5 jobs are staying up late just so they can listen to Steve's radio theatre of the absurd. There's nothing like it anywhere else in the country. Steve is pioneering something much more important than a new kind of music. He's starting a movement, a virtual groundswell that's changing people's lives, liberating teenagers from their dull, boring parents, and providing a public forum for the disenfranchised.

Plus, to everyone's delight, he becomes a real ham and it doesn't take him long to make a name for himself as his fan base grows exponentially. His audience is mainly comprised of the people who work the late shift and those free-spirited denizens of the dark who exist on the fringes of society. They run the gamut from rich to poor, old to young, and semi-literate to highly educated. He develops a huge following among this diverse group by making them an integral part of the show when they call his studio hotline.

He banters with them and tries to keep the conversation focused while knowing the show may spiral out of control at any given moment. This gives them the chance to vent their frustrations and he usually encourages their off-the-wall rants. He values their opinions and always treats them with respect, something they crave, but rarely get from anyone else. This sets him apart from all other DJ's who only play records and read commercials.

Some of his fans become regulars and call several times a week, especially when there's something important or controversial in the news. Steve starts calling them Rasco's Rascals and they love it. The vast majority of them are lovely people: warm, friendly, funny. As they get to know each other, they bicker, rib each other, and form a tight knit group of callers that listeners get to know. If one of them doesn't call in for a while, the others worry about them.

Murray, a cab driver, is one of Steve's favorites. He started saving the travel folders people left in his cab and now he and his wife Anne are hooked. If a place peaks their interest, they go to the library and learn everything they can about it. They also go to travel agencies, ask about tours to several different destinations, and usually walk out with a few more pamphlets and some posters to boot. Then they go home and pour over all the literature and imagine what it must be like to go to all those faraway places.

Now Murray's a travel expert in his own right and he can't wait to tell Steve about his newest exotic getaway. After he does this a few times, other people call in and ask his advice about a particular place or perhaps what kind of clothes to pack. He revels in the attention and happily offers tips to everyone who's interested.

And he loves it when foreign diplomats get in his cab. As soon as he hears their accent, he peppers them with questions about their native countries. Most of them are thrilled when any American shows an interest in their homeland and they give him names of restaurants and other places to go. Then Murray relays the most interesting tidbits to Steve and his listeners.

Tony, a short order cook who works until midnight, is also an amateur astronomer. Steve asks him why he's always so happy and excited about his hobby.

"Steve, I gotta be honest. I used to be depressed every night when I got off work. You see, I live with my sister and she's got arthritis so bad I have to wait on her hand and foot. Now, please don't think I'm a bad guy. I really don't mind taking care of her, but I always felt hemmed in until the time I happened to look up at the magnificent starry sky and everything changed. Then I remembered that I still had a little telescope that she gave me for my birthday many years ago. I started using it as an escape because of my fascination with the stars. I got books from the library and learned everything I could. The only problem was the telescope was little more than a toy and didn't have the magnification I needed. One day I spotted the perfect telescope in the window of a pawn shop and since then, it's been one discovery after another. Hey, if you don't mind, can I tell you about my favorite new constellation?"

"Sure, Tony, I'm sure everyone would love to hear about it."

"Well, it's called Hydra, the sea serpent. Believe it or not, it spans more than a quarter of the whole sky. It is so huge it amazes me very time I see, but that's not why it's my favorite. I love it because it's brightest star is named Alphard which means 'the lonely one.' Steve, that's who I was until I started listening to your show. Now I'm not lonely anymore. Steve, you're the greatest. Thanks for doing what you do."

"No, Tony, you're the greatest. You found a way to make your life more meaningful and now you want to share it with us. That's what the Rascals are all about."

Before long, Tony has his own following on the show. Other listeners are buying telescopes and trying to find the stars and the constellations he talks about. Tony also starts a discussion about astrology and how it makes sense when you consider the gravitational pull the planets exert on us just like the moon effects the tides. One night, a local cop seconds the notion when he calls in and tells Steve that more crimes are committed when there's a full moon.

Tony completely agrees, "Steve, when I was doing research on gravitation, I found that the word 'looney' comes from all the crazy stuff people do when there's a fun moon. Get it? Lunar calendar, lunar eclipse? I bet everyone has at least one looney relative."

Steve laughs, "You're absolutely right, but I think there's two or three in my family."

Trudy, another favorite, suffered greatly after her husband passed away. Married for over 36 years, her loneliness was a terribly painful, everyday reminder of just how much she missed her dear Charlie, but talking to Steve and interacting with other callers has given her hope for the future. Charlie's doctors had all but given up on him; Trudy never did. She became his primary caregiver for the last two years of his life and it started her on a path to rediscovering some of the old tried-and-true remedies people used to rely on.

"Hello, Steve, this is Trudy."

"Hi, Trudy, what's on your mind tonight?"

"I just heard you talking to Tony the astronomer and he mentioned he takes care of his sister who has arthritis real bad."

"Right, yeah, that's why he lives with her. Great guy, isn't he?"

"He sure is. I know what it's like to have your life consumed with the care of a loved one, but, hey, it's good work if you can get it. Right?"

"Trudy, that's why you and Tony are very special people."

"Oh, fiddlesticks, Steve, now you're embarrassing me. I called to recommend something I use for my arthritis. You know, most people over 50 have a touch of it."

"You're right about that. What are you suggesting?"

"I use Arnica Oil and it works great. Hopefully it'll help his sister."

"Wow, I've never heard of it. Where do you get it?"

"I get it from a mail order catalog called *Miracle Elixirs* that I found at the newsstand on 14th Street. It carries all the tonics and herbal remedies people used before all this modern medicine came along. Funny thing, the old stuff usually works better'n the new, expensive junk doctors peddle. I hope Tony's still listening. If not, please tell him where he can get his own copy of *Miracle Elixirs*."

"That's great news. I'll let him know. Thanks again, Trudy."

A city sanitation worker named Stan calls in one night and tells Steve how much he appreciates being able to listen to the show while he makes his rounds. He drives the truck and two other guys hop off, grab the cans, and empty them in the back.

"Steve, the main reason I'm calling is to tell you about my hobby, if you could call it that."

"Sounds interesting...what is it?"

"Don't laugh, but I guess you could say I'm a student, no, it's more than that. I'm a big fan, a real admirer of our democracy. I'm just so grateful for my job, our country, and our government. Look what the Germans and the Japanese did to people during the war and now look how badly the Russians treat their own people. I think we're all lucky to live here."

"Stan, you're absolutely right. We are lucky to live in a democracy."

"According to my research, the ancient Greeks came up with the idea, but no country ever put it into practice until our Constitution became the law of the land in 1789."

Steve laughs, "I'll have to take your word for it. I think I slept through that part of American history. No, to be honest, I think I slept through most of it."

"Sure, we all did. I only got interested in it when my mom showed me a pack of letters my dad sent her during the war. There he was, in the middle of battle, telling her how proud he was to be fighting for our country. After that, I learned all I could about our history, especially the Revolutionary War and, of course, the drafting of the Constitution."

"Wow, that's amazing. If you don't mind my asking, did your dad make it home?"

"No, I don't mind. Matter of fact, I'm proud to say he died a hero on Juno beach during the D-Day invasion. He singlehandedly took out a Nazi machine gun nest before he got shot and the Army gave him the Distinguished Service Cross."

This sends a chill up Steve's spine and he feels nauseous as his mind flashes back to the apothecary shop, the explosions, his dead buddies...the nagging horrors of war that constantly lurk beneath the surface of his everyday life.

"Steve, you still there?"

He shuts off his mic for a second and clears his throat before answering, "Uh, yeah, guess I kinda got lost in some of my own memories for a second there. Whew, hey, enough about me. I'm so sorry about your dad. You must be really proud."

"Yeah, we sure are. My mom never remarried. Said nobody could ever measure up to him."

"Stan, I want to thank you for telling us about yourself and your dad. Please call back soon and give us another history lesson, will ya?"

"You bet. And thanks again for doing your show."

"Hello, this is Steve. You're on the air."

A gravelly woman's voice crackles through the phone, "Oh, Steve, this is Dorothy. Your last caller really took me back. I worked for the USO during the war, you know, we entertained the troops? And I met so many wonderful, brave young men over there in England. Speaking of D-Day, we knew something was up because we did a show and there were only a few guys in the audience. Normally, the place was packed."

"Thanks for calling, Dorothy. Now tell me, did you sing and dance in the shows?"

"Steve, I was a child star in vaudeville. I can do it all. I can even juggle. Lemme tell you, I juggled a few soldiers over there," and she laughs heartily until she starts coughing.

He giggles, "Take it easy, Dorothy. You okay?"

"Yeah, guess I shouldn't be smoking so much at my age. I think it also upsets my stomach."

"Hmm, sounds like you should probably quit."

"Easy for you to say. Next you'll probably tell me I shouldn't drink so much whiskey."

Now he laughs out loud, "No, no, it's not my place to...I was only trying to help."

"Oh, I know. You sound like a nice young man. I'm sure you meant well. You married?"

He laughs again, "Why yes I am. Are you?"

"Oh, no, don't wanna be tied down. Bein' tied up can be fun, though."

He gasps, "Dorothy, you better behave."

She giggles, "Ah, life's too short for that? Gotta go now...stomach's startin' to give me a fit. Love your show, Steve."

"Thanks, Dorothy. Hope you feel better."

A few minutes later, Trudy calls back.

"Hi, Trudy, what's up?"

Well, Steve, that Dorothy is a lively one, isn't she?"

He laughs, "Oh, you heard that, eh?"

Yes, I did, a woman of her age...anyway, I have some advice for her."

"Oh, this should be interesting. What is it?"

She laughs, "No, it's not what you think. I think she should try cola syrup for her stomach. She can get it at most drug stores and it works like a charm."

"Wow, that's so nice of you, Trudy. Cola syrup...who knew?"

"I did, Steve."

He laughs, "Yes, you did and I hope Dorothy takes your advice. Thanks for calling."

Steve talks to a few more people and then a very angry Dorothy calls back, "How dare that woman, what's her name. You know who I mean, the one with the cola syrup?"

"Dorothy, what's wrong? I thought Trudy gave you some good advice."

"Ha, the advice might be good, but she said something about 'a woman of her age' and I resent that. Steve, she basically called me an old lady. Well, I may have a few years under my belt, but I am not old. I feel terrific, except for my stomach, that is."

"Okay, I'll tell you what I know about Trudy. She's kind, thoughtful, and she sincerely tries to help people. I'm sure she never meant to offend you. Now, I could be wrong, but you and she are probably around the same age and I'll bet you have a lot in common."

"Age is a state of mind and my mind is very young, thank you. I do appreciate the fact that she was trying to be helpful and all. So, if she's still listening, thanks Trudy. I'll try the cola syrup and let you know if it helps."

"There you go, Dorothy. I think you both just made a new friend and, if I may be so bold, I just made two new friends."

"I think you're right, Steve. Stay tuned, as they say."

About an hour later, Steve picks up a new line, "This is Steve and you're on the air."

"I hate to be a bother."

"That you, Trudy?"

"Oh, yes it is. I'm glad that Dorothy calmed down. She sounds real nice. I just thought I should tell you why I started using cola syrup for my upset stomach."

"Sure, go ahead."

"Well, my sweet Charlie came from a very large family, eight kids in all. His parents were quite affluent and they were able to provide very well for all their children.

However, when Charlie's father died, his mother said it was time for a little payback."

"What did she do?"

"She said it was time her children took care of her so she sold the family home and stayed with each kid for six weeks at a time. Then she'd travel to the next one and so on. Steve, she could could drive anyone nuts. She expected us to wait on her hand and foot, always saying it was the least we could do considering the inheritance we were gonna get. And that wasn't the half of it. Why, she'd tell Charlie's sisters how to raise their own kids and she'd chide him and his brothers for not being as successful as their father. You can see why I always had an upset stomach when she stayed with us."

"Yeah, she sounds like a real piece of work."

"Yeah, but she did hold up her end of the bargain. She left each of her children a nice chunk of change so I guess it was worth putting up with the old so-and-so."

Murray calls in right after Trudy hangs up, "Steve, I envy Trudy."

Steve laughs, "Oh? Because she and Charlie got a nice inheritance?"

"Uh, well, that too I guess, but I envy her because her mother-in-law only stayed for six weeks at a time. Now, my sister-in-law? She really is a piece of work."

"Your sister-in-law? You never mentioned her before."

"Yeah, well, haven't you ever wondered why I only talk about traveling, yet I never go anywhere?"

"Uh huh, I figured there had to be a good reason."

"Ha, I wouldn't necessarily call it a 'good' reason. You see, Anne's sister, Shari, moved in over a year ago and she won't leave. She has a good job at the automobile license bureau, but she's sickly and a lifelong spinster. We really had no choice. She doesn't have anyone else. We had to let her move in. Now we're trapped and that's why we can't go anywhere. We had several trips planned before she moved in…even put down deposits, but ended up losing our money.

Steve, we only have a one bedroom apartment and now this lunatic has completely taken over the living room. She sleeps on the sofa and, what's worse, she's a hoarder. She's hooked on those mail-order catalogs and she spends all her money on shoes and handbags that she never uses. Sometimes, she doesn't even open the packages; they just pile up in the living room."

"Well, doesn't she contribute money toward rent or groceries?"

"Omigod, that was my biggest mistake...asking her to pitch in."

"What happened?"

"She told us she had a better idea and she switched to buying cheap porcelain figurines because she thinks they're valuable collectibles that'll be worth a lot of money some day and she'll leave them to us when she dies. Steve, they're nothing but worthless junk."

Steve does his best to calm Murray down and is grateful for the opportunity to help him feel better. Obviously, Steve can't solve everyone's problems, but he gives his audience a broad shoulder to cry on which is something most of them have never had. More than that, he respects them regardless of how small or trivial their complaints might be. In turn, they love him for it and repay his kindness in a very important and unexpected way.

The next morning at breakfast, he gushes to Sonny, "You'll never believe what Ernie told me last night."

She smirks, "Ha, at this point, I'll believe anything he says. What was it this time?"

"Well, you know I don't just read commercials like other DJ's do. I kinda romance each product and give it my personal endorsement?"

"Yeah, I know and I bet the sponsors love it."

"Sure, they do, but now the Rascals have started buying the products and giving their own glowing reviews. To no one's surprise, sales are going through the roof and so am I. Sonny, I'm on cloud nine."

From that point forward, Murray, Tony, Trudy, Stan, and Dorothy make up the core of Rasco's Rascals. They call in most nights and are the best of friends. In fact, they become a true family and they act like it: they argue, laugh, and tease each other unmercifully, all in the spirit of good-natured fun. Steve loves listening to them, interacting with them, and learning from them. After all, he never had a family growing up; it was only him and his mom.

Other listeners become fans of the Rascals and they also talk about the sponsors' products. Thanks to the show, the Rascals and everyone else have become unfettered, no longer shackled by the stigmas thrust upon them by society like garbage man, taxi driver, widow, or short-order cook. Their insecurities and their feelings of inadequacy are jettisoned by their camaraderie and by the acceptance and admiration they lavish on each other. Steve loves it because the show suddenly has its own contented momentum. He doesn't have to stimulate the conversation anymore; now his main job is to make sure as many people as possible get to participate.

However, as the show gains in popularity, the Rascals are gradually joined by a more diverse, free-spirited bunch intent on pushing the limits of radio. Some of them are merely hell-bent on having fun while others seem to be equally determined to raise a ruckus by igniting controversies. Steve privately refers to them as his "late night loonies."

His favorite looney, who calls himself the Turtle, always starts off with, "This is the Turtle. I keep to myself and hide in my shell, secure in the knowledge that we're all going to Hell."

He complains about everything under the sun, especially politicians and big institutions which endears him to other listeners because he says things other people think, but are afraid to say. He's abrasive, intelligent, militant, and quite formidable because he's well-educated and extremely well-spoken. Many people, including Steve, will marvel at his insights and agree with him one minute, then turn right around and butt heads with him because he's being such a jerk.

His caustic, tormented personality is an understandably well-deserved consequence of the catastrophic car crash that took the lives of both his parents and his older brother. The other consequence, obviously unknown to Steve's radio audience, is that his four-year-old body barely survived, only to remain broken and grotesquely disfigured for the rest of his life. He was severely burned, both legs were broken, and one of his lungs was punctured by a splintered rib.

Presently in his mid-forties, Thomas Perkins lives as a recluse behind the gates of his family's estate in Potomac, Maryland, just north of DC. He was raised there by his wealthy grandparents who saw that he had the best available medical and rehabilitative care. He endured countless operations to repair the damage. Steel pins were inserted into his legs, yet he still had to walk on crutches until he was almost eight and limps badly to this day. A team of plastic surgeons attempted to restore his face with multiple skin grafts, but after a certain point, they realized it was a futile exercise that was only torturing the poor lad.

Most of his rigorous education came from tutors and as a result of his insatiable curiosity. He read all of Shakespeare's plays before he was nine, he speaks French, reads Latin and Greek, and plays chess though the mail with several different people around the world. His grandparents tried sending him to a respected private school when he was ten, but the other children bullied him unmercifully and named him the Turtle because of his leathery skin, mottled with brown and red scar tissue.

A by-product of this bullying was, and still is his, his obsession with weightlifting. He works out with a professional trainer every day and has the strength of a gorilla. He also trains with a Judo instructor on a regular basis. Nobody's going to bother him ever again. On the rare occasions that he ventures outside the confines of the estate, he wears dark glasses and a scarf around his neck to conceal most of his disfigurement, but he secretly hopes that he'll run into one of his old tormentors from school so he could settle the score with them.

Oddly enough, he now wears the name Turtle as a badge of honor and uses it as a protective buffer with his chess partners and other people with whom he corresponds. After all, that's who he is and his estate, replete with servants, coaches, and guards, is the impenetrable shell that protects him from the outside world.

Only Steve and his marvelous collection of clowns have given him the freedom and the opportunity to have actual conversations with people outside his enclave. For him, it's like going away to camp, something he obviously never did. While he may have the equivalent of a post-doctorate education, he has the emotional maturity of a young teenager. Now, for the first time in his life, he finally has some playmates and he's never been happier.

One night, while grousing about the IRS, he giggles so hard he has to catch his breath, "Ach, you know what's so funny, Steve?"

"No, but it must be good. Tell me."

He chuckles fiendishly, "I really shouldn't complain about them. They're so stupid, I cheat on my taxes and they never catch me."

"Uh, maybe you should say they haven't caught you yet."

"Nah, like I said, they're too stupid and they have no idea who I am. I'm just a voice on the radio. Everybody should cheat them out of every dollar they can because the IRS is evil. Hell, there was no Federal income tax before 1913. As far as I'm concerned, it's still 1912. How do you like that?"

For a time, the Turtle appears to be the most popular man in DC. Most callers love his irreverent refusal to pay taxes and someone even said he should run for office. Steve doesn't know what to do because he secretly admires and even identifies with many of the anti-establishment things the Turtle says, but if he publicly agrees with the Turtle, he could get in trouble. When he warns callers not to follow the Turtle's lead, especially on taxes, they often make fun of him and say he's a stick in the mud.

To make matters worse, other disgruntled anarchists, emboldened by the Turtle, emerge from the shadows and begin crowding out the friendly Rascals. And when someone vehemently disagrees with one of their maniacal tirades, all good humor evaporates and the show inevitably devolves into vicious arguments that force Steve to juggle several calls at once. He's very adept at going from one line to the next, punching the buttons with the skill of a jazz pianist. If someone gets too nasty or lewd, he instantly jumps to another caller.

Trouble is, many of his sponsors are complaining that the show has deteriorated into nothing but a nasty slugfest. What's worse, the disgruntled, anti-government radicals aren't buying any of the sponsors' products. And before you know it, the once-faithful Rascals have all but disappeared. Ernie is so concerned that he sits in the control room with the engineer two or three times a week and tries to figure out a way to turn the ship around before it sinks for good. He happens to be there when Stan, the democracy-loving sanitation worker, calls in and provokes the ultimate firestorm that gets real ugly real fast.

"Hi Steve, it's Stan. Remember me?"

"Stan, of course I remember you. How've you been? We've missed you."

"Well, Steve, in all honesty, it's so hard for me to listen to your show that I don't want to participate anymore now that certain people tend to steer the conversation into such dark places. And I don't want you to think that I'm being intolerant. After all, free speech is one of our most precious liberties."

"Stan, for what it's worth, I don't think you're being intolerant...I think you're right. I don't know why those people try to drag us down into the gutter with them. That's another reason I'm glad you called. We need to hear from more people like you. If the good guys stop calling, then the bullies win and that's never right."

"Good, I'm glad you see it my way. And since you mentioned free speech, I'd like to speak frankly about your worst offender."

"You go right ahead."

"Okay, I think the Turtle is, at base, nothing but a coward. He wouldn't brag about cheating on his taxes if he used his real name. In my book, a real man plants his feet and tells the truth. Plus, and it goes without saying, some of us are interested in helping people instead of giving up hope and resigning ourselves to an eternity in Hell."

"Wow, did you hear that, folks? One of our old friends just threw down the gauntlet big time. Proud of you, Stan."

"Thanks, Steve. I couldn't take it any longer. I had to say something. Oh, and I hope Trudy's still listening. I heard her recommend cola syrup to Dorothy so I got some for myself and it cured my upset stomach. Guess the smell of garbage caused it, but now it's gone. Thanks, Trudy."

"I also hope Trudy's listening. Thank you, Stan. Please call back."

"Uh, sorry, Steve, I really called to say 'Good bye' because you have disappointed and abandoned your most loyal fans by allowing the bad guys to take over. I may listen to your show every once in a while, but I won't be participating as long as the Turtle and his gang rule the roost."

Steve's heart skips beat and he breaks out on a cold sweat. His mind goes blank and he feels like throwing up.

"Steve, you still there?"

"Uh, dammit, Stan, you're absolutely right. I don't know what to say except that I miss you and all the other Rascals. Please don't give up on the show just yet."

There's an audible click and the line goes dead. Steve panics but he has to keep going so he hits another blinking light, "Hi, this is Steve and you're on the air."

A humble sanitation worker, an ardent student of our democracy, just took a valiant stand and for the rest of the show, the callers either agree with him and also chide Steve for losing control, or they make fun of him and the Rascals. They're like two schools of starving piranhas fighting over a carcass. After nearly three hours of nonstop bickering, the good guys appear to gain the upper hand and Steve begins to feel a glimmer of hope that the ugly tide has turned. Until…

"Hi, this is Steve, you're on the air."

"You and your sanctimonious garbage man make me sick. He's doling out nothing but delusional drivel full of pithy platitudes and most of your idiotic listeners are buying it. You and your Rascals are nothing more than a pathetic cadre of simple-minded kooks."

The Turtle commits the unforgivable sin of deliberately defaming the innocent inhabitants of Steve's sanctuary that shelters them from the cruel indifference of the outside world. Most things in life, including radio shows, eventually unravel and fall into disarray. The Turtle's assault is the exact opposite and, in one fell swoop, turns several months of ever-increasing good will, friendship, and a sense of real community into a nasty, divisive street brawl.

That does it. When Ernie hears the Turtle spout his vitriol, he knocks on the window and motions for Steve to hang up and play a record. Steve does as he's told and Ernie barges into the studio.

"There's no way that son of a bitch will ever be on your show again. I'm tired of making excuses for him and for you. The ratings are down and sponsors are threatening to leave, but you're oblivious. Look here, I'm not gonna take the fall for you, Steve, so here's what's gonna happen: I'll answer the calls tonight and hand the phone to you if it's not the Turtle. If it is, I'll hang up. And tomorrow morning I'll have all ten lines moved into the engineer's room and you'll only have a single phone in here. From now on, Jimmy'll screen the calls so the goddam Turtle can't get through. Got it?"

"Aw, c'mon, Ernie. I'm not disagreeing with you, but I just got really good at juggling all the calls. You know, going back and forth from one to another? How can I do that if Jimmy answers the phone?"

"Steve, I love you like a brother, but this isn't open for discussion. The truth is, the sponsors complained to the station owners and wanted me to fire you...yet I fought to keep you, but I'm done. I'm not gonna let you kill my Golden Goose. You've plumbed the depths of society, the last refuge of the truly desperate, and allowed those despicable bottom feeders to take over. We're almost at the point of no return so this, my dear friend, is it. Now we have to get the Rascals back and do whatever it takes to keep our sponsors happy.

Think about it: Jimmy can hold up a list of the callers and you can take your pick. Wow, I'm brilliant. This is a much better system than the one we've been using and it'll also weed out the bad guys. Get it?"

Steve shakes his head and chuckles, "Okay, okay, I get it. You're brilliant. So what should I say when I go back on the air?"

"That's easy. First, you say you're sorry people had to hear that and you promise it'll never happen again. Then tell 'em somebody else will answer the phone from now on just to make sure that sick bastard can't get through...period. Meanwhile, I'll pick up the first line and tell 'em to hold for you."

After he does, Steve stops the music and turns on his mic, "Hey, sorry about that folks. I'll honor and uphold the First Amendment until I hear that kind of vulgar, insulting language. From now on, somebody else will answer the calls to make sure the Turtle never gets on the show again. Yes, you heard me; he's permanently banned. Now let's pick up where we left off. Ah, I'm told we have a new caller on the line. Hi, this is Steve."

Sonny walks in the door after work and sees Steve lying on the couch, staring at the ceiling. Bo's lying next to the couch and thumps his tail loudly when he sees Sonny, but Steve doesn't move.

"Ahem, 'scuse me, are you daydreaming or what?"

Bo keeps thumping his tail, but Steve still ignores her. Not a good idea. She barges into the room and confronts him, "Hey, what the hell's wrong with you?"

He doesn't look at her and continues staring blankly into space, "Whew, it was a close one. The show almost came to a screeching halt until Ernie stepped in and turned it around. I mean, I hope it'll be okay. We'll just have to wait and see."

She plops down at the end of the couch and folds her arms, "I'm all ears."

"Remember that argument we had about the Turtle?"

"Yeah, you said he was the best thing that ever happened to the show and I said you were blind as a bat because I thought he was the worst thing."

"Well, he was the best thing…for a while anyway, but you were absolutely right. He got nastier and nastier. I completely lost my bearings and ignored my lovable Rascals so they stopped calling because they didn't want to suffer his abuse. Plus, he drew other mean people out of the woodwork who dispensed a disgusting litany of cultural grievances that took all the fun out of the show. But the Turtle finally went too far tonight so Ernie stepped in and ordered me to ban him from the show. Ernie also told me the advertisers were threatening to leave if we didn't do something about the Turtle."

"It's about time you banned him. What did he say?"

"Well, since the show had already become a soapbox for his hate, when one of the Rascals actually had the courage to call in, the Turtle insulted him and me in the most despicable terms. I really don't want to repeat what he said. It still makes me sick. Now I have to do everything in my power to get the Rascals back and have fun like we used to."

"Steve, get a grip. Merely getting rid of the Turtle won't be enough to turn it around. You've gotta come up with a gimmick, some way to combat the remaining bad element, and get the show back on track. You need a breakthrough that fosters a renaissance, a new beginning. That's the only antidote. "

"I know, but what? I wish you could be in the studio with me. We could banter back and forth, make short work of the awful people, and make the show fun again. That's the trouble with live radio...you open the door and a bunch of jerks can waltz right in and ruin it for everyone else."

Steve's not the only one who's been down in the dumps. Bo feels like he's been shunted aside because Sonny and Steve are too busy to give him the attention he craves. Sonny goes to work all day and Steve sleeps all day. When Sonny gets home from work, she and Steve spend most of their precious time together behind the closed bedroom door, making all those animal noises, and completely ignoring the real animal in the house. Then Steve goes to work and Sonny goes to sleep. As a result, Bo, who never sleeps, has way too much time on his paws and he's not happy about it.

His puppyhood was cut short due to the war, but he's retained his inner puppy and he had the most fun when he played pranks with Sally. Now that he's alone most of the time, he feels left out and desperate to find new ways for that puppy to have fun again. One night, after Sonny refuses to take him for a walk before she goes to bed, he can't stand it any longer so he hops out an open window, slithers down the fire escape, and disappears into the darkness. If his two best friends won't play with him, then he'll have to find some excitement on his own.

He's always liked the dark of night. For one thing, he can see perfectly well, unlike humans and most other animals. Ah, the dewy grass feels great underfoot, the air smells better, and it's quiet...a rare and valuable commodity in a bustling city like DC. Plus, he can go anywhere he wants and take his sweet time without having to be on somebody else's schedule. But as he wanders about, the trouble is, he's still alone. The streets are empty, save for a drunk staggering his way home and a couple of alley cats scrounging for food in a garbage can...not exactly the kind of action he's looking for.

Though his first outing proves to be rather uneventful, he decides to make it his nightly ritual and keep at it until he finds some new playmates. He bounds up the fire escape moments before Steve gets home and greets him at the front door like he always does. Secrets are fun. At least he has that to show for tonight's jaunt and now he can look forward to tomorrow's.

Several weeks go by and Bo's nightly forays into the city prove to be extremely eventful to the point that he's becoming something of an urban legend. One of his new friends runs a newsstand that opens at 4 AM when the morning papers are delivered. Bo had walked by several times and never stopped, but on one occasion, he saw an apple sitting atop a stack of magazines and paused to drool at it.

When the man noticed Bo, he picked up the apple and said, "You want some of this?"

Naturally, Bo licked his chops and nodded his head. The man laughed, carved off a piece with his penknife, and tossed it to Bo who inhaled it with one gulp. The man laughed again and carved a piece for himself. Bo cocked his head to one side and snorted softly.

"Oh, I get it. You think this is your apple, huh?"

Bo nodded again and sat up extra straight.

"Too bad...we'll have to share," and he tossed Bo another piece. When the apple was gone, Bo burped his thanks, and walked away.

The man yelled after him, "You're welcome. Come again."

And he did, at least twice a week from then on.

Another new friend is a doorman at a ritzy hotel. Bo noticed him several times before he approached him. The man usually stood all alone, first on one foot, then the other, whistling, clapping his white-gloved hands…anything to pass the time. Bo had a great idea and suddenly appeared, sitting next to the man with a tennis ball in his mouth.

The man jumped when he saw Bo, "Whoa, where'd you come from?"

Bo looked up at him, carefully placed the ball at his feet, backed up, and did his best impression of an Irish Setter pointing at a pheasant: his tail ramrod-straight behind him, one front leg curled up under him, and his eyes glued to the ball.

"Oh, you wanna play fetch, huh?'

Bo never took his eyes off the ball and didn't move a muscle.

"Okay, then," and he kicked the ball down the sidewalk. Bo grabbed it in a flash and placed it back at the man's feet, all in one fluid motion.

Startled by Bo's quickness, the man's mouth dropped open, "What the…?" but Bo was locked in the same pose.

The man chuckled, "Alright, Fella, let's see how fast you can fetch this one," then he picked up the ball and threw it as far as he could, well into the next block. Once again, Bo literally disappeared, reappeared, placed the ball at the man's feet, and resumed his point in a blurred gust of wind.

The man stumbled backward and collapsed on a bench beside the front door. Bo realized the man was scared, slowly walked over to him, placed a reassuring paw on his knee, and smiled.

The man recoiled at first, but somehow found the courage to reach out and pat Bo's head, "Good dog. Whew, good 'n fast. What's your name?" He reached for the dog tags around Bo's neck, but Bo backed up and scurried away, leaving the poor man utterly befuddled and mumbling to himself, "I can't tell anyone about this. Who'd believe me? I don't believe it myself."

While Steve's rascals thrived in a public forum, Bo's buddies were very private, known only to him. That is, until two separate incidents basically blew his cover.

The first one involved a taxi driver who was parked at a curb, counting his money when a man knocked on his window with the barrel of a gun. The man screamed, "Roll down your window and give me all your cash."

Bo was two blocks away when he heard it and he raced toward the sound of the man's voice. He wasn't sure what was going on, but he was all too familiar with the angry, threatening tone and he knew something was very wrong. When he saw the cab and the man sticking a gun in the driver's face, he crept on his belly until he was within striking distance, and lunged at the assailant. He ducked his head and rammed the man square in the chest. The gun flew out of the man's hand and he was unconscious before he hit the cement. It all happened so fast that the driver was in shock. He glanced back and forth from Bo to the man, his mouth agape, his body trembling uncontrollably. Bo looked at him and barked softly, as if to say, "Hey, snap out of it."

It worked. The driver shook his head to clear his mind, fumbled for his radio, and called his dispatcher, "Charlie, it's me, Sam. Hey, I was parked at a curb and a guy tried to rob me, but a dog clocked the asshole and he's out cold on the sidewalk. Yeah, you heard me…a dog. Call the cops and tell 'em I'm on 19th between Q & R just north of Dupont Circle." He put down the radio and turned to thank Bo, but he was gone. The driver jumped out of the cab and looked up and down the street. Nothing…no dog anywhere.

Shortly thereafter, a police car pulled up behind the cab and a cop jumped out with his gun drawn. He ran over to the man lying on the sidewalk and kicked him to see if he was awake. When the man didn't respond, the cop holstered his gun and checked the man's throat for a pulse. Then he looked at the driver and yelled, "He's alive. Get back in the cab and I'll call for an ambulance."

It's not easy for a young reporter to get started in this town. Most plum assignments go to grizzled veterans who've been around for a long time. Brett Horton figured the only way he'd get noticed at the Post was to camp out at the City Desk in the wee hours of the morning and listen to the police radio. Most calls were boring, routine, and definitely not newsworthy. This one was unique. A dog stopping a robbery? Horton grabbed a notepad and ran to his car.

He got there before the ambulance, parked in front of the cab, and ran up to the driver, "Brett Horton, Washington Post, what's you name? Can you tell me what happened?

The cop shoved him away from the cab and said, "Hey, back off. This is an active crime scene."

He obeyed and threw his hands in the air, "Okay, okay, we heard a dog knocked out a robber." He turned to the driver and yelled, "Is that true? Where's the dog? C'mon, was there really a dog?"

The driver stuck his head out of the cab, "Hell yeah, he was huge, black with brown markings, great lookin' dog, probably saved my life."

Horton pleaded with the cop, "Please, Officer, just let me give him my card."

The cop nods, "Alright, then beat it."

Horton walked to the cab and handed the driver his card, "Here, please call me if you see the dog again and what'd you say your name was."

The driver took the card and smiled, "Rather not say, but I'll call you if I see him again."

Horton shrugged and got back in his car. 'Gotta respect his privacy. Maybe he's moonlighting and doesn't want anyone to know. Not much of a story without his name and a shot of the dog. Oh well, I'll write it up anyway and see what the editor says.'

His luck was about to change. A call about a large dog and another robbery came over the police radio less than 30 minutes after he get back to the Post. This time the dog supposedly stopped a purse snatcher who was

254

accosting a nurse. What's more, the dog was still standing guard over the robber. It had to be the same dog. Horton woke up a photographer who was snoozing in a back office and convinced him to go along for the ride. They had to get there before the dog disappeared again.

This time they beat the cops. Sure enough, a nurse in a white uniform was cowering in a nearby phone booth and a large black and brown dog was standing over a man who was cringing in the gutter between two parked cars.

Horton and the photographer got out of the car and Horton whispered, "Quick, get a shot of the dog and the perp. Be careful. Don't spook the dog."

The photographer nodded and got into position. Horton waved at the the nurse to come out of the booth. She shook her head, "No" and held the door shut. He moved closer and smiled, "We're from the Post. What's your name?"

She looked at him and started to speak, but instead, she clasped her hands over her mouth and sobbed silently.

"Hey, take it easy. It looks like the dog's got everything under control and the cops'll be here soon." He pulled a hanky out of his pocket and held it up to the door. She opened the door a crack, grabbed it, closed the door again, and blew her nose. The she looked at him and mouthed, "Thank you."

The street was briefly illuminated by the pop of a flash bulb as a siren wailed ever closer. He smiled at her and winked, "Hear that? Cops'll be here soon." She smiled feebly in return and wiped her eyes as the police car screeched to a halt and two cops jumped out. One of them ran up to Horton and yelled, "Who are you and who's the guy with the camera?"

Horton fumbled in his pocket and handed the cop his card and said, "Brett Horton, we're with the Post and..."

The cop interrupted him and turned to his partner, "Hey, Al, these two are with the Post. Go ahead and cuff that guy."

When she heard that, the girl opened the phone booth and said, "Officer, is it safe to come out now?"

"Yeah, sure. You okay, Lady?"

She nodded and pointed at the dog, "Yes, I'm fine now. That dog saved me. He appeared out of nowhere and knocked the mugger flat. I was so scared I couldn't move.Then the dog looked at me and looked at this phone booth. I swear...he was telling me to call you."

The cop rolled his eyes at Horton and cleared his throat, "Sure, Lady, long as you're alright. That's all that matters."

Horton smiled and looked at the dog, but he was gone.

What a scoop. Horton got noticed alright; his story made the front page and so did Bo. There was a picture of him snarling at the horrified robber under the headline: *Canine Crime Fighter.* Horton told the taxi driver's story and then included an interview with the nurse who gave her firsthand account of Bo's heroics.

When the story broke the next day, Bo's pal at the newsstand, the doorman, and several other secret buddies called the Post and told Horton about their experiences. Now he had a terrific follow-up story for tomorrow's paper.

Jake Miller was not at all amused when he saw the story in the Post. He went nuts anytime a reporter from another news agency grabbed a great story, but this was about his star reporter's dog. The irony of it all was like a kick in the gut. He was pacing around the newsroom with the Post in his hand when Sonny ambled in that morning.

"Hey Sonny, seen the Post yet?"

She hadn't, but she and everybody else who worked for Jake never wanted to hear that question. It always meant that the AP was late to the party.

"Uh, no, why?"

He held the paper up so she could see the headline, "Why? The real question is: why is this story in the Post? If you knew Bo was roaming around the city like a vigilante, why the hell didn't you write the story?"

She grabbed the paper from him and read it with her mouth open and her eyes bugging out of her head. When she got to the end, she looked up and mumbled, "I, uh, we, uh, had no idea he was running around the city at night. Really, Jake…no idea whatsoever."

When Sonny gets home from work that evening, Bo greets her at the door like he always does, but she holds up the paper, points to his picture, and says, "Something you wanna tell me?"

He lowers his head, walks over to the corner of the living room, and curls up facing away from her.

"Hey, don't you dare ignore me. Bo, look at me."

He doesn't budge.

She stamps her foot and yells, "Bo, c'mere this instant."

He still doesn't move and Steve calls her from the kitchen, "Sonny, what's wrong?"

"Steve, could you please come in here?"

He walks into the room and she hands him the paper without taking her eyes off Bo, "Here, read the lead story… that's what's wrong."

He knows better than to argue when she's using this tone of voice so he obediently sits on the sofa and looks at the paper. He reads a little, frowns at her incredulously, then at Bo, and reads the rest of it. When he's finished, he dares to chuckle, "Bet Jake was pissed."

"Is that all you have to say?"

"Hey, don't get mad at me. I'm not doing anything wrong and it looks like Bo's been doing a lot of stuff right and, I might add, right under your nose."

As soon as he says it, he knows it was a mistake so he tries to cool things down, "C'mon, Sonny, nobody's blaming you. He can disappear into thin air and I bet he uses the window we leave open to make his way down the fire escape."

"He never did anything like this before. Why now?"

"Well, come to think of it, we haven't been paying as much attention to him as we used to. Maybe his feelings are hurt. We've both been neglecting him lately."

"Yeah, with our crazy schedules...I think you're right. Well, shame on us."

She walks over to Bo, kneels down next to him, and gently scratches his ear, "I love you, Bo. We love you. Please, don't ever run away again."

He whines softly and licks her face.

Steve walks up next to Sonny and leans down with his hands on his knees, "Bo, you know we love you. We're a family. You're just better at it than we are, but we're learning. From now on, you come first." Then he looks at Sonny, "I have a great idea and I hope you'll agree with me."

"I will...as long as it has to do with Bo."

"Oh, it sure does. Remember when I told you I wished you could be in the studio with me?"

"Yeah, but what...?"

"Hey, gimme a second...you can't be there, but Bo can."

Her mouth drops open, "Wow! That's a fantastic idea!"

"And now, thanks to that reporter Horton, Bo's a local hero and a celebrity in his own right...think about it: I can talk to him when one of those assholes starts trouble and use him to make fun of them. I'll ask him a question, use a hand signal, and he'll give me the answer I want. I honestly believe he could be the catalyst that'll lighten up the show and bring the good people back together."

"Yes, yes, yes, that's it. He'll be the show's official mascot and growl those bullies right into submission just like he did in his travels around the city."

Steve scratches Bo's ears, "What do you say, Bo. Wanna be my sidekick?"

Bo answers Steve with a nod and a "woof."

He giggles, "I may not even need hand signals."

"Hello, everybody, I want to start off this morning's show by introducing you to Bo, our newest Rascal. He's part of my family and now he'll be part of our radio family. Bo, say 'Hello' to our listeners."

Steve gives him the "bark" sign and Bo is so excited he happily obliges with a little gurgle deep in his throat that quickly builds into a thunderous bark. Unfortunately, it's so loud Jimmy goes cross-eyed and rips off his headset.

"Whoa, guess you can tell from his really loud bark that Bo's a really large dog. He sure is and I'm proud to say he's my dog. We met a long time ago, then we lost touch, but now we're back together and we'll never be apart again. Our story is a very long one and I hope to share it with you over time because I bet you'll end up loving Bo almost as much as I do. Oh, hey, looks like we have our first caller and it's one of our old friends. Hi Tony, how've you been? I've missed you."

"Hi, Steve. Yeah, it's been a while. I missed you and the rest of the gang, too."

"Tony, great to hear your voice. What's new with you?"

"Well, Steve, after you introduced Bo, I couldn't resist telling you about my favorite new constellation. Believe it or not, it's Canis Major which means the greater dog. Imagine that?"

"Wow, you know, Tony, some people think there's no such thing as a coincidence and right now...I have to agree."

"Yeah, me too. What are the odds? You got a big dog and my favorite constellation is named after a dog. And what's more, it contains Sirius, the Dog Star, which just happens to be the brightest star in the sky."

"You're kidding."

"No way, it's true. And I want you to know something, Steve. You used to be the brightest star for me, for all the other Rascals, and for everyone else who loved and appreciated your show. Now that you've gotten rid of you-know-who, can we please go back to the way it was?"

Steve swallows hard in a feeble attempt to get rid of the lump in his throat. It doesn't work so he tries again.

"Steve, you still there?"

He clears his throat, "Uh, yeah, uh, Tony, I gotta tell you, that's one of the nicest things anyone has ever said to me and I will do everything in my power to honor your request."

"Steve, I know you will. It's great to be together again. Talk to you soon. Bye now."

During the next hour, Steve hears from another Rascal.

"Murray, so glad you called. I just spoke with Tony. Did you hear?"

"Yeah, I figured since you got a dog and you sound like your old self, it'd be safe to give you a call. Guess what?"

"I give up...what?"

"My blankety-blank sister-in-law is still camped out in our living room and now there's even more of that junk porcelain everywhere. Steve, it's like walking through a minefield just to get to the front door and it's still driving us crazy, but we actually caught a break."

"Really? How?"

"Believe it or not, Shari met a guy at Bingo, a butcher named Harry who's a widower and he's very nice. Yeah, she's still living with us, but now there's hope. At any rate, we're eating a lot better. She always brings home delicious roasts and she insists, no matter what happens with her and Harry, she will still leave her 'fortune' to us. She's crazy, but her heart's in the right place. Anyway, the good news is... Anne and I will finally be taking our first real trip in a couple of weeks."

"Wow, that is good news. Guess this is one instance where you can honestly say, 'All's well that ends well.' Right, Murray?"

"Um, honestly, Steve, I really don't know.

Steve looks at Bo and a sly grin lights up his face.

"Bo, Murray's not so sure about all this. What do you think?"

Bo cocks his head to one side, doing his best to understand Steve's question. They stare at each other for a long moment then Steve nods his head in amazement as the answer suddenly comes to him, "Yeah, of course. Life always takes unexpected turns, but your wife is happy, you're certainly eating better, and you're finally going on a trip. That's all good news."

Bo barks his enthusiastic approval.

"Did you hear that, Murray?"

"Yes, you're absolutely right. You have a terrific way of seeing things so clearly."

"Hey, don't thank me; thank Bo. He's the one with the unique gift. He understands the human condition better than most people do."

Steve gets the chills as he hears his own words and he wisely spins a record to give himself time to calm down so he can try to figure out what just happened. He was joking around when he asked Bo's opinion, but something profound happened when he looked into those big golden eyes: the right answer instantly popped into his head.

'Did that really come from Bo? Nah, couldn't have...or could it? If not, then where the hell did it come from? I usually don't come up with profound shit like that, but hey, maybe staring at him forced me to think like him and that's always a good thing. Yeah...'

Bo became an integral part of the show ever since that first day when he eagerly sniffed his way into the studio. Now Steve has everything he needs to be a success and he attacks his job with an unshakable, newfound confidence. If there's a big disagreement about a particular issue and people even start to get ugly, Steve asks Bo to decide which caller is making sense and which one is being ridiculous. Obviously, nobody knows that Steve's giving Bo silent signals for barking, growling, whining, or panting. You name it, they have a signal for it.

In a few short months, the show's humming along better than ever. Matter of fact, it's the hottest show in the time slot again. The other troublemakers eventually fade away, and slowly but surely, all the old Rascals eagerly return to the fray. Bo quickly gets to know their voices and, without being prompted, barks "Hello" when he hears them. In fact, Trudy and Bo have regular "conversations" on the air that usually leave Trudy in stitches. Nothing brings a family back together like a dog.

And now, the sponsors are thrilled with Steve and his extraordinary creativity. His commercials always have crazy sound effects, background music, and they're punctuated with Bo's approval. The fans love them and they rave about the products when they call in. Ernie doesn't waste any time. He plasters pictures of Steve and Bo on billboards, city busses, and he books them on local TV shows. Soon, people start sending dog biscuits and toys to Bo and he gets almost as much fan mail as Steve.

24

Sonny has proudly watched Steve experience a great deal of success in the past three years and her eyes have been opened, as never before, by listening to him banter with his wild band of misfits on the radio. She's alone in the house when he's at work, but she isn't lonely because she recognizes and accepts the fact that Bo basically became Steve's dog when Steve realized that it was Bo, not Ben Harper, who dragged him out of that burning building and saved his life back in Belgium. In addition, Steve and Bo have teamed up to revolutionize the way people listen to the radio and, in the process, have empowered the voiceless multitudes to speak freely without censure or fear of reprisal. It would be hard to imagine a more perfect example of democracy in action.

Sonny's fine with it. Benjamin warned her that Bo will never belong to only one person. And how can she possibly be jealous of the time he spends with Steve when they always come home to her? She can't and her time alone gives her the chance to ponder her own professional quagmire. She's not in competition with Steve. On the contrary, his meteoric rise inspires her to relaunch her own career. She was raised by two renowned, overachieving parents and now she's married to an extremely successful man. No wonder she's restless.

There's so much happening beyond the confines of the White House and she yearns to be in the middle of it, not cut off from it. Eisenhower's administration is effectively on autopilot as he nears the end of his second term in office. Now he spends every spare moment on the golf course. Here's the most powerful man in the world, the brilliant general who pulled off the D-Day invasion, the best kept military secret since the Trojan Horse, merely biding his time until he can leave office and play golf every day. It's not what you'd call earth-shattering news.

True, she uncovered some juicy tidbits about certain presidential surrogates taking bribes and a couple of really big scandals involving the Secret Service that enhanced her reputation as a top journalist, but she couldn't care less. In her eyes, she's little more than a gossip columnist.

So what if she's the most prominent White House reporter. She's chomping at the bit to shift her career into overdrive and chase the most important stories out there in the rest of the world.

For one thing, Rock and Roll is starting to disrupt society and stands in stark contrast to the staid, boring White House. Sonny really doesn't understand why it's having such an incredible effect on the culture and it piques her reporter's curiosity. Suddenly, she smells blood: this new phenomenon could be the basis for a fabulous series of articles…if only she had the freedom to write them.

Until recently, popular music was little more than a soundtrack, always there, humming in the background, a pleasant thread woven into the fabric of American life. Sure, the big bands were fun to dance to and young girls went crazy over Frank Sinatra, but it was all so mainstream, so acceptable, so blasé.

Rock and Roll is anything but. It's raw, provocative, and naughty. TV cameras are only allowed to show Elvis from the waist up lest people see his wildly gyrating hips. Many parents try to stop their teenagers from listening to Rock and Roll. They confiscate phonographs and transistor radios, they throw away records…all to no avail because it's already too late. The kids have tasted something so new and exciting that they're addicted. They refuse to be denied and they clamor for more as does Sonny. She has Steve bring her all the extra 45's from the station and she plays them constantly, determined to unravel the mystique. She watches *American Bandstand* on TV and reads *Variety* to keep up with all the news about new artists and record companies.

Her boss, Jake Miller, has always been extremely supportive, but now he's holding her back by keeping her at the White House and that's the crux of her dilemma. She's eternally grateful for his help and support; that's the part that eats at her whenever she thinks about confronting him, but there's no way around it. She has to convince him to get her out of there and let her do what she wants.

After talking it over with Steve, she waits till the end of the day and knocks on Jake's door, something she never does. She's the only one in the office who barges in whether the door's open or not.

He yells, "I'm busy. Go away."

She knocks again.

He yells louder, "I said, 'Beat it.'"

She knocks once more.

She hears heavy footsteps accompanied by a barrage of mumbled profanity before the door swings open and Jake says, "What the hell, Sonny? Since when do you knock?"

Using her best southern accent, she replies, "Why, Mr. Miller, I'm applying for a job and I didn't want to be impolite. That's why I knocked."

"Have you lost your...?"

She bats her eyes and smiles innocently, "Please, Mr. Miller, if I could have but a moment of your precious time."

He looks past her through the doorway and sees the rest of the people in the office watching.

"Get in here."

She whisks past him and he pokes his head out, "Show's over. Get back to work," and he slams the door.

She sits in front of his desk and neatly folds her hands in her lap. He circles around her menacingly before he plops down in his desk chair and bellows, "Okay, cut the bullshit. What are you up to?"

She slaps her hands on his desk and bellows right back at him, "Jake, we have to talk about my career."

"Your career? What, do yo have another job offer? And since when are you Scarlet O'Hara?"

"Well, I didn't think I'd get anywhere if I acted like Rhett Butler. And, no, I don't have another job offer. Uh, not one that I would consider anyway."

"Oh, so you have other offers?"

"Yes, routinely, but that's not the point. I simply don't want to waste any more time at the White House. I feel like I'm handcuffed to a pipe in the basement and never get to see the light of day. Jake, you know me; I'm not good at beating around the bush."

"You're right. I'm glad you didn't pursue a career in diplomacy. It would have led to multiple disasters around the world."

"Thanks for the compliment."

"Oh, think nothing of it. Sonny, what the hell do you want, now that being the most visible reporter in DC isn't good enough for you?"

"Dammit, Jake, in my opinion, I'm visible for all the wrong reasons since I'm the only woman in the Press Corps and, rumor has it, I'm also rather attractive. I want to uncover the biggest stories in the real world, the whole world, instead of passing along the carefully edited fluff they hand me at the White House.

In case you haven't noticed, Rock and Roll is taking the country by storm and most news services, including the AP, hardly give it any traction at all. We treat it like it's just a passing fad, or at best, a cultural anomaly. Well, I'm here to tell you that it's the beginning of a massive shift in the culture. New recording companies are springing up and new artists are emerging almost every day. The business is growing exponentially because it's a wake-up call for a snoozing society that barely has a pulse. I want to get out there and report on it and all the other news that will light up the wires and my career in the process...for all the right reasons. Get it?"

"I get that you're way off base and I think your judgement has been clouded by Steve's success in radio."

"You're dead wrong. Steve doesn't play Rock and Roll; he talks to people about everything under the sun and much of what they discuss are the changes happening around the country. You could say the music is both a symptom of those changes and a cause as well."

"But there's an election coming up soon. Ike's done. You wanna talk about changes? One way or another, the next election will bring about massive changes. Don't you want to be around for all that?"

Dammit, Jake, Don't you see? I can have a better perspective from outside of the White House. You're right, it's going to be a tumultuous time in American politics, but I'm talking about the tumultuous time we're already experiencing. It's a helluva lot bigger than any presidential election."

Neither of them moves a muscle, for what seems like an eternity, until Jake smirks and says, "Ike will really miss you?"

"What are you saying? Did you just give me a 'get out of jail' card?"

"Aw, c'mon, has it really been that bad?"

She starts to point at him and say something, but she pauses and looks down, then smiles at him, "Know what? Yes, that's about the crux of it."

He frowns and nods his head, letting it all sink in for a moment before saying, "Well, in all honesty, you've been doing such a great job, naturally I thought you were happy. Now, you'll have to be patient. I can't make it happen over night. First, I'll have to find somebody else to cover the President. Boy, is he gonna be pissed. He adores you."

She smirks, "He'll get over it. Do we have a deal?"

"Yes, we have a deal, but you need to understand that you're buying a one-way ticket. It'll either take your career to the stratosphere or straight to Hell. Just keep this under your hat until I can find your replacement, okay?"

She runs around behind his desk and hugs him, "Oh, Jake, You're wonderful. And to think I used to fear you, even revile you. Now, there are no words to describe how much I adore you." She pulls back and looks him in the eye. "Can I tell Steve?"

"Sure, if anybody can keep a secret, he can."

"Believe it or not, when his career took off, it made me see things in a much broader sense and it made me realize that staying at the White House was too limiting for me, that I needed a bigger challenge."

"Well, there's a world full of important stories out there. Go get 'em."

Sonny doesn't waste any time settling into her new job. She takes off like a house afire with a scary level of enthusiasm, determined to ferret out the most consequential news in every arena. The White House and most people in DC, for that matter, only care about the business of government. They slog through their daily grind wearing bureaucratic blinders, numbly unaware of what's going on in the rest of the country.

Then she hits a wall. After trying unsuccessfully to uncover some juicy, inside stories about the record business, Sonny tries other areas like corporate scandals, labor unrest, immigration, transportation and infrastructure issues, medical care, and schools. She even frequents a couple of bars where foreign diplomats hang out. Yet despite all her efforts, most of her stories have about as much sizzle as a church bulletin. They're almost as bad as the boring drivel she used to write for the Stars and Stripes.

For example, when she tries to gin up some interest about corruption in the garbage business, she finds that nobody cares as long as their trash gets picked up. But just when she's beginning to think she should have stayed at the White House, her luck changes big time. Much to her surprise, the first ground-breaking story doesn't come from her own digging, it comes from Steve.

His career has exploded and he's become famous for his incredible nightly gabfest that's fueled by his innate ability to orchestrate extraordinary conversations between such interesting and diverse people. Plus, to no one's surprise, more and more puppies are being named Bo and one of his fans sends him a big water dish with his name on it. Ernie is so thrilled with Bo's popularity, he buys him his very own sofa that Steve calls the Bofa.

Obviously, very few DJ's have Steve's ability or his following. Rock and Roll isn't even his main focus, but if he likes a record, he tells his fans about it, and it sells like crazy. Now he's minting money for both the record companies and his sponsors while most DJ's don't have a clue. There were less than 250 of them at the start of the decade; now there are more than 5,000.

The big companies rely on promoters who travel all over the country bestowing certain gifts on the rest of the DJ's, thus buying valuable air time for their records. Guys in small rural towns are getting paid as much as $50 to play one record. That's big money, even in the big city. It's virtually irresistible and most of them happily go along with it. This blatant, thinly disguised bribery soon becomes known as "Payola" and it infests the music business like the plague. The word is a combination of "Pay" and "Victrola," the patented name for the first record player and the generic term most people still call any record player.

Enter the mob. Organized crime syndicates have always been very good at distributing things people crave the most like bootleg liquor, prostitutes, drugs, and gambling. Moreover, they are seriously organized. Their command structure would be the envy of any army and their leadership methods are extremely effective. If you work for the mob and you get arrested, you will be represented by the finest attorney money can buy. Likewise, your case will probably be thrown out of court by the most corrupt judge money can buy.

The underworld bosses see the burgeoning Rock and Roll scene as a bonanza ripe for the taking. Always looking for ways to launder their dirty money into legitimate businesses, this is a golden opportunity they can't resist. It's also a way for them to break the stranglehold that large record companies have on the music business. They start buying up smaller record labels, unscrupulously taking over others, and signing their own artists. Interestingly enough, many of them are minority artists who could never get deals with the big labels because their brand of Rock and Roll is too authentic, too visceral.

Unfortunately, the silver lining of getting a record deal amidst the pervasive cloud of racial prejudice often turns to dust. Most of the artists are forced to sign away their publishing rights for pennies and take long road trips to promote their records where they usually pay for their own food and lodging. Thus, they're lucky to break even and the record companies are making a ton of money.

While the big record companies and their promoters have turned Payola into an art form, the mob is even more adept at persuading people to cooperate. Their field soldiers can't exactly be called promoters. They're pros alright, but not in any positive sense of the word. They're commonly referred to as "muscle" and they know how to get their point across. In other words, they're the type of guys you shouldn't rub the wrong way. If they offer you money or another tawdry form of enticement to play certain records, you should cheerfully accept and do as you're told.

One of the most unscrupulous label owners is Maury Canter, a notorious bookie and loan shark, who's no stranger to the Philadelphia Police Department. He's been arrested several times for assault, racketeering, and even attempted murder, but always beats the rap thanks to his conniving attorneys and his ability to grease the right palms. Famous for being a snappy dresser, Canter is partial to custom tailored suits and Borsalino hats. He also teeters around on elevator shoes to compensate for his diminutive stature. He started his illustrious career as a numbers runner and found many of his patsies in Negro clubs where he became something of a fixture. He loved the action, the music, and especially the women.

You could say he inherited his record company after its former owner couldn't pay back the money Canter had loaned him. The guy knew that handing over the company was definitely more desirable than getting his legs broken... or worse. Canter immediately gave the company a new name that was anything but subtle: Revolver Records.

It soon becomes the scourge of the industry because Canter routinely strong-arms artists to sign with him and then rarely pays them what he promises. If they threaten to leave Revolver, his henchmen make it abundantly clear that such a move would be a big mistake. They also pay personal visits to several DJ's and deliver a similar message: "Play our records or else." Always looking for more ways to make money, Canter quickly expands his operation into DC because of all the Negro clubs there.

While attending a music industry convention in Atlantic City, Steve can't believe it when other big DJ's openly brag about all the cash they're raking in. Every so often, artists drop by Steve's station for an interview, they talk to callers, and become part of his radio family. Nobody can blame them for trying to get some free publicity, but so far, nobody has offered him any money, probably because he really isn't one of the key players in the industry. Those guys operate in the big markets, they only play Rock and Roll, and they have the prime slots in the late afternoon and the early evening.

Case in point: Rocky "Avalanche" Donovan, who has the biggest afternoon drive-time show in Chicago, is dying to know how much Steve is getting under the table. There's a tremendous amount of competition for the cash and Rocky wants to make sure Steve isn't raking in more than he is. He thinks he's being so clever when he casually tells Steve how much he's being paid as a way to draw Steve out. Highly offended, Steve tells him to take a flying leap and walks away. Then another DJ tells Steve about Maury Canter and he's all ears. He even buys the guy a few drinks to make sure he gets all the gory details and gory they are. So much so that he sits there with his mouth agape like a kid watching a high wire act at the circus, totally astounded at how rampant Payola has become and, in particular, how ruthless Canter is.

Sonny lights up like a Roman candle when Steve tells her what happened at the convention. This is the break she desperately needs. She knows this could be a huge story, maybe as big as the Russian story would have been, and she pounces on it. Later that day, she summons two trusted private investigators into her office and swears them to secrecy before charging them with the daunting task of uncovering all the dirt they can find on the Payola scandal in general and specifically on Revolver. She warns them that it will be a dangerous assignment and demands to know, right then and there, if they're both up to it. Otherwise, she'll find somebody else with the guts to see it through. It works. They swear they're committed to doing the job fearlessly and run out of her office before she can change her mind.

Now that they know where to look, it doesn't take long for Sonny and her team to uncover mounds of evidence against several high profile DJ's, their all-too-friendly promoters, and most of all, Canter himself. Next, they stage a two-pronged attack: one against the big companies and another against Revolver. They sprinkle scathing articles everywhere, provoking public outrage and forcing Congress to take action. Oren Harris, Chairman of the House Oversight Subcommittee, finally agrees to hold hearings on the Payola scandal.

However, before the hearings begin, the Federal Trade Commission files complaints against a number of the biggest record manufacturers and distributors and mysteriously gives them a way to escape prosecution if they agree to get rid of certain holdings and divulge certain information. Talk about an inside deal, somebody got to someone who made sure that almost everyone guilty of commercial bribery is literally given a free pass.

But poor Mr. Canter, despite all his efforts, is left hanging out there like a target in a shooting gallery. He certainly isn't the only underworld figure involved in the record business, but he's the only one presently under investigation. So far, there isn't enough hard evidence to indict him, but that makes Sonny even more determined to dig it up. He can't set foot outside of his house without being tailed and he knows it.

Not to be outdone, Canter does a little snooping of his own with the help of the people in his DC operation. They're able to identify one of Sonny's investigators and, with a little friendly persuasion, he tells them who hired him. As always, if you have enough money and enough muscle, you can find out almost anything. Canter will obviously do whatever it takes to kill this investigation because he plans to expand his operation into New York and he can't afford any more distractions.

Per their normal routine after signing off the air, Steve and Bo walk out of the station on an unusually crisp winter morning. Bo disappears around the corner of the building to do his business and Steve hobbles toward the car. The faintest hint of dawn glows over the Capitol as Steve grumbles to himself about having to scrape the frost off his windshield.

Suddenly, he's temporarily blinded when a parked car shines its bright lights at him. When he turns away and tries to regain his eyesight, three goons jump out of the car and surround him. One of them shoves him from behind and almost knocks him down. "Hey, Rasco, you need to tell your nosey wife to call off her investigation and leave Revolver Records alone."

A second man spins him around and drops him with a nasty gut punch, "Yeah, either she kills the story or we'll kill both of you."

Steve lands on all fours and tries to catch his breath, but   the   man grabs his cane, breaks it over his back, and he sprawls flat on the ground.   "Get the picture, Pretty Boy?"

Steve feels a rush of air as Bo leaps over him and flattens the man who hit him with the cane. Another man pulls a gun, but Bo swats it with his paw and sends it flying under a parked car.

He yells, "See that? He's not a real dog...he's some kind of monster. Let's get outta here."

Bo roars at them as they they stumble over each other and sprint toward their car. He could easily catch them, but he stays just far enough behind, nipping at their heels, terrifying them even more.

Steve finally gets to his feet and yells, "You'll regret this for the rest of your sorry ass lives."

The thugs jump into their car, but before they can speed away, Bo rips a chunk out of one of their tires and it sounds like a gun shot. The men duck down, totally convinced it is. The car lurches forward with the shredded tire flapping noisily, swerves out of control, and crashes headlong into another car. The radiator spews a geyser of steam and the engine gasps twice before dying.

Steve pumps his fists and yells, "Yes! Bo, c'mere."

They cautiously approach the wreck and see that all the men are out cold and one of them is bleeding profusely from a head wound.

"Bo, you stay here. If they wake up, make sure they don't get away. I'm gonna go call the police."

Steve's never been this angry in his entire life, nor can he remember being this frightened. Maybe it's because he's scared, not just for himself, but also for Sonny. By the time he returns, Bo is standing over one of the men who has crawled out of the car and is lying on the ground, cringing in fear as Bo snarls viciously at him. When he sees Steve, he screams, "Hey, call off your dog. "

"Hell no. You threatened my wife. I should let him tear you apart."

"Yeah, right."

"Try me. I'm sure he could chew you to pieces by the time the cops get here and don't forget, there's a pistol back there with your prints on it. I'll say he was just defending me."

The man glares at Steve with complete contempt, his mouth moves, but nothing comes out.

"Who sent you? Canter himself?"

He shakes his head, "Uh uh, I ain't, uh, he'll…"

"Are you crazy? You're worried about that little twerp? You'd better worry about this dog. He'd love to punch your ticket. He's already killed one man and you're about to be number two."

"Aw, bullshit. Go to hell."

Steve grins at him, "Bo, grab his knee."

Bo instantly obeys, wraps his jaws around the man's knee, and sits down as if he were holding a bone. Most of the man's body dangles off the ground with only his head and shoulders touching the pavement. Bo calmly looks up at Steve and waits for his next command.

"Hey, asshole, how fond are you of that knee?"

The man flails wildly, but hasn't a prayer of escaping. It looks like he's being held by a statue, "Why, you son of a bitch, you wouldn't dare…"

"I wouldn't, but he would. Bo, bite harder."

Nothing moves but his jaws and a loud crunching sound punctuates his vise grip.

The man slaps both hands to his face and screams, "Okay, okay, I'll tell you. Get him off me."

"And you'll tell the cops everything when they get here. Right?"

"Yeah, yeah…the dog."

"Uh uh, you first."

"Alright, it was Canter. He told us to rough you up and threaten you."

Steve snaps his fingers, "Bo, relax."

Bo merely opens his mouth and the man flops to the pavement sobbing in pain, clutching his bloody, mangled knee.

Within minutes, two police cars and an ambulance arrive with sirens wailing and lights flashing. One of the cops runs up to Steve and shakes his hand, "Hey, Mr. Rasco, you okay? I'm a big fan. Wow, Bo's even bigger than he looks on the billboards."

"Yeah, I'll be fine. Sure glad he was with me."

The officer points to the man on the ground, "He the one who pulled the gun?"

"Uh huh, and he has something to tell you."

The officer kicks him in the chest, "What is it, tough guy?"

The man groans, takes a deep breath, looks down at his knee, and sobs, "Canter sent us, uh, I mean, uh…"

The officer kicks him again and yells, "Can't hear you."

The man looks up and yells back, "Okay, goddammit, it was Maury Canter. He sent us."

Steve leans over the man, "Now tell the nice policeman what Canter told you to do?"

"He told us to give you a real beat down and threaten to kill you and your wife so she'd stop writing all that stuff about him."

After the police hear his confession, they notify the Philadelphia Police who instantly send a detail to arrest Canter. Later that morning, he's escorted out of his house, nattily attired in silk pajamas and handcuffs, where he's greeted by a horde of screaming reporters and a blinding barrage of flashbulbs. He responds with his own barrage of profanity-laced threats, "These stupid pricks can't arrest me. I'm innocent. Dumb sons 'o bitches. They'll pay for this."

Boy is he in for a surprise. Instead of taking him to the local precinct like they usually do, the police take him directly to the FBI office. Canter never dreamed he'd be interrogated by the Feds. He was accustomed to friendly questioning by the local Philly detectives who knew how to play the game and pick up some extra cash in the process, but not these guys. They won't budge an inch and none of his sleazy attorneys have any sway with them. After his own men provide additional evidence in court, Canter is convicted on several charges and sentenced to a long stretch at the

Federal Penitentiary in Leavenworth, Kansas, where he now peels potatoes for ten hours a day.

Hell hath no fury like the scorn of a woman whose family has been threatened. Soon, Sonny effectively becomes Everywoman. She's so emotionally involved in her quest for truth that she attacks the nationwide scandal with the viciousness of a champion prize fighter going for a knockout. She courageously jabs her way through their webs of deceit and then relentlessly wallops the corrupt individuals with coherent mountains of evidence. She constantly pummels DJ's and promoters with pointed questions, always knowing the answers beforehand, and when they lie, she decks them with truth-filled haymakers.

Starting with a detailed account of Steve's savage beating at the hands of Canter's goons, Sonny's bylines run day after day, week after week, giving absolutely no rest to the wicked and no quarter to the scoundrels. When people dodge her phone calls, she and her photographer make house calls, even if they have to drive for hours. It's amazing how many of her articles contain a picture of a DJ or a record company executive with their mouths agape and their faces twisted into a hideous scowl. But despite all her efforts, Revolver is the only independent label she's been able to expose. Another thing the mob is very good at is secrecy. Once Canter got nabbed, everybody clammed up and ordered all their people to do the same...or else.

It's a typical, sweltering summer day and Sonny's pounding away on her typewriter when Jake sticks his head out of his office and yells, "Sonny, c'mere, you got a long distance call."

She gives him a puzzled expression, but he waves insistently so she hurries into his office and closes the door. He's standing beside his desk with a silly grin on his face, holding the phone in one hand, and clasping his other hand over the mouthpiece.

He whispers, "You have a collect call from Maury Canter."

She mouths the the word, "What?"

He whispers louder, "You heard me." He motions for her to sit at his desk and after she does, he hands her the phone and a legal pad.

She gives Jake a wide-eyed look of utter disbelief, shakes her head, and speaks in a businesslike tone, "This is Sonny Daye."

She nods her head, "Yes, I'll accept." She picks up a pen and jots down the date and time.

"Why, hello, Mr. Canter."

"I am surprised. What's on your mind?"

Her mouth drops open and she grins wickedly at Jake, "You want to give me your side of the story and a lot more. Now, what exactly does 'a lot more' mean?"

"Ha! You want a deal first? What could you possibly tell me that's worth a deal? I've already uncovered tons of information about the big record companies and the DJ's they're bribing."

Her mouth drops open. "Okay, let me get this straight. You'll give me information about the big labels you say I could never get. Plus, you'll give me the names of other independent label owners like yourself and how they're connected?"

Jake nearly jumps out of his skin when he hears that and he scribbles "connected = Mafia" on her pad.

She nods her head, "Whoa, wait a minute. When you say 'connected' do you mean what I think you mean?"

She smirks and nods at Jake, "Well, then, Mr. Canter, if you're willing to provide that kind of information, I might be able to get you a deal. By the way, what do you want in return?"

"A reduced sentence in a cushy, minimum security prison, huh. Well, I can't promise anything, but I'll see what I can do."

"Yes, I'll hurry. I'm sure the food is terrible. Bye now."

She slams the phone down, jumps out of the chair, and cackles as she do-si-do's around the room with Jake until he pulls away and screams, "This is it. This is the inside track you've been looking for all along."

"Inside track? Shit, this is the mother lode, but how can we broker a deal? You got any ideas?"

"Leave it to me. I know a Senator who can make it happen."

Jake delivers on his promise within a matter of days. Canter can have his deal only if he discloses new information about the big companies and those "connected" small label owners he mentioned. Otherwise, the deal's off. When she tells Canter all this on the phone, he assures her that she'll be astounded at the mountain of information he'll give her.

Sonny meticulously plans her attack during the drive to Kansas. Her goal is to make sure Cantor delivers the goods he promised. She knows it won't be easy. He'll probably try to give her as little as possible, but a little won't cut it with the Senate committee.

She's right because his immediate goal is to give her just enough to convince her to write a favorable article so he'll get the deal. His ultimate goal, once he's out, will be to exact his gruesome revenge on her and Steve. It doesn't matter if he's in jail; his boundless ego can't be confined by concrete and steel, nor can his fiendish desire for retribution.

Sonny arrives at the prison and she's surprised when she's greeted by the warden himself. He tells her he's a big fan and that he's closely following her crusade against the corruption in the music business. He especially liked her story about Canter and was anxious to observe him when he arrived at Leavenworth. Sure, the warden has seen all kinds of dangerous criminals, but Canter is disturbingly unique. He's one of the toughest guys the warden has ever known...no fear, no conscience, as cold-blooded as they come.

The warden personally takes her to a small dank room that reeks of bleach and stale cigarettes. He motions toward the chair and she sits facing the heavy glass partition. There's a phone on the wall and a ledge in front of her where she puts her legal pad and her secret weapon: a Brownie Starflash camera. There's a mirror image room on the other side of the glass that also has one chair and a telephone on the wall. She takes a deep breath and nods at the warden. He tells her he'll wait outside, then he knocks three times on the window, and closes the door behind him.

Shortly after the warden leaves, two guards usher Canter into the room on the other side of the window. They shove him roughly into the chair and stand on either side of him with their hands behind their backs like soldiers at ease. He shakes it off and grins as he picks up his phone, determined to keep up his amicable charade. Without warning, Sonny raises her camera and blinds all three of them with a quick snapshot. The guards scowl at her, but neither of them moves a muscle. Canter blinks a few times, grits his teeth, and maintains his grin, pretending it doesn't bother him. She calmly picks up her phone and tries to provoke him again, "How's life treating you, Maury?"

Too cocky to lose his cool, he shrugs and says, "I've had better food, but hey, I'll be out of here soon, right?"

"Well, that depends on what you tell me. Doesn't it?"

"Oh, I'm gonna tell you plenty and you should be very glad I'm giving you this opportunity. It shows that I'm basically a very nice guy. Hey, I could have given this deal to a lot of other reporters. Do you know that?"

"Bullshit! First of all, you didn't give me this deal. I negotiated it with my contacts in the Senate, something no other reporter could have done.

So don't act like you're doing me any favors here. C'mon, let's have it."

"Yeah? You wanna hear about some real DJ's, the guys who actually play Rock and Roll? They're not like your husband. He's not a real DJ. He plays elevator music that nobody cares about and he shoots the breeze with those weirdos who manage to crawl out of the shadows long enough to dial a phone."

"Insulting my husband won't get you out of here so either keep up your end of the bargain or I'm gone."

With that, Canter promises to deliver the goods, but only gives her dribs and drabs of unsubstantiated gossip, most of which she's already heard, that amount to little more than a load of hot air. But now that he's talking, Sonny continues to patiently prod him for more detail by softening her tone, winking, cajoling, almost flirting. Even the guards become restless as if they just noticed how attractive she is, watching her every move, wondering what she's saying to Canter, amazed at how compelling she is. Then everything changes.

Canter's grin dissolves into a cold stare and he looks like he's about to explode: his face reddens, veins pop out on his forehead, his lower lip quivers, and drool runs out the corner of his mouth.

"Okay, you want names, you want dirt? Check out that guy Alan Freed. You know, the one who came up with the name Rock and Roll?"

Sonny matches his seriousness with her own icy glare, "Yes, I've heard of him. Go on."

"Rumor has it that he keeps it in a safe in his home. You know, the money?"

"What money?"

"Aw, come on now, what money. You can't be that slow."

"You mean the money from…?"

"Yes, the money from…"

Now the guards are really interested in the conversation and they glance back and forth at each other.

"Okay, who else do you know about?"

"Yeah, uh, that pretty boy, Dick Clark? He's got his fingers in a lot of pies he shouldn't."

"Like what?"

"You're such a great reporter. Do some digging. You'll find it."

"She smiles and calmly continues, "Well, well, never thought I'd get a compliment from you, but what I really need to know are the names of those 'connected' people you mentioned on the phone."

He holds up his hands, "Whoa…not so fast. I've already given you a lot of stuff, but that'll have to wait until I'm

transferred out of here. It's too dangerous." He rolls his eyes back at the guards, "Get my drift?"

"Hey, that's not our deal. You promised to give me everything…right here and right now."

"Too bad. That's my deal. Take it or leave it."

Sonny uses every bit of self control she can muster and raises one eyebrow, "I'll take it to the committee head. That's all I can do," and she starts to hang up.

Canter snarls, "Hey, make it fast or I might forget all those names."

She gives him the icy stare again and lays the phone down on the ledge. As she's leaving the room, she faintly hears him yell, "Hurry."

Sonny can't wait to get to her car so she can recopy her notes, add fresh insights, and begin the outline for her article chronicling Canter's incriminating revelations. She drives home in fits and starts, pulling over at regular intervals to jot down all the ideas careening around her brain. When she gets back to DC, she goes straight to the AP office and blasts out her story in one sitting.

It's no surprise that Sonny's article about her exclusive interview with Canter is picked up by every major newspaper and it's a page one blockbuster. The way she describes his efforts to soft talk her into getting him an early parole that backfired when he refused to give her the names of his fellow mobsters is, in short, utterly masterful. And she teases her readers with the prospect that the Senate may relent and transfer Canter to a safer facility so he can finally disclose all that he knows.

During the next few days, she submits an additional trove of information to Congress, including all her private notes from her meeting with Canter, and the committee subpoenas several top DJ's, most notably Dick Clark and Alan Freed, who quickly become the prime focus of the investigation.

Before testifying, Clark, who looks like a clean-cut frat boy, wisely agrees to sell his shares in various music publishing and recording companies. People are shocked when committee chairman Harris calls him "a fine young man" and he somehow escapes prosecution by the skin of his teeth even though most committee members don't believe he's innocent.

The swarthy, disheveled Freed, Mr. Rock and Roll, is defiant and refuses to deny any wrongdoing. Though he only receives a small fine and a six month suspended sentence for commercial bribery, he's fired from both his radio and TV jobs, effectively ending his career and accelerating his descent into a fatal alcoholic abyss.

Freed's head isn't the only one to roll. Several of Steve's friends and acquaintances are indicted for taking Payola and summarily dismissed from their jobs. Phil Lind, a Chicago DJ, confesses that he was paid $22,000 to play a single record. The biggest DJ's in the business, Joe Niagara from Philadelphia, Tom Clay from Detroit, Murray "The K" Kaufman from New York, and Stan Richards from Boston are all called to testify.

After determining that they already have enough evidence to go after many of the small independent labels and the shady characters who own them, the committee decides not to give Canter the transfer he requested. In reality, their real agenda can't wait and the more little guys they can get rid of, the easier it will be to protect the virtual monopoly the large companies have on the business.

In a very public attempt to stop the corruption, Congress eventually demands that station managers, not DJ's, should be in charge of the daily playlists. Everybody in the business is running scared, on the surface anyway, but greed rears its ugly head in new and somewhat predictable ways. The stations make a big show of cleaning up their acts by dutifully changing their policies. The Feds aren't stupid; they know the grease will keep flowing. The only difference is, now the mob and the promoters have fewer pockets to line so the station managers will be easier to catch.

The biggest shock for Steve is the arrest and subsequent indictment of his boss. The promoters who entice Ernie to accept a big wad of cash are actually undercover FBI agents and while they're preparing to take him away in handcuffs, Steve grabs his arm and wheels him around, "Goddam it, Ernie, is it true?"

One of the agents yells, "Sir, step away from Mr. Shiller."

Ernie shrugs his shoulders and smiles, "Stay out of it, Steve, and forget about me. You're on the right side of this and I'm not."

"Was it the money? You already make a shitload."

"Yeah, I know, but my wife wanted a new house and I still gotta pay alimony to my first wife. They offered me so much cash, well, obviously I couldn't refuse."

Steve shoves him, "You dumb son of a bitch."

The agent moves between them and points a finger at Steve, "Sir, I'm not going to warn you again. Step away."

Ernie looks at Steve, his mouth quivers, and he whispers, "I'm sorry."

Thus, the man who convinced Steve to go into radio, the man who changed his life, is out on his ear and the business itself will never be the same.

Sonny is sound asleep at 5:50 AM when the phone on her nightstand rings her awake. Her first thought is that something's wrong with Steve as she fumbles for the phone.

"What? Steve? You okay?"

"Uh, hello, is this Sonny Daye?"

"Why, uh, yes...who's this?"

"This is Sgt. Harris from Leavenworth. The warden told me to call you."

"Why? Is it Maury Canter? Does he want to speak to me?"

"Oh, no Ma'am. Canter's dead. The warden wanted you to be the first to know. Well, the first one outside the prison, anyway."

"What happened? How did he die?"

"He was murdered and we don't know who did it. We're still trying to figure that out. Warden said he'll call you when he knows more. He figured you'd wanna write a story about it."

"Hell yes...I sure do. If I'm not here, I'll be in my office."

"Yes, Ma'am. We have that number. It really hit the fan, if you know what I mean, and we're kinda busy."

"Yes, I'm sure you are. Thanks again."

She puts the phone down and screams, but it doesn't get rid of the inexplicable pang of guilt churning through her like a runaway bulldozer. She can't stop it and she can't explain it.

'It's not my fault. He called me. The deal was his idea. He volunteered the info. Well, not at first. I did sort of drag it out of him. That's what I'm supposed to do. That's my job so it's not my fault he was murdered. Obviously, somebody didn't want him to talk. Hell, several people were probably afraid he'd rat 'em out.'

Later that afternoon, the warden called her and asked if she had a fresh sheet of paper in her typewriter. That never happened before, but then again, nothing like this entire saga has ever been so meticulously described…by any reporter. Her headline screamed: *They Slit His Throat from Ear to Ear* . Her groundbreaking story instantly became a journalistic legend and so did she.

To no one's surprise, the reporter who exposed the corruption responsible for the seismic shift that changed an entire industry had already come to the attention of the Pulitzer Prize Board and her Canter story sealed the deal. They eagerly accepted Sonny's nomination from the Associated Press and promptly awarded her the Prize and the prestigious Gold Medal in the public service category of the journalism competition. How fitting. Her tireless efforts embody the very essence of public service and these accolades are sweet revenge for the one that got away.

When she calls her parents to tell them the news, her mother answers and almost drops the phone.

"Sonny, really? And the Gold Medal?"

"Yes…and the Gold Medal."

Elizabeth continues as if she's thinking out loud, "Why, I hardly know what to say. I, I'm surprised, but then again, I really shouldn't be surprised, should I. That story about Maury Canter was so scathing it was delicious, but we've been following all your stories, no, we've been following your mission. Yes, you are on a mission and it's all we ever talk about. Great reporting, yes, great reporting for sure. So great, the landscape of the entire music business has changed. No mean feat that."

"Mom? Hello, earth to Mom."

"What? Oh, Sonny, um, let me get your father."

There's a lot of commotion in the background and Archie says, "Sonny, your mother's babbling like a fool. What's wrong?"

"Nothing, Daddy, everything's great. I won a Pulitzer for my Payola story."

Silence.

"Daddy? Are you there?"

Silence.

"DADDY!"

He clears his throat and blows his nose.

"'Scuse me, Darlin', I thought I could never be prouder of you and now, by God, I am."

"Oh, Daddy, you're so sweet. You know I never could have done it without your support. After all, you taught me how to write."

"Yeah, maybe, but this goes way beyond writing. You have a calling, pure and simple. Your stories are so incisive, so beautifully written. We save all of them and keep them in a big folder."

There's more commotion and then, "Give me that phone. Sonny."

"Uh, yes, Mom."

"I have been a fool and I need to apologize to you and your father."

"Why? What for?"

"Isn't it obvious? All this time I wasn't satisfied with my career because I never got enough recognition; I never won any prizes. Yet the real prizes were right in front of me all along. You and your father are the greatest gifts anyone could ever wish for. Please know that I am profoundly sorry for being such a self-centered idiot all these years. Whatever it is you have with Steve and Bo, well, as far as I'm concerned, it's some sort of serendipitous magic. Congratulations, Sonny, and like your father, I couldn't be more proud of you."

Silence.

"Sonny? Do you hear me?"

She sniffs and says, "Yes, now you made me cry."

Steve's show has happily hummed along ever since he calmly kicked out the Turtle several months ago. Though thankfully forgotten by most people, the ogre suddenly emerges from the shadows to exact his revenge. He buys a full-page ad in the Washington Post:

That DJ, Steve Rasco, is really second-rate
What's more, as a friend, he's such an ingrate
My wit and my wisdom did make him a star
But he threw me aside after I took him so far
Now he has a dog that grunts and growls
A perfect mascot for the dumb night owls
Oh, I'll show the man with mind so feeble
I'll find a new way to reach more people
Don't believe for a moment that I am uncouth
For the world deserves to know my real truth
So I'll keep to myself and hide in my shell
Until I make sure that you all go to Hell

The Turtle

Instead of harming Steve, the Turtle's ad in the Post raises public   awareness for Steve's show. In fact, many people who had never heard of him start to tune in, call in, and happily join Rasco's Rascals. Now, the only complaints he gets are from some of the new recruits who say they fall asleep at work because they stay up way past their bedtimes listening to the show.

Sonny isn't getting much sleep either. Winning the Pulitzer has vaulted her into another dimension altogether and she's besieged by interview requests from both the famous and the infamous to the point that she has to be very selective and carefully weed out the opportunists from the serious subjects. More often than not, she tends to court those world leaders, business titans, and celebrities who don't chase her. They're the people who make the world go round and her innate ability to peel away the layers of their complex personalities makes for some very interesting, very revealing reading.

Sonny begins a cavalcade of interviews in 1959 that set her apart from any other journalist in the country, if not the entire world. Her favorite interview makes headlines far beyond the Associated Press. After not being allowed to visit Disneyland due to security concerns during his "goodwill" visit to the US, Soviet Premier Nikita Khrushchev meets with Eleanor Roosevelt at Springwood, her home in Hyde Park, New York. Jake calls in a favor so Sonny can attend the meeting and write the official account of the historic event. And he suggests that she take Bo along as her bodyguard and de facto wingman.

Khrushchev is startled when Sonny says, "Bo, introduce yourself to Mr. Khrushchev." Bo promptly sits in front of him and offers his right paw. Khrushchev hesitates and looks quizzically at Sonny before gingerly shaking Bo's paw. A mock headline flashes into Sonny's mind: "Blustery Russian Premier Dumbfounded by American Dog."

Something profound happens to Sonny during the course of the meeting as she begins operating on an entirely different level, transcending mere reporting, and hitting her stride as a masterful interviewer. Ostensibly, she's there to write an account of the two-way conversation between Mrs. Roosevelt and Khrushchev, but she begins interjecting disarming questions that elicit the same kind of candid responses that Steve gets from his callers. Now, both of them are tapping into the nation's psyche by allowing and encouraging people to bare their souls and speak openly about any number of personal subjects.

When she asks Khrushchev if he has a personal question for Mrs. Roosevelt, he's visibly taken aback. Then he clears his throat, turns to his interpreter, and says something in Russian. It turns out, he wants to know how her husband, Franklin Roosevelt, managed to be elected to four consecutive terms in a democracy since the only way Russian leaders stay in power is through brute force, intimidation, and murder. Mrs. Roosevelt calmly responds that our democracy is a miracle because it has fundamentally changed the way we treat one another as human beings. Thus, the conversation between Roosevelt, the tall upper crust American, and Khrushchev, the squat Russian peasant, quickly turns into a rather lopsided affair. Damn...dumbfounded again.

Sonny has a ball interviewing Rocky Marciano, the undefeated heavyweight boxing champion. What a great guy...humble, down to earth, a perfect gentleman. He was considering a comeback after retiring in 1956 with a 49-0 record, but after he sits down with Sonny, he quickly decides that it was a bad idea and thanks her for helping him figure it out.

Sonny's next interview proves to be more of a challenge. Fidel Castro, the new Prime Minister of Cuba, visits the US hoping to gain support from our government though he's an avowed Marxist revolutionary. After failing to curry favor with anyone in Washington, Castro and his entourage travel to New York City to blow off some steam.

Sonny gets a call from one of Castro's lieutenants, Che Guevara, who tells her that the Prime Minister of Cuba would like to grant an exclusive interview to the prize-winning AP reporter who wrote about the meeting between Premier Khrushchev and Mrs. Roosevelt. Jake loves the idea and gives her his blessing so off to New York she goes.

At first, she listens patiently as the long-winded revolutionary expounds on everything from Marxism to baseball to Latin jazz. Then she asks several pointed questions about his background, his education, and why he chose the Socialist path. In the end, his answers bring to light the private side of the complicated, brilliant man that no one has ever seen before and her article becomes a must-read for people from every walk of life.

Going forward, Sonny won't let anyone dodge a question with pithy platitudes and hollow generalizations. If a world leader tries to play the "classified" card, she gets even more suspicious and more determined to ferret out the truth. She prods, she pushes, she challenges, and always seems to be one step ahead of her subjects, ever ready with a swift rejoinder that will stop their evasive behavior. All the while, she never resorts to being combative, disrespectful, or threatening. She doesn't have to. Her disarming beauty coupled with her razor sharp intellect move men to ingratiate themselves with her and women to befriend her. Everyone knows what happened to the man who lied to her and, worse yet, tried to intimidate her. It didn't end well for him.

One day, as Sonny sits at her desk preparing for interviews with the presumptive nominees for the 1960 Presidential election, Vice-President Richard Nixon and

Senator John Kennedy, her phone rings and her life takes another exciting turn.

"Sonny Daye."

"Hello, Sonny. This is the Turtle."

After all her years of reporting and all the important people she's been around, the mere sound of his voice sends a shot of adrenaline through her body and she almost giggles out loud before composing herself.

"Why, hello. To what do I owe the honor?"

"Ah, the honor is all mine. I've been admiring your terrific reporting and your celebrity interviews. You really put Khrushchev through the wringer."

"Oh, I wasn't that hard on him. Mrs. Roosevelt did most of the heavy lifting. Now then, how can I help you?"

"Glad you asked. You know, I liked being on Steve's show alright, even though it was only a local program, but I really want to reach the entire country. Now that you're famous and have a national following, I think you should interview me."

She almost giggles again as she muses to herself, 'Wow, he really is a delusional egomaniac,' and she deadpans, "Um, let's set the record straight. Steve barred you from his show because your behavior was too despicable for radio and now you think you deserve a national audience? That'll never happen on my watch. Goodbye."

She quickly hangs up in the nick of time before she cracks up and yells, "What a freak. He'll be back...no doubt about it."

People in the newsroom stop what they're doing and stare at her as if she's lost her mind. When she notices them, she sobers up and mumbles into thin air, "Aw, just another crank call. Everybody wants to be famous." Then she stands up, heads straight for Jake's office, and walks right in as usual.

"Jake, guess what?"

He looks up from his desk with a fake smile, "Gee, Sonny, I can't imagine. Please tell me...what."

"The Turtle just called and wants me to interview him."

"You mean that lunatic Steve kicked off his show?"

"Yes. Can you believe it?"

He frowns and shakes his head, "What I can't believe is that you're excited about it for some odd reason. Have you run out of powerful, famous people to interview?"

"Oh, of course not, but he's more interesting than most of them."

"You're scaring me, Sonny."

"Jake, stop it. If you ever listened to him on Steve's show, you'd understand what an amazing character he is. Some of his ideas are wacky. I'll grant you that, but every once in a while, he comes up with some brilliant shit."

Yeah, and that's just what we need at the AP... some brilliant shit."

"Jake, trust me. I know what I'm doing."

"Well, what happened? Did you interview him on the phone?"

"No, I hung up on him, but when he calls back, I'll egg him on and see if he has any pearls of wisdom worth printing."

"You hung up on him and you're sure he'll call back. What if you pissed him off and he calls another reporter?"

"No way. He's all mine. You'll see." She storms out of his office laughing and slams the door behind her. He stares blankly into space for a moment before saying, "And I keep thinking I'm the boss. Ha, silly me."

Sonny is so excited about the Turtle, she can't wait to tell Steve and she literally accosts him when she gets home.

"You won't believe who called me at the office."

He grins and holds out his arms, "Hi, Steve. How was your day?"

She rolls her eyes, gives him a perfunctory peck on the cheek, and continues, "Oh, c'mon, can't you see I'm really excited?"

"Okay, okay, who called you?"

"The Turtle. He wants me to interview him."

"What? "The Turtle? Are you sure? I thought he fell off the face of the earth."

"Oh, it was him alright. I'd know that creepy voice anywhere."

"Well, I hope you didn't talk to him."

"I can't believe you're saying that. Why the hell did you spend so much time talking to him on the air?"

"You know why…because he was so entertaining?"

"Duh. So what's wrong with me wanting to talk to him for the very same reason?"

"Correct me if I'm wrong, but you're not an entertainment reporter. You deal in hard news and important interviews with prominent people, not someone who routinely goes off the deep end."

"But you told me the Turtle has the courage to say what a lot of people are thinking. He's kind of a nasty Everyman and I think it would be fun to draw him out on any number of issues."

"Look, I know enough not to tell you what to do, but you can't blame me for being a bit protective. He almost ruined my show and I don't want him to harm your career."

"Take it easy. In fact, I hung up on him when he said he wanted me to interview him."

"Why'd you do that if you think he'd be fun to talk to?"

"I didn't want to seem too eager. He'll call back. I know he will."

"You're probably right. He doesn't give up easily. Just be careful. Okay?"

She nuzzles up against him, "With him, I'll be careful. With you, I'll be daring," and she gives him a big, sloppy kiss.

Barring the Turtle from the show has made Steve a local folk hero and he needs Bo's help more than ever because he's busier than ever. Standing up to a bully is an almost impossible task for most people, but not for Steve. True, he did it because he was told to, but he was forceful, confident, and fearless…thus setting a standard for all.

While he had already broken some incredible new ground in radio, his courage has allowed the conversation to reach an entirely new level by engaging and empowering a larger group of silent people who never would have participated during the reign of the Turtle.

It also gets the attention of some very important advertising agencies and their clients because one of the most effective tools for any advertiser is a trusted, highly respected personality. Steve has now become an ideal spokesman and his career takes off in a whole new direction. He always had tremendous success doing local ads and now he starts getting offers to do regional and national commercials for ridiculous amounts of money.

His rich, baritone voice, his affable public persona, and his talented sidekick make him an irresistible force in advertising. He can't help finding the humor in the situation, especially since he never cared that much about money or notoriety. Throughout his adult life, he always seemed to have more than enough money and he never wanted to be famous. Now, thanks to Sonny, Bo, and his beloved Rascals, he's making terrific money and having a blast in the process.

Now that Steve is busy doing voice-overs in the afternoons and occasionally flies to New York to do commercials, Sonny gladly takes Bo to the office with her more often and he loves being around all his old pals again. He also senses that something of great importance is afoot and he's right. The 1960 presidential election is only a few months away and it has all the makings of being one for the history books.

Vice-President Richard Nixon is the Republican candidate, but the real news is the excitement surrounding the candidacy of the young, 43-year-old Democratic senator from Massachusetts, John Kennedy: the wealthy, strikingly handsome, decorated war hero, and Harvard grad, whose elegant wife, Jackie, looks like a Vogue model and speaks fluent French to boot.

Nixon is the stronger, incumbent candidate since he's been Eisenhower's VP for the last 8 years, but he's being overpowered by the Kennedy mystique that's sweeping the country. Kennedy's only real problem is the fact that he's Catholic and, so far, all our presidents have been Protestant. But none of that seems to matter to most women; they'd probably vote for him if he were a Communist.

And, for the first time in history, there are televised presidential debates. Nixon is no fool. He's a well-seasoned politician with excellent debating skills. Most of the people who listen to the debates on radio think he wins hands down. TV is a different story altogether and permanently turns the tide in the election. While he handles himself quite well, Nixon looks like he's scared stiff. He sweats profusely and has a grimy looking five o'clock shadow, but Kennedy has a gorgeous tan and professional makeup. He looks terrific and his suave Boston accent excites the general public to no end. Most people have never heard anything like it and they're mesmerized whenever he speaks.

All of this is nothing short of catnip for columnists and the rest of the news media as well, not to mention Steve's coterie of crackpots. All of a sudden, women start calling in and gushing about the dashing Senator. Save for Trudy and Dorothy, the vast majority of callers have always been men and this feminine intrusion irks some of Steve's regulars to no end. Not only has the grumpy fraternity been breached, these insurgent women are giddy with the prospect of a sexy young president instead of a stodgy old one.

Just when Sonny thinks she couldn't get any busier, the Turtle calls again.

"Sonny Daye."

"It's me."

She grins and cradles the phone on her shoulder while she grabs her notepad before responding, "Hello, Me, where've you been?"

"Well, I've been collecting some very important, secret facts to tell you."

"Really…and how do you find these secret facts?"

"I hire investigators, very special investigators. You know, Sonny, you can find out just about anything if you're willing to pay the right people to snoop around."

She laughs, "Is that your business? Snooping?"

"I beg your pardon. I'm interested in helping you divulge these nuggets of truth to the public."

"Okay, if your business isn't snooping, then what is it and how can you afford to hire all these special investigators?"

"Oh, money is no problem. I have quite a lot and you should be grateful I'm willing to spend it to help you."

"Ha, what makes you think I need your help?"

"Because I know things you don't."

"Try me."

"Uh, uh, not unless you promise to give me credit."

"No dice. I'm going to hang up now."

"No, wait."

"Why should I?"

"Because I'm going to tell you something that will change the course of history. Ready?"

"Alright, let's have it, but you'd better have some ironclad proof."

"Do you know the United States was founded by Freemasons?"

"Uh, that's not news. George Washington was a Freemason and people refer to him as the founder of our country."

"But do you know that Benjamin Franklin and James Monroe were also Masons?"

"No, what if they were? A lot of men are Masons."

"Yes, a lot of very powerful men. Do you know the real reason they started this new country with this new type of government, was so they could eventually rule the entire world?"

She rolls her eyes and looks at her watch, "Look, I really don't have time for your tall tales. Come back when you have something real to report."

"Why do you think, of all the countries in the world, we were the one that invented the A-bomb?"

"That's easy. We were damn lucky Einstein immigrated here from Germany before the war. Oh, wait, are you going to tell me that Einstein was a Freemason?"

"No, but the people who brought him here are the same Masons who run our shadow government."

'Now he's giving me the creeps.'

She laughs derisively, "Yeah, and I'm the Queen of England. Bye bye," and she hangs up.

Then she looks at her notes and tries to collect her thoughts, 'I wonder if…no, he's full of it. Yet, what if some of it's true? So what if the Masons are a secretive bunch…no crime in that. Maybe I should do some of my own research. Ugh, no way. I hardly have time to pee as it is.'

However, throughout the rest of the day, Sonny can't get the Turtle's accusations out of her mind. She prattles to Bo on their way home until he can't stand it any longer and sticks his head out the window, trying in vain to get some relief from her mental meanderings. When they walk into the apartment, they head straight to her study where she recopies her notes, and adds her own thoughts. Next, she clears off the bulletin board and pins her notes all over it. She stands back for a few moments to get some perspective, then lunges forward and rearranges the notes into distinct groups, always looking for correlations and especially the threads that align with her ideas, threads that could open up possible avenues of investigation. She stands back again, folds her arms in disgust, and mutters, "Just what I need…another job."

The front door slams and Steve's voice rudely invades her reverie, "Sonny, where are you?"

She doesn't move a muscle, "In here."

"Can you be more specific?"

Annoyed by the interruption, she answers sarcastically, "In my study?"

He walks into the room and he's welcomed by Bo's thumping tail, but ignored by Sonny who's glaring at the notes on the board. He leans down and gives Bo a good scratching, well-aware that Sonny is onto something big and he probably should leave her alone. He wisely starts to leave, but she blurts out, "He called again."

He stops and grins at her, "Is 'he' a reptile?"

"Yup. He sure is."

He motions at the board, "And what's all this?"

"It's my futile attempt to make sense of everything he told me."

"A conspiracy theory, perhaps?"

"How'd you know?"

"Easy...he's got a bunch of 'em. What was today's flavor?"

"Uh, the Freemasons secretly run the country?"

"Whoa, never heard that one. Was he convincing?"

"Don't laugh, but sort of?"

"Yeah, he's good at that. He could talk the bark off a tree."

"No shit. I kinda felt like a sucker, but at the same time, I was really intrigued."

"How'd the conversation end?"

"Oh, I hung up on him again."

He throws his head back and roars, "You do realize that you're in a cat and mouse game with a certified lunatic, don't you?"

"Shut up."

"Sonny."

"What?"

"No need to get defensive. I'm only trying to help."

"Don't need your help. Bo and I can figure this out."

"Well, up yours."

She laughs, "Ooo, sounds good to me."

Sonny finally gets to interview Kennedy and Nixon shortly after the debates. Naturally, she writes two incisive pieces that reveal more then anyone could have expected and much more than her subjects intended. Nixon really knows his stuff, chapter and verse. You name a subject and he's totally prepared to discuss it intelligently and concisely. Whereas, Kennedy tends to answer in broad strokes, filled with flowery language and bold promises, punctuated by an impish sense of humor. DC pundits are nearly universal in their praise for her interviews and laud her for getting both men to be so candid.

The Turtle has a much different opinion.

"Sonny Daye."

"Don't you dare hang up on me. I have extremely important information that you can't get anywhere else."

"I told you I don't have time for your verbal shenanigans. Either prove what you say or take a hike."

"I bet you've done your own investigating about the Freemasons, haven't you?"

Stunned again, 'How the hell did he know? Not that I was able to corroborate anything he said.'

She gets very businesslike, "Of course I did. I have to look under every rock, even when they're figments of an untethered imagination."

"Maybe you don't know where to look. Maybe my investigators are better at it than you are. Sonny, I'm only here to give you the benefit of my resources."

"Ha, nice try, but I'm going to hang up now."

"I know a secret about John Kennedy."

She chuckles to herself, 'What a conniving little shit. Okay, I'll listen to him once more, but that's it.'

"I don't have time for idle gossip."

"It isn't gossip and I can prove it. Why do you think I called you?"

"Just my lucky day?"

"Because the nation deserves me."

She laughs audibly, "And what have the American people done to deserve you?"

"It's not funny. I'm a patriot and they deserve to hear the truth from me because we're all in this together."

"Then, by all means, let's have it. What's the secret about John Kennedy that America deserves to know?"

"Are you ready?

"Pins and needles."

"First of all, let me remind you that our so-called democracy is only an illusion. The Freemasons control the Electoral College and they elect the President, we don't. As for Kennedy, he'll take orders from the Pope; all Catholic leaders do. Know why? The priests secretly record everything people say during confession so they can use it for blackmail."

"Never call me again," and she hangs up.

Because of their packed schedules and the additional time Sonny spends at the Library of Congress trying to make even a shred of sense out of the Turtle's flights of fancy, she and Steve are lucky if they see each other at all during a typical work week. They routinely forget who's supposed to take Bo and they also forget to buy groceries. Most of the time they end up living on leftover Chinese food. Bo prefers Moo Shu Pork and egg rolls with duck sauce. He also loves to watch Sonny and Steve try to use chopsticks because they're both clumsy and keep dropping their food.

She sees him staring at her and snaps, "Oh, gimme a break, Bo. I don't make fun of you when you burp after gulping your food down."

He looks away for the moment, then right back at her and laughs when she plops a big wonton in her soup and it splashes everywhere.

Steve giggles and says, "Why are you worried about him? We're both terrible with chopsticks. I think we should give up and use forks."

She grits her teeth. "Suit yourself, but I'm gonna master these goddam sticks as long as I don't starve in the process."

"Something bothering you?"

"Uh huh, but it shouldn't…ah, what the hell."

"Ooo, sounds juicy."

"Yeah, and then some. The Turtle called me again yesterday."

"Why are you just telling me now?"

"It's the first chance I've had. No, that's not true. I wasn't going to tell you because I thought it was stupid, but it's been gnawing at me."

"Why? What'd he say?"

"It wasn't so much what he said as the way he said it. He's so tricky with his words, he'd make a terrific politician if he weren't completely off his rocker."

He laughs, "Hey, as far as I'm concerned, several members of Congress are just as crazy as the Turtle and most of them aren't as smart."

"Steve, I'm serious. This guy may be more dangerous than we thought."

"Well, what exactly did he say?"

"Only that Kennedy takes orders from the Pope because priests secretly record people's confessions to use for blackmail. Oh, and our democracy is a farce because Freemasons control the Electoral College and they decide who'll be President."

"Wow, you're right. That really is dangerous. Can you imagine how much damage either of those rumors could cause? Trouble is, as wildly absurd as they sound, a helluva lot of people would probably believe both of them."

"I don't even want to think about it. It would have a catastrophic effect on the country, not to mention the election."

"You think the Turtle's saying that because he wants Nixon to win?"

"Nah, I think he's very well-spoken, very intelligent, and clinically insane."

"I know and I can't imagine a more dangerous combination."

"Me either. Anyway, I'll never talk to him again and you'll never let him back on your show so, hopefully, he won't be able to find a platform for his insanity."

What a challenge. Steve and Sonny go about their work with a clear sense of duty coupled with a nagging dose of dread. Jake keeps bugging Sonny about the Turtle, asking whether she's been able to substantiate any of his assertions. She says the only thing she's been able to substantiate is that he's dangerously deranged and that she finally got fed up and told him to stop calling her.

Luckily, the Turtle remains silent and the fierce campaign ends with Kennedy eking out a victory by the slimmest margin of popular votes in history: a scant 112 thousand out of 68 million total. That's roughly a tenth of a percent. However, in the Electoral College where it counts, he wins by a whopping 16 percent, thus becoming the youngest President ever elected and the first Catholic.

True to his patrician upbringing, he wears a silk top hat for his inauguration and ushers in an era that soon becomes known as our own Camelot. He and Jackie throw marvelous state dinners. She completely refurbishes the White House, changing the interior from staid to stunning with authentic period antiques, priceless art, and even oversees a complete reconfiguration of the President's Oval Office. America loves it. The country revels in a whirlwind of hope, strength, and daring to dream that Kennedy's promised "New Frontier" is truly within reach.

It's such a shame when the business of actually running the country interrupts your personal pursuit of greatness. Just when everything seems to be going along as planned for the fair-haired new President, a covert CIA operation known as the "Bay of Pigs Invasion" fails miserably and embarrasses Kennedy only three months after his inauguration. A year earlier, President Eisenhower approved of and funded the CIA proposed plan to overthrow the Communist-leaning revolutionary regime of Fidel Castro in Cuba. It was widely known that Castro and Russia shared not only the same ideological beliefs, they also shared an ingrained hatred of the United States.

After taking office, Kennedy is immediately briefed about the ongoing operation and bullied into giving his approval with the following statements: "Don't worry, Mr. President, we're using Cuban ex-pats and South American mercenaries to do the dirty work on the ground. We're overseeing the operation from a safe distance by supplying air support with unmarked planes. It'll look like the Cuban people rose up on their own to take their country back."

The invasion is successful at first, but Castro himself assumes command of the Cuban forces and soundly routs the invaders after three days of fighting. Several members of the CIA-led force are killed, many more are captured and executed, but before they die, they implicate the US, hoping to have their own lives spared. It doesn't work and we subsequently impose a complete trade embargo with Cuba which necessitates and strengthens Castro's relationship with Russia.

Two days after it's over, Sonny hugs Steve when he comes home after work and says, "How in the world are you able to handle the horrendous firestorm of hatred and confusion spewing from your listeners?"

"What else can I do. Everybody has to face the fact that our fair- haired new President just blew it big time. There's no way to sugarcoat it. The first major event of his presidency is a major disaster and my callers have every right to be upset. They're justifiably horrified that our big, powerful government could be so stupid. You're lucky the AP doesn't publish letters from your readers. If you did, you probably wouldn't have room for anything else."

"But you're so calm and collected on the air. Wow, you're good, better than I ever could have imagined. Oh, I meant to tell you, one of my Agency contacts said the Cubans knew about it ahead of time and they were obviously ready for it."

"Well, I have to stay calm and, more important, I have to stay neutral. If I get emotional or take a side, the whole show will go to hell in a hand basket. And yeah, it's always a bad idea to play where the other guy has the home field advantage, especially when he knows about your plan. We were blinded by our own bravado and ended up getting spanked.

As a result, a lot of people are genuinely shaken because their hopes for a fresh start with Kennedy have been dashed to pieces. There's an avalanche of new listeners who want a chance to vent their frustrations. I guess it's because we're the only game in town, the only outlet they have. It's crazy. It used to be easy to goof around with my old callers since most of them were completely off the wall, but these new people, whoa, they're serious as a heart attack.

One guy said Nixon never would have blown it the way Kennedy did and then he challenged me to a debate. When I said it was my job to facilitate the discussion, not to be a part of it, he said, 'Well, you're obviously a liberal pinko who voted for Kennedy and I dare you to defend him.' I couldn't help laughing which obviously pissed him off and he started cussing like a sailor so I cut him off."

"What happened then?"

"What happened? All hell broke loose. Jimmy, the engineer, said he thought the phone was gonna blow up...all ten lines were blinking like crazy during the entire show and they were still lit up when we left the studio. Some people agreed with the guy, others called him a fascist, then they started calling each other names.   By the way, I'm really glad Bo's been with me the past few days."

"Why? What does he do?"

"He lets me vent my frustrations during the commercials and helps me regain my composure. He also nuzzles his head under my hand so I'll scratch his ears or he sits up on his hind legs and makes me laugh. When he does those things, my anxiety literally floats away. If we could bottle him, we'd make a mint. So what's it been like at your office?"

"Ha, first of all, you know I stopped trying to corroborate all the Turtle's bullshit well before this Bay of Pigs thing happened, right?"

"Yeah, you took down all the notes on your bulletin board. By the way, I'm sure glad he wasn't a part of my show this week. He would've made it a lot worse."

"Well, speaking of a lot worse...wait here." She walks into her study and reappears with two Xerox copies. "This was sitting on my desk when I got to work this morning."

She holds up the first copy in front of his face and he looks at it with his mouth agape. It shows a regular envelope and, instead of being handwritten or typed, each individual letter of her name and the address of the AP office looks like it's been cut out of a magazine and pasted onto the envelope. There are only two words pasted in the upper left hand corner of the envelope: *The Turtle*. The whole thing resembles a typical ransom note you might see on a TV cop show.

What did you think when you saw it?"

"Think? I didn't think. After Bo sniffed it and growled at it, I screamed for Jake. He took one look, told me not to touch it, and called the FBI. They sent a forensic team within the hour. Steve, they all wore white gloves and they dusted the envelope for fingerprints. Next, they carefully opened it, took out the letter, and dusted it as well. They said he must have used tweezers to cut and paste the letters because there were no fingerprints anywhere. Plus, they told us they tried to track down the Turtle after he bought the ad in the Post that was aimed at you, but he paid for it with a cashier's check through the mail so they hit a dead end."

She hands him the second copy, "Here, this was inside."

It also has the same cut and paste letters.

> All great kingdoms will crumble
> When leaders begin to fumble
> Emperor, Führer, King, or Tsar
> It doesn't matter who you are
> When you lose the power to lead
> The people will make you bleed
> Then string you up and let you rot
> So they can forget your Camelot

After reading it several times, he looks up at her, his mouth moves, and nothing comes out.

She nods her head, "Exactly...Jake and I were speechless, too."

"What did the Feds say?"

"Not much...they never do, but they took the letter and the envelope with them. Jake said they'll definitely show it to the Secret Service. Obviously, it's one thing to foment unsubstantiated rumors, but this is a direct, craven threat against the President."

Thankfully, the letter is the last communication from the Turtle and he eventually falls off the FBI radar. Despite obvious chinks in the Camelot armor, most people regain faith in Kennedy and continue to be enamored with every aspect of the First Family. Women buy "Pillbox" hats like the ones Jackie wears. College kids are smitten with his brand of social idealism and thousands volunteer for his pet project, the Peace Corps, designed to help underdeveloped nations around the world and advocate American ideals.

Speaking of pets, Steve has a fantastic idea in the fall of 1962 when it dawns on him that Bo is 20 years old because they always figured he was born in 1942. This calls for a party, albeit a very private one. It's not like you can broadcast it on the evening news or send out an AP press release. First of all, nobody would believe it. Secondly, if people did believe it, it would almost certainly cause an uproar. Big dogs don't live this long. Only little pipsqueaks like Chihuahuas have a shot at getting to be this old. Not to mention the fact that Bo still doesn't have any gray whiskers. Steve's now in his early forties and has a dignified dusting of gray at his temples. Sonny, in her mid-thirties, goes nuts when she sees a gray hair and viciously plucks it out. Bo? He just keeps getting better and stronger as time goes by.

Sonny loves the idea of a birthday celebration, but the question is, what kind of a present can they get him? He can only eat so much and he doesn't really need anything.

Then she comes up with a great idea, "Steve, what's Bo's favorite thing?"

"Uh, besides food?"

"Yeah, what does he absolutely love the most?"

"Oh, I get it..water and swimming. Right?"

"Yes! Let's take him to the Delaware coast so he can swim in the ocean and run wild on the beach. What do you say?"

"Sure, I know a great place...Rehoboth Beach. It's practically deserted. He can go crazy and nobody will bother us."

They're able to rent the perfect little cabin on a quiet stretch of beach, but the three hour ride from DC is a tough one for Bo. He can hardly contain himself. Sonny and Steve keep humming *Happy Birthday* and he clearly understands that they're singing to him. He knows the song. Who doesn't? This difference is, nobody ever sang it to him before. Will there be balloons, cake, and presents? He doesn't like cake, though he'll dutifully eat a piece if they give him one.

When they arrive at the cottage, he bounds out of the car and runs around in gleeful circles, barking his head off. He skids to a stop and sits at attention in front of Sonny, begging for permission to play. She bends down and says, "Here, let me take off your dog tags so you don't lose them in the ocean."

He quickly backs away from her and defiantly shakes his head, "No!"

Steve puts his hand on her shoulder and says, "Sonny, those dog tags belong to him and I doubt he'll ever part with them. Let him go."

She laughs and says, "You're right. Here I am, acting like a protective mother when he's always two steps ahead of me."

She looks at Bo and says, "Go on, go play."

Swoosh...he's off in a blur, up and down the beach, back and forth countless times. Next, he walks up to the incoming surf and licks it. Phooey, it's too salty and he spits it out. Then he backs up, crouches down, streaks toward the water, and takes a giant leap that propels him a hundred feet out into the ocean. Sonny and Steve, dumbfounded once again, look at each other, and then at the vast expanse of water. Bo is nowhere in sight.

Sonny says, "Holy shit! Where is he? Can you see him?"

"No, hope he's okay. Ah, you know he is. He's probably..."

Bo explodes twenty feet straight out of the water, howling with glee, and dives back in. When he surfaces again, he starts jumping around on the surface of the water like a frog hopping from one lily pad to the next.

"Uh, yeah, like I was about to say, he's probably getting his sea legs, so to speak."

They giggle and hug each other. Sonny says, "Whew, guess we got him the right present."

"Yup, we sure did. C'mon, let's go inside and get settled. He'll come back when he's done acting like a manic dolphin."

As soon as they walk in, Steve turns on the radio, and some nice jazz wafts through the cabin. He grabs Sonny's hand and says in a southern drawl, "Excuse me, Ma'am, may I have this dance?"

"Why, I do declare, Sir. You are being rather forward, aren't you?"

"Oh, yes Ma'am. I don't know how much time we'll have before the birthday boy comes a runnin' in here all wet and smelly."

A frantic voice on the radio says, "We interrupt this program to bring you a special broadcast from the President of the United States."

They stare at each other in shocked disbelief as Kennedy calmly describes the dire situation at hand. American spy planes flying reconnaissance over Cuba have taken aerial photos that definitely show several Russian missiles that typically carry nuclear warheads. He finishes by announcing that he has ordered a military blockade to prevent any more missiles from entering Cuba. Then, in a very measured tone, he issues an ultimatum to Khrushchev: "Remove all of them immediately or run the risk of all-out war."

Sonny says, "Well, this has to be one of the shortest birthday parties on record." She runs outside and screams, "Bo, come!"

In an instant, he appears out of nowhere, sits at attention in front of her, and awaits her next command.

"Oh, Bo, I'm so sorry, but we have to go home now."

Without hesitation, he shakes himself dry, and waits by the car. Steve comes out of the cabin with all their luggage and finds Sonny wiping a tear from her eye.

"Sonny? What's wrong?"

"Oh, nothing's wrong. I just told him we had to leave and he's such a trooper, he didn't complain, he's waiting by the car. I feel terrible for him."

"Uh, I think he knows something big's going on from the tone of your voice and, anyway, he's just had the time of his life. We'll come back. I promise."

"Right, I hope we live long enough to come back."

Khrushchev's famous quote, "We will bury you," that he uttered at a diplomatic reception in 1956, is featured on radio, television, and in newspapers everywhere. The nation and the rest of the world remain in a state of mortal shock for thirteen horrible days. Sonny stays in her office at the AP and Steve bunks at the station with Bo. They only see each other once during that two week period. After eight days of non-stop terror, she can't take it any longer and she goes to see him late one night. To be honest, standing alone on the precipice of hell has been nerve-wracking. She needs a big hug and then some.

She runs into the station and heads straight for Steve's office. She opens the door and he's lying on his couch, taking a nap with a newspaper draped over his chest. Bo sits up and thumps his tail on the floor, but Steve doesn't move a muscle.

She goes, "Pssst." No response. She clears her throat. Still no response. She looks at Bo and nods toward Steve. He gets up close to Steve's face and snorts him awake with one breath.

"Whoa...what the..."

Bo laughs and then licks him mercilessly until he sits up.

"Take it easy. What're you doin', Boy?" Then he sees Sonny standing there with a huge grin on her face and he laughs, "And what're you doin', Woman?"

"Why, I'm doin' you, Man."

She leads Bo out the door and says, "You wait here for a minute, okay?" He lies down with a loud groan and rolls his eyes up at her. "Really, I'll just be a minute."

She goes back into the office, locks the door behind her, and walks over to the couch. She opens her coat to reveal that she's wearing absolutely nothing underneath and says, "Did you miss me?"

He covers his face with his hands and says, "Yes, but please be gentle. I'm fragile, you know."

Secret Service agents follow Kennedy and his brother Bobby, the Attorney General, as they walk around the outside of the White House for hours on end, whispering, arguing, laughing, and even crying as they struggle to find a solution. After long and laborious negotiations, Khrushchev blinks first, he and Kennedy finally reach an agreement, and the world breathes a collective sigh of relief.

Russia will remove all missiles from Cuba and allow the process to be verified by the United Nations. In return, the US publicly agrees never to invade Cuba unless provoked. While Kennedy is hailed as a hero by the news media, many government insiders are scared stiff by his seemingly capricious decision making process. They think he got lucky and they hate the fact that he and Bobby excluded other top advisors from most of their deliberations.

One of them grumbles, "For all we know, they make decisions with the flip of a coin."

Any President and his appointed Cabinet are generally viewed with utter disdain by the entrenched Washington bureaucracy as temporary employees at best. Kennedy's snotty, superior attitude makes the situation worse than usual and the Secret Service adds fuel to the fire by divulging some of the conversations they overhear to their old cronies.

However, once the crisis is over, Jack and Bobby go about their daily business with renewed vigor, one of Jack's favorite words, and an even greater sense of entitlement. Jack parties harder than ever and Bobby's new crusade is ridding the country of organized crime by any and all means, thus breaking the deal the brothers made to leave the mob alone if they delivered the union vote. The Kennedys don't understand that it doesn't matter who you are or how powerful your are, some dragons should never be poked.

In the months following the Cuban Missile Crisis, Sonny and Steve settle back into their jobs with more relief than anything else, happy to be focusing on the upcoming presidential election next year. After all that just happened, the daily grind isn't that bad at all. It's a pleasure to go to work, go home, walk Bo, watch some TV, and try to lower your blood pressure to pre-crisis levels. Mundane things are now preferable to nail-biting excitement; most people have had enough of that to last a lifetime.

Then the rumors that begin with a whisper slowly increase to a dull roar and proceed to ear-splitting levels. The clandestine information Sonny's getting from her sources at the CIA, the Secret Service, and the Defense Department, all echo a common theme: Kennedy isn't a team player and he's got to get with the program or else.

He's already made it quite clear that he's going to pull out of Vietnam after he's re-elected and stop one of the most promising gravy trains to come along since the Korean War. In 1960, Eisenhower started sending advisors, ostensibly to help the South Vietnamese government stave off the advances made by the Chinese Communist backed regime in North Vietnam. In reality, those "advisors" were covert CIA operatives whose real objective was to stir the pot and escalate the conflict, something they've been doing with great success ever since. Now we're sending actual ground troops, establishing air bases, and gearing up for a major conflict.

There's one thing you simply can't do in this country. The most grievous crime you can commit is interfering with the American money machine. Mess with business and you mess with our true state religion: capitalism. Al Capone wasn't jailed for bootlegging, murder, or racketeering; they got him for income tax evasion. You can pillage and plunder to your heart's content, but don't kill the Golden Goose that is the United States Treasury.

Oddly enough, it was Eisenhower who warned against what he called the "Military Industrial Complex" that threatens to erode our national moral fabric in its insatiable quest for profits because war is great business. The draft is still in effect so we have an endless supply of cannon fodder, aka soldiers. Stopping it now would waste a fantastic opportunity for a lot of people to make bundles of money and what could possibly go wrong?

Here again, Sonny and Steve are torn between what they now see as the true reality that exists in the shadow of the public's perceived reality. Kennedy's Vice-President, Lyndon Johnson, is convinced he should have been President and openly derides his boss. Robert McNamara, the Secretary of Defense, can't stand the thought of pulling out of Vietnam. After all, he's the main architect of our military buildup. Publicly humiliated, the Russians and the Cubans have an obvious vendetta against Kennedy, making the list of his powerful adversaries too long to comprehend, but the American public still can't get enough of him.

One man, however, has finally had enough of him and promises to take drastic action, but it's not one of the above, it's the Turtle. Sonny and Bo walk into the AP office one morning and he starts growling at another envelope on her desk with the same cut and paste letters as the first one. Jake immediately calls the FBI and they arrive in less than a half hour and confiscate the letter. Then they tell Sonny to wait outside as they file into Jake's office and shut the door. One of the agents stands in front of the door to prevent her or anyone else from entering.

Furious at being left out of the meeting, she paces back and forth, muttering under her breath, "Goddam letter was addressed to me. I should be in there. I know they're dusting for prints. What's the big secret?"

Bo, always a bit bemused when she gets like this, looks like he's watching a tennis match as she struts from one end of the office to the other. The door finally opens and Jake motions for them to come in.

She runs into his office and lets it fly, "Why the hell am I being excluded?"

The lead agent motions toward a chair and says, "Please, Miss Daye, let's sit down and discuss this calmly. Nobody else should hear what we're saying, okay?"

She starts to speak, but Jake loudly clears his throat and she reluctantly holds her tongue and sits down in a huff.

The agent continues, "Look, we know both you and your husband have quite a history with this Turtle character. Frankly, we believe you gave him an unwarranted platform for his abjectly depraved fantasies that have defamed any number of good people to include the Masons, the Catholic faith, and the President. Now we have an apparent escalation..."

She scowls at him and blurts out, "What are you saying? Are you blaming us for encouraging his lunacy? In case you haven't heard, both of us severed all ties with him."

"Yes, we're well aware of that, which leads me to the point I'm trying to make...if you let me finish."

"Fine, fine, so what's your point?"

"We started watching him, or I should say listening to him, when he was a regular part of Mr. Rasco's show. We always suspected that a man with his superior intelligence and his radical views could be very dangerous. When he put that nasty poem in the Post, it confirmed our suspicions. And now, the two poems he sent you, especially this last one, have convinced us that your abandoning him has only served to accelerate his insanity."

"Oh, thanks. First we created the monster and then we made him worse. Whoa, wait a minute. What did this one say? Did you find any prints on it? Can I see it?"

"No, there were no prints and yes, you can see it." He takes it out of a manila folder and hands it to her.

He sailed into office on a wave of hot air
Fooling us all with his enviable flair
But his words came cheap and rang so hollow
That we soon lost the urge his lead to follow
The Bay of Pigs gave us clear proof
The man is inept, vain, and aloof

He sits on a throne not his, it's ours
Abusing his constitutional powers
You needn't worry, our state shall prevail
For I'll do the deed that all will hail
Atop the lone place of a new beginning
To insure it's the end of his ninth inning

She scans it quickly and gasps, "He's promising to kill the President. That's exactly what it means." She looks around the room, expecting agreement, but she's even more disturbed when she sees everyone else rolling their eyes, trying to stifle a smirk.

Jake shakes his head sadly and says, "Sonny, you know I love and respect you, but you've got to let this go. The man is clinically insane, but they don't believe he poses any real threat except, perhaps, to himself. Sooner or later, the authorities will find him and they'll put him away somewhere."

"Now you're making me crazy. I know him better than anyone, especially the people in this room, and if I say he's planning to murder the President, you should goddam well believe me."

The agent takes the letter back and says, "Please, Miss Daye, you should listen to Mr. Miller. He's right. This man is disturbed; there's no doubt about that. However, we have voluminous files dedicated to people just like him, people who blow a lot of smoke, but who shouldn't be taken too seriously. He's just another loose cannon in a very crowded field. Let us know if he contacts you again and we'll take it from there."

Completely beside herself, yet wise enough to know when to hide her emotions, she appears to agree and says, "Well, okay, I'll tell you if I hear from him again. Could I have a copy of the letter?"

He opens the folder and pulls out another sheet of paper, "We knew you'd want a copy so we made one before you came in," and he hands it to her.

She snatches it from him and turns on her heel, "C'mon, Bo," and walks out, doing her level best not to let out a primal scream.

Steve is in the kitchen preparing dinner when the front door opens and slams so hard the dishes rattle in the cupboard. Figuring she's on the warpath, he girds himself for the onslaught and waits patiently. Bo slinks into the kitchen, hides behind Steve, and peeks at the doorway. Steve looks down at him and whispers, "That bad, huh?" Bo snorts and nods his head. Steve takes a deep breath and puffs out his cheeks as he exhales, "Oh, boy."

Sonny flies into the room, mumbling to herself, and throws her purse on the counter, "How can they be so stupid? What does he have to do, barge into the White House with a loaded gun?" She rummages around in her purse, pulls out a crumpled sheet of paper, and smooths it out on the counter. Without looking at Steve, she points at the paper and hisses, "See for yourself. See if you're smarter than those FBI idiots."

He looks at her, but her gaze is still locked on the paper and she points to it again, "Go on, read it…now."

He picks it up and steps back, keeping a safe distance from her. Bo wisely slithers under the table in an attempt to protect himself as well. Steve reads everything on the page a couple of times to make sure he doesn't miss anything because he knows she'll probably cross-examine him.

And, right on cue, she stomps her foot impatiently, "Well?"

Justifiably afraid to say anything, he takes the easy way out, "Well, what do you think?"

It backfires big time and she snatches the paper from him, "Holy shit. You're…you're as dumb as they are."

He smiles feebly, "Uh, can we start over?"

She puts one hand on her hip and shakes the paper in his face, "If Bo could read, I know he'd get it."

"Sonny, I can't win when you're like this. Gimme a break. Tell me what I'm supposed to get?"

She growls through clenched teeth, "The crazy son of a bitch is threatening to kill the President and I believe he's serious. I also believe he's quite capable of doing it."

"Oh, so do I."

She stomps her foot again, "Then why the hell didn't you say so in the first place?"

He can't help himself and he laughs out loud, "Okay, I'll take a wild stab here: Jake called the FBI, they did their number on the letter, and they decided it was no big deal."

"What the...did Jake call you?"

"No, I'm sure the FBI already has enough kooks to contend with."

"Shit, that's exactly that they said, but Steve, we know the Turtle better than anyone so it's our responsibility to stop him."

"Sonny, get a grip. If the Feds couldn't track him down, what makes you think we could?"

"The FBI agent said our history with this character may have prompted him to take his insanity to the next level."

"What? We're the cause of his threats against the President?"

"I don't know. Maybe they have a point. Think about it. At first, we both befriended him and then we both shunned him. People like him will do almost anything to get attention when they're pushed aside. Steve, he's baiting us. He's daring us to catch him. This is different than anything he's ever done in the past. The devious bastard is playing a game with us that will end with the death of the President. Don't you see? Hell, for all I know, he wants to get caught. That's why it's so hard to deal with the criminally insane; we don't think like they do."

"Hey, you're probably right. We might be the only friends he's ever had and, even though we both abandoned him, he still wants to play with us. But don't forget, you've done plenty of crime stories and we both have a lot of experience with the intelligence community. Let's analyze the letter and see if we can crack the idiot's code."

"Absolutely. He wants to play? Fine, we'll play and, by God, we'll catch him."

Two pots of coffee later, Sonny hasn't budged from the kitchen table. Steve fixed dinner and tried his best to help, but she hardly ate a bite and ignored most of his suggestions. He takes Bo for a walk, like he always does before they leave for the station, and when he tells Sonny "good-bye," she scowls at him, "What? Where are you going?"

"Uh, to work?"

"Oh, yeah, wow, uh, didn't realize what time it was, uh, is."

"Sonny?"

"Now what?"

"You're beginning to worry me. Why don't you get some sleep and start fresh in the morning?"

"No way. He made the mistake of pissing me off. This is war."

Steve doesn't say another word. He and Bo walk out to the car and when he pulls away from the curb, he looks at Bo and shakes his head, "She's possessed. Boy, am I glad we could leave."

He's also glad he can chat with his callers and get his mind off the Turtle and Sonny's manic determination to solve what might not even be a real puzzle, but somewhere around 2:30 in the morning, Jimmy knocks on the window and holds up a sign: *Sonny's holding for you.*

Steve quickly finishes his call, puts on a record, and picks up the phone, "Sonny, what…?"

She screams, "I got it."

He jerks the phone away from his ear and yells into it, "Hey, you trying to deafen me?"

Still screaming, "He's gonna do it in Dallas," and she hangs up.

Completely dazed, he stares at the phone for a long moment before he carefully hangs up, as if he's scared it might blow up. He turns to Bo and shakes his head, "We're not even safe here."

Later that morning, Steve and Bo carefully creep through the front door, fearful of being attacked by the wild animal lurking within. As soon as he shuts the door, Sonny yells, "C'mere, both of you…now."

Bo looks up at Steve who giggles, "Promise you'll protect me?"

Bo lowers his head and slinks toward Sonny's study like a lion stalking an antelope. Steve follows, trying his best not to laugh. When they enter the room, they see her staring at her bulletin board with her hands on her hips, still in the same outfit she was wearing last night, hair a mess, mumbling to herself. The Turtle's last poem sits in the middle of the board with scribbled notes thumbtacked all around it. Without turning around, she raises her right hand and motions for them to come closer. They obey and stand on either side of her facing the board.

She points at the bottom of the poem, "See the second to the last line where it says: *Atop the lone place of a new beginning*?"

Steve utters a simple, "Yes."

"Do you know Kennedy is scheduled to go to Dallas next week?"

"Yeah, but what makes you think…?"

"And do you know the official Texas nickname?"

"Omigod, it's the Lone Star State."

"And if he does away with the President, that would certainly be a new beginning, wouldn't it?"

"Damn right it would."

"But I'm still puzzled by the word 'Atop' and that's where I need your help. What do you think it means?"

"Uh, well, I uh…"

"Steve, he's describing the place where he intends to make his move. You were a soldier. Think like a soldier and help me figure out where that place is."

He turns to face her, "Sonny, slow down. You've obviously been at this all night. If you stop acting like a drill sergeant and give me a chance to catch up, we can brainstorm this thing together...okay?"

She rolls her eyes and takes a petulant deep breath, "Fine, storm away."

Try as they may, neither of them can figure out why the word *Atop* is there. The entire rest of the poem makes perfect sense and they firmly agree the Turtle is playing a deadly game with them, daring them to catch him, but what can they possibly do about it?

Now it's 10 am, Sonny's already late for work, Steve's exhausted, and they finally agree they're going to need outside help.

"Steve, I gotta go to work and you need to get some sleep."

"What about you? Maybe you should take the day off."

"Are you nuts? I'm going to the office and convince Jake to help us. He trusts my instincts and I don't think he agreed with the FBI anyway."

When Sonny and Bo walk into the AP office, everyone gawks at them with a mixture of fear and amusement because Sonny definitely looks like she pulled an all-nighter. What's more, Jake's office door is wide open and that's not normal.

"Nice of you to join us, Miss Daye," his voice booms from within.

She smiles at Bo, "Get ready for a big fork in the road. Let's go see which one we'll be taking."

They walk in, both still smiling, and she quietly shuts the door behind them.

Jake takes one look at her and frowns, "What the hell happened to you?"

"Ha, after you and the Feds were so fraught with indecision, so afraid to take action, I knew it was up to me to figure out the Turtle's message."

"Thats not entirely true. Well, did you figure it out?"

"What exactly do you mean by, 'not entirely true'?"

"Look, Sonny, the FBI deals in hard facts. They aren't wired to be creative like you. They can't deal in speculation and you know that as well as I do."

"But...?"

"But I have the faith in your instincts that they couldn't possibly have so don't lump me in with them. Now, answer me. Did you figure it out or not?"

"Sort of. I mean, yes, all but one word."

"And that word is...?"

"Atop?"

"Atop. What don't you understand? It's a fairly common word, you know."

"In context, I don't understand what it means in context. Look here." She reaches into her purse, pulls out her copy of the letter, and puts it on his desk.

"See the second to the last line where it says, 'Atop the lone place of a new beginning'?"

He squints at the page for a moment and says, "Goddam it, Sonny, what are you talking about? None of it makes any sense."

"Alright, I'm not being fair. I worked on this for several hours until it hit me: Kennedy's going to Dallas next week. Texas is the Lone Star State. Killing him would be one hell of a new beginning for the country, if not the world. Like I said, everything but 'Atop' makes perfect sense. Jake, don't you see? We gotta go to Dallas and figure out the rest of it so we can stop him."

He leans back in his chair, stares at the ceiling, and grits his teeth, "Give me strength."

"For what? Strength for what?"

He leans forward and smiles, "You're absolutely right. This guy's gone from annoyingly unbalanced to downright scary and we can't afford to ignore his threats. Now Sonny, you can't go this alone, you gotta have help, but even if we explain it to the FBI the way you just did, I doubt they'd be convinced."

She bites her lip, then her mouth flies open, and her eyes bug out, "We only have to convince one of them: Agent Hollis. Remember? He drove me to the Russian rooming house and walked me in? He was great and he's not your typical Fed. He has three degrees, and if I remember correctly, one is in psychology. He'll understand the Turtle better than those other agents. Plus, he knows me. He trusts me. He'll believe me. What do you think?"

He shakes his head and laughs, "Well, if anyone can convince him, you can and I'll be right there with you. I'll see if I can track him down. It's been a while, you know."

She runs around the desk and gives him a big hug, "Jake, you're my hero."

"Hey, gimme a break. I can't breathe."

The President's scheduled trip to Dallas worries a lot of people because it's hostile territory for the haughty Boston Brahmin. Some of his advisors try to convince him not to go, but he's adamant and refuses to listen. The election is less than a year away and he needs to shore up his support in the South and Texas is the jewel in that crown. Its's also home to Lyndon Johnson, his detested VP, the man Bobby Kennedy humiliates at every turn, yet the man who delivered Texas in the 1960 election. For some inexplicable reason, both Kennedy brothers have an enormously irritating habit of forgetting who butters their bread.

It only takes a day for Jake to find Hollis who's on some kind of classified mission in Chicago. When Jake tells him Sonny's on the warpath again, he smirks "What? Has she uncovered another international spy ring?"

"No, this is much more serious than her escapade at the rooming house. I firmly believe she's uncovered a plot to assassinate President Kennedy. She can give you all the details. Hold on a second and I'll get her."

He puts his hand over the phone and bellows, "Sonny, get in here."

After she and Bo come in, he motions for her to close the door. Then he hands her the phone and whispers, "Hollis."

Smiling broadly and barely able to contain herself, she grabs the phone and tries to speak in her most businesslike tone, "Hollis, how are you?"

"I'm fine, Miss Daye. I see you've done rather well since we parted, winning a Pulitzer and all."

"Oh, uh, you know about that?"

As dry as always, "I do read a newspaper now and again."

She can't help giggling, "Hollis, you're such a card. How've you been?"

"Busier than ever. People keep breaking laws. Now, Mr. Miller tells me you're on to something big. Tell me about it."

She carefully lays out the whole story from the Turtle's emergence as the de facto star of Steve's radio show all the way to his last gruesome poem. She ends with her final assessment and tells Hollis they desperately need his help.

There's a long silence followed by some odd, rustling sounds and some garbled conversation until Hollis says, "Say no more. I'll be in your office tomorrow morning. Please bring all correspondence and any other pertinent evidence you may have. Also, since Mr. Rasco figures greatly in your equation, please have him attend the meeting as well. Oh, one more thing, I know your dog Bo was badly injured at the rooming house. Is he still around?"

She almost chokes up, "Is he ever. He's right here by my side. It's so kind of you to ask about him."

"Is he still in good shape?"

"Ha, he's in much better shape than the rest of us. You'll see for yourself tomorrow. And thanks again for asking."

"Well, in all honesty, if we're going to Dallas to hunt down this lunatic, I'll feel much better if Bo's part of the team."

"Absolutely, I'm only this brave when he's around. See you in the morning."

After she hangs up, she puts on her little girl face and stares at Jake, "Daddy, I wanna go to Dallas next week. Can I have the company plane? Huh, Daddy, can I?"

The next morning, Steve drives to work with Sonny and Bo and they hammer out a plan with Hollis and Jake. There's no way to know for sure if they're chasing the Turtle or a wild goose, but the risk is too great to ignore and the stakes couldn't be higher.

Sonny, Steve, Bo, and Hollis will fly to Dallas the day before Kennedy gets there, ostensibly to cover the President's trip. Naturally, they won't tell the AP pilot the real reason they're going. Other news agencies will be there so the trip will appear routine and they'll introduce Agent Hollis as a new reporter from New York. Once they get there, they'll analyze the President's itinerary to look for obvious security weaknesses that might give the Turtle the best opportunities to strike.

Steve wisely doesn't mention anything to his listeners about being out for a few days because he doesn't want to arouse the Turtle's suspicions in case he's listening. In fact, Steve waits until the last minute to tell the station manager that he needs some personal time off. It doesn't sit well, but the manager has no choice. Once again, he'll have to get another DJ to fill in for Steve and play records during his time slot. It'll probably drive his listeners a bit crazier than they already are, but Steve can deal with them when he returns.

Bo's first plane ride is just about the most delicious experience of his entire life. He stays glued to the window, squinting into the sunlight, memorizing everything he sees, barking at clouds, howling at a flight of geese. Sonny and Steve are glad he's preoccupied since they have the gargantuan task of narrowing their search for the Turtle's point of attack. His phrase, "Atop the lone place of a new beginning," tantalizes them, haunts them, and tortures them. It may be the key, but how can they find the lock?

Sonny is horrified when she hears that Kennedy will be riding in an open limousine, but Steve and Hollis agree that it might be the break they've been looking for because the parade route will present the best opportunity for the Turtle. At least they can narrow their focus to a few city blocks in downtown Dallas. It isn't much, but it's a start.

When they land, they all pile into a waiting car and head into the city. Hollis drives and Sonny sits up front with him. Steve and Bo ride in the back seat and Steve studies a map of the planned parade route. They decide to start at the very beginning and look for any clues as they go along, a thankless task when you don't have the foggiest idea what you're looking for. They get out of the car periodically to look at every detail of the city for any possible hint and to let Bo douse yet another fire hydrant. They cover the entire route once and then go back over it from the other direction. Still nothing, that is, until Hollis looks up at a tall building under construction about block away and says, "Guess the oil business is really booming here. Look at the size of that new building."

Sonny agrees with a little giggle, "Yeah, it's huge, gotta be at least thirty stories. I think I'm in the wrong..."

Steve yells, "New building...get it? New beginning? Maybe that's the beginning he was talking about and what a great place for a sniper. The top two floors are still open; there's no outside walls. He'll have a great vantage point from up there and all the workers will be off tomorrow so nobody will be there to stop him."

All three of them are frozen in place, mouths agape, staring up at the building. Only Bo seems disinterested and tugs at his leash toward the next hydrant. This jolts Sonny back to her senses and she hisses at Steve,

"Quiet! You may be right, but we don't know what the bastard looks like. Maybe he's close by and heard what you said."

They check out the people around them, silently nod in agreement, and hustle back to the car. Once the doors are closed, they all start yelling at the same time until Bo can't stand it any longer and barks his displeasure.

Sonny gets it, "Okay, you guys, stop. Bo's right. We gotta get a grip here. Steve, you first. Talk to me about snipers."

"Well, that's exactly what struck me. Snipers love a high perch. It gives them the best angle for a shot, and the higher they are, the harder they are to spot. Right, Hollis?"

"Absolutely, but we still have to make sure it's the only building within striking distance that's either under construction or brand new."

Back they go, up and down the route, two more times, until their craning necks ache like crazy. It's worth it. This is the only place that fits the Turtle's clue like a glove. Now they have to come up with a strategy to stop the bastard.

They're able to gain access to the building when Sonny flashes her AP badge to the construction chief. They take the elevator to the top floor and decide that Steve, Bo, and Hollis will hide themselves on separate floors as best they can. Naturally, Hollis will be armed and he'll be on the roof, the likeliest place for a sniper. Steve will be on the top floor and Bo one floor below. Sonny, Steve, and Hollis will each have a small walkie talkie. Sonny will stay on the ground across the street, watch through binoculars, and alert them if she sees something.

She looks at all the huge piles of trash and debris scattered everywhere and giggles, "Jeez, this looks more like a high-rise dump. Construction guys are really messy, aren't they."

Steve winks at Hollis and snickers, "Yeah, when there's no women around to complain about it, you can throw your garbage anywhere and nobody gives a shit."

She gives him a stiff punch on the arm, "Wise ass."

He grabs his arm, "Ow, that hurt."

"Yeah? Serves you right."

There's no way to tell when the Turtle will enter the building so they grab a quick bite nearby and head back. They get out of the car and Steve gives Sonny a big hug and whispers, "It's showtime, Baby."

She whispers back, "Promise me you won't try to be a hero, okay?"

He kisses her and nods, "I promise."

She reaches out and grabs Hollis by the arm, "Please protect my guys."

"Yes, Ma'am. Will do."

She kneels down, hugs Bo, and whispers, "I'm counting on you more than ever."

He pulls back, puts one paw on her shoulder, and nods with a little growl. Then he follows the two men into the building, up the elevator, and they take their places. Sonny gets back in the car and makes sure her walkie talkie is on and her binoculars are at hand. Now the arduous wait begins and her mind goes a million different places, then it stays put because she knows conjecture yields nothing but idle worry and confusion. She has to stay alert and focused on the here and now which shouldn't be a problem considering the amount of adrenalin coursing through her body.

Steve gets as comfortable as he can amidst a large pile of debris behind the stairs. It's impossible not to think about being in battle. Then as now, wondering if today's the day he dies. It's all anyone ever thinks about when they're fighting a war and, by God, this is war. Maybe he should have kept Bo with him. No, they need to guard each of the three possible vantage points and this is the only way they can.

Hollis crouches behind a large pillar at one end of the floor so he can see everything in front of him. It reminds him of hiding behind a tree after being shot down over North Korea, wondering if he'd ever find his way back through enemy lines. He obviously did and he has the faith he'll make it through this as well. Plus, this is a lot more exciting than sitting in a van, listening to wiretapped gangsters argue about drug deals back in Chicago.

Bo is quite content to lie behind a pile of lumber with his head between his paws and rely on his keen senses to alert him if anything happens while he fondly remembers the great cheeseburger he just inhaled. He's very aware of the anxiety in the air. Sonny and Steve have never been wound so tight and he wishes their pain would subside. Yet, he's always prepared for anything so this day isn't markedly different from any other.

Right on schedule, the President and First Lady land in Dallas the next morning and they're greeted at the airport by Texas Governor John Connelly and his wife. The four of them are promptly seated in the specially designed, open Lincoln limousine. The Kennedy's sit in the back row and Connelly and his wife sit in front of them. One Secret Service Agent drives and another agent sits next to him. Other agents walk alongside the limo and a dozen motorcycle cops ride in front and behind. In all, there are a total of 19 vehicles in the procession.

When Sonny sees the motorcade approaching a few blocks away, she raises her walkie talkie and whispers, "Here they come." When the lead car is a block away, she whispers, "Now."

At the same time, Steve hears something in front of him. He pokes his head up and sees a short, stocky man with a hump on his back emerge from the stairwell. He's wearing a long overcoat and has a scoped high powered rifle slung on his back. The man gets down on his belly, crawls toward the edge of the floor, and peers over the edge at the street below. Steve's heart jumps into his throat because the guy really does resemble a turtle. Yeah, a turtle with a rifle on his back.

Steve raises his walkie talkie and whispers, "Hollis, c'mere, he's right in front of me."

When Sonny hears that, she grabs her binoculars, looks up at Steve's floor, and gasps when she sees a hideous red face looking down at the street. A horrible thought crosses her mind, 'So that's what the Devil looks like.'

Steve creeps toward the man as quietly as he can despite his limp, but he stubs his toe and stumbles forward. The Turtle hears him and jumps to his feet, "Why it's Steve Rasco. You fell for it. Now I can get rid of you and the goddamn President on the same day."

Steve yells, "Good luck with that you sick son of a bitch," and he lunges toward him with all his might. The Turtle pulls the rifle off his back and Steve grabs it at the same time. They struggle face-to-face, each trying to wrest the weapon away from the other.

Steve's aghast, not only by the fact that he's fighting for his life, he's done that before, but more so by the horribly disfigured ogre grimacing demonically at him. The man is hideously repugnant; he really does look like a turtle. His skin resembles a ghoulish patchwork of ragged, crimson leather. He must have been brutally burned and his neck is virtually nonexistent. His head sits right on his shoulders.

Steve can't believe how strong the Turtle is. It's like grappling with a gorilla. Suddenly, the Turtle kicks Steve's bad leg and forces him to his knees. Then the Turtle head-butts him, kicks him in the chest, and yanks the rifle away from him. Next, he savagely pounds Steve with the rifle butt and hisses, "Why should I shoot you when I can savor the thrill of beating you to death?"

When Bo heard Steve call Hollis, he immediately ran up the stairs just as Hollis ran down from the roof. They bound out of the stairwell together and see a grotesque man thrashing Steve with his rifle. The Turtle sees them coming and fires a shot at Hollis that wings him in the shoulder and sends his pistol flying into a pile of trash.

He screams, "I'm hit," and falls to the ground clutching his shoulder. Bo lunges at the Turtle, rips the rifle from his hands, and smashes it on the concrete.

The Turtle jumps on Bo's back and begins choking him. Bo tries to shake him off, but the Turtle doesn't budge and squeezes with all his might. Bo even tries to claw himself free and rips the Turtle's arm to gory shreds, but the monster hangs on. Hollis frantically searches through the trash for his pistol and comes up empty. Steve's scared shitless because Bo appears to be weakening and he slowly sinks to the ground with the Turtle clinging to his back. He's confused more than anything; he's never had trouble breathing before.

The Turtle sneers at Steve who tries to get up and can't, "You wait your turn, Rasco. As soon as I finish off your dog, I'll do the same to you and your buddy."

When Sonny hears that on her walkie talkie, she screams at the top of her lungs, "Bo! Steve!"

Her voice jolts Bo out of his daze, he springs to his feet, and gallops toward the edge of the floor. As he skids to a stop, he ducks his head between his legs and bucks the Turtle off his back, but the Turtle manages to keep his death grip on Bo's neck. Fatally entwined, they somersault over the edge and hurl to the pavement below. **Bo lands right on top of the Turtle** as the President's motorcade heads toward Dealey Plaza.

Sonny recoils in abject horror when she hears them hit with a blood-curdling splat. She jumps out of the car, runs toward Bo, and stumbles when she sees what's left of the Turtle lying lifeless a few feet away.

"Bo! Oh no, Bo!" She throws herself on Bo's limp form, cradling him in her arms...crying, sobbing, cursing.

Having raced down from the building, Steve limps his way toward them and cries, "Sonny, I'm right here."

"Steve, this can't happen. He's our blood…our family."

"He did what he had to do. That's our boy. At least he stopped that son of a bitch from murdering the President."

She looks up at the sky and murmurs, "What are we going to do? How can we live without him?"

Suddenly, Bo wheezes, takes in a huge breath of air, and coughs loudly. Sonny is so startled she falls backwards and screams, "Bo, Bo, are you alright?"

He coughs again and pants happily at Sonny. He appears to be unhurt and perfectly normal.

Steve yells, "He just had the wind knocked out of him. He's fine."

She looks at Steve and laughs, "Well of course he is. He's Bo."   She scrambles to her knees and cries, "C'mere, Boy."

Bo shakes himself all over, sits in front of her, and puts his paws around her neck. She hugs him tightly and sobs uncontrollably. He leans back and licks away her tears, but it's no use. They keep cascading down her face and she gets the giggles.

CRACK   CRACK   CRACK

Three gunshots echo through the streets, time stands still, and a massive psychic tremor rocks the world.

EPILOGUE

A terrible tragedy will mire some people in a quicksand of despair while others refuse to be discouraged and forge ahead with renewed resolve. Then there's Bo who treats each new day as an opportunity to love, to have fun, and to be of service.

That's why he's a bit confused by all the extra attention he's been getting since returning from Dallas last night. Sonny showers him with an overabundance of hugs and kisses and Steve prepares his favorite apple pancakes for breakfast; a delicacy usually reserved for birthdays and special occasions.

Steve muses, "Maybe I'll take the day off and stay home with Bo."

"No you won't. This may be a sad day for the country, but it's all the more reason for us to keep busy."

"You're right. It's time to get back to my Rascals even though there's a rumor the new management is switching to pre-programmed music. If so, there goes my show."

"Hey, you can't worry about rumors. We'll just have to see what happens. By the way, the pancakes were delicious. Give me a kiss. Bye Bo."

Sonny strolls into the AP office with a mixture of strong confidence and great trepidation.

Jake pokes his head out of his office and yells, "Well, Sonny, it's about time you got back from your silly vacation. There are rumors of everything from a foreign conspiracy to the Mafia being responsible for the assassination. The cops have a suspect in custody, but some people don't believe he acted alone."

"Relax. What do you want me to do? I'll carry the load."

"Nah, I put Hartman and Goodwin on Kennedy. I've got something else for you." He pops back into his office and slams the door.

She chuckles to herself, 'Ha, guess I'll have my own share of rumors to deal with. Probably not the best time to bring up the Turtle.'

She starts rummaging through the Dallas papers for any mention of their incident and finds a small blurb about a homeless man who fell to his death from a construction site. Strange…no gun…no bullet holes…nothing. Case closed.

Her phone rings and it's Jake, "Sonny, please come in now."

As she approaches his office, the door opens and four Feds walk out and silently head for the elevator.

When she walks in, Jake motions toward the door, "Close it and have a seat. Sonny, it may or may not be a coincidence, but there's been a series of high profile bank robberies throughout the country and millions of dollars of Treasury Notes were taken. The government isn't sure if it's a coordinated attack by a hostile power or some domestic group. Regardless, it's undermining our country's economy and we want you to investigate it. Now, you'll only be working with the FBI and staying within the confines of this office. Got it?"

"Yeah, sure, got it. Uh, Chief, there's something you should know…"

"What?"

"Oh, it's nothing. I'm on it."

"And take your giant mutt with you."

"Thanks, I was going to anyway."

Made in the USA
Monee, IL
05 March 2020